KT-548-930

Sharon Kendrick once won a national writing competition by describing her ideal date: being flown to an exotic island by a gorgeous and powerful man. Little did she realise that she'd just wandered into her dream job! Today she writes for Mills & Boon, and her books feature often stubborn but always to-die-for heroes and the women who bring them to their knees. She believes that the best books are those you never want to end. Just like life…

USA TODAY bestselling author **Natalie Anderson** writes emotional contemporary romance full of sparkling banter, sizzling heat and uplifting endings—perfect for readers who love to escape with empowered heroines and arrogant alphas who are too sexy for their own good. When not writing, you'll find her wrangling her four children, three cats, two goldfish and one dog…and snuggled in a heap on the sofa with her husband at the end of the day. Follow her at natalie-anderson.com.

ACC. No: 05202550

Also by Sharon Kendrick

Cinderella in the Sicilian's World
The Sheikh's Royal Announcement
Cinderella's Christmas Secret
One Night Before the Royal Wedding

The Legendary Argentinian Billionaires miniseries

Bought Bride for the Argentinian
The Argentinian's Baby of Scandal

Also by Natalie Anderson

The Greek's One-Night Heir
Secrets Made in Paradise

Once Upon a Temptation collection

Shy Queen in the Royal Spotlight

Rebels, Brothers, Billionaires miniseries

Stranded for One Scandalous Week

The Christmas Princess Swap collection

The Queen's Impossible Boss

Discover more at millsandboon.co.uk.

SECRETS OF CINDERELLA'S AWAKENING

SHARON KENDRICK

NINE MONTHS TO CLAIM HER

NATALIE ANDERSON

MILLS & BOON

All rights reserved including the right of reproduction
in whole or in part in any form. This edition is published
by arrangement with Harlequin Books S.A.

This is a work of fiction. Names, characters, places, locations
and incidents are purely fictional and bear no relationship to
any real life individuals, living or dead, or to any actual places,
business establishments, locations, events or incidents.
Any resemblance is entirely coincidental.

This book is sold subject to the condition that it shall not,
by way of trade or otherwise, be lent, resold, hired out
or otherwise circulated without the prior consent of the publisher
in any form of binding or cover other than that in which it is published
and without a similar condition including this condition
being imposed on the subsequent purchaser.

® and TM are trademarks owned and used by the trademark owner
and/or its licensee. Trademarks marked with ® are registered with the
United Kingdom Patent Office and/or the Office for Harmonisation
in the Internal Market and in other countries.

First Published in Great Britain 2021
by Mills & Boon, an imprint of HarperCollins*Publishers* Ltd,
1 London Bridge Street, London, SE1 9GF

www.harpercollins.co.uk

HarperCollins*Publishers*
1st Floor, Watermarque Building,
Ringsend Road, Dublin 4, Ireland

Secrets of Cinderella's Awakening © 2021 Sharon Kendrick

Nine Months to Claim Her © 2021 Natalie Anderson

ISBN: 978-0-263-28249-8

06/21

This book is produced from independently certified FSC™ paper
to ensure responsible forest management.
For more information visit www.harpercollins.co.uk/green.

Printed and bound in Spain
by CPI, Barcelona

SECRETS OF CINDERELLA'S AWAKENING

SHARON KENDRICK

MILLS & BOON

Big thanks must go to:

The lovely Emily, owner of Hair Jungle, Plymouth—
for her insights on hairdressing.

And the fabulous criminal lawyer Janie Heard—
for advising me on Pansy's fate.

CHAPTER ONE

IT HURT. It really hurt.

Marnie opened her mouth and yelled as she hadn't yelled in years. Crawling out of the water, she slumped onto the hard sand, shivering uncontrollably in her stupid orange bikini despite the heat from the late afternoon sun.

Just her luck.

Or maybe not. Unless she stupidly believed that fate wouldn't be cruel enough to throw anything else at her. Because since when had fate ever been *fair*? Fairness was what happened to other people. To people with homes and parents and food in their belly, and no reason to fear the creak on the landing.

Biting her lip, she tried to conquer the pain, which was coming at her from all directions. Because wasn't her twin sister in prison, grimly fulfilling the predictions made by so many foster parents all those years ago, while she was alone on a faraway Greek island, which suddenly felt more like a battlefield than the paradise she'd been promised?

Twisting her head, she surveyed her foot and a heel which was scarlet and speckled with black. She let out a whimper, barely noticing the shadow which was falling over her shivering flesh.

'What the hell has happened?'

The voice was deep. Authoritative. Marnie jerked her chin up to see the silhouette of a man blocking out the sun and she squinted. His torso was covered with droplets of water, which glittered like diamonds on his powerful frame, and he was out of breath—as if he'd been running. Rather distractingly his hand was positioned over his groin and she realised he was just zipping up a pair of faded jeans.

And despite her throbbing heel, Marnie felt a punch of vivid awareness because it was him. The swimmer. The man she'd noticed before she'd been bitten—if indeed she *had* been bitten—and not just because he'd been the only other person on the beach. Who wouldn't have noticed his wild, almost feral beauty when he'd arrived on a noisy old motorbike and laid it down on the wide strip of sand?

With uncharacteristic fascination she had watched as he'd stripped off his jeans and T-shirt before running into the sea and diving beneath the sapphire froth of the waves. He had moved with a kind of elemental grace as he'd ploughed his way through the water—but his determined progress had looked more mechanical than joyful.

'Are you okay?' he probed, his rich voice edged with urgency. 'I heard you scream.'

Now her eyes had adjusted she could see him more clearly but despite his solicitous question, his face was hard, his mouth unsmiling. The sculpted contours of his features were unmoving, as if they had been hammered from some cold and unforgiving metal. Only his eyes looked alive as they raked over her and she wished she hadn't worn this bikini, which her workmates had given her before she'd left London, more as a joke than because they actually thought she'd wear it. And if the elastic on her ancient one-piece hadn't finally snapped the flimsy garment wouldn't have made it out of the carrier bag. It was too tight, too small, too everything really and it was making her feel almost naked beneath the man's burning gaze.

Marnie shook her head, wet strands of hair flopping onto her shoulders. And because she was in pain and because he was making her feel something she wasn't used to feeling and didn't particularly like, she took refuge in sarcasm. 'Does it look like I'm okay?' she demanded.

He looked slightly surprised and then irritated, as if he weren't used to women talking to him that way. 'What have you done?'

'I don't *know*!' she wailed. 'It's my foot.'

'Let me see.'

She wanted to tell him to go away. She wanted to tell him she could take care of herself because that was always her default mechanism, but he was crouching down and cradling her foot in the palm of his hand, before running the edge of his thumb over the heel with what felt like consummate expertise. And that one simple act made Marnie's stomach turn to jelly.

She wasn't used to being handled by anyone, but especially not by a man. Parentless kids didn't get cuddled much in her experience—and when you did, you viewed it with suspicion and tried to avoid it wherever possible for there was usually some sort of agenda involved. That habit had carried over into adulthood and avoiding physical contact had made her life less complicated. Unlike her friends, she didn't have sex only to regret it afterwards, and she'd never suffered from unrequited love or a broken heart. She feared intimacy with the natural aversion of someone who had never come into contact with it and the only person she had ever loved had been her twin sister.

But the stranger's touch was having a potent effect on her—it was driving everything from her mind other than how *good* he was making her feel and the sensation took her by surprise because it felt irrational. It also felt like emotion—and Marnie didn't do *that* either. She'd taught herself not to care because you didn't get hurt if you didn't care.

'So what's happened? Have I been bitten by some deadly Greek sea serpent or something?' she questioned.

He lifted his head then and she almost wished he hadn't because his eyes were so blue that they made the sky behind him fade into insignificance.

'A sea urchin, actually,' he amended coolly. 'And they do have the potential to be dangerous. Certainly not something you can ignore, or be flippant about. I have something in my bike which can sort it out for you. Wait here.'

His response sounded halfway between a reprimand and an order and Marnie opened her mouth to tell him not to bother, but thought better of it and shut it again because really—what choice did she have?

'Suit yourself,' she said.

Leon scowled as he turned away, retracing his route

across the beach towards his motorbike and wondering why the hell he had made the mistake of getting involved with such a fractious female. Afternoons off in his crazy busy life were rare and riding to the top of the island to watch the sunset had been his only plan for the rest of the day, before the whirl of the upcoming weekend descended on him.

It was strange being back in Greece. It always was. He'd been away for a long time and trips to his homeland had been erratic, for he had made his fortune in America and Europe. But there had been a couple of tentative meetings with his father over recent years, leading to an uneasy reconciliation after a long period of estrangement. Soon he would attend the wedding of the man who had sired him, telling himself it was the right thing to do, even if found the prospect distasteful. But his father was an old man now and who knew how long he had left?

With an effort, Leon pushed the thought away and regarded instead the weekend which lay ahead of him. His mouth relaxed by a fraction. He owed it to one of his oldest friends to put in an appearance for his birthday celebrations and at least he'd be able to enjoy some down time. At least, that was the theory. In truth he didn't really *do* relaxation, no matter how much he tried. He did adrenalin and hunger and drive. He worked better with projects than with people and nothing distracted him from his primary purpose—of remaining one of the most successful self-made men to ever come out of Greece. And that was important to him. It had been the main salvage to his pride and self-respect after the bitter chaos of the past.

His scowl deepened as he reached his bike and opened up one of the dusty panniers, because rescuing damsels in distress certainly hadn't been on his agenda, especially one who answered back as much as this one did. But despite the bitter accusations sometimes levelled at him by women who had tried and failed to pin him down, he wasn't *completely* devoid of conscience. What else could he do but help the stricken blonde, even if she seemed remarkably ungrateful that he was putting himself out for her?

He dug around until he found what he was looking for and returned to find her lying prone on the sand, her eyes closed. For a moment he registered her laboured breathing and the way it made her breasts rise and fall so rapidly. He noticed droplets of sea water drying into dots of salt on the faint curve of her belly and something shifted inside him. Something dark and powerful and strong. As he pulled out an old army knife and extracted a pair of tweezers, he realised his mouth had suddenly grown dry. 'You've got some spikes in your heel,' he said unevenly.

'You don't say?'

He gritted his teeth. What *was* her problem? 'Which I'm now going to remove.'

Her eyelids shot open as he spoke and as she stared at him he noticed her eyes for the first time. They were wary eyes, the colour of one of those wintry skies you sometimes saw over Paris. Beautiful eyes, he thought suddenly as another whisper of awareness rippled over his skin.

'Will it hurt?' she said.

'Probably. But there's no alternative. Are you brave?'

She shrugged. 'I suppose so.'

He almost smiled as he saw the defiant tilt of her chin. He wasn't used to prickly women. To women who were doing their damnedest *not* to react to him, even though the outline of her nipples against the stretched fabric of her bright bikini told a different story. 'What's your name?'

'Marnie. Marnie Porter.'

'Okay, Marnie Porter. Why don't you close your eyes again and try to relax while I remove the spikes?'

'*Relax?* Is that supposed to be a joke? Do you have any idea what this feels like?'

'Actually, I do. It happened to me some years ago. I'll be as gentle as I can.'

'I…*ouch*!' She glared at him, dark lashes fluttering like demented butterflies. 'If that's what you call being gentle, I'd hate to see you being rough!'

'Impossible to make it a completely pain-free experience, I'm afraid.'

'Oh, yeah?' She viewed him with a renewed look of suspicion. 'Are you a doctor, or something?'

Her random question was way off mark but for some reason it pleased him. Mostly because it was rare to meet someone who didn't know who he was, who had no idea of all the baggage which came with having been born a Kanonidou. Even though he'd been away for a long time, the burden of his heritage never really left him and it came rushing back whenever he returned. And why *should* she know? She was obviously British—one of the thousands of tourists who visited this part of the world every year and spent the rest of their lives wistfully remembering its beauty. She wouldn't know about the intrigues of Greek society, or the fact that the lives of some of its better-known billionaires were not as unruffled as they appeared on the surface. 'No, I'm not a doctor. Do I look like one?'

'Not really,' she said, directing a pointed look at his faded jeans before closing her eyes again. 'More like a beach bum.'

As Leon's lips curved, he realised it was a long time since a woman had made him smile. He really *had* been working too hard. 'Am I hurting you?'

'A bit—but it's bearable.'

The biting of her lip indicated otherwise and Leon worked quickly to remove the last spike from her flesh, aware that she was clenching her fingers into white-knuckled fists.

'It's okay,' he said, at last. 'You can open your eyes now.'

Confronted again by that pewter gaze, he felt a wave of desire sweep over him as potent as anything he could ever remember. It made his heart pound. It made his groin ache with a rush of urgent need. It made him want to take her in his arms and kiss her. To lay her down in the sand and get physical with her.

As she sat up to examine her foot he was able to study her objectively, telling himself she was nothing special. Long, thick hair the colour of wet sand and killer curves contained in a very cheap bikini. But the shiny fabric looked good on her. Much better than it should have done. He was used to women who wore dazzling couture, not something which looked as if it had been picked up from a market stall. And wasn't it refreshing to see someone dressed in clothes which didn't cost the equivalent of a small national debt? A woman who didn't seem to care that her belly was a little rounded as she leaned over to survey his handiwork. A woman without diamonds, or gold, or bling.

'They've all gone!' she exclaimed.

'Yes,' he agreed gravely. 'They have.'

'Wow. Thank you.'

'It's nothing,' he said. 'But you should keep an eye on it. Make sure you keep it clean. Where are your shoes?'

'Over there.' She pointed to a small heap of clothing, sheltered by an overhanging rock.

'I'll get them for you.'

'There's no need.'

'I *said*, I'll get them for you.'

Marnie heard the ring of command in his voice, thinking, *This is someone who's used to being obeyed.* And although she didn't normally let herself get bossed around, there was no reason to object to what seemed like courtesy. Especially when he'd already gone out of his way to be so kind to her—and kindness could be compelling, she realised suddenly. Especially when you weren't used to it.

She watched as he headed towards her clothes, thinking that she could have watched him all day, because he was...magnificent. Tall and strong and rippling with muscle. Above the hard thrust of his thighs, his hips were narrow—the denim jeans clinging to the high curve of his buttocks, making her wonder what he might look like naked.

Her cheeks grew hot as she wondered where on earth *that* had come from because she'd never even *seen* a naked man before! Not unless you counted those marble statues with tiny genitals in the museums which some of her more ambitious foster parents had dragged her round when she was younger, until they'd realised that she and her twin sister weren't ideal candidates for lessons in culture and had sent them packing back to the children's home.

The memory was more painful than it should have been and so Marnie forced her attention back to the man who had rescued her. His hair was damp and unruly black tendrils were dangling around his neck, making her itch to tame them into some kind of order. But she wanted other things, too. Things which had nothing to do with giving him an impromptu haircut. Things she'd never wanted before. Suddenly her breasts were aching and there was a strange, sweet clenching in her core.

She knew exactly what it was but the knowledge was freaking her out because she didn't *do* desire. Men left her cold—they always had—even gorgeous men like this one. She was employed by an upmarket unisex hair salon in London and met plenty of lookers in the course of her working week, but to Marnie they were just pretty wallpaper. She didn't trust beauty. Actually, she didn't place her trust in much at all because too many times she'd had it thrown back in her face.

He bent to retrieve her clothing and she wished she hadn't been so caught up in her daydreams. Because when he turned he caught her staring and as their eyes met something passed between them—a wordless sensation which slid over her skin like honey. And it was weird. On some fundamental level it was almost as if she recognised him. As if he were capable of knowing her like no other man ever could, even though they'd never met before. She shook her head. She was going mad. She must be. Now might be the moment to stop reading those time-slip novels she loved so much. Either that or the strain of the past few months had finally caught up with her.

And it still isn't over, she reminded herself bitterly. *In fact, it has barely begun.*

She started to scramble to her feet but he must have seen her sway because as he reached her, he extended his hand to support her.

'Hey,' he said softly. 'Watch out.'

Those fingers which had ministered so expertly to her foot were now cupping her elbow and although Marnie wanted to revel in the sweet sensation of having him touch her, she forced herself to draw away.

'I'm fine,' she said stiffly, waving away his attempts to help as she wriggled into her loose-fitting T-shirt dress. Gingerly, she slid her injured foot into one sandal, then put on the other and gave her head a quick shake, feeling the warmth of her drying hair as it brushed against her back. 'Right. Well, that's all done. I ought to get going. Thanks again for coming to my aid. I'm very...grateful.'

Leon told himself to let her go. She had managed to find her way down to this small private beach on her own, so presumably she could make her own way back again. He glanced at the discreet golden and coral sign of the upmarket Paradeisos hotel complex which hung in front of a coded wooden gate, and idly wondered if she was trespassing. Probably.

Should he offer her a lift to where she was staying?

His final duty done and his conscience fully satisfied as he saw her safely home?

But her hair was almost dry now and he realised it wasn't the colour of wet sand at all. It was as pale as silver. As moonlight.

His voice wasn't quite steady as he spoke. It was as uneven as that of a teenage boy who had just realised how a woman could make him feel. Blood was pounding powerfully at all his pulse points and a sense of being properly *alive* flooded through him. 'I could give you a lift back if you like,' he said. 'Better still, I could drive you round the island first. Have you seen much of it?'

She shrugged, before lifting her gaze to his. 'Not as much as I'd like. The trouble is that I work long hours and I often work on my day off because…'

'Because?'

She shook her head. 'It doesn't matter. I went on a round-the-island coach trip when I first arrived but we didn't see very much of it. The organiser seemed more concerned with getting us to buy vases than wanting to show us the place.'

He shuddered. 'I know those vases.'

'Ugly.'

'*Neh.* As you say, ugly. Yet this island has her secrets. Places where the tourists tend not to go. We could drive through some of the villages. Watch the sunset from the Dhassos Rock. Maybe find ourselves something to eat.'

Her grey eyes regarded him suspiciously and this was definitely *not* a reaction he was used to.

'Are you asking me to have dinner with you?'

'Sure. Why not?'

'Well, for a start, I don't even know your name.'

Conditioned by a lifetime of expectations, Leon felt an instinctive tension enter his body. 'It's Leonidas. Leonidas Kanonidou.' He watched for some sort of reaction but when there was none, he relaxed a little. 'Most people call me Leon.'

'Like a lion,' she said slowly.

'Exactly like a lion. Do you speak Greek?'

'Very funny. That would be the hardest thing in the world.'

No, not quite the hardest, he thought ruefully, aware of the exquisite throb at his groin. 'So, now you know who I am, are you going to have dinner with me?'

She didn't answer straight away and even her hesitation was a turn-on. He was used to capitulation. To women being available at the metaphorical snap of his fingers. To being hit on—sometimes subtly, sometimes not. His growing reputation as one of the world's most eligible men had contributed to his recent absence from the dating scene, his appetite jaded by too much choice and too much opportunity.

What Leon wasn't used to was being kept waiting, because people went out of their way to please him. As if his gratitude would somehow improve the quality of their lives. Hoping he would give them a break, or a job, or a wedding ring. He was used to people laughing at his jokes, even if they weren't funny—which wasn't often. Was this what happened to men who were not billionaires, he wondered idly—were they judged on their merits rather than the size of their wallet? Was this unknown Englishwoman destined to be remembered as the only woman who had ever turned him down?

But she didn't.

Of course she didn't.

'Okay.' She shrugged. 'Why not?'

Her reluctance was possibly contrived—yet Leon didn't care. He seemed to have stopped caring about anything right now, other than this diminutive woman with attitude. He watched her lift her arms to tie her hair back then almost wished she hadn't because it drew his attention to the heavy curve of her breasts. Had she been intending to showcase the nipples which had tightened so enticingly and was she aware of her power over him at that moment? Another surge of hunger flooded through him, which was crazy.

Crazy.

He thought about the busy timetable for the weekend ahead. The selected cream of young Grecian society would be in attendance, eager to participate in the lavish events lined up for them. There certainly hadn't been many slots available to accommodate the reckless acquisition of a new lover he'd only just met. Plus, there would be an available slew of far more suitable hookups than this spiky blonde with the wintry eyes. Leon swallowed. Maybe this wasn't such a good idea after all.

But common sense was no match for the heavy slug of his heart or the growing heat of his blood. It certainly wasn't powerful enough to stop him grabbing his T-shirt from the back of his motorbike and pulling it roughly over a body which once again was exquisitely aroused.

'Then let's go,' he said roughly.

CHAPTER TWO

'SO WHAT DO you think? Like it?'

The drawled questions, delivered in Leon Kanonidou's knockout velvety voice made Marnie's cheeks grow hot and, hoping he hadn't noticed—she looked around the restaurant.

It was gorgeous. Like something you might see in a film. Just a few tables perched on a dramatic rocky outcrop above the sea, into which the sun was sinking like a giant red ball. Beneath them was a long beach of fine sand, lit crimson and mauve by the dying light. Still early, the place was empty except for them—though surprisingly for such an out-of-the-way location, every table was reserved. In fact, the proprietor had borne down on them rather forbiddingly when they'd arrived, all windswept and dishevelled and she'd thought they were going to be turned away. Until Leon had spoken to him in Greek and Marnie had watched an astonishing transformation take place. The man had almost done a double take before nodding his head, quickly removing a 'Reserved' notice and reverentially ushering them to the table with the best view.

Marnie thought she could understand why. Had her

companion used his lazy charm to get what he wanted, or had he simply turned on the full force of his charismatic personality which made it hard to imagine refusing him anything?

She felt supremely relaxed, sitting here with him. The tiny place had none of the unashamed opulence of the Paradeisos complex where she worked, which sometimes made her feel a little bit uncomfortable. Yet as she shifted her bottom on the chair, she found herself wondering what she *was* comfortable with—because climbing onto the back of a total stranger's motorbike and speeding off in a cloud of dust wasn't her kind of thing at all.

Usually she was cautious with men and as unlike her twin sister as it was possible to be. She had never acted impetuously with a member of the opposite sex because up until now there hadn't been a good reason. Was feeling as if someone had reached inside her body to stir up her senses a good enough reason? As Leon's eyes met hers she saw his lips curve into a faintly mocking smile—almost as if he'd guessed at her thoughts. Yet instead of bristling defensively, Marnie found herself grinning back and that was addictive too. For a moment she felt as if she were somebody else. One of her clients, maybe. One of those rich, confident women who breezed into the salon and seemed to smile for no reason at all. Who studied their phones with expressions of pleasure, not dread. She stared down at the dish of shiny olives and wondered if it would be wise to eat one before deciding to err on the side of caution because black teeth were never a good look, except maybe at Halloween.

Instead she sat back and luxuriated in the fact that for the first time since she'd been on Paramenios, she actually felt as if she were on holiday.

Leon had driven her all the way round the tiny island, past postcard images of sleepy white villages with purple bougainvillea scrambling around bright blue doors. She'd marvelled at crystalline turquoise waters fringed with unexpected greenery and the soar of distant mountains. They'd skirted tiny shops bursting with trays of ripe, plump peaches, and seen lines of drying octopi, which stretched in front of the dancing sea. Yet all the time she had been acutely aware of the Greek's hard body as she clung to his waist. Had found herself *grateful* that her pillion position gave her a legitimate excuse to wrap her arms around him and feel all that hard muscle rippling beneath his black T-shirt. Which came as a bit of a shock to someone who wasn't remotely tactile. Who found it hard not to recoil if someone touched her. The truth was that she'd never met a man she considered irresistible.

But Leon Kanonidou was another matter…

And now, sitting opposite him sipping a delicious drink he'd told her was made from almonds and cinnamon, she luxuriated in the sensation of being happy in her own skin. Until she remembered Pansy, miserable and scared in her prison cell in England, and a shiver of guilt ran down her spine.

Aware that Leon was regarding her expectantly as if awaiting a reply to his question, she dragged her thoughts back to the present. 'I love it,' she said. 'It's the prettiest restaurant I've ever seen.'

'And does it make up for the coach trip to see the vases?'

'Oh, I think you could definitely say that. Not an ugly vase in sight.'

He smiled, lifting his fingertips to summon a waiter, but the proprietor himself came scurrying over, nodding his head intently while the order was given in Greek.

Once the man had departed, Leon leaned back in his chair. 'I've ordered fish. I hope you like it. It's the only thing on the menu.'

She hesitated, aware that so far he had made all the decisions and although she was quite enjoying somebody else being in charge for a change, maybe it was time she asserted herself. She looked at him with challenge in her eyes. 'What would you say if I said I hated it?'

'I'd say you'd never eaten fresh fish which had been hauled out of the water just a few hours before and then thrown on a fire scented with herbs fresh from the mountainside, so that the flesh is as soft as butter melting in your mouth.'

His voice was caressing now and Marnie was suddenly aware of the weight of her hair as it fell over her breasts and the sweet, tight tug of her nipples. And suddenly Pansy was forgotten. Everything was forgotten except for the way he was looking at her and making her feel. Was that why she blurted out her next words, which afterwards would make her cringe for being so unbelievably naïve? 'You make everything sound so…'

'So?'

His gaze pierced through her like a blue sword aimed straight at her heart. Marnie wanted to say *romantic*, but suspected that wasn't the right word. Because romance was soft, wasn't it? And there was nothing soft about this man, no matter how silken his question. There was something hard and invulnerable about him—something which attracted yet cautioned her at the same time. She wanted him to kiss her, she realised. She wanted it in a way which was inexplicable—yet she didn't know a thing about him. She smiled up at the proprietor as a delicious-looking platter of sizzling fish was deposited on the table, alongside a bowl of Greek salad and two plates.

'Why don't you tell me something about yourself?' she said, her years as a hairdresser reminding her that people liked nothing better than to talk about themselves.

'Ohi.' He shook his head, tendrils of dark hair moving sinuously against the olive glow of his skin. 'I'm far more interested in you, Marnie Porter. Who you are and how you came to be here.'

She felt a sudden rush of nerves, though she kept her face impassive—the result of years of knowing that social workers would be studying your expression and trying to work out what you were really thinking. But Marnie didn't want to talk about her past, which had been rubbish. She didn't want to consider the equally scary future either, with all the worrying possibilities which lay ahead. She just wanted this. Now. Whatever *this* was. So she stalled. She was an old hand at stalling. 'What exactly do you want to know?'

'You're English?'

'Yes, I am. From London. Well, Acton.'

'Act On,' he repeated, making it sound like two

words instead of one. 'I know London very well but I don't think I've heard of Act On.'

'There's no reason why you should—it's hardly in the buzzing epicentre of the city, though there is a transport museum, which is very popular with schoolboys.'

'But not with you, I think?'

'No. Not with me.'

He smiled as a waiter slid a sizzling fish onto each of their plates, before raising his dark eyebrows at her. 'And this is your first time in Greece?'

She nodded. 'It is.'

'Where are you staying?'

'You don't think I could be staying where you found me?' she questioned innocently. 'At the Paradeisos? Don't I look like their usual type of client?'

There was a pause. 'If you want the truth, then no.'

Marnie stiffened because this was familiar territory. Who could blame her for being defensive when she'd been considered second-best for most of her life? Being second-best was the reason she'd worn hand-me-down clothes and shoes. And why she'd been stuck in the homes of people who didn't really want her, or her sister. 'Too trashy, I suppose?' she demanded hotly.

But he shook his tousled head. 'No, not at all. Too… normal, I guess.'

Oh, how wrong could he be? *Normal?* Marnie almost laughed. An outsider, yes. And a freak too, very occasionally. Both those things. But a human being who blended in with the rest of the world? Never.

'I *am* staying there, if you must know,' she countered, enjoying the surprise which flickered over his face. And then, because he had been kind to her and because she liked him, she shrugged before making her admission. 'I work there. In the spa.'

'You work there?'

'That's right. I'm a hairdresser, though I'm also qualified as a manicurist and a beauty therapist. And obviously I can do brows and waxing. Not my favourite part of the job, I have to admit.' She pulled a face. 'Whoops. Probably too much information.'

Leon felt a rush of something he didn't recognise. Was it her deadpan delivery which was making him smile, or her refreshing outspokenness? She certainly wasn't the usual kind of woman he had dinner with. He mixed with investment bankers and CEOs. With models who commanded a king's ransom for photographers to capture their matchless faces and incredible bodies. With actresses who kept gold-plated awards rather pretentiously on the shelves of their downstairs closet.

And usually he would be bored out of his skull by this stage of the meal.

He felt his pulse quicken as he acknowledged the steely throb at his groin. She wasn't his usual *type*, that was for sure—and not just because she was blonde. She was pretty enough. Not beautiful, no—the set of her jaw was too firm and her lips weren't full enough for conventional beauty—though her dark-lashed eyes were remarkable. She was no traffic-stopper, yet there was something about her which was so out of his comfort zone that Leon felt curiously *alive* in her company.

'A hairdresser,' he observed softly.

She pursed her lips together, as if he had criticised her. 'I'm actually a very good hairdresser, which is how

I got a job in a place like the Paradeisos, which—in case you didn't know—is a very high-end hotel complex.'

'Yes, it is,' he agreed gravely.

'In fact, I can give you a trim some time, if you like. Those ends don't look in great condition to me and it's long enough for you to be able to lose a bit. Call it payback for having come to my aid, if you like.'

Leon nearly laughed as he wondered how the prohibitively expensive hairdressers he visited in London and Paris and New York would react to the suggestion that his hair wasn't being properly maintained. 'Maybe I'll take you up on that,' he murmured. 'But in the meantime—don't you think we should eat? Any minute now and the chef will come storming over here to demand to know what's wrong with the food.'

She looked startled. As if she had forgotten that they were in a restaurant and that the proprietor was casting worried looks over their untouched meal.

'I guess we should,' she said.

But he noticed that she was spooning salad onto her plate without enthusiasm, and chewing fish in a way which seemed almost mechanical. Did the food taste like sawdust on her tongue, as it did for him? Yet that should come as no surprise when eating was the last thing he needed right now. He wondered if she was aware that he wanted to taste nothing more complex than her skin. To slowly lick his tongue over every salt-covered atom of her curvy body, to discover her scent and her flavour.

Yet he didn't *do* casual hook-ups. It didn't suit his fastidious nature. Maybe it was arrogant of him to think that his cool intellect was always capable of conquering his baser instincts, because hadn't he been on fire with need since she'd slid onto the back of his bike? Hadn't it taken all the concentration he possessed—which was usually formidable—to focus on the journey and not the heavy throb between his legs? As an exercise in self-control, it had been considerable.

'Your turn now,' she said.

Her words shattered his erotic fantasy. 'My turn?' he questioned throatily.

'I don't really know anything about you, do I? Other than the fact you were named after a lion and you're very handy with a pair of tweezers.'

He started to laugh. Maybe *that* was the secret of her unexpected allure. She was quick-tongued. Bright. Plus she was treating him with an irreverence he wasn't used to, which he was discovering he liked. Would she continue to behave in the same way towards him once she discovered who he really was? He doubted it.

All the more reason not to tell her.

'I'm Greek,' he informed her.

'Obviously.'

'And I came to Paramenios for the weekend because work has been pretty full-on lately.'

He watched as she bit into a slice of tomato and found himself wanting to lick away the gleam of juice which lingered on her lips.

'What kind of work do you do?'

The question was unwelcome and Leon wondered how to avoid it. If he told her, it would change everything. It always did. His billionaire status altered the way women viewed him—hadn't that been demonstrated time after time, and contributed to his innate cynicism?

'I'm a builder,' he said.

'Ah. I *thought* so!'

'You did?'

'Uh-huh.' Pushing away her barely touched plate, she smiled. 'I can imagine you wielding a sledgehammer on a building site. You've definitely got the build for it—no joke intended.'

For some reason, Leon found her remark slightly insulting. Was she implying he was all brawn and no brains? For a moment he was tempted to tell her that he'd been offered a place at Stanford at a precociously young age, until he'd decided that his future didn't lie in academia and he needed to get out there and make some money. But then he wondered what he was thinking. This wasn't some sort of boasting exercise. He certainly wasn't there in order to establish his intellectual credentials, or *prove* himself to her. He knew exactly why he was there—and judging from the sexual energy which had been fizzing between them from the get-go, she knew it too.

'Have you finished?' he asked.

She surveyed her plate. 'Well, I have and I haven't. I really don't want to offend the chef, but I'm not hungry.'

'Me, neither.'

'Must be the heat.'

'Must be.' There was a long pause. 'Don't worry about the chef,' he said softly. 'We'll make sure we tip generously.'

'Yes. Yes, of course.' Hastily, she reached for her beach bag and a sandy shell fell onto the table as she started to rummage around inside. 'I'll get my purse—when I can find it, that is. I'm happy to split the bill.'

Leon's eyes narrowed. It was a novel experience to have a woman offer to pay and for a moment he thought about letting her, because novel experiences were rare in his world. Until he reminded himself that despite the clifftop restaurant's deceptively rustic appearance, the food commanded prices far beyond the reach of most mortals. He shook his head. 'No, you won't—but thanks for the offer. I'll see to it.'

'But—'

'I *said*, I'll pay. Now, would you like to look at the desserts before I ask for the check, or would you prefer to walk on the beach and catch the last of the sunset?'

His words floated on the warm air and as Marnie stared into his sculpted face, she was unbearably tempted. Until he'd suggested it, she hadn't been aware of just how much she wanted to be alone with him—away from the frankly intrusive glances of the attendant staff who seemed to be hovering around their table quite unnecessarily in her opinion, considering they were the only customers in the place.

But she wasn't stupid and she knew how the world worked. If it were possible for a person to be aware of the corrupting power of sex without ever having had any actual experience of it—then Marnie *was* that person. She had been brought up to fear it. To be aware of all the trouble it could get a woman into. It was why it hadn't particularly bothered her when men had accused her of being frigid or cold, whenever she'd failed to respond to their fumbling kisses. But those kisses had felt like ambushes, whereas the thought of Leon's lips pressing down on hers was making her feel quite dizzy with need.

He was making it clear that he found her attractive and maybe she should be scared by the knowledge of where that could lead. Maybe she should tell him that if he wanted to see her again, then he should take her number and call her and then arrange a second date. That was what you were *supposed* to do, wasn't it?

But she wasn't going to.

Because Marnie knew better than anyone how fleeting happiness could be and something was telling her that if she didn't grab at whatever he was offering, she might never get the chance again. Why *wouldn't* she want to take a walk with this gorgeous man whose black waves tumbled so riotously against his darkly golden skin?

Which was why she nodded. Why she rose to her feet with a solemn expression. Why she accepted that she was about to break one of her most fundamental rules—and break it big time. 'I'd like that very much.' Her fingers tightened around the strap of her beach bag. 'I'll just use the bathroom and then I'm all yours.'

Her words were clumsy and open to misinterpretation and she wished she could take them back. But there again, why should she?

They both knew what was on the menu for tonight and it certainly wasn't fish and salad.

CHAPTER THREE

HIS LIPS WERE SOFT. Surprisingly soft. Marnie had thought they would be hard. Hard like his body. Hard like the fierce blue glint of his eyes. But what did she know, other than when Leon Kanonidou pulled her into his arms it felt as if this were the reason she'd been born?

They had left the restaurant and walked slowly along the sand, the pain in her heel gradually receding as they watched the setting sun make its slow descent in the sky before finally slipping into the sea. Their arms brushing occasionally, they had commented on the soft sound of the waves and the fiery glow of the dying embers. But that conversation had felt *mechanical*, rather than natural, and it had filled Marnie with all kinds of fears—the main one being that she had totally misjudged the situation and maybe the attraction she felt for him was one-sided.

She'd found herself wishing he would touch her. But he hadn't. They'd just walked and walked until all the daylight had disappeared and faint stars had begun to puncture the moonless sky, before turning to retrace their steps towards his motorbike. And the more he had kept his distance, the more she had wanted him.

They had turned to retrace their steps and Marnie had seen the restaurant in the distance—all brightly lit up like a cruise liner. They must have started playing music after they'd left but as they stopped to listen to the faint chords of a bouzouki drifting on the warm air, she had been acutely aware of a sinking sense of disappointment.

So was this *it*? Was her determination to do something wild and free for the first time in her life about to amount to nothing, because the man she was with wasn't interested in her? Maybe he really had just been acting as an impromptu guide, eager to show the English tourist the hidden delights of Paramenios.

And then, almost as if he'd read her mind, Leon caught hold of her and turned her round, his hands on either side of her waist. She held her breath because his touch felt *electric* and he studied her upturned face for what felt like a long time, before lowering his head to kiss her.

It was…dynamite.

It was…life-changing.

Marnie swayed in disbelief, her limbs growing instantly boneless. How was it possible for a kiss to feel this *good*? How could *anything* feel this good? At first there was barely any contact between them—just the intoxicating graze of his mouth over hers. Did he know how desperately frustrating that was? Was that why he deepened the kiss so that, suddenly, everything changed? The pressure of his lips became seeking. Super-charged and somehow *profound*. As if she were the sleeping princess in the pages of a fairy story, who had been woken by a gorgeous prince.

He deepened the kiss and began to stroke one of her breasts. Her nipple was pushing against her baggy T-shirt dress towards the circling of his thumb. She could feel the syrupy rush to her bikini bottoms and realised she wanted him to touch her there, too. She wanted things she'd never wanted before and she wanted them very badly. Was it that which made her writhe her hips against his with instinctive hunger, causing him to utter something in Greek which sounded almost *despairing*?

The sound broke the spell and she drew back, though in the faint light all she could see was the hectic glitter of his eyes. 'What...what did you just say?'

'I said that you set my blood on fire, *agape mou*. And that I want you very much. But you already know that.'

Well, she knew he wanted her, yes. She wasn't actually sure about the 'blood on fire' bit, because nobody had ever said anything like that to her before. And although she liked it, her instinct was not to believe him because even if they were true, she knew compliments always came with a price.

Yet what was the *point* of all this if she was just going to pepper the experience with her usual doubts, and spoil it? Couldn't she have a holiday from her normal self and shake off all the worries which had been weighing her down for so long? Couldn't she be a different Marnie tonight—one who was seeking nothing but uncomplicated pleasure? She had always been the responsible one. The one who looked out for other people, always preparing herself for the shadows which inevitably hovered just out of sight. Wasn't it time to articulate what *she* wanted for a change?

She cleared her throat. 'Would you mind speaking in English so I can understand what you're saying?'

She could hear the amusement which deepened his voice.

'Are we planning to do a lot of talking then, Marnie? Is that what turns you on?'

Something warned her she'd be straying into dangerous territory if she told him she didn't *know* what turned her on because she'd never given herself the chance to find out. But while she didn't want to lie to him, that didn't mean she couldn't tell a different kind of truth.

'*You* turn me on,' she said boldly and something about the breathless rush of her words made his powerful body tense.

'Oh, *do* I?' he questioned, tilting her chin with his fingers so that their darkened gazes clashed. 'So what are we going to do about that, I wonder?'

She didn't dare answer in case she said the wrong thing. In case she frightened him away with her appalling lack of experience—because her gorgeous biker looked and kissed like someone who knew his way around the block. So instead, she just did what she'd been aching to do all evening, which was to touch his face—grazing her fingertips down over its sculpted planes, as if she were committing them to memory.

Did his quick intake of breath mean he liked it—was that why he pulled her back into his arms and hauled her up close to his body, so that they felt glued together? Her nipples were stony and she could feel the hot slick of desire between her legs. As he moulded the curve of her buttocks with his open palms, she became aware of the rocky outline of his erection, which was pressing through the soft denim of his jeans against her.

'Can you feel how much I want you?' he taunted softly.

Maybe she should have been daunted by all that virile power, but weirdly enough she wasn't. Because it all seemed so *natural*. As if it was meant to be. As if her life up until now had been nothing but a preparation for this moment. 'Yes,' she breathed. 'Yes, I can.'

His fingertips were hovering close to the hemline of her dress. 'I want to see you,' he husked. 'I want to see your body, Marnie.'

Marnie closed her eyes. She could hear the raw hunger underpinning his words and sense the barely restrained need in them. And didn't that match her own hunger and make it easy to know how to respond to him, despite her pitiful innocence? No need to point out that the moonless night would make twenty-twenty vision impossible and it would be practically impossible for him to see her with any degree of detail. 'I'm not stopping you,' she whispered boldly. 'Go ahead.'

'*Meta haras.*' His words sounded like dark honey coating her skin with sweetness. With a fluid movement he peeled the dress over her head and let it fall to the sand, one-handedly unclipping the fastening of her now-dry bikini top, so that her breasts came tumbling free. And if at times Marnie had despaired about her disproportionately large bust, Leon Kanonidou's murmur of appreciation was enough to banish those complaints for ever.

'My turn, I think,' he said, pulling off his T-shirt

and dropping it to the ground, so that his torso was as bare as hers.

He pulled her into his arms and that first contact of skin against skin felt so delicious that Marnie gave a little gurgle of joy. He was smoothing his fingers through her hair. He was kissing her and kissing her, until once again she was in that blissful state of molten compliance. He slid his fingers between her legs and she held her breath as they pushed aside the panel of her bikini bottoms—terrified he was going to stop his intimate exploration.

But he didn't stop.

He started to stroke his fingers over her and a ragged moan escaped from her lips.

Maybe it was the shock of discovery which made her so instantly responsive or maybe it was the things he was saying to her, some in English and some in Greek. She no longer cared which language he was using—all she cared about was the way he was making her feel. That sweet, savage tightening in her groin and exquisite aching of her breasts. Her heart was racing as waves of something unbearably beautiful beckoned her towards an unknown destination. The tension grew and her body felt so taut that she didn't think she could bear it any longer. And then she went under—or was it over?

His kiss drowned out her spiralling cries of pleasure as Marnie began to spasm around his finger, trying like mad to hold onto the feeling until her body gradually grew still. She was dimly aware of him supporting her weight while he bent to smooth his T-shirt over the sand to form a makeshift sheet—admittedly on the small side—before very gently easing her down on top of it. His shadow fell over her as his hand went to the button of his jeans and the image was reminiscent of when she'd seen him on the beach earlier. And that was when reality hit her befuddled brain with a bombardment of urgent questions.

You realise what you're about to do? You're about to have sex with a man you barely know. All those things which have scared you all your life are right here. Things you were determined never to do. Things you know you shouldn't do.

That reality hit should have been enough to make her stop but it wasn't. Because as he slithered out of his jeans, Marnie was able to ignore the voice of her conscience by noticing several things. Firstly, that he wasn't wearing any underpants—which seemed more erotic than shocking. Secondly, that he was withdrawing a foil packet from his back pocket—making her wonder if he *always* carried a condom with him. And if that were the case—then didn't that make her just one in a long line of conquests of women he barely knew?

But those discoveries were quickly eclipsed by another—which was that she had been completely wrong about the available light. Because while there was no moon, the sky of Paramenios was incredibly clear and the millions of stars were certainly bright enough to illuminate Leon Kanonidou's magnificent body. Twenty-twenty vision it might not be, but the starlight was strong enough to emphasise the rippling muscles and honed flesh. She gazed at the hair-roughened chest and narrow hips, which led down to those long, powerful legs coated in a silvery gleam.

Naked, Leon Kanonidou was the most beautiful sight

she'd ever seen. Even the proud pale pole of his erection springing from a dark blur of hair wasn't enough to daunt the innocent Marnie as she opened her arms to him.

Her soft curves accommodated his hard planes and sculpted limbs as if they'd been designed for that purpose. Was it always like this? she wondered dizzily as he moved over her. So…*easy*? His lips began to explore her skin, his tongue sliding over her as if he had all the time in the world ahead of him. He licked her nipples and belly and then the delicate skin between her thighs and she shivered. His fingers moved to reacquaint themselves with the slickness between her legs, feathering her with that dextrous touch which made her feel as if she were drowning in sweetness. Should she be doing something back? she wondered. Actively participate by touching *him*, even though her clumsy movements might give away the fact that he was with a novice?

But while she was plucking up the courage to curl her fingers around his rocky shaft, he dissolved all rational thought by kissing her again.

'You taste salty,' he murmured, against her lips.

'So do you,' she murmured back—and something about that small interchange felt as intimate as anything else they'd done and filled her with a newfound confidence, so that when he reached for the condom which lay on the sand beside them, Marnie felt nothing but eager for what was about to happen. She watched as he stroked on the protection, his starlit expression a study in concentration until he had sheathed himself, his lazy smile of complicity emphasising the closeness of the moment.

'Now, where was I?'

He was right here. Holding her, and stroking her, and Marnie was touching him back and he was almost purring with pleasure. His fingers were tangled in her hair and his body was pressing down on hers so that she could feel the soft sand at her back. There was a sudden rapid escalation of need and a subtle shift in tension and her thighs parted eagerly as if some unseen force was choreographing her movements. She held her breath as he made that first deep thrust inside her, her quick cry the only indication that pain had momentarily eclipsed the pleasure.

But Leon must have heard it. Or felt it. Or something. Because he stilled inside her, and when she looked up into his face all she could see was confusion glinting from his narrowed eyes.

'Please don't stop,' she whispered, and afterwards she would be ashamed at having said that. For *pleading* with him, almost.

But his answer took her by surprise.

'I can't stop,' he said, almost bitterly, and began to move again.

She'd thought that this unmistakable disconnect would be enough to shatter the magic so that she would feel nothing—but she had been wrong. Because Leon immediately adapted to what he'd just discovered by moving inside her at a completely changed pace. At first, his thrusts were performed with almost exaggerated care, until her newly awakened body had adjusted itself to the rocky width of him and to what was happening to her. He took it slow. So very slow. Until she had completely relaxed.

'Oh, Leon,' she cried out.

Until that sweet urgency had flared up inside her again, building into such a pitch until she could hold it back no longer. And this time when she came, his body bucked in perfect time with hers.

But this time he did not kiss her quiet.

Leon rolled off Marnie's soft body with a reluctance which unsettled him even more than what he had just discovered. He wanted to feel anger and indignation. He wanted to accuse her of misrepresentation. Yet all he could think about was the moment when he'd entered her—recalling that fleeting sensation of resistance before being encased in her molten tightness. He had wanted a novel experience, he reminded himself bitterly. Well, this one had certainly ticked all the right boxes. Or the wrong ones. He gazed up into the star-punctured vault of the black sky and even though he told himself he wasn't in the least bit interested in her motivations, he found himself biting out a single word.

'Why?'

'Why what?' she questioned, her voice soft and replete.

He rolled onto his side to look at her and instantly regretted the action, for her cushioned flesh looked utterly inviting and he could detect the musky perfume of her sex on the air. Leon swallowed, hovering on the brink of unbearable temptation. He wanted to touch those peaking breasts again. He wanted to part those silken folds and plunge into her with the erection which was already growing rigid against his belly.

'You were a virgin!' he accused.

Her eyes fluttered open. 'So what?'

'Are you kidding me? Virgins don't just have random sex on beaches with men they've just met.'

'You mean, they should save it for their wedding night?' Her laugh was tinged with a cynicism he recognised as something regularly found in his own repertoire. She sat up, her hair falling over her breasts. 'Oh, don't worry, Leon—you can wipe that look of horror from your face. I'm not about to start demanding you provide me with a gold ring and white dress!'

'Because I'd say the white dress would be redundant by now, wouldn't you?' he drawled.

'And a marriage would be a lot harder to walk away from than this!'

He watched as she scrambled to her feet with an innate sexiness which made him want to pull her back down again, but she cursed as she put her weight onto her injured foot and, instinctively, he frowned. 'Careful with that foot.'

'Just leave my damned foot out of it, will you?'

He wished he could. He wished he'd never heard her stricken scream. He wished he were a million miles away from here, but he felt a responsibility towards her—one he didn't want, but which he would honour. It was the least he could do in the circumstances. Rising to his feet, he reached for his jeans. 'You'd better get dressed,' he said abruptly. 'I'll take you back.'

'That won't be necessary!' Speaking through gritted teeth, she stepped into her bikini bottoms and hauled them up over her hips. 'I certainly don't need your grudging charity. Don't worry about it. I can make my own way back.'

The sting of pride in her words made him feel an unexpected wash of gentleness towards her. 'Marnie,' he said patiently. 'It's getting late and you're in one of the most remote parts of the island. How are you proposing to get back on your own? It's not like we're in Act On. There isn't a reliable bus service.'

'You've obviously never been to Acton, or you'd know that reliable is the last word you could ever use to describe our bus service!'

He could see her struggling to do up her bikini top and instinctively reached out to help her but she batted him away. 'I can do it myself. Though I expect you're far more practised at it than I am!'

Half in amusement, he watched while she fumbled with the clip until her magnificent breasts were constrained once more, and then pulled on the rather ugly T-shirt dress, which successfully concealed all her curvy magnificence. Lastly, she shook her hair and ran her fingers through it, but still it looked wild and indescribably sexy as she turned to face him. She was struggling to control her rapid breathing and appeared to be choosing her words with care. 'Look, what just happened was obviously a huge mistake.'

'It's done now,' he returned, slightly irritated by the less than flattering sentiment. Was she trying to imply that she hadn't enjoyed it? Or that she regretted it? 'You're sure you're okay?'

'Well, it doesn't hurt, if that's what you mean,' she responded bluntly. 'Or is this the moment when I'm supposed to pour on copious amounts of praise about your skill as a lover?'

Easing the zip over his hardness with difficulty, he winced. 'That is what usually happens.'

'Oh!'

For a moment he thought she was going to launch herself at him and start drumming her fists against his chest and wasn't there a part of him which wanted her to do that, because the fury on her face was turning him on more than it should have done and if she attacked him then surely he would be justified in kissing her? Yet even as he rejected such a scenario as folly, Leon couldn't shake off the sensation of being...cheated. Feeling as if she had lured him into a honey trap with the skills of an ancient siren. Lured him into something he'd been having second thoughts about and then delivered something he hadn't been expecting.

All through dinner he had acknowledged the powerful chemistry sizzling between them, but during their walk on the beach he had forced good sense to prevail. As the soft sand had ridged between his bare toes, he had silently listed the reasons why making love to Marnie Porter was a bad idea—and there were plenty. They were strangers. They were from different worlds. It was why he hadn't kissed her. Why he had walked chastely by her side even though he had been aching with desire and frustration, and her body language had indicated she felt the same way.

Yet as the throbbing in his groin had become unbearable, he had wondered just who he was protecting. Just because he'd never done a casual hookup before, didn't mean it couldn't happen. He wanted it and she wanted it. Where was the problem? They were both adults. But he'd *assumed* she was similarly experienced. Why wouldn't he? He had always steered clear of virgins—and for precisely the reasons she had sarcastically joked about. Because women didn't just give their innocence to a passing stranger, did they—not without wanting something in return? Especially when the stranger in question possessed riches beyond most people's wildest dreams.

His mouth flattened. Maybe *he* was the one who was being naïve, not her. Maybe she *did* know his true identity and she had been saving herself for someone from whom she could reap some very attractive benefits. Someone with money. He shook his head. Wouldn't it be almost easier if that *were* the case? If he were able to place her into the well-worn compartment in his life labelled *gold-digger*? But deep down he didn't really believe that. There was something too proud about her to let him believe she was motivated by greed.

Yet whatever her intentions had been, it mustn't happen again. Because for all her bravado, Leon had detected an unmistakable trace of tenderness when she had opened her arms to him. And because he hadn't been expecting that either, it had thrown him. He had briefly lost himself in her softness, disorientated by a swirl of conflicting and unrecognisable emotions, which had troubled him. He was the only man she'd ever had sex with, he reminded himself, and, despite her insolence towards him afterwards, she would inevitably read too much into it. Women always did. They were experts at seeing what they wanted to see. At obscuring and manipulating the truth if it didn't fit in with their own needs.

His jaw tightened. Hadn't he learnt that to his own

detriment—and hadn't the fallout turned him into a man who had been accused too often of having a lump of ice for a heart? He was certainly not the kind of person this little innocent should be associating with.

So he would make her realise she would be better off without him. And the sooner she was out of his life, the sooner he would forget her.

Digging into the back pocket of his jeans for his keys, he turned to her—steeling himself against the soft quivering bow of her lips, made silver by the starlight. 'Grab your helmet, Marnie,' he instructed coldly. 'I'll take you back to the hotel.'

CHAPTER FOUR

'MARNIE, YOU'RE GOING to have to do an emergency manicure!'

Marnie glanced up, emerging from the uncomfortable swirl of her thoughts to focus on her boss, a wiry and very dynamic Scotswoman called Jodie, who had worked on Paramenios for almost a decade. It was Jodie who'd been responsible for getting her this prestigious summer job on a Greek island and Jodie who had persuaded her salon in London to allow her to have unpaid leave for the summer so she could double or even triple her salary in this luxury resort. Thus it was important not to annoy someone who'd done her a number of favours. But, really, how on earth could a manicure ever be described as an emergency?

'Can't someone else do it?' Marnie questioned. 'I'm not feeling that great, to be honest.'

'Yeah, I can tell. You look terrible,' said Jodie bluntly. 'What happened?'

Marnie bit her lip, because how could she possibly confide the reason for her washed-out appearance or inability to concentrate for most of the morning? She could just imagine Jodie's reaction if she explained that yesterday she'd met a gorgeous stranger, had let him take her to dinner—then ended up losing her virginity to him on a beach. Or that he'd dropped her off near her staff accommodation without even a farewell kiss to remember him by. And hadn't that bit hurt the most of all, even though she'd tried to convince herself it didn't matter? He'd been deep inside her body in the most intimate of ways and that didn't even warrant a goodnight kiss.

She'd spent the rest of the night tossing and turning in her narrow bed, unable to get rid of the memory of Leon as he had ridden her to fulfilment. She kept remembering the way she had cried out in rapture. She'd lain there in the claustrophobic staff accommodation, beating herself up about her behaviour—until the morning light had helped her put things in perspective.

She had been foolish and impulsive in a way which was totally out of character, that was all. She'd been living on her nerves since Pansy's arrest and maybe it was inevitable that sooner or later something was bound to give. But she hadn't hurt anyone—except perhaps herself—and she was going to draw a very firm line under the whole episode. The sex had been amazing—she wasn't going to deny that—but it wasn't going to lead anywhere. She was never going to see Leon again—he'd made it perfectly clear he didn't want to, and she had pretended she felt the same. And even though she had just been saving face, it was probably a good thing they *weren't* on schedule for a repeat performance. Because Leon Kanonidou had made her feel…*vulnerable*, and vulnerability had no place in her life. Didn't she have enough on her plate, without pin-ing after some boho biker who probably slept with a different woman every night of the week?

She could feel her cheeks growing hot as she met Jodie's curious stare. 'I just didn't sleep very well last night,' she said truthfully. 'I think a mosquito must have got into the room because every time I closed my eyes I could hear that awful high-pitched whining sound buzzing around the room.'

Jodie shuddered. 'Tell me about it. I hate mosquitos. Get some of the spray they sell in the hotel shop—the one with the red label. I know it's expensive but it works wonders.'

'I will. Though I'm not sure it's great for the lungs. Anyway—' Marnie forced a smile '—who's this manicure for?'

Her nails glinting coral in the bright Greek sunshine, Jodie glanced down at her clipboard. 'One of the women in that party who've taken over the western side of the hotel. You know—the billionaire who's having the birthday celebrations. Her name is Ariane Paparizou and she's requested a mini manicure. Poolside.'

'And when does she want it?'

'Are you kidding me?' Jodie pulled a comic face. 'Like *yesterday*? You know what these wealthy women are like.'

Marnie nodded. She certainly did. A few seemed like perfectly decent people but many of them were spoiled and, in her experience, nearly all of them were demanding. So she tidied her hair, checked her portable nail kit and then made her way through the sprawling Paradeisos complex towards the upmarket Ouranos section. She'd never actually done a treatment here before—Jodie usually kept the jobs with the greatest tip potential for herself—and ordinarily Marnie might have been excited at the thought of having a peek round this most exclusive area of the hotel. But today didn't feel ordinary. Not at all. She still had that strange feeling of being disconnected from her own body. As if being given two orgasms in quick succession by a man she barely knew had shaken the foundations of her world and made her realise she didn't really know herself very well at all.

Abundant pink and white flowers framed the interconnecting buildings surrounding the different-sized swimming pools which made the Ouranos complex so distinct, though naturally it had its own private beach. It was just unfortunate that the thought of any kind of beach made Marnie want to shudder. It made her think of grains of sand falling onto the floor of her tiny shower cubicle and swirling down the plughole as she'd tried to wash away the memories of Leon's lovemaking. But his scent had clung stubbornly to her hair and her skin and it had taken a full twenty minutes of fierce scrubbing before she'd finally felt free of him and able to fall into bed last night.

She could hear the chink of glasses and as she approached, her gaze took in the kind of scene which looked like an advertiser's dream. Around a vast azure pool stood a cluster of rich and beautiful people—all speaking in Greek and laughing while waiters topped up their crystal goblets with champagne. Several of the women lay sprawled on sun loungers and they were all wearing tiny scraps of swimwear which looked hugely expensive. But that was because they were. Marnie had seen the discreet price tags in the hotel boutique and marvelled at the fact that anyone would ever spend that much on a bikini.

From beneath the wide brim of her straw hat, one of the women spotted her and lifted her hand in careless greeting. 'Ah! My manicurist is here. At last!' she exclaimed, in perfect if slightly dramatic English. 'Never has the sight of someone been so welcome!'

Everyone turned to stare at her, their voices growing silent as Marnie walked towards the group. Finding herself the unwilling focus of attention made it difficult to avoid becoming self-conscious as she moved across the terrace. She was dimly aware of the women's collective beauty and that the men were all tall and devastatingly handsome. But her unease quickly became acute as the identity of one of the guests seared itself onto her disbelieving brain and at first she thought it must be some sort of mirage. *Please, no,* she thought. *Please don't do this to me.* She could feel the savage pounding of her heart as she risked a glance towards the most captivating member of the group and could see that her prayers hadn't been answered.

Because it was Leon.

Leon the biker, who'd picked her up on the beach.

Lion-like Leon, to whom she'd given her virginity.

But this Leon looked nothing like the man she'd kissed so passionately last night while his fingers had been playing a rhapsody between her legs. Today there were no faded denims. No close-fitting black T which caressed his ripped torso—and definitely no sign of a dusty old motorbike. He wore an expensive linen shirt, unbuttoned at the neck, and navy swim shorts.

His black hair was tamed and sleek, not windswept and ruffled. He was looking cool and immaculate, yes—but his head-turning qualities were due to much more than his rugged good looks and muscular body, for he radiated power and privilege in the way that only the truly wealthy ever could. Marnie wanted to look away but somehow she couldn't. She was mesmerised by those eyes which rivalled the sky behind him, for they were dominating her line of vision and burning into her like blue fire. Was his expression mocking her, she wondered, or was he just acutely embarrassed to see her here?

Awkwardly, she moved towards the woman who was beckoning her with a rather impatient finger, and realised that if she didn't get it together, she would start stockpiling complaints about her lack of professionalism—and that was the last thing she could afford to happen. But the efficient smile she was usually able to summon up at will for clients seemed to have deserted her. 'Ariane Paparizou?' she croaked.

'That's me! Don't just stand there. Come and sit down.' Ariane turned her head with a swish of a glossy black ponytail and flashed the onlookers a wide smile. 'I'm sure the others don't mind watching while…what's your name, dear?'

'Marnie.'

'While Marnie works her magic on me!' A small chair beside the lounger was patted and Marnie padded her way over to it, wishing the ground would open up and swallow her. Wishing she'd never met him. Wishing she were anywhere other than here. Taking the colour swatch of varnishes from her little bag, she splayed it out for Ariane's attention, but her head was buzzing with questions which seemed impossible to answer.

Like, *what was he doing here*? He was supposed to be a builder, wasn't he? Yet he was standing fraternising with these privileged people as if he had every right to be here and, judging from their fawning body language—he did. Suddenly, she realised that, whoever he was, he wasn't the man he had appeared to be—and that she had made a very bad choice for her first lover. Not just that, but she had been totally naïve—she, who always prided herself on being street-smart. She, the wisecracking victim of circumstance who was never going to allow herself to be conned by a smooth-talking man.

Of *course* he wasn't a builder! Yes, he'd been dressed in a laid-back way—but what else would he have been wearing if he'd been out in the hot sun all day, pelting around a Greek island on a motorbike in the height of summer? She remembered the restaurant where all the tables had supposedly been reserved…until Leon had appeared and one had miraculously been made available by a proprietor who had been fawning over them all evening. Would they have done that for an ordinary builder? Of course they wouldn't!

Flicking him another glance, she could see he was the only one not drinking champagne, for he was holding a glass of water. His expression was dark and brooding and he was still staring at her. Staring very hard. Any minute now and someone might notice that his attention was—inappropriately—fixed on the visiting beautician and start to wonder why. Or was she flattering herself? Were casual sexual games with staff members par for the course for these kind of people?

Pulling out her kit bag, she began to rummage inside it but all she could think about was that bright gaze which had burned itself into her consciousness.

'Leon…'

Marnie almost dropped her cuticle-pusher as Ariane said the name she had cried out last night, and the little hairs on the back of her neck stood to attention as she heard his murmured response.

'Mmm?'

'Would you like to help me choose a colour?'

There was a pause. 'Nail polish isn't really my area of expertise I'm afraid, Ariane.'

Sweat began to bead on Marnie's brow as she found herself thinking the unthinkable. *Because what if Ariane and Leon were lovers and he'd taken a few hours out to be unfaithful to her last night?* It was a grim possibility but it was still a possibility and, in the sort of world in which she'd grown up, it remained a very real one.

'Marnie?'

Ariane's voice broke into her thoughts and Marnie felt another trickle of fear sliding down the back of her neck. What if the gorgeous Greek woman knew exactly what had happened? Maybe they'd even discussed it and laughed about it—in a very modern way? *I know I shouldn't have done it, agape mou, but she kind of threw herself at me.*

She swallowed. What if Ariane called the hotel management and dobbed her in for being intimate with one of the guests—something which was strictly forbidden?

What if she was sent home in disgrace with a black mark on her CV and, much more importantly, without the inflated bonus she had been relying on to help her twin sister when she got out of prison?

'Y-yes?' Marnie questioned, her cheeks burning with dread.

'I'll have the Early Sunrise, please.'

Marnie blinked as Ariane jabbed her broken fingernail in the direction of a vivid orangey hue, and she stared at it as if she had never seen that particular shade of varnish before. 'Yes, yes. Of course. A…a very good choice. It's been very popular with all our clients this summer.' She flashed a smile. 'Is there somewhere I can go to fill up my nail bath?'

Ariane flicked a hand in the direction of one of the sleek white buildings. 'There's a bathroom in there—first on the left. You can't miss it.'

As Marnie began to walk across the sunlit patio, Leon couldn't tear his gaze away from her because right now she seemed like the personification of his perfect dream.

Or his perfect nightmare.

He was having difficulty breathing. Difficulty thinking of anything other than the way she had wrapped her legs around his back last night while he had thrust deep into her virgin tightness. Had he thought he would never run into her again? Yes—and a million times yes. Because that was for the best. He was all wrong for her and she was definitely all wrong for him. Not just because she was unsophisticated and innocent and would never have fitted into his world—nor he into hers—but because he didn't recognise the man he had become in her company.

Wild—tick. Reckless—another tick. But it had been the way he had lost control which had so disturbed him. Or rather, the realisation that someone else had the power to take that control away from him which had bothered him most. As a child he had been manipulated by the subterfuge of his mother and the widespread influence of his father and at times had felt powerless. *That* was the feeling he'd been determined never to revisit but, last night, he had done just that—and it had scared him. He, who despised fear almost as much as he despised lies.

Which was why, when he had dropped Marnie off, he had resisted the urge to kiss her—despite the red-hot invitation of her lips. Just as he hadn't taken her back to her room and made love to her again, even though powerful desire had raged inside his body. He had forced himself to listen to the voice of reason and had said nothing but a terse goodnight as she slid from the back of his bike.

But now she was here and he knew he had to get her alone, though he didn't stop to ask himself why. Putting his glass down on a nearby table, he began to follow her into the shady interior of the villa. He could hear the sound of running water and there, in the open doorway of a bathroom, stood Marnie, bending over a sink. He saw her shoulders stiffening and her head jerking up, as if she'd sensed someone was behind her and that it was him. Was she as acutely aware of his presence as he was of hers, he wondered distractedly, even from this distance? But no, she was actually looking at him in the mirror and her furious expression was reflected back at him.

'Go away,' she snapped.

'I need to talk to you.'

'To say *what*?' Holding her little container of water, she turned to face him and her anger was far more intense when witnessed face-on, rather than through the cool barrier of the glass. 'To explain how you got invited to a fancy party like this? They don't look like the kind of people who would be hobnobbing with their builder, unless society is a lot more equal here than I thought it was. What happened, Leon—did you decide to leave your trowel and cement behind, or did I arrive too late to see you scaling up a ladder? Because you're not a builder at all, are you?'

'In a way, I am—'

'Please don't insult my intelligence by playing with words! You know exactly what I mean.'

Leon's mouth flattened. Her fury was delectable enough to make him want to smile, but he sensed the embarrassment behind the words she flung at him. 'There's a reason I didn't tell you.'

'I'm sure there is. And what might that be, I wonder?' Her gaze raked over his body, but it was a cold and damning assessment and nothing like the hungry gaze she had subjected him to over dinner last night. 'You're obviously a very rich man, Leon. I guess you need to hide that fact away from casual hook-ups, in case they start making demands on your wealth!'

'But I don't *do* casual hook-ups!'

'Really? So did I just dream what happened last night? Was it all a figment of my imagination?' There was the faintest, telltale wobble of her lips before she looked over his shoulder and her angry expression quickly morphed into a brisk and professional smile. 'Kyria Paparizou!' she gushed. 'I'm so *sorry* to have kept you—I was just running the water to get it to exactly the right temperature for your nails. Certainly. Yes, of course! I'll be right there!'

Leon was so taken aback by the unwanted interruption that he stepped aside to let her pass, tantalisingly aware of her scent before reluctantly turning and wondering how the persistent Ariane Paparizou was going to react when she saw him talking to the manicurist.

Until he realised that the Greek heiress was nowhere to be seen! Only Marnie herself, sashaying across the brilliant patio, with the white material of her uniform stretched alluringly over her buttocks and her hair a million different shades of gold. His body tensed. So, it had been nothing but a ruse to get her away from him—and he had fallen for it! He wasn't used to being wrong-footed and for a moment he just stood there, watching her retreat.

Suddenly she turned and flashed him a triumphant look—as if she was enjoying having outsmarted him—and Leon felt the corresponding stir of hunger in his blood. As she sat down on the stool to start working on Ariane's nails, he walked out onto the terrace.

A waiter handed him a drink and he knew he ought to join one of the small clusters of people who were laughing and drinking beneath the shade of big white umbrellas. But all he wanted to do was to stare at Marnie and drink in the way the sunlight was gleaming on her bare legs. Last night he had been determined he wasn't going to see her again—but in the bright light of day, that suddenly didn't seem like such a good idea.

'So, Leon. This is where you're hiding.'

A male voice shattered his contemplation and Leon glanced across at the man who had joined him—Xenon Zafiris, heir to a massive shipping line. The two men had moved in similar circles when they'd been teenagers but had never really been friends.

He flicked Xenon a cool smile. 'As you see, I'm in plain sight.'

'So you are. How was America?'

'Oh, you know. Big.'

'And England?'

'Pretty small.'

'I hear you've been doing stuff in Northern Greece.' Xenon raised his eyebrows. 'Drilling for wells, on a no-profit basis.'

'That's right.' Leon's voice became thoughtful. 'The land up there badly needs water. There's no limit to the possibilities for future farming, if we just get the irrigation right.'

'Philanthropy is always such an admirable trait,' observed Xenon softly, before curving his lips into a smile. 'But on a more personal level… I gather your father is getting married again. Are you planning to attend the wedding?'

'I'm sure I'll be able to fit it in,' answered Leon, with a shrug.

There was a pause. 'Which number is that, I wonder? It's so easy to lose count.'

'Four, I believe.' Leon's voice was dismissive, because he didn't want to talk about his father, or his wives, or to inform a man whose imagination was so limited that he used his leisure time to gossip. He wanted to be left alone to study Marnie Porter, even though she had just slanted him a look of pure ice. He took a sip of water to ease the dryness in his throat. Was he discovering a previously unknown streak of masochism? he wondered wryly. No woman had ever looked at him that way before and his pulse was pounding like a piston in response.

'Easy on the eye, isn't she?' said Xenon, following the direction of his gaze. 'Though I can't quite work out what the attraction is. I mean, she's wearing a pretty unflattering uniform and those rubber-heeled shoes make her look a bit like a nurse, and yet…'

Leon's body stiffened as Xenon's speculative observation died away. He knew that men often discussed a woman's appearance, in the same way you might admire an amazing sunset or a good wine. His friends' wives told him that women sometimes did the same. It was no big deal and in many cases it wasn't even predatory. But this felt predatory and suddenly he felt the build-up of something unfamiliar. A slow, simmering rage that the renowned playboy Zafiris should dare to look at *his* lover in such a way.

But Leon didn't *do* jealousy. His eyes narrowed. Just as he didn't do commitment.

Or trust.

In fact, there was a whole list of no-go areas in his life, which helped shore up his determination never to get married, or have children.

Yet Marnie Porter had managed to achieve something which no other woman had succeeded in doing before, because there had been no need. She had turned him into a hunter.

Yet women usually came to *him*. They flocked to him like wasps to honey. They didn't freeze him out with withering looks which seemed genuine rather than fabricated.

So why was his blood pulsing with the hottest desire he could ever remember?

He frowned.

What did the little hairdresser from Acton have which so entranced him?

CHAPTER FIVE

THE KNOCK ON the door was quiet yet insistent, but Marnie ignored it. She didn't want to see anyone and she *definitely* didn't want to speak to anyone. The hurt and humiliation she'd felt when she'd seen Leon Kanonidou down by the poolside with all his sophisticated buddies had been bad enough but she probably could have coped with it. Of course she could, because didn't it only reinforce what she had already known? That she could trust nobody. Nobody at all. The only person she could rely on was herself and she should forget that at her peril.

She had gone through the rest of the day on autopilot and returned to her room in time to receive a call from her twin in England—a short and deeply upsetting exchange before Pansy's prison phone credit ran out, which it always did. But the gist of the conversation had been devastating. Her twin's lawyer had announced that she probably *was* looking at a jail sentence and Marnie had listened to her sister's rising hysteria, feeling impotent and useless and too far away.

It had been the final straw and she had given into a violent flurry of tears which had taken her by surprise, because crying was something she rarely succumbed to.

Had her sexual awakening made her more susceptible to the great swings of emotion which were barrelling through her and if that were the case, then wasn't that yet another reason to steer clear of men in future? Her sobs had subsided now and she had scrubbed at her face with a hankie, but someone knocking on her door was the last thing she wanted.

She didn't *care* if it was Jodie calling to see if she was feeling better, or one of the hotel waitresses enquiring whether she'd be interested in going out for a drink later, which she never was. Basically, she just wanted to tick off the hours until she could fly back to London and discover for herself if Pansy's lawyer was as bad as her sister claimed. And she would prefer to do it by burying her head underneath a duvet, and sleeping through the next twenty-four hours.

But it was only six in the evening and there was no duvet to be seen since, according to the hotel guidebook, the temperature on Paramenios was always warm—even in winter. And now, at the tail end of summer, it was almost unbearably hot in this cramped little room—with the noisy fan whirring away in one corner a poor substitute for air conditioning. And somehow she couldn't escape from the taunting memories which seemed determined to plague her.

Pushing a clump of hair away from her sticky brow, she remembered Leon watching while she painted the glamorous Ariane's nails. His gaze had been unsettlingly intense, as if he were examining her underneath a microscope, and she had felt…

No. She didn't really want to think about how she had felt—because it wasn't very helpful to realise that he had the ability to make her react in a way which was reminiscent of a helpless turtle which had just had the shell ripped from its back. She didn't want to dwell on her rush of mortification either, when Ariane had pressed a large banknote into her hand as a tip. Obviously, the money would come in very useful, but the ultra-generous amount had made her feel awkward—and Marnie had only just stopped herself from declaring that she didn't need it.

As if.

But as she had scuttled away from that glittering group of revellers, she had felt *less than*. Just as she'd felt throughout most of her life. An outsider. The odd one out. The object of ridicule and scorn.

The knock was repeated.

'Will you go *away*?' she said. But the caller was nothing if not persistent, so eventually Marnie got up from the lumpy mattress and opened the door—her heart clenching like a vice when she saw Leon standing there. He had changed from his pool attire into a pair of tailored trousers and a charcoal-coloured shirt, which emphasised the blackness of his hair. These clothes were also screamingly expensive and hugged his muscular frame as if they'd been designed for him—which they probably had—and once again he seemed to represent a personification of virile power.

His unexpected appearance was a massive shock to the system but not as unwelcome as it should have been and instantly Marnie could feel her body begin to betray her again. Beneath the uniform dress, which she hadn't bothered to remove, she could feel her breasts springing into rampant life.

What was the *matter* with her? she wondered furiously. Why was she still attracted to such a deceiving cheat? Yet it horrified her to realise she was also worrying about how awful she must look, with her tear-streaked face and bedhead hair. Her hand tightened on the door handle as she tried not to think about the way he had kissed her. Tried to forget the hard warmth of his body and the way his fingers had stroked over her skin as her yelps of pleasure had subsided into purring little sighs. 'Go away right now or I'll slam the door in your face,' she vowed softly. 'And don't think I won't.'

'Are you sure you want to do that, Marnie?'

'Nothing would give me greater pleasure!'

'I would have to disagree with you on that particular point,' he remarked coolly and she blushed at the implication.

'Do you really think trying to ignore me is the best way to deal with our predicament?' he continued.

'The only *predicament* we have, Leon,' she echoed sarcastically, 'is two strangers standing looking at one another, with one of them wishing they'd never met.'

'So would that be you, I wonder, *agape mou*? Or me?'

'Oh!' she said, as wrong-footed by his silken retort as by his use of the word he'd murmured against her neck last night just before he'd made his fateful discovery of her innocence. But she didn't want to think about that either. She wanted to remind herself that he was trespassing and she had the upper hand. 'I'm not going to say it again,' she vowed.

'Five minutes. That's all.'

'And then you'll go?'

He shrugged. 'If you still want me to.'

He sounded so sure of himself, she thought furiously. So completely certain that she would comply with his wishes. She supposed the subtext was that no woman in her right mind would ever eject a man like him from the premises. Which was exactly what she *should* do. But his gaze was so steady and compelling and once again he was managing to exude an aura of power so spellbinding that, stupidly, she didn't want him to go. At least, not yet. Surely it wouldn't hurt to hear him out, especially as they had been so intimate. Because what if someone saw him and worked out what he was doing on her doorstep? Hadn't one of the waitresses recently been sacked for skinny-dipping with one of the clientele? She mustn't forget that she was leaving the day after tomorrow—so why jeopardise her much-needed bonus, by risking someone discovering she'd had sex with one of the hotel's most important guests?

She opened the door a little wider. 'I suppose you'd better come in,' she said.

'Efharisto.'

'I'd like to say *you're welcome*, but I'm not that much of a hypocrite!'

He smiled and instantly his powerful body seemed to suck up all the available light and air, as if the universe were silently acknowledging his formidable presence. Clicking the door shut, Marnie moved as far away from him as possible—not terribly easy in this confined space—because close up he was making her feel helpless. And she wasn't helpless. That was what she needed to remember. She was strong. That was her trademark. Her legacy from having been ejected from her mother's womb a full five minutes before her sister, and then left to deal with the dreadful fallout of that day. She tilted her chin and regarded him unwaveringly.

'Okay. You've got five minutes, and the clock is ticking.'

He didn't seem in the least bit fazed by her attitude—in fact, he was behaving as if he was enjoying the challenge rather than being annoyed by it. And didn't his unflustered air only add to his lazy confidence, which had been one of the things which had attracted her to him in the first place?

'You're angry,' he mused.

'Yes, I'm angry. But I'll get over it.'

'And you've been crying.'

'So? That's not a crime, is it?'

'Is it because I didn't ask to see you again?'

'Oh, the arrogance! Is that what you really think? That I've been sobbing into my pillow because you made clear it wasn't going to happen again?' She gave what she hoped was a liberated smile instead of the bitter laugh which was hovering on her lips. 'I may not have had much experience with men, but I've listened to enough people over the years to understand the meaning of a casual hook-up. Don't worry about it, Leon. I certainly wasn't expecting a repeat performance.'

'So what's the problem?'

Her smile vanished as quickly as it had appeared. The problem was that she felt overwhelmed by all her emotions—concern for her sister in prison but also how to deal with him. She'd been hurt before—many times—but never by a man, because she'd never put herself into a position where that could happen. And none of her usual coping mechanisms seemed to be working. She could admit that she'd found it humiliating to rock up with her manicure kit while he was standing quaffing champagne with his billionaire mates, but that wasn't really what all this was about.

'I thought you were like me,' she said.

He frowned. 'In what way?'

'Ordinary.' The word puffed out of her mouth. 'Not...'

'Rich?' he prompted, into the pause which followed.

'Rich?' she echoed. 'Oh, come on, Leon. I suspect that's a pretty modest assessment, judging by the bar bill which your party apparently ran up at lunch time, and by the way all the hotel staff keep referring to you all as if you're some kind of royalty.' She shook her head. 'Why didn't you tell me you were staying here when you dropped me off last night, instead of letting me run across you while I was working? I felt completely disoriented when I saw you down by the pool.'

'If you must know, I felt pretty disoriented myself.'

'My heart bleeds for you.'

'It doesn't show,' he said softly, his gaze flicking to the bodice of her white dress.

'Someone in the spa was talking about you just before I finished my shift earlier,' she said, wishing he wouldn't look at her that way. Wishing he'd pull her into his arms and kiss her as she wanted to be kissed. She swallowed in an attempt to dissolve the erotic image. 'And that's when I discovered how inaccurately you had described yourself. Because you're not a *builder*, are you, Leon? You're one of the biggest property developers around. One of the richest men in the world apparently.'

'I don't deny it.' He shrugged. 'Perhaps now you can understand why I didn't tell you.'

'Actually, I don't. So why don't you enlighten me?'

Leon's eyes narrowed. Did she really need him to spell it out? Usually, he would have sidestepped her questions because analysis was something he avoided whenever possible. But as he stared into her defiant face he honestly thought he would answer anything she asked of him right then. Was it her innate impishness, or the memory of her tight body which made him unusually indulgent with her? 'The Kanonidou name carries a lot of baggage,' he said heavily. 'And a lot of expectations.'

'And, *what*? Did you imagine I'd be trying to extract some of your fortune if I'd had any idea how rich you were? Demanding to know why you hadn't used a gold-plated pair of tweezers to remove the sea-urchin spines?'

'Do tweezers actually come in gold plate?'

'I expect so,' she said, pursing her lips as if she were trying not to laugh. 'You can get pretty much anything you want if the price is right.'

'You think I don't know that?' he demanded. 'For once in my life I was enjoying the fact that you didn't know who I was, or what I was worth, or what the papers are saying about my family. I can't remember the last time that happened.' He paused. 'And I've never had dinner with a woman who offered to split the bill before.'

The look on her face became proud—the light in her eyes very bright.

'I've always paid my way!' she declared. 'And it wouldn't have made the slightest bit of difference if I'd known how much you had in your bank account, because I don't care. That wasn't the reason I had sex with you.'

'I know, that was what was different for me. But I'm confused—what was the reason, then? Because that's the bit that puzzles me, Marnie. For most women their virginity is a big deal. Why give your innocence to someone you've only just met?'

As he stared her down Marnie realised she had backed herself into a corner. Naturally, she was reluctant to admit how special he'd made her feel because it was, well...irrelevant. It would make her appear needy—as if nobody else had ever made her feel so desired, which also happened to be true. *And* it would undoubtedly feed his ego, which seemed inflated enough already. Yet if all the things she'd heard were correct, sex was mostly about the *physical* not the emotional, especially where men were concerned.

So what was wrong with identifying with that part of the equation?

Who wasn't to say that, when she got back to England and managed to sort out Pansy's current problems, she might actually find herself a permanent boyfriend? Someone more on her own wavelength. An ordinary man with an ordinary job, not some unreachable Greek tycoon with the face of a fallen angel. And if that were the case, then surely it would be better to be a little bit experienced. Men had always made her super-cautious but now she'd lost her virginity—and, given how much she'd enjoyed it, why shouldn't she explore her own sexuality a little? Leon Kanonidou had asked her a straightforward question, so why not give him a straightforward answer?

'Because I wanted to,' she said bluntly. 'I wanted to forget the outside world and everything which was going on in my life and somehow you made me…' She shrugged. 'You made me…'

'I made you, what?'

The air seemed to grow very still. 'Desire you,' she breathed, her words sounding deliberate, and heavy.

'Wow.' His shuttered gaze made his eyes resemble splinters of sapphire as he breathed out his reaction. 'That's quite some testimony.'

'You aren't used to women praising your prowess?'

'Not like that.'

'Well, I give you full permission to use it on your CV,' she said flippantly. 'But I'd prefer the source to remain anonymous, if it's all the same to you.'

'I'll bear that in mind,' he said, and gave a low growl of laughter.

The sound was rich and sexy but Marnie forced herself to remember that it meant nothing. It was an illusion. She'd just made a powerful man laugh—so what? Nothing had changed. He was still a billionaire who had preferred to keep his identity private in case she started muscling in on his wealth, and she was still a tear-stained misfit standing in an overheated room, due to go back to England where a mountain of problems awaited her.

'So now you know and you can go,' she said quietly.

'But I don't know. Your explanation has only thrown up more questions.' He stood there like a dark and immovable force, his eyes glittering as they stared her down. 'And now I'm curious to know what was going on in your life which you so badly wanted to forget.'

If only his words weren't softened with what sounded like genuine concern. Something which resembled *kindness*. Because that was Marnie's undoing. That was what made her defences begin to weaken. She curled her hands into two tight fists, her fight-or-flight instinct kicking into action. After a childhood of being let down so many times, she wasn't used to people being kind because she never let them close enough to try. The habit of a lifetime had taught her to guard her secrets and lock them away, because that was the safest thing to do.

But Leon Kanonidou knew her more intimately than anyone else. He had been deep inside her, his hard flesh united with hers so that for a while she had actually felt as if they were one person. Was it that which made her hesitate and foolishly give him the opening he was seeking?

'It's my…sister,' she said. 'My twin sister, Pansy. I've been worried about her, that's all.'

She recovered enough to follow this up with a dismissive nod, indicating that the subject was closed—but Leon Kanonidou was either oblivious to the hint or deliberately choosing to ignore it.

'What's happened to her?'

'I didn't say anything had happened to her.'

'But that's what you implied.' His gaze was very steady. 'Tell me.'

Was this how people got so powerful? Marnie wondered wildly. Did they just use the compelling force of their personalities to make you feel you actually *wanted* to confide in them? Well, maybe Leon would get more than he bargained for. She couldn't imagine him hanging around to investigate further once he discovered the facts. 'She's in trouble with the law,' she said, the words sticking like glue to her throat.

'Why?'

She shook her head. 'It doesn't matter.'

'Tell me,' he said again.

Oh, but his voice was so soft, so deep, so cajoling. It lulled her into a false sense of security. It made her imagine—for one brief and shining moment—how it might feel to have someone you could lean on.

'She's always been a bad judge of men. Maybe it's congenital.' She gave a short laugh and had the pleasure of seeing him flinch. 'Her latest boyfriend asked her to carry a bag to Monaco for him and she agreed. I'm sure you can guess the rest.'

'Drugs?' he said quietly, his expression grim.

'Diamonds, actually.' But then Marnie stopped thinking about Leon—stopped thinking about anything other than lovely Pansy, who should have known better, but who trusted people way more than she ever should. 'But she didn't know what was in it!' she burst out passionately. 'She honestly didn't know. You could rightly accuse her of being too gullible, but she's not a criminal. She's innocent!'

His blue eyes were very intense. 'That's what they all say.'

His cynical assessment made Marnie furious that she'd told him, and as angry tears sprang to her eyes she tried to turn away from him. But he stopped her. He put his hands on her shoulders and she could feel the power which flowed from their steady weight. And then he did the most unexpected thing. He reached one hand to her face to slowly wipe away the track of wetness which had trickled down her cheek. Somehow the gesture disarmed her and she couldn't afford to let it. She jerked away from him, aware and afraid of what his touch could do to her.

'Don't you dare judge her!'

'I'm not judging her,' he said. 'I'm just telling you how a prosecution lawyer would look at it.'

'Oh, so you're an expert in law as well, are you?'

'Let's just say I have a working knowledge of legal matters,' he answered drily. 'Where is she now?'

'In prison. In London.' She stared at him defiantly. 'There! Shocked?'

'It takes a lot to shock me, *agape*,' he demurred. 'Won't they grant her bail?'

She moved her shoulders uncomfortably, knowing that she had said too much, but something about his response made her want to continue—because hadn't she been bottling this up for so long? 'No,' she said flatly. 'No bail. They think she might be vulnerable to outside influence—which is probably true.'

'From the boyfriend?' he interjected.

She pulled a face. 'Yeah. The ex-boyfriend now. The case comes to court soon but the lawyer they've given her is rubbish. That's the reason I came to Greece. It's pretty much a certainty that Pansy's going to get a custodial sentence, so I took this job because it's unbelievably well paid and my salon in London gave me a leave of absence.' The words were bubbling out now. Bubbling out in a torrent she couldn't seem to stop. Yet wasn't it a relief to say this stuff out loud, instead of letting it join all the other dark secrets which hung heavy on her shoulders? 'At first I was determined to get her a better lawyer but when I discovered how much they charge per hour, I realised how naïve I was being. So instead I thought…'

Sapphire eyes speared into her. 'You thought what?'

She shook her head. 'It doesn't matter.'

'Marnie.' There was a pause. 'Please.'

It was a request but it was also a command and Marnie sucked in a breath, hating the way he seemed to be taking control. *Hating it, yet revelling in it all at the same time.* 'I thought I could save some money for her. So she'd have something to support herself with when she was set free. A nest-egg to get her started. At least that's something I *can* achieve.'

Leon watched as she fished a tissue from the pocket of her uniform and blew her nose, and afterwards surveyed him with an expression of defiance and vulnerability. He noted the untidy spill of her hair and the pinkness around her eyes and felt a tug of something he didn't recognise deep inside him.

'And what about your parents?' he said. 'Where do they come in all this? Can't they help?'

He saw her stiffen.

'My mother is dead and I never…' She lifted her jaw almost pugnaciously. 'I never knew my father. So now you know. You've heard everything and you can go.' Her gaze was very steady. 'Can't you?'

All her defiance was still there but so too was a

sudden sense of wariness which had made her words so brittle. Leon wondered if she was expecting condolences about her parents, but he made none. He couldn't be that hypocritical and, besides, wouldn't she be appalled if he told her the truth? That part of him envied her the inevitable freedom which resulted from being orphaned?

But she had painted a bleak picture of her life. Of someone struggling on her own and fighting against the odds. He looked around the small room, which was so hot it felt like being in a sauna. At the hairbrush lying on a table, next to a pile of well-read books and a photo of a beautiful woman who looked a lot like her. Was that her sister? A large, half-filled suitcase lay open on the floor in one corner and his gaze lingered on it for a moment longer. Did that mean she was leaving? And despite the inner voice of caution which was urging him to stay out of her troubles, he found himself ignoring it.

'I can help you,' he said suddenly.

Her suspicious eyes became iron-hard as she shook her head. 'I don't want your help.'

Leon frowned, for this was the last thing he had expected. In a world where wealth talked, he'd never met anyone who wasn't eager to have a conversation. People never refused his money or influence. But then, he'd never met anyone like Marnie Porter before and the fierce pride radiating from her tiny frame drew from him an unwilling sense of admiration. 'I have the wherewithal and the resources to help your sister,' he growled. 'Let me put them at your disposal.'

'Thank you for the offer. It's very kind of you and I appreciate it,' she said. 'But no.'

'Why not?'

She considered his question for a moment. 'Because I don't really know you,' she said at last. 'And I don't want to be beholden to you. I don't want to be beholden to anyone.'

He stared into her determined face and could see she meant it. But he could also see that she was far from immune to him.

Nor he to her.

Her eyes had grown dark and the way she was chewing on her bottom lip was failing to conceal its telltale tremble. Against the bodice of the white uniform dress he could see the tantalising thrust of her nipples as they silently acknowledged his proximity—just as the hard ache at his groin acknowledged hers. He could feel the throb of mutual desire which flowed between them like like some tangible life-force. The sexual chemistry between them had been intense and powerful from the start—and, oh, the temptation to capitalise on it was overwhelming.

He knew he could pull her into his arms and kiss her and within minutes she would be kissing him back with the same hunger which had captivated him on the beach last night. He swallowed, tortured by all the possibilities which might follow such a move. He pictured his hands exploring her newly awoken body, hearing those mewling little cries of hunger as she touched him back. He imagined his fingers rucking up her uniform dress to slide down panties he suspected would already be wet. Would she instinctively tilt her pelvis towards him—inviting him to ravish her here, where she stood, her back pressed up against the wall and her legs wrapped around his back? Or would she lead him over to that lumpy-looking bed where they could spend a long and sticky night together?

But that would be wrong, on so many levels. He needed an outspoken hairdresser with a sister in jail like he needed a hole in the head.

The aching in his body was almost unendurable but Leon forced himself to project an indifference which, for once, was proving elusive.

'If that's what you want.'

'It is.'

'Then I guess I must wish you well. Goodbye, Marnie.'

'Goodbye, Leon.'

He saw the shadow which flickered over her face just before he turned his back on her and wondered if she would break in the short time it took for him to walk to the door. Would she call him back and tell him she'd changed her mind? Tell him that she wanted his money *and* his body—and didn't the prospect of that fill him with heady anticipation?

But she didn't.

She didn't say another word as he let himself out into the sultry darkness of the Greek evening and Leon experienced a powerful sense of disappointment.

And surprise.

CHAPTER SIX

AMBER SUNLIGHT SLANTED in through the windows of the tiny London pub and although a TV screen was showing highlights of a hugely anticipated football match, most people were watching the bubbly blonde who was waving a half-empty champagne flute in the air.

'Ooh, I'm just so thrilled! I can't believe it, Marnie,' she was cooing. 'After all the dire predictions the court just *threw* the case out!'

Marnie shook her head and smiled. 'It's wonderful,' she breathed. 'And no, I can't quite believe it either.'

They were sitting in the nearest pub to the courthouse in central London, while her sister celebrated her acquittal in typical, flamboyant style. She was wearing a leopard-skin jacket over a very short black dress and her bottom-length blonde hair was accessorised with a glittering gold headband. It probably wasn't the best choice of clothing in which to attend an important court hearing and Marnie had been amazed at the eventual outcome. All charges against her sister had been quashed, the surprising verdict no doubt due to Pansy's slick new barrister who had defeated the prosecution lawyer with his clever arguments and was now joining them for a celebratory glass of prosecco.

Pansy's new barrister.

As the euphoria following the verdict began to evaporate, Marnie's buzzing mind started focussing on Walker Lapthorne, who had made a dramatic, eleventh-hour appearance at the beginning of the trial. A handsome and sophisticated lawyer who didn't come cheap. Marnie had looked up his rates soon after his unexpected appearance at the start of the case and had stared at them in disbelieving horror. Who on earth could afford to employ someone of his calibre? She remembered the panic which had flooded through her. What if Pansy had done something completely dumb—like taking out a bank loan to hire one of the country's best barristers to defend her? And why was she now batting her eyelashes at the russet-haired attorney as if she were completely smitten? Marnie had tried to get her sister alone ever since they'd sat down in the pub, but had met with a deliberate stonewalling by her twin, and a refusal to budge from Walker's side.

Well, there was nothing else for it but to ask the question out loud.

Marnie cleared her throat. 'Mr Lapthorne?'

'Walker, please.'

'Walker. Firstly, a great big thank you for helping my sister get the justice she deserves.'

The lawyer smiled. 'My pleasure.'

Marnie lowered her voice. 'I'm assuming you weren't appointed to be Pansy's lawyer through legal aid?'

He nodded, his expression growing slightly veiled. 'Your assumption is correct.'

'And I know she couldn't possibly afford to pay your fees.' Marnie fixed her twin with a questioning look. 'You didn't pay them, did you, Pan?'

'Of course I didn't,' spluttered her twin. 'How could I?'

Her innocence sounded genuine and Marnie found herself despairing at the way her sister had always operated. She had always closed her mind off to the unpleasant things in life if she suspected they might compromise her in some way. It was presumably why she had agreed to carry a bag which wasn't hers for a smooth-talking boyfriend. And if a mysterious lawyer had appeared out of the blue and informed her he was going to be her saviour, Pansy would simply have smiled and said yes, please.

But if Pansy hadn't paid for the services of Walker Lapthorne, then who had?

Briefly, Marnie closed her eyes as an unwanted image swam into her mind. Of a man with blue eyes which blazed like sapphires and a naked body bathed silver by the light of the stars.

He wouldn't.

Would he?

Not when she had expressly told him not to.

She forced herself to continue. 'So, who *did* employ you to take on this job, Mr Lapthorne?'

The lawyer's voice acquired a little edge. 'I'm really not at liberty to say, Miss Porter.'

Marnie nodded. She wanted to ask him more but acknowledged the finality in his tone. And anyway—if her suspicions were correct—how on earth could she explain away such a random and generous action on the part of the Greek tycoon? Would she honestly want Pansy to know the reason *why* Leon had done it—or Walker, if he hadn't already guessed?

Repeating her congratulations, she rose to her feet, kissed her sister goodbye and let herself out of the pub, stepping into a flurry of leaves, their dark swirl controlled by an autumn wind which had suddenly grown biting. Although she had the rest of the day off, she was reluctant to go home just yet—not with all these unanswered questions swirling around in her head. She bought herself a takeaway coffee, carried it to one of the nearby garden squares and sat down on an iron bench.

It had to be Leon.

But Leon lived in Greece.

A wave of confusion washed over her. He hadn't actually told her that, had he? In fact, he had told her remarkably little about himself—something she could strongly identify with, but not in these particular circumstances.

Putting her coffee down, she took out her phone and tapped his name into the search engine and there it was. Thousands of entries about the Kanonidou empire, less so about the man himself. But several things became instantly apparent. That Leon had a home and a branch of his company in central London—*and he had flown into the capital just the week before*!

So it could have been him.

Who else would have done it?

Marnie's throat dried and her heart began to race. She needed to find out for sure and then to…to what? To thank him? Of course she was grateful—hugely grateful—but she couldn't quite shake off her air of suspicion. She'd never met anyone who did something for nothing—which made her wonder just *why* he had done it.

But these thoughts were nothing but self-indulgence. If her hunch was correct then Leon had been unbelievably generous towards her sister and she needed to tell him that. What was she so afraid of? But she knew that, too. She was scared of the way he made her feel. Scared of the things he made her want. She'd been thinking of little other than him since she'd flown back from Greece and touched down at a rainy Stansted airport. Hadn't she returned to work at the salon unable to stop fixating on him, causing a couple of her colleagues to remark that she had been unusually quiet and preoccupied? And they had been right.

She focussed her search on the whereabouts of his London offices and discovered they were in Mayfair, not far from Bond Street Tube station. Soon she was standing outside a small, modern block of offices which sat comfortably beside the imposing splendour of its eighteenth-century neighbours.

As she headed towards a discreet smoked glass door bearing the Kanonidou name, Marnie felt a sudden onset of nerves. Couldn't she have sent him a thank-you card, or a bottle of whisky in a flashy wooden box? She found herself wondering if she was using his interference as an excuse to see him again and whether this was the start of a slippery slope which was only ever going to lead downwards.

Her mind kept returning to their last meeting, when she'd told him about Pansy and had refused the help he'd offered. She remembered feeling empowered as she had announced that she didn't want to be beholden to anyone. *But he had ridden roughshod over her wishes and done it anyway, hadn't he? What kind of arrogance was that?*

She remembered the terrible, sweet tension which had sizzled between them, with her alternately praying he would kiss her, then praying he wouldn't. And he hadn't. He had walked away without a backward glance and that had made her feel dark and lonely inside, her stomach twisted into knots of regret and rejection.

She caught a glance of herself reflected back in the glass of the Kanonidou building. The wind had managed to free some of the hair which she had coiled into a sensible updo for the court hearing, and the sober charcoal suit she had hoped would reflect well on her wayward sister made her look as if she were moonlighting as a bailiff. But she wasn't here because she wanted to appear attractive to the Greek billionaire. She was here to say her thanks, and then leave.

What if he wasn't here?

Well, it was too late to change her mind because a revolving door was expelling her into a huge reception area, filled with jungle-like foliage, and Marnie felt as out of place as she'd ever felt—especially when she noticed a uniformed security guard studying her from between narrowed eyes. A beautiful brunette behind a wide desk was sending a questioning look in her direction, the angle of her jaw suggesting that Marnie had no right to be here.

But she did.

She most certainly did.

Trying not to feel overwhelmed by the cavernous dimensions of the place, she made her way to the desk—fixing her face with the determined expression she'd used with social workers during most of her turbulent childhood.

'I'd like to see Leon Kanonidou, please,' she said.

'I'm afraid Mr Kanonidou doesn't see anyone without an appointment.'

'How do you know I haven't got an appointment?'

The brunette gave a serene smile. 'Because I have his diary sitting right in front of me and your name isn't on it.'

'But you don't know my name.'

'No, but I do know all the people on his list and you aren't among them.'

Marnie chewed on her lip. In a way she admired the woman's resolve, which was easily a match with her own—but if this receptionist thought she was going to slink away from here with her tail between her legs, then she thought wrong.

'Tell him Marnie Porter is here,' she said quietly. 'He'll see me.'

It was amazing how many insecurities you could hide behind a mask of bravado, but for once in her life Marnie was sure of herself, confident that Leon *would* see her. Because wasn't there something powerful which pulled her to him and vice versa? Some unseen force which flowed between them—as strong as molten metal. Wasn't it that same force which had made him hire an expensive lawyer to get her sister out of a fix? Which had brought her here today, even though every atom of her body was telling her it was dangerous.

The receptionist's perfect brow pleated into a frown

as she picked up a phone and had a brief conversation which resulted in her giving a grudging nod. But any triumph Marnie felt at having got her own way was short-lived, because the realisation that she was actually going to face Leon again was making her feel dizzy. Would she have gained some kind of immunity to him by now? Would she be able to look at him without wanting him to pin her down onto the nearest horizonal surface?

As a flash elevator swished her upwards, she wished she'd had the good sense to use a bathroom to repair her wayward hair and perhaps apply a slick of lipstick. She had already decided she didn't particularly care about impressing him, but she didn't want to come over as looking a total mess. But the elevator doors were sliding open and another gorgeous brunette was waiting outside. Did he order them from a catalogue? she wondered. This one was dressed in a neat black pencil skirt, a pristine white silk shirt and vertiginous black heels.

'Miss Porter?' the woman questioned.

Marnie nodded. 'That's me. I've come to see Leon.'

'If you'd like to come this way. Kyrios Kanonidou is expecting you.'

No time for second thoughts, just time to breathe deeply in a vain attempt to calm the wild thunder of her heart—while Marnie followed the black pencil skirt over a softly carpeted floor and into a vast office, whose windows overlooked the carefully tended grass of Hanover Square.

A lifetime of being summoned into alien offices had honed her ability to take a rapid measure of the tycoon's inner lair and, naturally, it was impressive. Spectacular paintings covered the walls, making it far less impersonal than most offices. There were big windows with amazing views and an even bigger desk, on which she could see a fancy cream card edged in gleaming gold, which looked like an invitation.

And then she noticed Leon standing on the other side of the room, watching her—the faintest of curves tilting his hard mouth into an ironic smile. As if he were used to being the first thing someone looked at, not the last. What did his expression tell her? Was that bemusement she could read? It was difficult to tell. She blinked, trying to adjust her eyes to the bright light—trying to get her head around the fact that this was the man who had kissed her, and held her. Who had taken her virginity with a consummate skill which had made her want to weep with disbelieving joy.

Yet today he looked like a stranger in his smart city clothes. An intimate stranger in a dark suit and a sapphire tie which echoed his spectacular eyes. She felt poleaxed by his presence, aware of her stinging breasts, which had started rubbing against her bra, and the rush of syrupy heat to her panties. It was as if her body were acknowledging him with ecstatic familiarity, even if her mind remained deeply mistrustful. She had certainly not acquired any desired immunity, she realised, too late.

'Marnie,' he said, his rich voice caressing her skin like velvet. 'This is an unexpected surprise.'

'Is it really?' she questioned quietly and when he didn't answer, she continued. 'Did you pay for my sister's defence lawyer, Leon?'

His eyes narrowed. 'Did Walker tell you?'

She shook her head. 'He didn't break any confidentiality clause, if that's what you mean.'

'Then how did you find out?'

'I guessed it was you. Who else could it have been?'

He met her gaze. 'My actions were intended to be anonymous.'

'But you must have known I would try to find out.'

'Your powers of detection weren't my primary concern at the time, Marnie,' he said drily.

She flushed. 'No, of course not.'

He stared at her, eyebrows raised. 'So?'

'I came here to…to thank you. And to ask…' She swallowed before the words came tumbling out in a rush. 'To ask why you did it.'

The sigh Leon had been holding back left his lips at last because here came the infernal conundrum. Why *had* he done it? He had admired Marnie's passionate defence of her sister and her total belief in her innocence, that was for sure. The matter had been none of his business and she had told him to stay out of it, yet he despised unfairness and knew how situations could be weighted against you because of prejudice, or because you didn't have enough money to fight your corner.

But his interjection had been motivated by factors other than sympathy and the ability to help, and one of those had been a deep and lingering frustration. Had he subconsciously envisaged this very scenario, that she would come to him like this? Yes, he had. Of course he had. Initially, he'd thought that out of sight would be out of mind and he would quickly forget the feisty little blonde. It had been both irritating and perplexing to discover that hadn't been the case at all, and that he'd been thinking about her far more than was necessary. In fact, he'd been thinking about her a lot.

Maybe it was because Marnie Porter had given him a glimpse into a different kind of world—the kind he wasn't familiar with. One where the odds were stacked up against you if you happened to be poor. His own upbringing had been far from perfect but it had always been affluent. He'd always had the best that money could buy. And yet that made no difference. Money didn't make you happy.

His mouth hardened.

Wasn't he the living proof of that?

He watched as she readjusted the strap of her shoulder bag and thought how uncomfortable she looked in her 'smart' clothes. Yet, ironically, the badly cut jacket and skirt somehow managed to tantalise him. Was it because they hinted at the delicious flesh he knew lay beneath, rather than clinging to her voluptuous frame and announcing it to the world? Had bedding a virgin turned him into a latter-day prude? he wondered wryly.

'I did it because of what you told me,' he explained slowly. 'Your anger at your sister's imprisonment was very...affecting. As was your belief in her innocence. I don't like injustice and I was in a position to do something about it. So I did.'

'Just like that?' she said faintly.

He shrugged. 'Walker is a top-class lawyer who has done some brilliant work over the years. I had him take a look at your sister's case and he concurred that she was likely to be given a custodial sentence. So I asked if he would investigate further and he agreed. He went to see her in jail, believed in her innocence and then took her on as his client. You know the rest.'

She fixed that grey gaze on him, fierce and unwavering. 'Even though I'd explicitly said I didn't want to be beholden to you?'

'But you aren't,' he objected. 'Not in any way. If the money I paid to employ Walker is really bugging you, you can walk straight out of here, speak to one of my assistants and arrange to pay back the fees. Take as long as you like—a lifetime if you wish—I don't care. But we both know that would be a futile gesture because I don't need the money. I already have more than I know what to do with.'

'Then maybe you should try giving some away to charity!' she challenged.

'I already do.'

'And I suppose you consider me and my sister to be your latest charity?'

'Now there's a thought. What would we call it, I wonder?' he mused. 'The Proud Porter Charity?'

She pursed her lips in what looked like a disapproving gesture but a brief giggle escaped from them nonetheless, and Leon felt an unexpected flicker of achievement—as if he had done something remarkable by coaxing a smile from her. As if a man would have to work very hard to amuse this little hairdresser—and since he had never had to put in much effort for a woman before, the novelty value of that was also appealing. And didn't her smile kick-start his imagination? Didn't the soft curve of her lips plant a very graphic picture in his mind about on which particular part of his anatomy he'd like to feel them?

'Anyway,' she said, shifting a little awkwardly on a pair of extremely unflattering shoes. 'I've said thank you and I'm sure Pansy would echo that.'

'Shall we go and have a drink to toast her freedom?'

She regarded him suspiciously. 'When?'

He glanced at his watch. 'What about right now?'

'It's the middle of the afternoon!'

'So? Haven't you ever drunk champagne in the middle of the afternoon?'

The look on her face suggested she had not and, even though Leon was already doubting the wisdom of his invitation, he seemed powerless to stop himself from pursuing it.

'Come on, Marnie,' he continued softly. 'What do you have to lose?'

But she shook her head. 'Thanks, but no thanks. I have to get home and anyway, I'm not dressed to go for a drink.'

For a moment Leon was so surprised and yes, so *irritated* by her refusal that he was tempted to let her walk right out of that door. And then his gaze was drawn to the unwanted invitation to his father's wedding, which was lying in a prominent position on his desk, and he reminded himself that sometimes life's pleasures needed to be grabbed at.

'Then how about you let me give you a lift home instead?' he questioned evenly. 'To Act On.'

CHAPTER SEVEN

'What do you have to lose?' Leon had demanded when he'd invited her to toast her sister's freedom, and Marnie could have answered in an instant.

Her sanity?

Her composure?

Most of all, the sense that she still had some element of control over her life.

She had refused the drink and not just because she was wearing clothes which would have made her stand out like a sore thumb. It was more to do with the fact that Leon was such a big personality. He was so handsome and charismatic that people would be bound to stare at them if he took them to a fancy venue, which undoubtedly he would. What if people saw them together and started asking questions about her? It was a risk she wasn't prepared to take, having kept herself below the radar all through her life. But Leon was nothing if not persistent and eventually Marnie had agreed to a lift home, thinking he might send her off in a flashy car with a chauffeur at the wheel. That part of the equation had been correct—she just hadn't been expecting Leon to slide into the back seat beside her, his powerful presence immediately dominating everything around him.

Despite the vast dimensions of the luxury car, the atmosphere inside felt claustrophobic and not just because the windows were tinted, concealing them from the outside world. It was more to do with the realisation that she badly wanted him to touch her again, even though every instinct was telling her that was a terrible idea. He was powerful and autocratic. He was right out of her league. It was just a pity that her traitorous body didn't seem to agree. Her palms were sweaty. Her knees were trembling. Worst of all, they were already snarled up in traffic and Acton was a long way from the West End. She swallowed, aware of the silken throb of desire low in her belly. Would she be able to endure another thirty minutes of this torture? She wasn't sure.

'Shouldn't you be at work?' she demanded when he crossed one long leg over another and she found herself following the movement like a dog eyeing the revolution of a can-opener.

'I'm the boss. My hours are my own and I can do whatever I like—within reason. What's the matter, Marnie?' he questioned softly, stilling her by putting his hand on her arm. 'You seem very fidgety.'

'Is it any wonder? I wasn't expecting company.'

'And is my company so very awful?'

'It's not that. It's more a case of… Leon! What…what the *hell* do you…' Her question tailed off as his thumb began to caress her through the thin material of her jacket and she wondered if he could feel her shiver. Just as she wondered how it was possible to feel so aroused when all he was stroking was her arm. '…do you think you're doing?' she whispered.

'I think you know perfectly well what I'm doing. I'm trying to find out whether your skin is as deliciously soft as I remember and it most certainly is.' Without missing a beat he moved his hand down to her leg. 'I'm also a little surprised to discover that you're wearing stockings, since you didn't strike me as a stockings kind of woman, Miss Porter.'

'What's that supposed to mean?'

'I thought you were prim.' A skim of fingertips against the quiver of flesh, as his voice deepened. 'And these don't feel remotely prim.'

His fingers were inching up beneath her skirt and Marnie knew now was not the moment to enlighten him that she found tights constricting and liked her skin to be able to breathe properly. She swallowed but that didn't affect the terrible dust-dry feeling in her throat. She knew she ought to slap his hand away and stop him, but the trouble was that she didn't *want* to stop him. She wanted his hand to continue creeping up towards its drenched and aching destination. Would it be so wrong to allow herself a few moments of bliss before telling him this was a bad idea, or could he then rightly accuse her of leading him on? But she was powerless to prevent her eyes from closing as he drew a light circle over one trembling thigh and she wondered if he'd noticed the spill of flesh over the top of her hold-ups.

But suddenly all her perceived imperfections didn't matter because his slow stroking was becoming more and more irresistible and it was taking all her willpower not to whimper her approval, especially since he had bent his head and begun trailing soft kisses across her neck.

'Leon,' she whispered, but that throaty murmur sounded nothing like her normal voice.

'Shh…'

His velvety cajolement made the words die on her lips because he had reached her panties at last and was pushing the moist fabric aside and her eyes snapped open in alarm.

'Your…driver,' she gasped.

'There's a screen between us and him,' he murmured. 'And it's one-way. He can't see us and he can't hear us.'

Afterwards Marnie would marvel at the fact that they'd been discussing the inner workings of a luxury car at such a moment, but right now she was busy having Leon kiss away her little cries of pleasure while his unseen fingers worked their magic. She told herself to call a halt to it before it was too late, but she didn't think there was anything on earth which would have given her the strength to do that. Her breasts were tingling. Her flesh was dissolving—that silken beat impossible to ignore—the pump of her blood gathering pace like a piston. And then she was coming. Coming hard against the pressure of his palm. Trying not to buck or to cry out, despite his reassurance about the privacy of the one-way screen. Her attempts to keep her orgasm secret seemed only to intensify the sensations which were pulsing through her. It was…incredible. It seemed to go on and on for ever.

Eventually, he withdrew his hand and she was aware of the faint smell of her sex in the air. In a daze her eyelids fluttered open to find Leon regarding her, a look of feral satisfaction on his face, a soft smile at his lips.

'Did you like that?' he questioned silkily.

'I hated every minute of it.' She hit the button of the electric window and it slid soundlessly down. 'Couldn't you tell?'

A rush of cold air swirled in and he laughed but that didn't quite disguise the shifting frustration on his features and Marnie boldly reached out to rub her fingers over the hardness which the expert cut of his expensive trousers was failing to hide. For a moment he groaned as she feathered her fingers up and down his rocky shaft, before firmly removing her hand and putting it on her lap.

'No,' he advised sternly.

'Don't you want to?' she questioned, confused.

'What do you think, Marnie? Of course I do. It just happens to be a slightly less discreet operation for men.'

'I wouldn't know,' she said sulkily.

'Neither would I.'

She turned to him, blinking very hard, unable to hide the surprise from her voice. Or the leap of pleasure in her heart. 'Are you saying—?'

'That I've never made a woman come on the back seat of my car? *Neh*, that's exactly what I'm saying,' he growled. 'Just like I've never had sex on a beach with someone I've only just met. I don't know what it is you do to me, Marnie Porter—only that I find I want you. I want you very badly.'

It was a heartfelt declaration and it startled her. A little flustered now, Marnie turned her head to stare out of the open window to see that Shepherd's Bush had come into view. They must have been in the car longer than she'd thought. Her heart began to race. What did they say about time passing quickly when you were having fun—and wasn't that the best fun she'd had in years?

She turned back to find him studying her. In the dim light his features were shadowed, making the brilliance of his eyes stand out like jewels. And suddenly she thought, why *shouldn't* they carry on what they'd just started? Mutual pleasure between two consenting adults wasn't any sort of crime, was it? Because yes, she'd just had the most amazing orgasm but Leon must be extremely frustrated, judging from the tension which was hardening his amazing features. And she wanted him inside her again. Deep and properly inside her. She wanted that more than anything.

'Would you like to come in for coffee?' she questioned carelessly.

His eyes gleamed as his tone matched hers. 'Why not?'

It was weird having the limo purr to a halt outside the purpose-built block which housed her humble bedsit and even weirder to walk into the thankfully litter-free—for once—entrance hall with Leon by her side. She wasn't used to having a man around and she certainly wasn't used to the wild flutter of her heart, or the urgent need which fired up inside her when she closed the front door and he pulled her hungrily into his arms and started kissing her as if his life depended on it.

'Leon!' she moaned and was rewarded with a taunting thrust of his hips against hers. He had pushed her jacket from her shoulders with an impatience which made her heart sing and now he was tugging frantically on the zip of her skirt, so that it pooled to a heap on the well-worn rug. Fingers flying, she did the same—easing his jacket off so that it concertinaed to the ground.

He removed her shoes and the sensible white blouse she'd worn for the court case. Next, off came her bra and panties and although both were plain and not in the least bit provocative, they still elicited a husky groan when he saw them. She could see him scanning the small room with dazed eyes before backing her towards the sofa and laying her down on it.

He hauled his silk shirt over his head without even bothering to undo all the buttons, before turning his attention to his trousers. 'Don't move,' he commanded, for he must have seen her wriggle.

But that was a big ask. Marnie could barely keep still. She wanted to writhe her bottom against the narrow sofa in joyful anticipation. It seemed so long since that night on Paramenios, and although he had just subjected her to that blissful experience in the back of his car, she wanted something more intimate than that and didn't know how much longer she could wait.

Not much longer, it would seem as he came towards her with a look of dark intent on his face which thrilled her to the core. And it was only when he was finally and magnificently naked that Marnie realised that she hadn't been able to appreciate him properly last time. The afternoon sun was far more revealing than the Greek starlight had been, accentuating the honed contours of his incredible body so that he looked like a living statue—and much better endowed than any of those museum sculptures of her childhood.

'You're…you're beautiful,' she blurted out before she

could stop herself, and the surprised flare of pleasure in his eyes gave *her* pleasure.

'So are you,' he husked.

She wasn't—she knew that—but by then he was bending his head to kiss each peaking nipple as if paying homage to her breasts—so that she actually *felt* beautiful. She could feel each mound fill with heat and fire, their tips so exquisitely aroused by the graze of his teeth that it felt as if she were hovering tantalisingly between pleasure and pain. He slid his hand between her legs, a moan sliding from his lips as he found her sticky warmth and began to strum against the sensitive bud until once again, Marnie found herself on the brink.

And then he was straddling her. Sliding a condom into place before entering her with one long, slick thrust. She felt him still as her body readjusted itself to his size and his width and when she looked up into his face, it was a study of concentration and fierce pleasure as he began to move.

It was incredible. It was everything Marnie had imagined it could be. It was also over very quickly. She didn't think it was possible to orgasm so rapidly, and as her body pulsed out its climax she heard the broken exclamation he made in Greek and that thrilled her too.

'Where's the bedroom?' he growled, when they finally came up for air.

She pressed her fingers into his back. 'You're in it.'

'I meant, where's the bed?'

'You're lying on it.'

'What?' Propping himself up on his elbow, he frowned.

'This is a studio flat,' she explained. 'Everything's in one room, including the kitchen—although the bathroom's off the hall. Haven't you ever seen a sofa bed before, Leon? If I had the energy I could demonstrate how you can tug the mattress out from underneath to make a very small double bed.'

Leon started to laugh. No, he had never seen a sofa bed before. Just as he'd never been somewhere where you shared a sleeping space with a kitchen. He yawned. 'Why don't you show me in a while and we can spend the rest of the evening here?'

She hesitated, a look of uncertainty crossing her face. 'If you're expecting dinner, I've only got leftover lasagne in the fridge.'

'I don't care what you've got in your damned fridge, Marnie. The only thing I want to feast on is you. Now stop blushing and go and get us something to drink.'

He almost regretted asking when she removed her delicious warmth from his proximity and he wished she hadn't pulled that unprepossessing white blouse over her head. Pillowing his head on his folded arms, he watched her walk across the limited space to a tiny fridge, thinking that maybe the blouse wasn't such a bad idea after all, for it ended midway down her bottom, allowing him to fully appreciate the abundant flesh of those peachy curves. She was still wearing the hold-ups—although now with a tear snaking down the back of her left leg. Should he arrange to have some silk stockings delivered? he wondered idly, before dismissing the thought. Given her spiky independence, she was more likely to garotte him with them than wear them.

She turned round, a glass of water in each hand, and as their eyes met a punch of something he didn't recognise slammed at his heart. It was desire. It must be. What else could it be? How did she do it? he wondered feverishly as he felt the inevitable hot hardening at his groin. How did she make him want her this much?

He waited until she had returned to the sofa bed and they'd drunk some water—until he had made her come with the flick of his tongue and afterwards she had licked him back as if she were slowly working her way through a large ice-cream cone. It was only then that he pushed away the pale tumble of her mussed hair.

'I think we should do this again, don't you?' he questioned idly.

He felt the sudden tension in her body.

'This?' she queried, lifting her head from his chest to stare at him, as if seeking clarification. 'Celebrating my sister's acquittal? I'm hoping she's going to avoid any more court cases, if that's what you mean.'

'You know damned well that's not what I meant, Marnie.'

'I'm a hairdresser, not a mind-reader. Could you be a bit more specific?'

Leon frowned. He would have preferred she had worked this out for herself rather than him having to spell it out. But maybe it was better this way. There would be no way she could misinterpret his bald words, nor attach any kind of unwanted significance to them.

'I'm talking about seeing one another again when I'm in town.'

'You mean for sex?' she questioned carefully.

'I suppose that's one way of describing it.' There was a pause. 'I prefer to think of it as mutual enjoyment.'

She was still regarding him with that unblinking stare. 'And you would expect me to be *available*?'

He shrugged. 'Only if you wanted to be.'

A long silence followed his remark. He realised he was hanging onto her every word and for one insane moment he actually thought she might be about to turn him down, but then those wintry eyes narrowed speculatively.

'No strings?' she said.

That was supposed to be *his* line.

'No strings,' he concurred.

'Because I'm not looking for a relationship at the moment.'

'Neither am I,' he said faintly. 'I don't want marriage and I definitely don't want children, but I—'

'You, what?' She tipped her head to one side, her blond hair falling untidily over her breasts, drawing his attention to them and making it imperative that he flick his tongue over their puckering surface as soon as possible.

'I want you,' he concluded huskily.

'Yet you're still looking shell-shocked,' she observed caustically. 'What's the matter, Leon? Haven't I been eager enough in accepting your offer? Do women usually cling to you like limpets in this kind of situation?'

'You could say that.'

'I just did.'

He smiled. 'Do you know, I don't think I've ever met a woman who answers back quite as much as you do,' he murmured as he brushed another thick and wayward strand of hair back from her face. 'But I know one guaranteed method of keeping you quiet.'

'Oh, really?' she questioned innocently. 'And what's that?'

But he shut off any further lines of questioning with a hard and demanding kiss.

CHAPTER EIGHT

THE RATHER BATTERED old Mercedes came to a halt outside the salon, the profile of the man behind the wheel darkly rugged and unmistakable, and Marnie's heart performed a predictable somersault when she saw him.

'Ooh, look—here's your boyfriend, Marnie!' Hayley, the salon junior, sounded excited as she peered out through the plate-glass windows, watching the yellow gleam of the headlights cutting through the late-September dusk. 'Haven't seen him in a while.'

'No. That's right. He's been away,' said Marnie, grabbing her coat and feasting her eyes on her Greek lover, who was waiting for her in his old car. The ten-year-old car he kept in his garage for solo anonymous driving trips until she'd confessed she much preferred it to his sleek, chauffeur-driven limo. Just as she'd explained she'd rather get the bus than be driven around by someone wearing a cap and uniform who insisted on leaping to open the door for her as if she were infirm, and bowing to her every wish. At first Leon had thought she was joking—as if nobody in their right mind wouldn't like being ferried around by a driver. But Marnie hadn't been joking. What was happening to her was surreal enough anyway—without throwing into the mix the sort of hands-on luxury most people only dreamed about. His massive apartment she could just about cope with, along with the staff he employed there—but anything else would be stretching it. And why get used to something which was only ever intended to be temporary? Wouldn't that make the inevitable comedown even worse?

Wasn't she already terrified of how much she was going to miss him once it ended?

'Where's he been?'

Marnie turned to look at the salon junior. 'Oh, you know. Abroad. On business.'

Hayley frowned. 'You've never really said what it is he does, Marnie.'

'Something to do with property?' Marnie said, turning the answer into a question. 'I'm never really sure what it is myself.'

Slinging her handbag over her shoulder, she grimaced. She hadn't actually *lied* to the staff at Hair Heaven about the identity of her 'boyfriend', and particularly not to young Hayley, whom she'd been mentoring for years—she'd just played down Leon's international status and achievements. Because the reasons for her caginess had the same root as her preference for travelling in a nondescript rather than a head-turning car. It was easier to let her colleagues believe she was going out with an ordinary man, rather than an international property tycoon, and it stopped them from asking too many questions.

She licked her lips. Not that 'going out' was a particularly accurate description of their set-up. They didn't really travel anywhere much beyond the walls of his vast apartment—although, to be fair, he often asked if she wanted to go out for dinner, or the theatre, or even the opera. But Marnie invariably refused and not just because she was paranoid about their relationship going public. She liked being alone with him best of all, without the pressure of wondering whether she was using the correct knife and fork. And besides, she didn't have the clothes to wear to those places and she didn't want people staring at them, thinking what an odd couple they made. She could never quite shrug off the feeling that others were judging her and deciding she didn't have a right to be there. She knew that was called imposter syndrome.

Because you are an imposter. If Leon knew the person you really were, you wouldn't get within five yards of his home.

Because that was the bottom line, wasn't it? The ever-present fear which always gnawed away at the back of her mind, that her true identity would be rumbled. And not just that. Years of being rejected and subjected to the harsh regimes within the many institutions which had housed her had planted in her the seeds of doubt. Of not being good enough—certainly not good enough for a man of Leon's calibre. Cocooned in the roomy opulence of his London home, she was safe from speculation, and safety was something she had always rated highly.

Only Pansy knew the truth about Marnie's new lover and Pansy most definitely did not approve. She seemed to have become a worrier on her sister's behalf and, in a slightly ironic twist, their lifelong roles seemed to have become reversed.

'Is that why he bailed me out?' her twin had demanded. 'Just so he could get inside your knickers? You do know that he has a terrible reputation with women, don't you, Marnie? I looked him up on the internet. Why, even *I* wouldn't dream of getting involved with a man like that, and I'm way more experienced than you!'

That last bit had been particularly wounding and Marnie had railed at her sister's ungratefulness, closing her mind to the fears which Pansy's words had produced. If her twin was determined to be cynical, that was up to her. She had agreed to a no-strings fling with Leon. She had laid down those terms herself and the billionaire tycoon had agreed to them. She'd done that mostly to protect herself, to try to shield herself against any hurt she might feel when it all ended—and if she was being naïve, then so what? Naivety wasn't a crime, was it? He had given her the opportunity to walk away from him and she had chosen not to take it.

Hayley's question broke into her thoughts.

'He's still keen, then, I take it?'

Marnie gave a ghost of a smile as she made her way towards the door. 'That's a question you'd have to ask him, I guess.'

But one word spun around in her head as she bade goodnight to the junior and pushed open the salon door.

Keen?

He was keen for sex, that was for sure. Just like she was. And that was what all this was about, she reminded herself fiercely. A grown-up relationship which revolved around the physical, with no unrealistic promises and definitely no glimpses into a possible future. They never discussed next month, let alone next year. He hadn't asked how she was spending Christmas or quizzed her about what she wanted for her birthday. In fact, he had no idea when her birthday was, and she didn't know his either. And since Marnie had never pursued a happy-ever-after, she had convinced herself that she was contented with what Leon was offering.

Sometimes she couldn't quite believe the situation in which she found herself, because in a sense she was betraying everything she held dear. Sometimes, in the dead of night, she found herself unable to escape the mocking thoughts which taunted her. That she had become something she'd never set out to be. A rich man's plaything. Something she'd never planned but which had been driven by her fierce desire for him. Because she just couldn't resist him. Never. He only had to look at her to make her boneless with longing, and when he touched her she went up in flames.

She'd let down the defences she'd spent a lifetime erecting and knew that made her vulnerable. But Marnie had convinced herself that as long as she compartmentalised everything—if she kept her feelings in check and just enjoyed the sex—she would be able to keep emotional danger at bay.

Hayley was still standing at the salon window watching as Marnie opened the car door and there was Leon in the driver's seat, his jaw shadowed, his black hair ruffled. She felt her pulse pick up speed as he turned to slant her that slow and sexy smile.

'Hi,' he said softly.

'Hi.'

Keeping her greeting as casual as his, Marnie slid into the passenger seat and snapped her seat belt shut. How quickly she had adapted to being a rich man's lover! His discreet squeeze of her thigh made her shiver and a rush of something powerful flooded through her as their gazes met. But there was no kiss. Nothing to indicate he'd been missing her while he'd been away. Leon Kanonidou didn't do public declarations of affection. Just as he didn't do romance, or commitment, or marriage—though he'd never told her why and she'd never asked. They didn't have that kind of soul-searching relationship.

But that was okay.

That was what she had signed up for, wasn't it?

'Like to go for a drive?' he questioned as he started up the engine. 'We could watch the sun go down somewhere along the river. Maybe have a drink on the way.'

The dying September day might be growing dusky, but it was still light enough for Marnie to notice the tension which was forming deep grooves on either side of his lips. Was that jet lag? she wondered. 'We don't have to. You look tired—and I've been on my feet all day,' she said, suddenly realising how much the backs of her calves were aching. 'Why don't we go…' she nearly said home, until she realised that sounded a little presumptuous, so she quickly changed course '…back to yours?'

'Okay. Back to mine it is.' Leon switched on the ignition and glanced in his rear-view mirror as he pulled away. 'Why don't you tell me about your day?'

Out of the corner of his eye Leon could see her clasping her hands together on her lap, before beginning to chat. Slowly at first and then, as she got more into her stride, her account became rapidly laced with irreverent anecdotes and a few impersonations of the salon's clientele, which for once failed to make him smile.

His mouth hardened as he drove into the underground garage of his block. Deep down, he was grateful she had refused his offer of a drive because he was worn out after his trip and dreading the week ahead. He switched off the engine. Sex would ease some of the tension. It always did.

The elevator from the garage took them straight to his apartment and as Marnie removed her rather ugly coat he felt the instant flare of hunger. He stared at her with a bemusement which was rapidly overtaken by desire, despite her sartorial shortcomings. Beneath the coat she wore a plain and frumpy blouse and skirt, along with a pair of shoes whose only possible attribute—surely—was that they could be described as *comfortable.* But at least she had untied her hair, letting it fall into a silken tumble which rippled down over her luscious breasts, in the style she knew he liked. She was the sexiest woman he'd ever met and yet she dressed like a middle-aged secretary.

He shook his head a little, still slightly irritated by her stubborn rebuttal of his suggested gifts, despite the fact that they'd been seeing each other for weeks now. She hadn't let him buy her anything. No clothes. No jewels. No shoes. Nothing. Not a single trinket had ever made its way from him to her and he found that deeply frustrating. No woman had ever refused his gifts before and sometimes he found himself wondering if she thought he would regard her more favourably if she rejected his generosity.

But at other times he chided himself for his cynicism because—quite simply—she took his breath away. He let his gaze drift over her now, unable to lose his faint air of incredulity. Wondering how it was that, despite her modest wardrobe and lack of sophistication, Marnie Porter could provoke in him the most powerful physical response he'd ever experienced. A response which was all-consuming, instant and automatic. She was doing it now, without doing *anything*—just regarding him with those watchful grey eyes which gave nothing away.

He had tried to analyse her appeal, with varying degrees of success. Sometimes he thought it was because she made him laugh and challenged him all at the same time. At others, because she seemed genuinely unimpressed by his wealth. Was it because she didn't bore him with questions about how he *felt*—or, even worse, give him chapter on verse on her own feelings? Or was it more primitive than that? Maybe it was all tied up with him having been her only lover. Maybe he was more old-fashioned than he'd thought.

Exclusivity was a powerful entity, he concluded wryly, his lips softening in anticipation. And purity was a surprisingly potent concept. He could feel a sweet aching in his balls as hot, hard desire flooded through him. A desire strong enough to take his mind off the forthcoming engagement which was looming ever closer in his diary with all the allure of an execution.

Deliberately, he leaned back against the wall. 'Come here,' he instructed softly, his concerns drifting away as she went straight into his waiting arms. Wasn't it remarkable that she knew intuitively when to be docile and when to be dominant and, right now, he was the one who needed to be in total control. He kissed her for a while. A long while. Until her breath had begun to quicken. Until he was so hard that he wanted to explode. But he liked making himself hold back—and that was part of the control too.

'How…how was your trip?' she asked breathlessly, as he slid her blouse from her shoulders.

'Predictable.'

'Oh?'

As her skirt pooled to the ground, he put his hand between her thighs and felt her shiver as his thumb alighted on her sensitive nub, already slick with desire. 'Well, we *could* talk about my trip,' he said unevenly, flipping her round so that now it was *her* back pressed against the wall. 'Or we could talk about how wet you are and how much I want to be inside you again, after a wait which has felt almost unendurable.' He swallowed. 'The choice is yours, Marnie.'

'That's not…fair,' she said weakly as he pushed aside the damp gusset of her panties and grazed his fingertip down over her soft folds.

'Isn't it? How would you like me to be fair, then, *agape mou*?' he mocked, his movement pausing. 'Do you want me to stop? To fix you a drink, and remark how beautiful the trees look from the terrace?'

'No,' she husked. 'You know I don't.'

He gave a soft laugh as he unzipped himself and let his trousers fall, before stroking on a condom and hooking up her legs, so that her thighs clamped themselves deliciously around his hips.

He could have come immediately but tempered his own desire until she was engulfed by satisfaction, until her curvy body tensed with waves of release and she shuddered out his name. With one final jerk he let go and spilled his seed—pumping ecstatically until at last he stilled inside her spasming flesh.

Afterwards, he kicked off his jeans and carried her into the bedroom, laying her down in the centre of his bed so that her hair was spread like rippling gold against the pristine white of the pillow, thinking how exquisite she looked with her eyelids hooded and that dreamy smile curving her lips. Deftly, he removed the rest of their clothes and pulled her into his arms, so that her soft flesh moulded against his beneath the duvet.

'I really am the most inattentive of hosts.' He pressed his lips into her hair. 'Want me to get you a drink now?'

'No, thanks. And for what it's worth—I have no complaints about your hosting skills,' she said, rolling over onto her stomach and fixing him with that curious grey gaze. 'I'm more interested in how you are. You look stressed.'

'Not any more, I hope.' He yawned. 'Orgasm is supposed to release stress.'

'Temporarily, I believe. But now it's back again. I can tell.'

'You're very observant.' He yawned again.

'Mmm. I know. It's an acquired skill. Comes from years of watching people in the mirror. I can always tell if there's something on their mind. And there's definitely something on yours.' She hesitated for a moment before she started speaking very carefully, as if she were reading from a crib sheet. 'Do you want to… to move on?'

'Move on?' He looked at her with genuine bewilderment. 'Move on where?'

'From me.'

His eyes narrowed as it slowly dawned on him what she meant. It was honest and upfront but if she was expecting him to make a declaration that he would never leave her, then she was about to be disappointed. 'No, Marnie. I don't want that but when I do, I can assure you that you'll be the first to know. Is that a deal?' He wondered if she would find his honesty unsettling, but her careless shrug reassured him.

'Deal,' she said, turning onto her side to face him. 'So, now do you want to tell me what's bothering you?'

'You don't usually ask questions.'

'No, but you don't usually keep scowling like that either.'

Leon stared into the up-close focus of her features because the crazy thing was that he *did* want to tell her. Crazy because his usual instinct would be to shut the topic right down. But there was something about the way she was talking which felt more like concern than prying. He didn't get the feeling she wanted to discover more about him because that would increase her influence over him, or because one day she might try to use it against him. He was no stranger to power games with women, but there had never been any with her. In fact, she had been the soul of discretion since their affair had begun. She'd explained that she hadn't told anyone at work about it—'They'd only try to talk me out of it, like my sister.'—which he had found slightly insulting. Her words had been backed up by a lack of prurient calls from diary columnists, trying to find out why he was dating someone like her.

He swallowed. She was unlike any woman he'd ever known, that was for sure. She confounded his expectations at every turn. Was that why he was tempted to confide in her? Because, on some unfamiliar level, he felt he could trust her not to take this any further?

'My father is getting married and I have to go to the wedding.'

'Have to?' Her grey eyes narrowed. 'I can't imagine you doing anything you don't want to, Leon.'

'Your faith is touching.' His voice hardened. 'Put it this way—the publicity and conjecture surrounding a no-show would be far worse.'

She pushed a thick handful of hair away from her flushed face. 'Let me guess. You don't like your new stepmother?'

The suggestion was almost comic in the circumstances but Leon didn't smile. 'It would be difficult to attribute that particular role to a woman who, at twenty-four, is almost a decade my junior.'

'So she's—'

'I think the term you might be looking for is trophy wife,' he offered caustically. 'And there's no need to look so concerned, Marnie—I'm used to it. This will be my father's fourth wedding, but the third was far worse—or rather, that particular stepmother was.'

There was a pause. Her soft lips became suddenly sombre, as if she had detected the new and bitter note which had entered his voice.

'So was she *cruel*, like in all the fairy tales?'

The silence which followed was broken only by the

sound of their breathing. 'No,' he said, at last. 'I almost wish she had been.' He waited for her to comment because that would have been a distraction—an intrusion—and might have halted the dark flow of his words. But when she didn't, he found himself lost in the past. Talking as if nobody were listening. Saying things to Marnie Porter that he'd never told another soul.

CHAPTER NINE

'MY FATHER WAS a shipbuilder,' Leon began, pushing the sheet away from his bare torso. 'And one of the wealthiest men in Greece.'

His words faded away and for a moment Marnie thought he'd forgotten she was there. 'That explains how you got so rich, I guess,' she prompted.

'Actually, it doesn't.' His words became coated with acid. 'I took nothing from him.'

'Isn't that unusual?' she questioned slowly. 'For a man not to help his kids out financially?'

'I believe so. Though he certainly didn't have any problem showering wealth on my two older stepbrothers from his first marriage. But by the time I was a teenager, we were estranged.'

There was a space in the conversation which demanded to be filled. 'Why was that?'

He shrugged. 'It's a long story.'

'Most stories are.'

He was staring at her, but it was as though he were looking right through her, and suddenly Marnie found herself wishing they were making love again or that she'd let him fix her that drink after all. Something which might have distracted him long enough to change his mind about telling her this. Because wasn't that the trouble when you found out more about someone—that you might not necessarily like what you heard? That once you had started exchanging confidences it changed the nature of a relationship and meant you might never be able to return to an earlier, easier place? Wasn't there the fear that he might expect her to tell him stuff about herself?

And she could never risk that happening.

She swallowed down the lump in her throat, knowing it would be better to halt the conversation right now. Make an excuse to leave their sex-rumpled bed to get them a drink or something and hope that he'd forgotten about it by the time she returned.

But it was too late for any U-turn. She could feel the rough brush of his thigh against hers as he changed position on the bed and turned to face her, his handsome features hard as granite, with an expression she'd never seen there before. 'My mother died when I was sixteen,' he began.

'I'm sorry,' she said, but she spoke with almost exaggerated care, because life with mothers was not her favourite topic. 'What happened?'

'She had cancer for a long time.' He paused. 'A fact made worse by the fact she didn't tell me how bad it was. She pretended there was nothing wrong right up until the end and by the time I found out...'

She saw and heard the pain as his words faded out and wished she could take it away. 'I think terminal illness was handled very differently when we were growing up,' she said, with some degree of calm. 'They tried to protect children from the truth without recognising the damage they were doing in the process. Didn't your father say anything to you, or did he collude with her?'

He shook his head. 'It wasn't a case of collusion. They barely spoke. He was never around and I don't think he particularly cared what happened to her,' he said, and now she could hear a different kind of bitterness in his voice. 'It was his second marriage and not a particularly happy one, but at that stage in his life I don't think he had the appetite for another divorce. So he just carried on seeing his long-term mistress and once my mother had died, he married her.'

She took a moment to absorb this. 'So what was that like? For you?'

He turned away from her, lying on his back to stare up at the ceiling—but not before Marnie had seen the flicker of something unbearably bleak in his eyes. It was only afterwards that she realised it was disgust.

'It was hell,' he said bitterly. 'She…'

'She what?' she prompted softly.

'My stepmother was a very beautiful woman and very conscious of that fact, in the way that beautiful women sometimes are,' he said. 'My father was in his fifties when I was born, so by the time he remarried, he was relatively old.'

'While you were just on the brink of manhood,' she observed. 'I'm guessing the atmosphere in the house wasn't great.'

'It was toxic. There were warped undercurrents everywhere you moved and you wouldn't need to be a genius to work out what happened.' He turned back towards her. 'Or rather, what my stepmother intended to happen.'

She didn't like what she could see in his eyes now, but she could hardly deny the truth when it was staring her in the face. 'She…' Marnie's stomach gave a sickening lurch. 'She wanted you?'

He nodded. 'Oh, she wanted me, all right. It was a silent form of seduction, conducted in total secrecy. Lingering glances which used to make my flesh crawl. She used to slide her tongue over her lips whenever she stared at me and she stared at me a *lot*. Nobody but me would have known it was happening, but I knew. It's what made me despise women who use and abuse their sexuality.' His words were tight and clipped. 'I kept away from the house as much as I could, but soon my absences started to be noticed. My father wanted to know why I was never there.'

'And you couldn't tell him, I suppose.'

'Of course I couldn't tell him. It would have ruined him. Smashed his pride and his ego, and no way did I hate him enough to want to do that.' He gave a contemptuous laugh. 'I don't think he would have believed me anyway—for what man likes to believe he's being cuckolded? The upshot was that I felt like a stranger in my own house. As if I were trespassing within the hallowed sanctuary of their marital home—and my father reinforced that feeling in his attitude towards me. Maybe I reminded him too much of the wife he had cheated on, or maybe on some subliminal level he *did* guess what my stepmother's intentions were.' A muscle began to work at his temple. 'All I know is that he was totally in thrall to that woman in a way I've never forgotten, nor wanted to replicate.'

His words unsettled her—sent alarm bells ringing—but Marnie told herself this wasn't about her, or her insipient fears about *their* relationship. 'Don't they call it the young lion syndrome?' she questioned slowly. 'Who is driven out of the pack by the older, jealous male.'

'I guess.'

She took the opportunity to snuggle up to him. 'So what did you do?'

'I took the route of disenchanted sons the world over and ran away to America. To Chicago, which has a big Greek community. I found myself a job and a mentor who told me what I needed to do. And with his backing, eventually I got lucky.'

'That sounds a very modest assessment, Leon,' she said, drawing a circle over his belly with the tip of her finger.

'Are you implying that I'm usually immodest?' he mocked, shifting his weight slightly to give her better access.

'I wouldn't dream of it!' Her face grew serious. 'But now you're reconciled with him? You must be, if you're going to his wedding.'

He shrugged. 'In theory—though it was never a total severing of relations, for that would have caused gossip and I had no desire to bring shame upon the family name. Whenever I visited my homeland I made sure I saw him, though I never visited the family house because I didn't want to run into my stepmother. But there was a definite thawing when he finally divorced her on grounds of infidelity.' He let out a frustrated sigh. 'And then came the news that he was planning to marry a woman in her twenties. Nearly sixty years his junior this time round.'

'And he wants you there.'

'He wants me there.'

'But you don't want to go?'

His mouth twisted. 'What do you think?'

'I'm thinking that maybe your conscience is nudging you to,' she answered quietly. 'Because he's an old man and it probably means a lot to him.'

Leon tensed, aware that again she had surprised him with her perception and quiet lack of judgement. She had listened to his words but his confidences hadn't brought forth a torrent of prurient questions. It was as though he'd dropped a stone into a pool, leaving behind no ripples. As if the things he had told her had vanished without trace.

And suddenly it occurred to him that perhaps Marnie Porter would be the ideal person to take to the wedding as his plus-one. Wouldn't she be like a breath of fresh air in that stale and echoing mansion? Someone innocent and straightforward who wasn't motivated by avarice, or greed. Someone honest and truthful, who could provide him with enough entertainment and satisfaction to make the whole damned occasion bearable.

He reached up to twirl a strand of pale hair around his finger and when he let it go it dangled in a perfect spiral against her heart-shaped face. 'Want to come with me?' he asked.

She blinked. 'Where?'

'To Syros, for my father's wedding.'

'You mean to the marriage of a child bride to a man you have a rocky relationship with? You haven't exactly sold it to me, Leon,' she said, but the waver in her voice betrayed a sudden sense of nervousness. 'I'm guessing it'll be a big, glittering affair?'

'Not at all. My father assures me it will be very low-key. A handful of guests, that's all.'

She still didn't look convinced. 'When is it?'

'Next weekend. The wedding is on Sunday,' he said. 'We could fly out on Thursday and come back on Monday. Make a break of it. We don't have to stay on Syros. I've recently bought a property in Thessaloniki. I think you'd like it.'

'I'm sure I would, but I happen to be working on Saturday.'

His eyes narrowed thoughtfully. Most women would have walked over broken glass to get an invitation to a party at the famous Kanonidou mansion and Marnie's reluctance was only firing his determination to have her there. Idly, he reached for her breast and began to caress the pliant flesh. 'But surely—'

'Surely what, Leon?' Pushing his hand away, she sat up and glared at him. 'You think I can just drop everything and come with you when you snap your fingers? You obviously have no idea how a hairdressing salon works! I have a client list which I've built up over years and which I'm not going to jeopardise for some random last-minute invitation.'

'"Some random last-minute invitation..."' he repeated faintly as he pulled her back down and into his arms, and this time she didn't resist.

'Well, how else would you describe it? You've hardly given me weeks to prepare, have you?' Undoubtedly influenced by the fingers which were edging towards her inner thigh, her voice became smoky. 'If I were to agree to come—*if*—it would have to be when I've finished work on Saturday afternoon.'

'That won't be a problem. We can fly out that night. You've never been on my plane, have you?'

'No, I've never been on your plane, but I haven't been losing any sleep over it.'

'That's a surprise. Most women are turned on by the size of a man's jet,' he said softly as he pinned his thigh over hers.

'Oh, you're impossible!'

'Am I?'

'Totally.'

He grazed his mouth over hers. 'But you're going to have to let me buy you some clothes for the wedding.'

Her eyes snapped open. 'No.'

'Yes,' he insisted softly.

'You know how I feel about you buying me things.'

'I don't think I could ever be in any doubt about that, Marnie,' he said drily. 'But this is different.'

'Because I dress so terribly, you mean?'

He chose his words with care. 'Because otherwise, I think you might feel out of place. And that would draw attention to you, which I know you don't like.'

She went very quiet then, as if she were weighing up her options. 'I'm not going into one of those fancy stores where the assistants look you up and down as if you're a nasty smell,' she said eventually.

A smile touched his lips, because this felt something close to triumph. 'That isn't going to happen. You don't have to do anything you don't want to, Marnie.'

CHAPTER TEN

THE PILE OF glossy merchandise was piled high on the floor of Leon's dressing room and Marnie came to a sudden halt when she saw it. Taking off her coat, she draped it over the back of a chair, conscious of his bright blue gaze boring into her. 'What's all this?' she asked slowly.

'Why don't you take a look?'

She regarded the boxes and upmarket carrier bags as warily as if they contained a set of unexploded bombs, but really it had been a disingenuous question. She knew exactly what would be inside—outfits for her to wear to his father's wedding, which she had grudgingly agreed to accept. She'd told herself that such a move made sense because if she turned up looking like a poor relation, wouldn't that make her stand out even more? But now the moment had arrived, her heart was thumping and she couldn't seem to shake off a gnawing feeling of anxiety. Was that because accepting his gifts seemed to signify a subtle shift of power between them? Or was she being delusional in denying that Leon had *always* possessed the power in their relationship? She wasn't sure—all she did know was that she felt as if she had crossed a line and the boundaries between them were becoming blurred.

Leon had suggested she choose the clothes herself but she had refused—citing busyness at work making it impossible for her to find the time. But the truth—which she didn't tell him—was that she wouldn't have known where to start looking. What if she'd broken some fundamental style rule and turned up wearing something horribly unsuitable? More than that, she couldn't bear the thought of walking into an intimidating store brandishing a rich man's credit card because that would have made her feel like…like a cliché.

She bit her lip.

Like a kept woman.

Perhaps if she'd been able to get hold of her sister she might have asked her to accompany her, because Pansy was super-confident, even if their taste in clothes clashed. But her twin wasn't answering her phone and, besides, Marnie couldn't bear to endure another lecture on Leon's unsuitability as a lover.

The upshot was that Leon had announced he would sort it out himself—and it appeared he had done just that. Was there anything a rich man couldn't do? she marvelled silently.

She walked across the room towards the goodies, telling herself she didn't particularly *care* what he'd bought her, but that certainty was fading by the second and suddenly Marnie was back to being that little girl at Christmas time. The one who never got any decent presents, even though she'd never stopped hoping. Even when she and Pansy were being considered for adoption, the gifts they received were always second-rate. It was as if their prospective parents didn't want to waste any money in case it didn't work out, which, of course, it never did—which meant that her mistrust of generosity ran deep. But Leon was looking at her questioningly as she stood in front of all the designer-store bounty—and surely it would be rude not to take a peek…

Crouching down, she began to untie the silken ribbons, delving between rustling layers of tissue paper to pull out the kind of clothes she'd only ever seen her most upmarket clients wearing. Several filmy day dresses, a couple of delicate blouses and butter-soft T-shirts. Pale jeans and a beautifully-cut skirt, as well as a kaftan, sandals and swimwear—all with co-ordinating accessories. There was underwear, too. Flimsy little scraps of fine lace and satin. High-cut panties designed to flatter a woman's legs and bras whose sole purpose, she suspected, would be to accentuate cleavage. Yet instinctively she knew that all these colours were *her* colours and that everything would flatter her and fit her perfectly. They were exactly the kind of clothes she might have chosen if she had lived a different life and been a different person.

But it was the dress which had obviously been chosen for the ceremony itself which commanded centre stage. In the softest scarlet silk imaginable, it was the loveliest thing she had ever seen. Marnie swallowed as she ran her fingertips over the slippery fabric, slightly scared by just how much she longed to wear it, but her natural suspicion was never far from the surface.

'Where did all these things come from?' she questioned, forcing herself to let the garment slide from her fingers. 'Did the good fairy drop them by?'

'The stylist delivered them this afternoon.'

'A stylist who's never met me?' She raised her eyebrows. 'She must be very perceptive.'

'Actually, the stylist was a he.'

'Oh. Right. And how did *he* know my size?'

'I gave him your measurements.'

'I wasn't aware you *knew* my measurements, Leon!'

He gave a slow smile. 'Let's just say I have a good eye for dimensions.'

The ugly twist of jealousy inside her made Marnie unable to hold back her feelings, even though caution advised her against expressing them. 'I suppose you've kitted out countless women like this in the past?'

'No, I haven't,' he negated silkily. 'And I've certainly never gone to the trouble of finding the best stylist in the business and telling him exactly what I thought you needed.'

Her voice was cautious. 'And what was that?'

His gaze swept over her. 'Beautiful things which weren't too revealing, because you have an essential modesty about you, Marnie, and I like that. In fact, I like it a lot. Call me old-fashioned but the possession of virtue is a dying art and it's seriously underrated.' His voice deepened. 'Though I can't understand why you insist on covering up so much, when you have the most beautiful body I've ever seen.'

It was a rare compliment, which made her heart stab with joy and apprehension, and Marnie busied herself with scouring through another bag, hoping the movement would hide the sudden hotness in her cheeks. He was making her sound like the personification of all that was good and innocent, but the woman he was talking about was nothing but a fiction. Yes, she had been a virgin, but he was making her sound like some kind of saint and she definitely did not have a saint's pedigree.

Worry began to gnaw away at the pit of her stomach as she wondered just where this affair of theirs was going.

Ever since he'd asked her to accompany him to the wedding, she had been aware of straying into perilous waters. With each day that passed, she felt the growing danger of remaining in this relationship. It was as though she were sleepwalking her way towards the inevitable pain of rejection, by a man whose company was never intended to be anything other than temporary.

And all the warning signs were staring her in the face—signs she had been stubbornly refusing to heed. Leon had told her about his surprisingly painful past. His mother's failure to disclose her terminal illness must have seemed like a terrible betrayal. He had witnessed other betrayals, too. His father's infidelity and slavish devotion to a new wife, who had tried to seduce his son.

No wonder he was so set against marriage and permanence.

And if he was? So what? What on earth did that have to do with her?

Her flush deepened.

Unless she was seriously considering herself in the role of Leon Kanonidou's wife! What had happened to the stubborn sense of determination with which she had entered into this affair? Hadn't her number one criterion for agreeing to become his de facto mistress been that it could only succeed if she kept the physical and the emotional separate? It was supposed to be about sex. Nothing else.

Nothing else.

'Well?'

She looked up to see Leon staring at her, his expression indicating he was awaiting her verdict, and she realised how ungrateful she must seem. He'd obviously gone to a lot of trouble to buy these gorgeous clothes, yet she was acting as if he'd committed a crime. And she had agreed to this, hadn't she? She had agreed to let him dress her up like a doll. Rising to her feet, she walked towards him, wrapping her arms around his neck and kissing him on the lips. 'I love them—every one of them,' she said truthfully.

'So why don't you try on the red dress?' he suggested.

She took a step back. 'What, now?'

'Don't you want to see what it looks like on?' His voice deepened. 'I know I do.'

It was a tacit request to take off her dowdy work clothes and replace them with a fairy-tale dress and, although Marnie tried to convince herself that would be a lovely thing to do, she suddenly felt stricken with shyness. Leon had watched her undress countless times before, so why did this feel so *different*?

Beneath the burn of his gaze she self-consciously removed her jumper and skirt and laid them on the chair to join her coat. She felt like one of those snakes she'd once seen on a TV documentary. As if she were shedding her old skin and taking on a brand-new persona—someone she didn't know or recognise.

She was down to just her underwear when Leon

began to walk towards her and she knew from his expression—which was hard and hot and hungry—just what he wanted. What *she* wanted, too—because wouldn't sex successfully eradicate the muddle of her thoughts?

'On second thought,' he said, 'the dress can wait.'

And the crazy thing was that Marnie didn't make a single objection to his masterful assertion. As he pulled her into his arms she shivered with anticipation, her stomach dissolving, her blood growing heated with need. Because that was the fundamental weakness which flew in the face of her certainty that she was getting in too deep—that the moment Leon touched her, she couldn't think straight.

His kiss was urgent and she moaned beneath the seeking pressure of his lips. As he slid her panties down over her trembling thighs something told her she would never wear this old underwear again. That from now on she would be dressed in fine satin and silk and lace, like a pampered woman.

Like a mistress.

She felt him tugging urgently at his belt as vulnerability and desire washed over her. 'I haven't had a shower yet. I still smell of the salon,' she whispered.

'I like the smell of the salon, but all I can smell is you,' he growled, kicking off the remainder of his clothes and carrying her next door into the bedroom, where he laid her down on the huge bed, and straddled her.

He took his time. He stroked her, knowing exactly how she liked to be touched—but something told her he was teasing her, too. By now she badly wanted him inside her but still he held back. As if he were hell-bent on demonstrating his steely self-control—or her lack of it—as she begged him to take her. As if it gave him a heady kick of power when he elicited her first helpless orgasm with the quick dart of his tongue. 'Oh!' she cried. 'Oh!'

He entered her when she was still caught up in those powerful spasms and as he filled her a soft warmth flooded through her body. She must have gasped something appreciative because his gaze was now focussed on her intently. And when he looked at her that way at a time like this she felt closer to him than she'd ever felt to anyone. 'Leon,' she breathed, overcome with an unwanted emotion which threatened to rock the foundations of her world.

'What is it, Marnie?' he mocked.

Closing her eyes, she bit back the tender words which were threatening to spill from her lips and concentrated on the ripples of pleasure instead. Already so close to the edge, she buried her head in his neck and began to husk out another orgasm, her fingernails digging into his broad shoulders as he followed her, choking out that incomprehensible sound he always made when he was coming and which had become so familiar to her. They lay there for a while in silence, his fingers running through her hair, when his question came right out of the blue.

'So what happened to make you so modest and shy, Marnie Porter?'

She fought her instinct to freeze, in case she looked as though she had something to hide.

Because you have.

'I don't know if that's a very accurate description.' She forced herself to smile. 'People always say I'm very mouthy.'

'Well, you are. Sometimes.' He smoothed a lock of hair away from her cheek. 'But you are also very reserved. And I'm curious why.'

She wanted to jump up from the bed and run away. She wanted to tell him it was none of his business and if this was only supposed to be a casual relationship, then he had no right to ask her questions. But he had told her all that stuff about himself and if she kept quiet that would only make him suspicious. Men like him didn't like having things denied them. He would probably start probing and she would have to stonewall him and then they'd have a terrible row.

And she didn't want it to end like this.

She chewed on the inside of her mouth. She could explain some things. Just not all of them. That was a compromise of sorts, wasn't it? 'You haven't actually met my sister, have you?'

'No, but I've seen a photo of her.'

'Then you will have seen for yourself how beautiful she is.'

'She's certainly a dramatic dresser.' He shrugged. 'If you must know, I don't think she's nearly as beautiful as you.'

'Oh, come *on*, Leon,' she said crossly, edging away a fraction. 'You don't have to flatter me because we've just had sex! We're non-identical twins and, yes, we're very similar, but beauty is notoriously difficult to define. A centimetre here and a centimetre there makes all the difference and it's Pansy who has the biggest eyes and the better figure and she was the one who...'

'The one who, what?' he questioned softly as her voice tailed away.

'It doesn't matter.'

'Or maybe it does.'

His voice was compelling. It was binding her to him like the strong silk of a spider's web. It enveloped her and in that present moment it made her feel safe and protected. Was it that which made her speak almost without thinking? 'I told you how we spent a lot of our time in the care system—'

'Sure. Because your mother—'

'Died,' she said quickly and now she was *keen* to talk to him, because surely one frank disclosure would rule out the need for another. 'We had no other relatives. And back then—it may have changed now—the care system used to employ some pretty dodgy people. The sort of people who might take an unhealthy interest in a pretty little blonde girl. I was always looking out for Pansy and I tried...'

'You tried to shield her,' he said, his voice tight with repressed fury. 'Let me guess. You did everything you could to help conceal her burgeoning sexuality from those bastards.'

Marnie stared at him. 'How can you even *know* that?'

'It's pretty obvious. I'm also guessing you taught yourself to hide behind concealing clothes and made Pansy do the same—and the moment she was able to take care of herself, she probably rebelled against that. You, on the other hand, kept up the habit.' He frowned. 'One thing which has always puzzled me is why you were wearing that uncharacteristically flimsy orange bikini when we met.'

'Oh, that. My work colleagues in London gave it to me before I flew out to Greece, mainly as a joke.' She turned her face towards his. 'If it hadn't been for that—if I'd been wearing one of my all-concealing swimsuits—do you think you'd still have taken me out on your motorbike and then to dinner?'

'Truthfully?' He shrugged. 'I have no idea. I certainly wasn't impervious to the very obvious visual stimulus of your barely clothed body, but there was also a powerful spark between us which went beyond the merely physical, Marnie.' There was a pause. 'There still is,' he concluded silkily.

Marnie pursed her lips together, trying to keep her reaction hidden. She wanted to thank him for saying that, which probably said a lot about her lack of self-esteem. But the trouble was that his murmured words gave her hope—and false hope could have painful consequences. Sexual chemistry was nothing special. It was fleeting and transient. Everyone knew that—and woe betide the person who thought otherwise.

'I'm going for a shower,' she said, sliding out of bed before he could try to change her mind, and it wasn't until she was standing beneath the steaming jets that she realised she was shaking.

She closed her eyes as hot water rained down on her face. Leon had asked all the right questions—or maybe they were the wrong questions—because she had ended up revealing more about herself than she ever did. More than she was comfortable with. And confidences were like standing at the top of a slippery slope. Once she'd told him one thing, he would want to hear more. And still more. Her sleazy beginnings were fascinating to other people—she remembered that much from school, when someone had found out about their mother. She remembered the row which had resulted after she and Pansy had been taunted and how the school had asked for them to be removed, because they really couldn't have little girls fighting like that. And yet another set of foster parents had explained to the authorities that they wouldn't be adopting the twin girls, with the faces of angels.

There was a *reason* why she had always felt as if she were on the outside, looking in—and why she would always stay that way. Because she was. People like her were scarred by their experiences and sometimes those scars were too deep to ever heal properly. She had never felt 'normal' and probably never would. She had always accepted that, until she had met Leon. He had made her want to step out of her comfort zone. He had made her want things which had never even been on her radar before and that was so dangerous.

She went back into the bedroom to get dressed, relieved he was nowhere to be seen, and as she pulled on some of her new lingerie she knew she couldn't carry on like this, no matter how much she liked Leon Kanonidou.

Liked?

She almost laughed out loud. Who was she trying to kid?

'Liked' was a lacklustre description of her feelings for him. Lately Leon had been dominating her thoughts like an addiction, and whenever she saw him it was as if an invisible fist had reached inside her chest and squeezed her heart very hard. She'd never felt love before but that didn't mean she was immune to it or its power. Did it? And if that was the case it was only going to get worse. If she allowed her feelings free rein they could easily overwhelm her, and then who would she be? Just another foolish woman sobbing into her pillow because she'd fallen into the trap of thinking a man might change.

Leon had told her from the start what he didn't want and she had gone along with that. And surely if he got any inkling that she'd started to want more, he would move to end it anyway.

She sucked in a deep breath.

She would go to the wedding, as planned. She would provide him with the support she suspected he needed, and afterwards…

She pulled on some pale cotton jeans.

Afterwards she would make her exit from his life.

She would walk, before she was pushed.

CHAPTER ELEVEN

THE MANSION ROSE up before them. A monstrous monolith which dominated the land around and Leon could do nothing to prevent the shudder of distaste which ran down his spine. The last time he had seen this place he had been walking out with a rucksack and the predatory eyes of a frustrated woman burning into his back. Had Marnie detected the bitterness of his feelings and was it that which had prompted her to lay her fingers over his tensed biceps and to give it a soft squeeze? He swallowed. Did she realise what her touch could *do* to him? That sometimes she had the power to take some of the darkness away?

She was staring up at the multi-tiered concoction, her lips falling open as if she couldn't quite believe what she was seeing.

'This is your *home*?' she verified, but he shook his head in grim denial.

'This is where I grew up and lived until the age of sixteen,' he amended grimly. 'Do you like it?'

'Honestly?'

'Are you ever anything *but* honest, Marnie?'

He saw her swallow. 'I can't imagine ever living

somewhere this big,' she whispered. 'It looks more like a museum.'

Leon rang the bell and waited but there was no welcoming committee to greet them. No sign of his father. Instead, the door was opened by a housekeeper—a stranger to him, obviously. Her hooded gaze ran over them both with calculating precision, her greeting more formal than warm.

'Kyrios Kanonidou has been making some last-minute adjustments before the ceremony and would like you to join him on the eastern terrace for a drink straight away,' she announced. 'If you would like to follow me, I will make sure your bags are taken up to your suite. Once your meeting with your father is finished, I will send one of the servants to accompany you there.'

Leon was about to inform the woman that he was in no need of any direction before reminding himself that he was here as a guest, not to stamp his mark or assert his ownership—which was non-existent anyway. And nothing ever stayed the same, he reminded himself—wasn't that apparent with every step they took? As they walked through the wide corridors, he became aware of how much had changed.

The route was familiar, the décor was not. Within its ornate elaborate shell, the building had changed out of all recognition in the years since Leon had last been here. All traces of his childhood gone. It was as though he had never been there—his presence wiped clean. In some ways it felt liberating to acknowledge this break with the past, but it still came as a relief to step outside onto the sun-washed tiles of the eastern terrace. Lush lemon trees in pots adorned a space used mostly used for breakfast and morning coffee and which was currently deserted. A white balustrade framed the dark blue sea and there were steps leading down to a beach of silvery white sand.

'Wow. What a view,' said Marnie, her long blonde hair blowing lightly in the breeze.

He turned to look at her, remembering the first time he'd met her. Looking defiant and wounded as she lay on the sand—those stormy eyes and killer curves luring him into the most memorable sexual encounter of his life. Whoever would have thought that one day he would bring her here and she would stand overlooking the beach from where he used to take his morning swim? He realised how uniquely comfortable he felt in her company. 'You're ready to meet my father?'

'I think so,' she said, smoothing down her skirt. 'Is he *very* intimidating?'

'I'll leave you to judge for yourself,' said Leon, because suddenly Stavros was bearing down on them, sweeping onto the terrace accompanied by a small retinue of servants carrying trays covered with drinks and canapés. It had been a year since he'd last seen his father and, although he was definitely a little frailer, his posture was as upright as ever, resplendent in a fine wedding suit of silver-grey, a waxy white flower in his buttonhole. But Leon noticed as if for the first time how excess rather than age had carved out the deep ravines which made his features seem more ravaged than he remembered, and how the once-handsome face was now a pastiche of what it had once been. An unmistakable coldness flickered through his faded eyes as turned to survey his son, though Leon noticed how quickly he hid his reaction behind a pasted-on smile.

'Leonidas! I was worried you might not make it in time,' Stavros observed in perfect English as he made his way towards them.

'I said I would be here—and here I am,' replied Leon steadily. 'I'd like you to meet Marnie. Marnie Porter. You remember, I told you about her?'

'Ah, yes. The hairdresser.' The octogenarian's eyes narrowed. 'I understand we missed your company at dinner last night because of your dedication to your job, Miss Porter? I am in awe of such a work ethic. My son must be, too—for I have never been permitted to meet any of his girlfriends before!'

There was no doubt that Stavros was being mischievous and Leon wondered how Marnie would react to his teasing. But she seemed in no need of token reassurance, her familiar determination emerging as a gritty smile as she shook hands with his father. 'I'm delighted to meet you, Kyrios Kanonidou. Thank you for inviting me to your beautiful home,' she said firmly. 'I'm sure you must have plenty to talk about with your son, so I'll leave you to it.' Diplomatically, she walked across the terrace to gaze out at sea, leaving the two men alone to converse.

Leon didn't know what he had been expecting from this particular reunion, but it wasn't the unedifying discussion which followed. At times his father seemed almost...*jittery*, while at others almost borderline aggressive as he spoke to his son in voluble Greek. Leon wondered if the reality of marriage to a woman so young was losing some of its allure as the wedding approached—if perhaps his child bride was more demanding than Stavros had anticipated. Was history going to cruelly repeat itself by giving him another predatory wife with a wandering eye? As the conversation ended, Leon was aware that the vague suspicion with which he had initially viewed this wedding invitation had been eclipsed by a quiet and simmering anger.

He saw Marnie's eyes fixed on him as his father swept away with his entourage and as she came towards him he wished they could leave now. Board the luxury yacht which was moored and waiting in the marina in Phoinikas to take them to his house on the Thessaloniki coast. And although nothing was stopping them other than a misplaced sense of filial duty, Leon had given his word he would attend the ceremony and therefore he would do it, even if it was with gritted teeth.

'So. How did that go?' she questioned.

'If you don't mind, I'd rather not talk about it at the moment.' His words were clipped and he saw from her reaction that she had interpreted this as a put-down, but the reality was that a manservant had appeared to take them to their suite and, once there, Marnie realised she had very little time to get changed.

His own dressing swiftly completed, Leon walked over to the window while he waited for her, and stared outside, but the sight which greeted him did little to quell the tide of cynicism rising up inside him. Below, against the glittering backdrop of the sea, stood a wedding arch with rows and rows of chairs before it. Long tables were covered with white drapery, their surfaces crowded with silver and crystal. On the other side of the terrace, a wooden dance floor had been erected with a small dais at the back—presumably to house the band. And there were flowers everywhere. He'd never seen so many flowers. There were even small posies sitting on each of the seats, presumably one for each of the guests, who he could see were starting to arrive in a flurry of finery.

Leon's eyes narrowed. His father had insisted this would be a small and discreet ceremony. It certainly didn't look that way from here.

He heard a sound behind him and the moment Marnie walked into the room all his disdain evaporated, a pulse thundering at his temple as he acknowledged her stunning transformation. She was wearing a simple full-length dress in a blue as vivid as the Grecian sky, which skimmed her luscious curves and emphasised the pale curtain of her hair. She looked young and firm and fresh and he felt the tug of something deep inside him. He didn't know what he had been expecting, but it certainly wasn't *this*…

Her gaze was searching his face, as if she were trying to gauge his reaction. 'I know this is slightly different,' she said nervously, smoothing her palms over the material.

'Turn around for me,' he instructed silkily. 'What happened to the red dress you were supposed to be wearing?'

Marnie nodded as she did as he asked, unable to allay her sudden rush of nerves and wondering if she'd been too headstrong in her choice as she faced him. 'You would have preferred me to wear that instead? Do you mind?'

'Are you crazy? Why would I mind? You look absolutely sensational, Marnie. You must know that.'

Did she? Marnie swallowed. She looked more like herself—that was for sure. Most of the clothes his fancy stylist had purchased were perfect, but the red dress had felt like a step too far. Despite his assurances that the outfits were modest it had seemed too clingy and too provocative and when she'd stared at herself in the mirror, her shocked breath had frozen in her throat—but she couldn't possibly tell Leon the reason why.

Imagine his face if she did.

Imagine the dilemma he would face as a result of her disclosure—if he realised why it should disturb her so much.

It makes me look like my mother.

She'd used some of the money she'd been saving for Pansy to nip out from the salon with Hayley the following lunchtime to buy something different. Something more suited to a hairdresser's salary—although Hayley had persuaded her to be a bit more daring than usual. But at least now she didn't look a rich man's mistress, because that wasn't how she wanted Leon to remember her. Hadn't she already decided this wedding was going to be their swansong and she was going to make a graceful exit from his life when they arrived back in London? Her mouth dried. Even though the thought of leaving him was making her heart want to shatter into a million pieces…

'What's wrong?' he demanded. 'Your face has gone as pale as milk. What is it that you say in England—as if someone had walked over your grave?'

The pound of her heart felt like guilt and Marnie

scrabbled around to come up with a reasonable explanation, because what would be the point of coming here if she was going to spoil the event with all her fears about the future? 'I guess meeting your dad was more nerve-racking than I'd anticipated and I'm wondering what on earth I'm going to say to the bride,' she babbled. 'You do realise she's younger than I am?'

'I think I've been quietly blocking out that fact,' he offered drily. 'Don't worry about it, Marnie. Just be yourself.'

She wondered how she could be 'herself' when she wasn't even sure she knew who that person was any more. Beneath her dress, she was still wearing some of the lingerie Leon had bought—which probably cost more than an entire month's pay cheque. Yet if she was being brutally honest, didn't she *like* the sensation of fine silk sliding over her skin? Sometimes she wondered what it was going to be like returning to 'normal' life when their affair was over—if she was going to find it a sobering comedown.

But her reservations were forgotten as he pulled her into his arms to graze his mouth over hers in a teasing kind of kiss. As his fingertips skimmed over her bottom, Marnie felt the inevitable ripple of desire and Leon must have felt it too because his hold on her tightened, his palms pressing against her buttocks.

'*Neh.* You and me both,' he murmured complicitly, his breath fanning her mouth. 'If you must know, I'd like to fast-forward the next few hours because I can think of some far more enjoyable ways of spending a weekend in Greece.'

'You want to go and visit some crumbling temples?' she questioned innocently.

'I want to take your panties off as quickly as possible but that will have to wait until later. Come on. Let's go.'

He laced her fingers with his as they began to make their way through the maze-like property—and if Marnie was surprised at this unusually tactile display, she guessed it was because there was nobody around to see them. As they passed beneath elaborately painted ceilings and tall columns which emphasised the dizzying scale of the house, the touch of his skin felt electric. She told herself it didn't mean anything—even if she was discovering how much she liked this languid gesture of possession which marked her out as Leon's woman.

Which she wasn't.

Get real, she reminded herself fiercely. *That would imply some measure of permanence which has never been up for grabs. Your position in his life is short-lived and temporary.*

And very soon it was going to be over.

And the moment they stepped outside, everything changed. An instant buzz zipped around the grounds as people spotted them and started to converge on them, or rather—on Leon. When he let go of her hand Marnie felt as though she'd lost her anchor. This was way more than *a handful of guests*, she thought desperately. She was completely alone in a bobbing sea of bodies but she forced herself to smile brightly and to nod as if she understood, even though everyone was speaking in Greek.

Suddenly Leon was back by her side, a glitter of fury icing his blue eyes as he touched his fingertips to her waist. 'This place is like a damned circus,' he hissed. 'I feel like leaving right now.'

'We can't go yet. Come on, let's go and sit down.'

The scent of the flowers was so strong it was cloying and as they walked towards their seats Marnie could see heads turning to watch them. Was that because Leon was just so outrageously handsome, with the sunlight turning his skin to bronze and making his eyes look bluer than the nearby sea? Or were they wondering why he'd brought this unknown woman from England as his guest, instead of leaving himself free to chat up one of the many gorgeous women here?

As they sat down a sudden silence descended on the congregation and, along with everyone else, Marnie turned to see Stavros standing in the doorway of the enormous mansion. To the sound of loud cheers, he began to almost *sprint* towards the wedding arch and Marnie couldn't help thinking how sad it was. It was such an inappropriate speed for someone to make their way up the aisle and supposedly designed to imply that, despite his great age, he was still very fit.

The bride was fashionably late, her eye-popping figure revealed by a dress designed to do just that. The white satin gown was backless, plunging and split to the thigh—caressing every gym-honed curve of her incredible body. Despite her startling youth, she appeared to have had some work done on her face—either that or she'd had an allergic reaction to her lipstick.

Marnie had been to several weddings of questionable taste in her time, but surely you'd have to travel a long way to find one as awful as this. Her heart went out to Leon as his father kissed his new wife for much longer than was necessary. A man with waist-length hair who had been eyeing up the bride throughout the ceremony perched himself on a stool and started to croon a song to the newly-weds, even though he was obviously tone deaf.

And then, mercifully, it was over. Clouds of rose petals fluttered in the air as the couple turned towards the congregation and began to walk, arm in arm. Music began to be played—thankfully by some excellent bazooka players—and glasses of champagne were offered around.

But beside her Leon stood tense and unmoving, and as Marnie glanced up into his stony features, another feeling of concern flickered over her. 'Are you okay?'

His smile was edged with grit. 'It wasn't the most palatable occasion of my life, but at least it's over. I think we should have something to drink to celebrate that fact, don't you?'

He handed her a goblet of champagne but it tasted vinegary and Marnie surreptitiously tipped it into a nearby plant pot while nobody was looking. But Leon was looking. She glanced up to find his gaze fixed on her and suddenly she was transported back to those times when the foster home insisted on giving her macaroni cheese and standing over her while she ate it, even though they knew it made her retch. Once she'd been caught hiding the cold lump of food in her handkerchief and the red marks on her knuckles from the resulting caning had taken days to disappear. She shifted uncomfortably on her high heels.

'I didn't mean to—'

'Don't worry about it.' A wry smiled touched the

edges of his lips. 'It's fine. I agree. The champagne leaves a lot to be desired. I wonder if my new stepmother had a hand in choosing it—she doesn't exactly look like a woman of taste, does she?'

She followed the direction of his gaze to see that the newlyweds had taken to the floor for the first dance and the bride was strutting her stuff—seemingly oblivious to the presence of her new husband, who was jigging awkwardly by her side. It was excruciating to watch, but when the music came to an end and other couples started taking to the floor, Leon took the empty glass from Marnie's suddenly nerveless fingers and put it down.

'Come on, Marnie,' he said. 'Dance with me.'

Marnie glanced up at his stony features as they found a deserted space on the dance floor, thinking that there was a new brittleness about him all of a sudden. A sombreness which seemed to have settled over him like a dark mantle. She thought about the way his face had hardened when he'd been talking to his father on the terrace and she asked him again.

'What did Stavros say to you back there?'

There was a pause before he answered. A pause which went on for so long that she wondered if he'd heard her question, or whether he was just blanking it. And when he began to speak, his words were edged with iron.

'He thanked me for coming. He said it was important to him because it enhanced his reputation as a father, as well as giving my tacit seal of approval to the marriage. He also said he was pleased I'd done so well for myself, because all his money would be going to his new wife and her large and apparently impoverished family. Oh, and to my two stepbrothers, who have never done a day's work in their lives.'

'Oh, Leon.'

He shook his head. 'I don't want your pity, Marnie,' he said softly. 'Just like I don't want his damned money. I never did. That much hasn't changed. I'm just not sure why he made such a damned fuss about me coming here, if all he wanted to do was to inform me of the terms of his will.'

She hesitated. 'Maybe you being here means more to him than he's letting on and he's just being clumsy about expressing it.'

'Please don't go getting all sentimental on me.'

'I can assure you I'm the last person who could ever be accused of being sentimental.'

But as his arms tightened around her waist, Marnie realised that maybe some of her old ideas *did* need revisiting. It was weird. She'd always been envious of people who hadn't been poor, or who'd had a permanent home when they were growing up. And even more envious of those kids with parents, even if they weren't happy—because at least divorced or separated parents were *around*. But Leon had described the atmosphere in this place as toxic and not much had changed. It seemed there was to be no fairy-tale ending. Even now, after all these years.

And hadn't she wanted that to happen? Deep down, hadn't she hoped that Leon's icy heart might melt a bit, if he was successfully reunited with his father? And then what? That he'd suddenly realise he wanted more from their relationship than he'd previously imagined? Well, more fool her. Hope really *did* spring eternal.

She almost wished they weren't dancing because it felt so poignant as she realised this was probably the first and last time they would ever dance like this. As they moved in time to the music, she could feel the strength radiating from his powerful body as he pulled her closer, even though from the corner of her eye she could see people watching them. Too many people, she thought fleetingly before another wave of physical reaction blotted out her reservations. She thought how perfectly their bodies fitted together, despite the fact that he was so tall and she was so short. As if they had been designed to match like this.

Her heart contracted. She was going to miss him. More than she could ever say. How long would it take to forget a man who was so unforgettable? She realised how naïve she had been in believing that having Leon teach her about sex might help in any future new relationship. How was that ever going to be possible when the thought of being in another man's arms made her feel sick?

'Do you want…do you want to go and circulate?' she whispered, because now the dance was beginning to feel dangerously erotic. Her breasts were throbbing and tender and her skin was on fire. She could feel a silken tug at the juncture of her thighs as he tightened his hold on her and she swayed in his arms.

'No, Marnie.' His voice was uneven. 'The only thing I want to circulate is you.'

But that wasn't strictly true. Leon felt so turned on by having her in his arms like this that he could barely move. Against the musculature of his body her light weight and soft curves were tantalising, her subtle scent causing his heart to race like a train. With the tips of his fingers he began stroking her back, unable to resist touching her. He felt her instant shiver in response. He swallowed. It felt as though he were touching her bare skin and the provocation of that was making him grow hard. He thought her breasts seemed bigger than usual, as if they had expanded in the warmth of the Greek day. Or maybe the bodice of her dress could no longer defy gravity and contain their lush weight. He could feel her nipples getting tauter against his chest—and he buried his face in her hair, overcome by a sudden sensation which made him feel almost light-headed.

She was so different from any other woman he'd ever met and suddenly he found himself listing all the reasons why. She wasn't *pretending* to feel things in order to impress him. She didn't want his money and worked hard to pay her own way. She was here because she wanted to be and not because she wanted to be *seen* with him—indeed hadn't she been noticeably uncomfortable when she'd seen the crush of people when they'd arrived? His billionaire status meant nothing to her—she had proved that over and over again. Was it possible that this woman—the most unlikely candidate of all—should make him rethink what he wanted from life?

'Marnie,' he said huskily.

'Mmm?' She dragged her head away from where it had been resting against his chest and looked up into his face.

Her eyes were wide and her lips utterly irresistible and something clenched deep inside his chest. Oblivious to the watching eyes and his usual restraint in public, he started to kiss her. And suddenly the world tipped on its axis. He could feel the tremble of her lips and heard the sigh of pleasure she gave as his tongue began to explore her mouth. Or was he confusing that sound with his own shuddered groan, as he revelled in the taste of her and found himself thinking that he'd never known anything quite so delicious as this kiss.

He knew he should stop what they were doing and move this upstairs to the bedroom, but for once his famously steely self-control was eluding him. What the hell did she *do* to him, that all his certainties suddenly seemed as insubstantial as dust? He was fired up by something he'd never felt before, something he couldn't seem to evaluate. It was a feeling of excitement, tempered with calm. It was comfort and joy. It was anticipation and serenity—all spiced with a powerful sense of desire which pulsed through his veins like a fever. It was feeling as if he'd come home at last. Properly home. Not to a vast, cold mansion where he'd spent so much time alone, nor to any number of lonely luxury houses in enviable locations, but to a place of sanctuary which wasn't defined by bricks and mortar but by the soft, giving woman he was holding.

He kissed her again. And again. And perhaps if he hadn't been so captivated by her, he might have noticed the dark-clad figure moving stealthily around the edge of the dance floor. But he didn't. He didn't notice anything except the shining blonde in his arms.

CHAPTER TWELVE

IT WAS A NIGHTMARE.

It couldn't be happening.

But it was. It was happening right now and right here.

Marnie's first clue that something was wrong was an early-morning phone check to discover dozens of missed calls from numbers she didn't recognise, including several from Pansy, who *never* called at this time in the morning.

Sitting bolt upright in bed, she raked her hair out of her eyes and stared down at the screen, but even in the midst of such unusual telephone activity her thoughts were flitting elsewhere and there was no mystery about who was dominating them.

Leon.

She puffed out a sigh of sheer pleasure. He had taken his jet to Paris at some unearthly hour and she must have fallen asleep after he'd gone, but not before he'd kissed her with a hard stamp of possession which had made her toes curl. Her finger hovering above the call button, she couldn't prevent a smile of satisfaction from creeping over her lips.

They'd only arrived back from Greece late last night,

leaving his father's house straight after the wedding—thank goodness—and then taking a yacht down to Leon's new property in Thessaloniki. And she had loved it. Just loved it. Its spectacular position on the edge of the sea was the only thing the house had in common with Leon's forbidding childhood home. With light-filled and airy rooms, it had been the antithesis of the cold mansion they'd just left.

In the warm October sunshine, they had picnicked on the beach and swum in the sea. Marnie had sailed for the first time in her life and surprised herself by enjoying it, although Leon was an excellent and very patient teacher. They'd even had a midnight skinny dip in his enormous infinity pool, with a giant moon reflected silver in the rippling waters. And they'd been having sex. Non-stop sex, actually.

Marnie leaned back against the pillows and stared dreamily at the ceiling. At times, she'd thought Leon had been almost…

Loving?

No. Surely that was nothing but wishful thinking. But he had definitely been behaving differently towards her. For a start, he had practically ravished her on the dance floor at the wedding—something she *hadn't* been expecting. And it hadn't stopped there. It was difficult to put it into words, exactly, but his behaviour had made her decide that maybe she didn't need to walk away from the relationship quite yet. As long as she kept her emotions in check—and surely she'd had enough practice to be able to do *that*?—and they continued to be discreet now they were back in England, there was no reason why this blissful state of affairs shouldn't continue for a little while longer.

She stared at her phone but before she'd a chance to hit the call button an icon of a pouting Pansy began flashing on the screen and Marnie answered immediately.

'Morning,' she said cheerfully.

'Have you seen the online edition of the *Daily View*?' demanded her twin, without bothering to return her greeting.

'You know I never read the tabloids.'

'Well, maybe you should. In fact, I would study that one with particular care. And then you'd better call me back. And just to let you know—one of the stylists from Hair Heaven has put a link to the piece on social media and it's already had hundreds of "likes".' There was a short, tense pause. 'Oh, Marnie, what *have* you got yourself into? I knew getting yourself mixed up with Leon Kanonidou was only ever going to end in tears. Have you told him?'

'Told him *what*?'

'About mum.'

There was a pause as a trickle of fear started sliding down Marnie's spine. 'No,' she whispered. 'No, I've never told him.'

'Why *not*? When are you going to get it into your thick head that it's not your fault, Marnie?'

'He doesn't need to know,' she answered, her voice hollow.

Pansy gave a laugh which sounded bitter. 'Well, good luck with that. I think he's about to find out—if he doesn't know already.'

Now in a state of terror, Pansy cut the call and went straight into the sitting room to find her laptop. Plonking herself down on the sofa, she scrolled to the free, online version of the *Daily View* newspaper, which apparently had one of the biggest circulations on the planet.

It didn't take long to find it—not when it was splashed all over the top of the page. Marnie's stomach twisted into a writhe of knots as she stared at it. Because there, in glorious Technicolor, was a photo of her dancing with Leon at his father's wedding. Only dancing didn't seem a very accurate way of describing what the camera had captured. They were all over each other. As if their bodies had been joined together with superglue. There were accompanying comments from some of the other guests saying how *close* they'd been, along with snatched photos which had obviously been taken on people's phones.

It was bad, but the headline made it even worse.

Upstaging his father's wedding!

Marnie's heart contracted as she read the piece.

When Greek shipping magnate Stavros Kanonidou (eighty-five) tied the knot with his latest young bride this weekend, his billionaire son, Leonidas (thirty-three), made sure all eyes were focussed on him. It seems heart-throb Leon has exited the marriage market at last, judging by his tactile display on the dance floor with nubile blonde English hairdresser Marnie Porter.

Just who is Marnie Porter and how has she managed to land herself one of the world's most eligible bachelors?

Phone this number if you know. (We pay for any information used.)

Marnie felt faint. Dizzy. A wave of pain and regret made her glad she was sitting down because she honestly didn't think her trembling knees could have supported her. When her phone began to buzz, she looked down to see another unknown number flashing on the screen. A journalist? She didn't know and she didn't care. She turned it to silent just as Leon's chef tiptoed in to deposit a cup of steaming black coffee in front of her, but when she mimed eating—presumably asking if she wanted breakfast—Marnie shook her head because the thought of food made her want to heave.

But as well as the pain, the irony of the situation didn't miss her. It seemed that just as she'd got used to this rarefied life with its servants and planes and luxury yachts it was about to be taken away from her. She didn't *care* about the trappings, the only thing she cared about was the man and she needed to speak to Leon. She badly needed to tell him before anyone else did.

He didn't answer. Not the first time she tried, nor even the fifth. After an hour had gone by, she sent him a text.

Please ring. It's urgent.

But Leon didn't ring, or text, and after she'd sent the chef away for the rest of the day Marnie began to pace around the huge apartment like a caged animal, staring out of the vast windows without really noticing the park's blazing autumnal display. It was past noon when she realised she hadn't even taken a shower and she was just emerging from the bathroom, wrapped in a towel, when she heard the sound of a key being turned in the lock.

She froze. And wasn't it funny the things which crossed your mind at moments of high tension? So that instead of wondering just how she was going to tell him, she found herself wondering whether or not she should call his name and let him know where she was.

But it seemed there was no need, because she could hear Leon striding down the corridor and when he walked into the bedroom, loosening his tie, she couldn't seem to read anything from the tight, closed look on his face. His icy gaze scanned over her and she thought about how he'd made amazing love to her that very morning and somehow she couldn't imagine that ever happening again.

'Get dressed and then come to my office,' he ordered succinctly. 'I'll be waiting.'

Here came another stupid dilemma—deciding what to wear. And although there were plenty of exquisite clothes in the wardrobe which Leon had bought for her, Marnie couldn't bring herself to put any of them on. The clock had struck midnight. It was time to return to her familiar rags. Wriggling into a pair of tracksuit bottoms, she swathed her bosom in a roomy top, unable to miss the faintly contemptuous curve of his lips as she walked into his office, where he was sitting perched on the edge of his desk.

'Sit down,' he said, gesturing towards the brown leather sofa on which they'd once spent a very passionate couple of hours one rainy Sunday afternoon.

'I'll stand if you don't mind,' she declined stiffly. As a doyenne of the formal reprimand, she was conscious that he might be employing a touch of psychological warfare here. Did he want her passively seated—and was he intending to make it seem as if he were interviewing her, as if she were his subordinate?

And aren't you?

Aren't you?

Had she ever imagined for more than a second that she was really his equal?

There was silence for a moment while he studied a paperweight containing an iridescent shell, before lifting his gaze to hers—and it seemed she had forgotten how beautiful his eyes were and how sometimes his gaze could wash over you, as brilliant and as blue as the ocean itself.

'So, where do we begin, Marnie?' he questioned heavily.

'That's up to you,' she answered, in a low voice. 'How much do you know? Have you been told that my mother was a prostitute?'

'Yes.'

She nodded. Had one of the journalists prised out that particular nugget and presented it to him, or had someone in his office been tasked with uncovering her past? It didn't matter. She had often wondered how it would feel to talk about this to someone, to open the door on a room which had been kept closed and locked for so long. And although she knew that what she was about to say was going to bring to an end this part of her life with Leon, wasn't there another part of her which felt a funny sense of relief to be able to unload the dark and heavy burden, after so many years of carrying it around?

'Do you want to hear why?'

'Not really.'

It hurt to think he didn't care enough to want to find out more—but wasn't that just another layer of hurt to add to all the others which were building up inside her?

'Well, I'm going to tell you anyway,' she said, suddenly fierce—and Marnie realised that maybe she *was* defending the indefensible. But really, she was defending her mum.

'She came from the north of England,' she said slowly. 'They said she'd had a tough childhood. A father who drank and who liked to beat her mother. He beat my mum, too, and I think…' For a moment her voice faded away as she recalled the other things she'd heard. Things buried too deep ever to be resurrected. Dark things hinted at by social workers, too tired and overworked to know how to deal with two angry and confused little girls.

'Anyway, she ran away to London and got in with a bad crowd. It's as simple as that, really. There was no safety net—and if there was she had no idea how to access it. Nobody to look out for her. She got pregnant by one of her clients.' Her mouth was working like crazy now, but years of practice meant she was able to keep the prick of tears at bay. 'I guess I should be grateful that she kept us.'

She lifted her chin, aware that her voice was trembling, waiting for him to prompt her—and when he didn't, she continued of her own accord.

'I told you I didn't remember anything about my early years, but, of course, I did.'

'Yes,' he breathed. 'I imagine you did.'

'I remember we used to have to stay very quiet whenever she had clients round. I remember the sounds they used to make.' She pulled a face. 'That was probably what put me off sex for so long. We used to sit upstairs in our bedroom and I would whisper little games for Pansy to play to keep her amused. We always kept the door locked, of course. And it wasn't all bad. If...' Her voice wavered again. 'If mum had had a particularly good night, then she used to go to the corner shop next day and buy us a cake, for tea. Ch-cherry was our favourite.'

'Go on,' he said grimly.

Marnie nodded, but the bitter lump which had risen in her throat was suddenly making it very difficult for her to breathe. 'Then she got pneumonia. It was all very quick. One minute we were being taken into care while mum went into hospital and the next we were told she'd died.' She shrugged. 'And it was as if she had never existed.'

'You didn't go to the funeral?' he said, as though this mattered, as though he were remembering the secrecy surrounding his own mother's illness.

'No. Things were different then. As you know yourself. Apparently they thought we would get over the whole experience more quickly if we moved on. So we did. We were sent to a children's home and from there we were farmed out to various foster families, but nobody wanted to adopt us.'

'Why not?'

She shrugged. 'We were too damaged, I guess. Too suspicious and too close and too much of a handful. They tried to split us up but I made sure that was never going to happen.'

Marnie's knees felt wobbly and she would have loved to have taken Leon up on his offer and to have sunk into that squishy sofa, but that would mean she was looking up at him and would definitely put him at an advantage. And he certainly didn't need any more advantages. Besides, how would she be able to leave quickly and with dignity if she had to haul herself up? 'It's okay, Leon. You don't have to worry about how to tell me. It's over. I know that. Who wants a girlfriend with a past like mine?'

He stood up then and she could see the shadows which were flitting like dark clouds across his face, making him look like a Leon she didn't recognise. His blue eyes were boring into her with a coldness she'd never seen directed at her before.

'It's not okay,' he negated harshly. 'It might have been if you'd told me all this right from the start.'

'Really? And how would that have worked?' She gave a bitter laugh. 'Should I have thrown it into the conversation on our first date? Maybe confided it when I came to see you at your office, or murmured it as pillow talk a little further down the line? At what stage of our relationship should I have told you the truth, Leon?'

'But surely that's the whole damned point!' he ground out. '*That you didn't tell me the truth.* That you feigned ignorance and pretended. That in essence you *lied* to me, Marnie. And I can bear a lot of things, but not lies.'

Leon tugged off his tie and flung it to the ground as if it were choking him. And in a way, it was. Because her words had taken him hurtling right back to his own childhood. To the mother who had always appeared startled whenever he caught her taking tablets, explaining them away by saying she had a headache. A mother who told him she much preferred the shiny new wig to her own wispy hair—though he'd never really understood until afterwards why all those gloriously thick black locks had fallen out so suddenly. Not one honest answer had she given to any of his questions and he'd felt sidelined. As if he didn't count enough to be told the truth. As if he didn't matter. And that feeling had stayed with him, lying dormant inside him—always ready to rise to the surface if someone was deliberately dishonest.

'You didn't tell me the truth, Marnie,' he repeated quietly. 'And I'm afraid that's a deal-breaker for me.'

He saw all the colour leach from her face and thought the clipped finality of his final statement would be enough to send her running from the room, saving them face and saving them both from any more soul-bearing or heartache. And didn't he want that? Wouldn't that have made it—not easy—but easier for them both? But she didn't go. She just stood her ground like an immovable force. Dignified and proud, despite the sloppy clothes and her diminutive height, as she tilted a mulish face at him.

'And being used is a deal-breaker for *me*!' she hissed back.

Mutual mud-slinging was the last thing he wanted

to engage in right now but he couldn't let her furious accusation pass. 'Being used?' he verified icily. 'And just how did I do that?'

'You used me to upstage your father on his wedding day!'

'You believe all that rubbish you read on the website?'

'Yes! Because that's what happened! I was there, remember? You must have realised that everyone was watching you, because they'd been watching you from the moment we arrived. What better way to pay your father back than by stealing all his thunder? By showcasing your own youth and vitality in contrast with a man in his declining years?' She drew in a deep breath and he could see a tiny pulse hammering away at her temple, close to the moonlight sheen of her hair. 'You told me you were angry with him. Angry that he'd duped you into attending a wedding you secretly disapproved of, but you did it because you were hoping for some kind of closure and reconciliation, which he failed to provide. You don't want or need his fortune, but the fact that he's doling it out to other people must have hurt you more than you care to admit, because that's human nature.'

Her words faded away but Leon shook his head. 'You can't possibly stop now, Marnie,' he said grimly. 'Not when this is just starting to get interesting.'

She stared at him and he could see the hurt in her eyes, but was able to steel his heart against it because the slow pulse of anger in his blood was dominating everything.

'You didn't stop to think how all this might impact

on me, did you, Leon?' she questioned quietly. 'I mean, you were never demonstrative with me before, were you? You never so much as held my hand or kissed me in public and I was okay with that because I sensed that was the sort of man you were. Yet suddenly, you're all over me. I couldn't believe the way you were acting on the dance floor.'

He gave a short laugh. 'Neither could I.'

'So why do it?'

It was a question he wished she hadn't asked. A question he was under no obligation to answer. But he was aware that he couldn't chastise her for refusing to tell the truth and then do the same thing himself. 'Because I was going to suggest taking our relationship to the next level,' he said, his words deliberately flat, as if that would take the emotional sting out of them. 'I thought I was in love with you.'

Surely that was the key in getting her to leave. The deliberate use of the past tense, indicating he felt that way no longer. Surely she would be too proud to want him to witness the tears which were currently filling her beautiful grey eyes. But no. It seemed he had underestimated her tenacity, for she drew her shoulders back as if she were squaring up to him in a boxing ring.

'Ah, so *now* I understand,' she said. 'You didn't want to fall in love, did you? Not with me and not with anyone. You told me that right from the start. But emotions are messy things, aren't they, Leon? Sometimes they creep up on you when you're least expecting them. So I imagine finding out about my hidden past must have come as a huge relief to you. It gave you all the ammunition you needed to shoot our relationship down in flames. You could classify my behaviour as an abuse of trust when the reality is that it presented you with a handy get-out clause from having to commit.'

She sucked in a shuddering breath. 'And you want to know something, Leon?' she continued. 'I understand. In a way, I almost expected it. I mean, who would ever want to get involved with a woman like me? I know I'm not good enough. Don't you think I've always known that? But please don't make out that I'm the only one of us who resorted to subterfuge when it suited them!'

'Marnie—'

'No!' She dabbed a furious fist against each wet eye before fixing him with a glare. 'You make a big deal about me keeping parts of my life secret, but didn't you do exactly the same when we first met? Pretending to be some boho biker, rather than a billionaire tycoon?'

'You know why I did that,' he growled.

'I know what you told me. That you didn't want people muscling in on you and knowing how rich you are and that's why you keep a beaten-up old car in every place where you have a home. You had your reasons, Leon, just like I had mine. Do you really think yours are somehow more valid because you're so powerful?'

'You're twisting this, Marnie.'

'No. I'm telling you how I feel, but it's done now. Don't worry. I get it. It's over. It should never really have begun. And I'm out of here.'

She moved towards the door and instantly he slid from the desk. 'Where are you going?'

'That's none of your business.'

'It *is* my business if you're being hounded by journalists because of your association with me.'

‘But I live in Acton and nobody knows that.’ She gave a laugh which was edged with hysteria. ‘Because I *am* a nobody!’

‘Don’t be so naïve, Marnie,’ he snapped. ‘Finding out where you live will be a piece of cake and if you try to use public transport you’ll be a target. My driver will take you anywhere you need to go. If you like, I can send someone from my security team to keep their eye on you. And I’ll leave a credit card on the side. Use it for whatever you need.’

She shook her head in disbelief. ‘Have you even listened to a word I’ve been saying?’ she demanded. ‘Do you think that’s the answer to everything—that you can just buy your way out of things, when the going gets tough? I don’t want your damned money, Leon, and I don’t want your damned driver—or your security team!’

And Leon was left with nothing but the sound of loud slamming as she stormed her way out of his office.

CHAPTER THIRTEEN

IT WAS ACTUALLY quite easy to 'disappear'.

Marnie realised she'd spent most of her working life influenced by the faint fear of not knowing what the future held. She'd been saving for that mythical rainy day for a very long time, which meant she'd accumulated quite a lot of cash which she could now use.

Because that rainy day had arrived.

Accompanied by her sister, she had left London—sneaking away as dawn was breaking over the city, with Pansy driving a borrowed and rather fancy car, although refusing to say whose car it was—'I'll tell you later…'

Hair Heaven had told her to take as much time as she needed and, at very short notice, Marnie had found a tiny cottage to rent on the edge of the Yorkshire Moors—chosen mostly because it reminded her of one of her favourite books from childhood and seemed to fit with the bleak mood she was trying to hide from her sister.

'It's good to be able to help you for a change,' Pansy said, once they'd managed to push open the rather stiff front door and she'd placed a steaming mug of tea in front of Marnie, as though she were recovering from some kind of sickness.

Which in a way, Marnie guessed, she was. There was obviously a reason why the expression *lovesick* had come about—and she was certainly portraying all the symptoms of it. She couldn't eat. Couldn't sleep. Couldn't stop thinking about the man who had stolen her heart and left her wondering how she was ever going to get it back.

Pansy waved a packet of chocolate biscuits in front of her but Marnie shook her head. 'I won't, thanks.'

'You should. You're looking peaky,' said Pansy disapprovingly.

'Unlike you,' said Marnie, eyeing her sister.

It was true. Pansy was positively glowing and had toned down the sequins and too-tight tops. She'd also had her hair cut so that it swung in a sleek blonde bob around her shoulders, instead of falling to just above her bottom in that retro hippie style. 'Why didn't you ask me to cut your hair for you?' she added suspiciously.

'You were too busy jetting off in private planes, weren't you?'

A lump rose in Marnie's throat and, quickly, she changed the subject. 'Whatever you're doing, just keep doing it. You look fantastic,' she said huskily.

The biscuit she'd been just about to munch into forgotten, Pansy smiled—a soft, sweet smile edged with contentment. Marnie had never seen her sister look like that before and suddenly the penny dropped, and she wondered what had taken her so long to work it out. 'You're in love?' she asked.

Pansy nodded. 'I am. I've been seeing Walker. Quite a lot, actually.'

'The barrister who defended you?'

'That's right.'

A flare of anxiety washed through her. 'Pansy, is that even *legal*?'

Her twin shot her a reproving look. 'Of course it is. It happens all the time, lawyers falling in love with their clients—although apparently it's always best to wait until the case is over.' She grinned. 'And Walker is way too ambitious to ever risk breaking the law.'

'And he doesn't mind—'

'That my mum was on the game and that I spent time in prison myself?' Pansy sighed and shrugged her shoulders. 'Well, obviously it's not the perfect CV for a barrister's wife but he says those experiences are what made me the woman I am today, and he loves that woman. Anyway, isn't the whole point of life supposed to be about learning from our mistakes and other people's? About redemption?'

'I'm sure it is,' said Marnie gruffly, knowing she had to get her twin out of here because any minute now she was going to break down and cry. 'Anyway, you'd better get back to him.'

'Marnie—'

'No. Honestly. I really don't want to hear it.'

'But you don't know what I was going to say.'

'Yes, I do. We're twins, Pan, and sometimes I know what you're thinking, though that's going to happen less and less, the closer you get to Walker. And that's the way it should be. I'm so happy for you. Really, I am. I think it's a wonderful love story, but I don't want to talk about Leon. Not now and not ever. I just don't. It…it hurts too much.' She drew in a deep breath, aware of just how much vulnerability she was revealing to her younger sister. And that was a first. 'Do you understand?'

Pressing her lips together as if she too was trying not to cry, Pansy nodded. 'I understand perfectly,' she whispered, and suddenly the two sisters were embracing, more tightly than they'd done in years. 'Just keep in touch, won't you?'

'Try stopping me,' answered Marnie fiercely, but once her twin had driven away in Walker's strangely silent electric car, she didn't have to pretend any more. For a while, she sat on an overstuffed armchair, buried her face in her hands and wept. She wept as tears trickled out from between her fingers and dripped onto her jeans. Until she felt exhausted, but in a way washed clean. And lighter, somehow—although the terrible ache in her heart hadn't gone away.

But as the next few days passed, Marnie tried to come to terms with what had happened, convincing herself that it was nothing more than she had ever expected. Like Pansy said, it was always going to end in tears. She couldn't allow what had happened with Leon to define her life in a negative way, she just couldn't. She needed to extract all the lovely elements they'd shared and remind herself that she was capable of a lot more things than she'd previously imagined. Of love, for a start—and how could any experience which had given her that ever be described as bad? It wasn't as if she'd ever *seriously* considered a future with him, was it? She'd get over it eventually, because people did. Every day thousands of people were getting their hearts broken and picking themselves up and carrying on.

Well, so would she.

Leon had managed to do it. Obviously. He hadn't tried to reach out and connect with her since she'd stormed from his Kensington apartment, had he? And she told herself she was glad about that. It would have been torture to speak to him, or see him and pretend that her heart wasn't shattering into a million pieces. She might have announced that her love for *him* was in the past tense but that wasn't true, was it? Love didn't disappear overnight, more was the pity.

Each day she would pull on some wellington boots, a waterproof coat and wide-brimmed hat and set off across the green-grey landscape of the brooding moorland, her stride lengthening as she got further away from the cottage. She'd bought herself an ordnance survey map and had started to explore the area in detail. It was so beautiful out here—in a very stark and elemental way. There were rocks and waterfalls and circling birds of prey. She was completely alone and yet somehow that felt okay.

One afternoon she had a slight wobble on her way back to the cottage, when she thought she spotted a man on the horizon, surveying the landscape through a pair of binoculars which glinted in the winter sun. The tall and brooding figure so reminded her of Leon that her heart constricted very painfully and tears sprang to her eyes. But thankfully the sound of a bird distracted her and when she turned back again, the man had gone. And that was normal too. *You're not going mad at all,* she reassured herself. It was probably a common phenomenon to imagine you'd seen someone when you'd been thinking about them as obsessively as she had about Leon Kanonidou.

She was tired when she let herself back into the cottage, but it was a very satisfying sort of tiredness. It wasn't like working out at the gym but a much more gratifying form of exercise, she decided. Peering into the tiny mirror over the bathroom sink, she appeared to have lost some of the haunted look which had made her face look so sallow recently and she wondered if it was time to leave London for good. Perhaps she should make the break from Hair Heaven permanent. She could move to somewhere like Yorkshire and see if she could get the backing to set up a little salon of her own. It was good to make plans. It made the future seem less bleak.

It was growing dark and she was deciding which book she would start reading this evening, having told the cottage owner that she didn't mind not having any broadband—how stupid was that?—when she saw the flare of headlights on the approaching track and heard the purr of a car drawing up outside the cottage.

Her heart raced and she knew then that she hadn't *imagined* a man who looked like Leon on the Yorkshire Moors. Because no other man looked like Leon and no other man ever could. He was here. Somehow he had managed to track down where she was staying. On the other side of that door was the man she loved with all her heart.

And she didn't know if she could face him.

Wouldn't it set her recovery back and prolong the torture if she allowed her eyes to feast on him once more?

The loud knock reinforced his identity as much as

the powerful car he was driving. She'd heard a knock like that once before when she'd been in Greece, feeling miserable and foolish after losing her virginity to him and realising he wasn't the man she thought he was. But she was a different Marnie now. She might be badly hurt, but she had always been strong. The question was whether she was strong enough to cope with seeing him again.

He was probably expecting her to play push-pull. To act all coy while not quite managing to hide her excitement at the realisation that he'd driven all this way to see her. Telling him to go away while expecting him to kiss her into changing her mind. He probably thought she would allow him to seduce her in front of that stupid damp fire, which she had been trying unsuccessfully to light. Well, he could go to hell!

She walked over to the door and pulled it open, trying not to react to his dark and windswept beauty as, coolly, she met his gaze.

'Who do you think you are? Heathcliff?'

'I hope not.' His voice was wry. 'Because I haven't come here to see a ghost.'

'I can't believe you've read *Wuthering Heights*.'

'Why? Because I'm Greek, or because I'm a man?'

Suddenly her knees sagged. She mustn't allow herself to get distracted. She mustn't. She must not put herself in emotional danger. Because suddenly the idea that she possessed some kind of inner strength was in grave doubt. 'Why are you here, Leon?'

'You must know why I'm here.'

'I'm afraid I don't. I think I may have mentioned before that I'm a hairdresser, not a mind-reader.'

'I'd like to come in.'

She made a play of hesitating but she knew it was a lost cause. Because no way was she going to send him away without hearing what he had to say—he knew that and she knew that. But that didn't mean she had to take his coat, or offer him a drink, did it? Why was he here? she wondered caustically. Had he been warned that a journalist had contacted her last week, offering her an eye-watering amount of money if she agreed to cooperate on a profile piece about the enigmatic billionaire—and was he seriously worried that she might go ahead and do it?

She stared at him. 'So?' she questioned, as coldly as she could.

Leon nodded in response to her terse greeting but he didn't speak straight away, knowing he had to choose his words carefully because surely these were the most important words he would ever say. He could see she was still angry and hurt—and he couldn't blame her for that. Not for the first time, he recognised that the forgiveness he sought from Marnie Porter was by no means guaranteed and she might not *want* to forgive him. What if it was already too late—if she had decided that she was well rid of his privileged but strangely antiseptic life? He felt the thud of pain. Of dread. Of fear. And he wondered how he could have been so emotionally brutal with her.

'I thought a lot about what you said, Marnie.'

'Good. I hope you can learn from it. I hope we both can.'

'Marnie…' He shook his head in frustration, realising that he had wanted her to make it easy for him by guessing what was on his mind. That she would be able to detect his pain and begin the healing process by forgiving him. But she was right. She wasn't a mind-reader, nor should he expect her to be. And he couldn't escape from his feelings or from learning to express them, not if he wanted her.

'What you said—'

'I said a lot of things, Leon.'

'I know you did—but one of them stuck in my mind more than any of the others.'

She stared at him. 'About my mum?'

'No. Not at all. Nobody should be blamed for their parentage, because that's something over which we have no choice or control.' He raked his fingers back through his windswept hair. 'I'm talking about when you told me you weren't good enough.'

She shifted awkwardly and stared down at the flagstone floor. 'Oh, that.'

'Yes, that. Because that's the craziest thing I've ever heard. You protected your sister through the most difficult of circumstances, all through your childhood. You forged a career for yourself and you've stuck at it. You made your own way in the world and took less from me than anyone else I've ever met. You have suffered knock-backs and the sort of prejudice which would have felled most other people, but not you. And somehow, along the way, you made me realise I was capable of feeling stuff. Stuff I'd always run away from before. You're more than good enough by anyone's reckoning, but especially by mine.'

'Thanks,' she said woodenly, her head still bent.

'And I realised something else,' he said slowly. 'That

maybe I deliberately failed to give you the opening to tell me about your mother before. There were plenty of times I could have asked you more, but I *liked* your reluctance to talk about the past. It seemed to offer a protection against the true intimacy I had spent my life trying to avoid. Do you understand what I'm trying to say to you, Marnie? That in a way, I condoned your secrecy.'

She shrugged. 'Sure.'

'I've missed you so much.' He swallowed. 'And the question I need to ask you now is whether you could forgive me?' he questioned unsteadily. 'Because I love you, Marnie Porter. I love you in a way I never believed I could love anyone and I can't imagine spending my life without you.'

She looked up then and, though her eyes were very bright, she was shaking her head, a blonde halo of hair shimmering in the lamplight. 'I'm afraid that's not enough, Leon,' she said. 'The trust between us has been broken.'

'Then let's repair it.'

'I don't want to repair it.'

His heart was pounding—its loud thunder edged with fear. 'Why not?'

'Because…'

Her mouth was working and he could see her trying to keep a rein on her own emotions.

'Because I don't want to get hurt again,' she burst out. 'I've had a lot of trouble adjusting to life without you, but I'm managing and every day it's getting easier. If we start seeing one another again, then we run the risk of breaking up all over again and I couldn't bear it.' She sucked in a deep breath and looked him straight in the eye. 'I'm strong,' she added. 'But I really don't think I'm that strong.'

He wanted so much to hold her—to comfort and kiss her—but the flash of her eyes was very definitely telling him not to touch. 'What if I told you that I want to spend the rest of my life with you? That I want to marry you?' he said huskily. 'What if I told you that I've sold off two large divisions of my company, which means we can live wherever you want to live. Maybe Thessaloniki? If you'd like that,' he amended hastily.

'You've *sold* part of your company?'

'Sure.' He shrugged. 'I've been simplifying my life so that I could devote the next section of it to you—that's what's been keeping me busy. You haven't seen the news? It's been all over the internet.'

'I haven't got any internet here. And even if I had, I certainly wouldn't have been reading anything about *you*.'

Leon's heart was beating very fast as he realised that this woman needed a declaration of love so powerful that never again would she be in any doubt of his feelings for her. She'd said she didn't know if she had the strength to risk having a relationship with him again, but he knew she did. He just had to convince her of that.

'I love and admire you more than anyone I have ever met, Marnie,' he said slowly, and very deliberately. 'I love your pride and feistiness and your ability to make me laugh. I love waking up in the morning and finding you there beside me, so that I can kiss you. I like your company more than anyone else's and I like you lying next to me when I wake in the darkness of the night. And I find myself imagining…' For some reason, his voice had started to crack. 'Imagining you,' he breathed unevenly. 'With a baby at your breast. Our child. A child we would love and protect with all our hearts. A child we would be honest with. There will be no more secrets between us from now on, my love. *Agape mou.* Just a shared life together. Will you share that vision with me, Marnie—will you journey down that road with me?'

As she heard the emotion underpinning his words, Marnie could feel the tears welling up in her eyes as she looked up into his beloved face. At the bronzed beauty of his sculpted features and the mouth she had thought so hard and unforgiving the first time she'd ever seen him. But Leon had crafted himself a mask to present to the world, the same as she had, she realised. A mask intended to conceal the pain they'd both suffered—a pain which had made them keep people at arm's length.

Yet somehow the two of them had come together—and how. They had got it wrong the first time around but he was right, they could start again. Because that was what life was all about.

About hope. And redemption. And renewal.

And love. Most of all it was about love. A love she had never imagined could be hers.

'Yes,' she whispered. 'Yes, I will journey down that road with you. Because I love you too, with all my heart. I think I've loved you from the moment I first set eyes on you, Leon Kanonidou.'

'So you'll marry me?' he verified fiercely. 'As soon as possible?'

She smiled. 'Yes, I'll marry you. But will you please hold me now? Because more than anything, I badly need you to kiss me.'

As his arms went round her, she sank lovingly into his embrace, feeling his warmth and protection as the sheer joy of being reunited with him flooded through her body. With tender fingers he dried the tracks of her tears and brushed the awry hair away from her cheeks and he lowered his lips to hers in what felt like slow motion.

But it was worth the wait.

Oh, yes. Definitely worth the wait.

Because that one kiss healed their past and sealed their future and made them realise how glorious their shared present was.

In fact, it was safe to say that it was the best kiss of their lives.

EPILOGUE

MARNIE HAD JUST positioned the final fondant dinosaur on top of the cake when the sound of movement outside the window captured her attention. With sunlight glittering off the nearby sea, she glanced up to see Leon approaching and thought—as she always did—what perfect timing he had. A visual feast in sawn-off jeans and a black T-shirt, he was running to keep up with two sand-covered little boys. Their sons. Their twin sons. Their two beautiful boys who would be four years old tomorrow, and who brought their besotted parents unimaginable amounts of joy. She swallowed, overcome with emotion which was never far from the surface—particularly during the last few weeks.

Every day she gave thanks for her life and her marriage because it hadn't all been plain sailing. Conceived early in their marriage, and born seven weeks prematurely, Theo and Atlas had been terrifyingly tiny when they had been delivered in Athens. Their parents had kept a tense vigil on the neonatal unit and Marnie had been shocked by the waxen pallor of her husband's face and the bleak terror she could read in his eyes.

But those little boys had come battling through and

today were as healthy and robust as any of their friends, five of whom would be joining them tomorrow for a raucous birthday picnic on the beach, along with their aunt and uncle. Pansy and Warren were flying in later on Leon's private jet, along with their russet-haired daughter, Bryony—who was a loveable little terror. Warren was now one of the most successful barristers in the country and Pansy had become a valued prison visitor in London. She was even on the lecture circuit, giving increasingly popular talks about the realities of women's experiences in jail. As she was fond of telling anyone who asked—nobody knew the inside of a cell as well as she did.

Marnie sighed. Who would ever have thought that fate could have done such a satisfying flip-flop and allowed the two Porter sisters to find true happiness?

'That was a very big sigh,' came a silken comment from behind her and Marnie felt a shiver of inevitable expectation rippling down her spine as she heard Leon's voice.

She turned round, her heart clenching with pleasure. His blue eyes were bright against the bronzed gleam of his skin, but these days his raven-dark hair was styled a little longer and looked *very* sexy. She cut it herself, of course. In fact, lots of his friends had asked if she would cut theirs, too, but Marnie had resisted. She had loved her time as a hairdresser but other things beckoned to her now. With the help of their beloved nanny, Christina, she took an inordinate amount of pleasure from being a mother. She was on the board of trustees of a children's home and, assisted by the philanthropic arm of Leon's pared-down business, she hoped she was helping to make a real difference in the lives of those children. In fact, next week a tiny orphaned baby girl they were fostering was coming to the newly decorated pink nursery upstairs, which had been prepared just for her. She bit her lip. Well, that had been the theory.

'It was a sigh of contentment,' she informed her husband as he slid his arms around her waist.

'But also one of faint concern,' he noted as he traced the tiny frown on her brow with the tip of one finger.

'Where are the boys?'

'Christina has insisted they remove all that sand in the bath and, afterwards, they've decided they want to make welcome cards to give to their new baby sister next week.'

She grinned. 'Aw. That's so sweet.'

'Mmm. And then they're going to "play" chess.'

Marnie grimaced. 'I hope they don't start fighting again.'

'Only time will tell.' He smiled. 'Which gave me the opportunity to come and find my beautiful wife, to admire the birthday cake she's made and to wonder why she's looking a little worried.'

He was so perceptive! Marnie touched her fingers to his shadowed jaw—treasuring a moment she'd prayed for but which she'd thought would be denied them for ever. Because even though the doctors had told her it was fine for her to have another baby, up until now it had never happened. She had convinced herself she was okay with that, and revelled in the fact that she had lots of blessings to count. Twin blessings, actually—as well as an adorable baby girl who was soon going to be joining their family. But now…

'I'm pregnant, Leon,' she whispered, watching the series of emotions which crossed the face of a man who no longer kept his feelings hidden away. She could see hope and fear and joy—all those things which most people felt every day of their lives. 'I'm… I'm having your baby,' she said, just in case it hadn't registered. 'Are you happy?'

Leon hoped his tight embrace reassured her on that point and as he pulled her closer he could hear the combined thunder of their hearts. *'Agape,'* he said shakily, coming to terms with what she had just told him before uttering a silent prayer of gratitude. Because he had never imagined life could be like this. With his loving wife and two amazing sons, they had created the perfect family. He had thought things couldn't get any better, but he had been wrong. But then, he had been wrong about so many things before he had met Marnie.

'Am I happy?' he echoed slowly. 'Let me tell you that my happiness is right off the scale.'

'But we're going to have *two* new babies in the house now! And four children in total.'

'Shh.' He kissed the tremble of her lips. 'We'll cope. We coped with our two boys, just as we will with little Athena and her new brother or sister. We have enough love between us for an army of children in our lives, Marnie. Surely you know that?'

She nodded, smiling through the tears he recognised as tears of joy. He thought of all the ways he could respond to her news. Later, he would take her to their room and pay homage to her with his body. He would spoil her and cherish her and insist she rested. But for now there was only one thing she needed to hear, which happened to be the only thing he wanted to say.

‘I love you, Marnie. *Se agapo.* For the rest of my days, and beyond.’

Their kiss was slow and very passionate, interrupted only by a furious accusation from upstairs, shouted in perfect English.

‘Atlas, you’re *cheating*!’

* * * * *

NINE MONTHS TO CLAIM HER

NATALIE ANDERSON

MILLS & BOON

For Jo.

Thank you so much for our weekend escape
to the seaside and time to stare at pretty cows. Lol.

I so appreciate your friendship and support.

Here's to some more fabulous time away writing.

CHAPTER ONE

'Rose Gold? It's been for ever!'

Rosanna Gold smiled through gritted teeth, inwardly groaning—yet again—that her parents had thought it clever and cute to name her Rose. It had even been part of their marketing plan for when she took over the family business from her father Red. But it wasn't clever or cute. It was cringeworthy, even more so given she was never going to take over the company. When she was introduced, people invariably giggled then commented on the fact that her hair was far more carrot than rose gold. She'd heard the same jokes a million times and when she'd finally moved out she'd lengthened her name to Rosanna. But tonight, she was back home. Back to being 'Rose'. Back to trying to please her parents. Back to being less than either the beauty or treasure her name suggested.

And it turned out that the opening celebration of the latest luxury apartment complex in central Sydney, built by property conglomerate Castle Holdings, was basically a horror of a high-school reunion: 'Ten Years On'—and it was still terrible.

'Mae, how lovely to see you.' Rosanna hoped her inevitable blush would recede quickly—she'd been flushing stop-sign-red all night.

Born and bred Sydney society elite, Mae Wilson had been in the year below Rosanna at school, but she'd always been decades ahead in style. So, of course, she was one of the well-heeled new residents of Kingston Towers. Only the absolute cream of Sydney society could afford one of the ultra-stylish inner-city apartments with their sleek security systems and every convenience imaginable.

'What brings you here tonight?' Mae asked.

The surprise in Mae's tone, and the mere fact that she'd even asked, hammered it home. Rosanna didn't belong in Kingston Towers. She probably would never have set foot in the place had her mother not begged.

She'd been woken early this morning by an awful call informing her that her parents had been in a car accident and she was needed in Sydney urgently. Freaked out, she'd raced from her town a few hours north, panicking the whole way. Only when she'd arrived at the hospital it was to discover she wasn't there for a bedside vigil. While her father would be in plaster for the next few weeks, he would recover fully, and fortunately her mother had only bruises… No, it turned out their 'SOS' summons had been about this *party* and how crucial it was that a Gold family member attended. And the only one able to go now was Rosanna.

Her initial relief that they weren't badly hurt had been washed over by the old frustration of past years. She shouldn't have been surprised. Her parents' business had always been the priority in their lives—coming ahead of everything and everyone else, even themselves and their *own* well-being and certainly Rosanna's as well. She'd tried to convince her mother that one party didn't matter. But, apparently, it did.

'My parents did the fit-out of some of the lounge spaces.' Rosanna maintained her smile.

For the last two decades her parents' company, Gold Style, had done the interior design for Castle Holdings properties. But when Hugh Castle had died a year ago things had changed. While they'd all expected Ash, Hugh's legitimate—albeit wayward—heir to assume control, it had been Leo Castle, Hugh's illegitimate son, who'd taken over as CEO of the conglomerate. It had been a shock, given Hugh had refused to recognise Leo right till the end. The shocks had kept coming since. A 'control freak' was how Rosanna's mother had described Leo this morning. A 'workaholic' who already headed another business in insurance and now ruled Castle Holdings with an iron fist and an acute eye. Apparently he was fiercely driven and uncompromising and in her parents' view that *wasn't* a good thing. Because he'd put Castle Holdings' interiors contracts out to tender, inviting proposals from her parents' competitors. Gold Style would no longer automatically secure them—and hadn't, in fact.

'Oh, Gold Style.' Mae nodded dismissively. 'Of course, I'd forgotten you were connected to them.'

Not just connected, she was their *daughter*. Their only child. And honestly? Their greatest disappointment.

'Wear that navy empire line dress,' her mother had shrilly instructed in amongst her barrage of information this morning. 'It's more flattering.'

Because Rosanna's body *needed* flattering—as always her pale freckled skin and uneven posture needed to be concealed. Appearances mattered to maintain and build the success of the business and imperfections were not allowed—not speckled skin, or a spine so curved by scoliosis that not even surgery could properly straighten it, at least not to the point of pleasing her perfectionist parents. But while Rosanna had obeyed the instruction to attend the party, she hadn't been able to wear that particular dress. She'd had only a few things at her parents' apartment and had opted for a silk black blouse and skirt. Her mother had always preferred Rosanna didn't wear skirts because the hemlines reflected the unevenness of her waist, but this one was long and hopefully that slight tilt on one side wasn't noticeable. But even though her outfit fulfilled the covering-up element, it wasn't really good enough for Kingston Towers society.

She'd let her parents down again and that hurt. That her mother had even *asked* had made her want to succeed just this *once* for them. Of course she'd yes, even though parties this fancy, in places this elite, weren't her forte. She'd always felt shy and awkward. But this morning her mother had been more upset than Rosanna had ever seen her. She knew their company was everything, but she'd wondered if the accident had shaken her mother more than she was admitting. She'd repeatedly insisted that Rosanna attend—someone from the Gold family needed to be 'seen' by the CEO himself.

But two hours in and Rosanna had yet to meet Leo Castle. It was her own fault, given she didn't even know what he looked like. She didn't bother much with Sydney society nor with social media either. However, she *had* briefly seen Leo's half-brother, Ash Castle—the 'legitimate' heir who'd rebelled and refused to have anything to do with his late father's company. That Ash had even been here tonight was a surprise because he'd avoided anything related to Hugh Castle for years. He must have a better relationship with his half-brother than he'd ever had with his father. Even so, Rosanna hadn't had the confidence to ask Ash to introduce her to Leo because unfortunately Ash Castle was the source of Rosanna's most mortifying teen moment. While it had been public humiliation of the online kind—and the reason she preferred to live a social-media-free life—the worst had been her parents' reaction. They'd placed the blame squarely on Rosanna's uneven shoulders and the impact of their displeasure still weighed on her today. That was why she was here now—still trying to please them for once.

But while Ash had been unusually quiet and courteous, it had been yet another awkward high-school reunion—especially when he'd briefly brought up that cringe thing in their past. She'd only got through it because she'd realised just what hell he'd have been under at the time. But maybe the fact that she'd spoken to *him* for the first time in a decade would suffice for her parents' expectations for the evening? He was a Castle, after all.

'I heard something about you being a university professor now,' Mae said, drawing her attention back to the present. 'You always were a brain box.'

Rosanna inwardly groaned again at her parents' inflated description of her job. When reality wasn't good enough, they embellished—always over the top. In fact she was a laboratory technician at the school of Biological Sciences at East River University, a couple of hours north of Sydney. As for being a brain box? That was only because she'd spent her life working insanely hard to maintain the grades that were the one thing her parents seemed to be proud of her for. Not that it had ever garnered her any social currency—Mae was one of those people who'd only ever spoken to Rosanna when she'd wanted to borrow her study notes.

'Not a professor.' She smiled resolutely. 'I take some lectures.'

Even that was a stretch. She tutored first-year science students because, according to her boss, she was 'good at instilling scrupulous understanding of the scientific method'. But the work had become repetitive and frustrating. Yet again she'd not lived up to expectations because she should, at the very least, be a full-time lecturer by now if only she'd lived up to her 'potential'.

And as she determinedly chatted with Mae, her energy wilted.

'I'm sorry, I've just got to go and talk to…' Rosanna glanced around the room, hoping to spot someone—*anyone* '… Harry.'

Her excuse to end the current conversation worked again. It had been working well all evening.

Breathing out, Rosanna walked away from the other guests, wondering whether it was too soon to sneak away or if she ought to 'fly the family flag' a little longer.

It had been a failed mission from the beginning. She knew her glamorous, party-professional parents had been disappointed in her reserved nature as a child, in her increasingly flawed appearance. They'd been disappointed by her decision not to stay in Sydney and follow them into the family business after 'all they'd done', and they'd *definitely* been disappointed by her inability to secure a society son-in-law of their dreams to lift their profile all the more…

But the fact was, Rosanna had never satisfied *anyone's* dreams. Not even her own.

She laughed beneath her breath at her self-piteous moment. She'd been so busy trying to meet the impossible dreams of her parents she'd not stopped to actually dream any of her own. And now? Now she had no clue what it was *she* wanted.

But Kingston Towers? The whole complex was dreamy. The party was on the penultimate level of the East Tower with stunning views across the city and to the second, slightly taller tower. She'd toured the two apartments open for viewing already, but from here she could glimpse the West Tower penthouse. Was that a hint of a terraced garden? Her curiosity was piqued and temptation stirred. Rosanna couldn't resist a garden. And it was a showing, after all. Given she was unlikely to ever get the opportunity again, she walked to the central elevators—taking a moment from the horrible party for herself. One elevator opened the second she summoned it and inside she pressed the very top button.

Moments later she arrived at the penthouse. She stepped out, savouring the silence and the sensation of *escape.* The tranquillity was a welcome contrast to the heavy bass downstairs and the hum of people loudly talking to counter it. The other guests couldn't yet have realised they could inspect this apartment as well. Rosanna was glad to explore it alone. No more awkward reunions for just a minute.

The glass doors leading out to the terrace were thrown wide open in invitation, so what else was to be done? Outside she breathed deeply, appreciating the scent of summer and the warm breeze. As she'd suspected, the terrace garden was a gorgeous space brimming with verdant vitality. There were cleverly placed trellises covered with foliage and structural plants that provided privacy and shelter around a comfortable seating area. In an instant she felt better. With all the greenery she could almost forget she was in the middle of a large city. Though if she glanced beyond the leaf-woven trellis, the view of the gleaming harbour was incredible. But it was the garden that truly entranced her.

As she explored the deceptively large space the sky began to turn. Small lights hidden amongst the foliage automatically beamed on. It softened the atmosphere and made it even more intimate. To her wonderment, tucked away on the other side of the trellis was a small pool. She knew there was a lane pool on the recreation level for the residents but this was smaller, a place to plunge rather than exhaust oneself with endless laps. The surrounding plants were flowering and had luscious deep green leaves and with the lights it made the place feel like a magical den. A sensation of peace and pleasure washed over her as one plant in particular caught her eye with its contrasting green foliage.

She'd found not just a sanctuary, but a *paradise*.

Leo Castle sprawled in the large chair in the study, silently watching the uninvited woman wander around his private terrace. She wasn't supposed to be here. Then again, nor was he. He was supposed to be downstairs talking with the new and prospective owners of the luxury apartments Castle Holdings had just completed. Socialising was his most loathed business task—mainly because it interrupted the actual business of doing business. His phone had been humming in his pocket when he was talking to guests downstairs, vibrating with notification after notification. In the end he couldn't resist stealing up here to check in because his favourite aspect was the deal—sale and purchase, the constant accumulation of security. He liked to work fast, accurately, viciously, relentlessly. So missing messages when he had a new deal on a knife-edge was not his idea of fun. But since he'd come up here he'd more than caught up. The outstanding deal had just come through. In theory he should now go down and celebrate the lot. In theory he should be the happiest he'd ever been. Because in theory, he finally had everything he'd ever wanted.

For almost thirty years—his entire life—he'd fought to get to this position. Fighting for recognition, for *justice...*for everything that had been denied him for so long. His name and honour, respect and reputation, fortune... all were finally fully within his control. And nothing mattered to him more than having complete control over his own damned destiny.

Kingston Towers—his first major project as the new CEO of Castle Holdings—was an undeniable success. The man who'd built the company from the ground up, Hugh Castle, had died a year ago. Leo had taken over from the man who'd not only refused to acknowledge Leo's existence, but done everything possible to deny him his rights. But Leo had no intention of letting that happen for ever. He'd talked to his half-brother, Ash, the 'rightful' heir. Ash hadn't wanted anything to do with their father's business—he'd have been happy to see it burn. But Leo had been determined to make the company what it *should* have been and so he and Ash had agreed he'd take the reins. In this last year he'd carved out the cronyism, the favours, the hidden deceitful deals—battling the resentment of the old guard wanting to hold on to their unearned privileges and the pressure to prove himself worthy when he'd been unrecognised for so long. But he'd accomplished what he'd wanted—all while maintaining the success of his own company that he'd built simply to prove he could. He'd worked every minute he'd been awake for *years* to get here. Hours of stress and toil and sacrifice. And he'd done it. He'd even claimed this jewel at the top of the tower for himself. Yet now he was here he didn't feel any real satisfaction. He felt…*nothing.*

Well, not *nothing.*

Because there was—as always—that acidic burning regret in the pit of his stomach that his mother wasn't alive to see any of it. She was never to know *her* honour had been restored, never to feel any peace or security or enjoyment of the rewards…which meant that he couldn't either. Because it was *his* fault she couldn't. Leo rolled his shoulders, unable to dwell on that most painful of wounds.

Maybe he was tired, but he didn't want to return to his duty downstairs yet. And he didn't have to, right? Because Ash had made an appearance. Ash, who'd tracked Leo down when they were both angry teens. Rebellious Ash, who'd enabled Leo to prove their shared parentage. Ash, who'd stepped aside and been an ally ever since.

Leo would always owe him. But their bond was built on more than mutual loathing of their father now. There was respect and loyalty. Ash had signalled his support of Leo's leadership of the company and Leo had done all he could to support Ash's fiercely independent business in return. It was the one relationship in Leo's life now that actually worked and Ash was the only family Leo would ever have. Leo hadn't failed to notice how haunted he'd looked earlier today. He suspected there might be a woman involved but he'd not asked. He'd have been unable to offer any advice anyway; it was for Ash to work out alone. But for now Ash was downstairs doing what he did best—avoiding whatever it was causing him grief by outrageously charming everyone he encountered.

Which meant Leo didn't have to. Leo didn't have to even *be* 'Leo Castle', right now. He could just be a man watching a mysterious, pretty woman out on the terrace.

The elevator had chimed its low warning a few moments ago. He'd neglected to lock it again when he'd come up, but now he swiped through a couple of screens on his phone, adjusting settings so the elevator couldn't come back to this floor unless summoned by him. No more intruders today. No one but the female currently prowling through his plants.

He didn't think she was a guest. Clad in a black blouse and black skirt and black heels that were more sensible than skyscraper, she was staff, he guessed. A waitress escaping all those trays of hors d'oeuvres for a few minutes. He didn't blame her for wanting some peace, he'd wanted it himself.

He watched her explore the terrace, increasingly fascinated by her unguarded demeanour. She was a slim shadow and even though her hair was tied back he could see it was more flaming orange tones than rich auburn—like bonfire night. Despite the distance and even as the sky turned dusky, he could see her skin was pale. She breathed deeply, taking in the view before turning back to the small garden again. Her hand lightly touched the blooms with a reverence and care that he appreciated. He felt a fleeting desire for her to look up and inspect him with the same deliberate concentration, as if there were nothing and no one else in the world she had any interest in.

Ridiculous.

He half laughed beneath his breath at his fanciful thinking. He *must* be tired. He didn't get distracted. Ever. But with that deal now completed, the party a success, maybe he could have a moment to enjoy the scenery. To stop and smell the roses like his interloper out there…

She cupped one of the flowers with a gentle touch and intense focus. But she didn't pick the bloom. He was glad;

he liked those flowers even if they only survived because of the people he paid to take care of them. More importantly, they were his. Not hers. But she suddenly turned to another plant. Her fingers slid across the large, flat leaf and down the stem. A second later she snapped it.

Leo stiffened in incredulity and a second later amusement washed over him.

Little thief.

She'd picked, not a flower, but a stem from an ugly-assin plant. Not quite Beauty stealing roses then, and nor was he about to be a Beast and keep her here for his entertainment. But given he'd caught her in the act, he *was* going to call her on it.

'And you are...?'

Rosanna jumped and turned at the low voice. Her reply caught in her throat as she saw him. First impression? Intimidating size. Second? *Eyes.*

They were so blue they were almost indigo and it took only one look at them for her brain to slither into irrelevance and leave her simply staring. Tall, muscular, *magnificent*. He moved towards her slowly, almost carefully, which allowed other details to slowly seep in. His dark suit accentuated his height and the breadth of his shoulders. The man had muscles and he moved with lethal grace, which meant he must use those muscles well and often. His close-cropped hair and chiselled jaw added to his aura of discipline. Adding this to his *very* serious countenance, she guessed he was on the security team. As he moved nearer she saw those blue eyes sharpen, revealing intelligence, alertness and a faint hint of condemnation.

Rosanna was poleaxed. And why on earth was she suddenly thinking a man *magnificent*?

'You know you're not supposed to be here,' he added, overlooking the fact she'd not answered his first question.

'Are you?' she deflected while attempting to catch both her breath and brain and hoping her flash-flood auto-blush would recede quickly.

'I am.' All authority.

'Security detail?' Catching her breath was impossible. Apparently all the oxygen had been sucked from the world and the plants surrounding her were no help whatsoever.

His shockingly vibrant eyes narrowed. 'You're…on service here?'

Service? She frowned before it dawned. The security guy thought she was a waitress—meaning he had no idea who she was. Rightly so—she really had no influence here, no matter how hard her parents wished it.

'Escaping duty for a little while,' she offered warily. It wasn't a complete lie. 'Besides, won't other—?' She broke off, realising she'd almost given herself away. 'Won't some of the guests be arriving up here shortly?'

His head moved almost imperceptibly. 'No one is supposed to be up here.'

No one? Too late she realised that maybe more people weren't up here because it was supposed to be off-limits.

'Why not?' she asked awkwardly. 'It's the best bit of the whole building.'

There was a hesitation. 'Some of the interior isn't finished so it's not open for a tour tonight.'

'Yet I got up here without any problems.'

'That was a mistake.'

His gaze was so unrelenting she couldn't resist a slight dig.

'Lax security?' she muttered innocently.

'Apparently so,' he acknowledged seriously. 'But I've locked the elevators now so no one can come up without the code.'

Her breath caught again—he'd *locked* the lift? 'What about getting back down?'

He didn't blink but his mouth twitched almost imperceptibly. Rosanna stared back at him, her own intrigue growing. Had that been a glimmer of *amusement*?

'Are you concerned that you're now stuck up here?' he enquired softly. The edge of tease was so faint. But it was there.

'Not in the least,' she lied, instinctively going for self-preservation.

'Not worried about losing your job?'

'They won't notice for a while.' That wasn't a lie at all.

'I don't believe you,' he said. 'I think the world would notice if you were absent.'

He was *so* far from right but, for just this once, it was nice to go along with it and believe a slightly cheesy line delivered by a sinfully serious man. Her nerves sharpened as awareness shivered along her veins. The sky had darkened further and now they were softly lit by the glow of those small bulbs. It could so easily be mistaken for a fairy den of magic and mystery and enticing amusement… And this flight of flirtish fancy? This ripple of temptation? This was not her. *Ever.*

She didn't think it was him either. But he wasn't moving and nor was she because there was *something* in the air.

She made herself swallow. 'Shouldn't you get back to doing your security rounds?'

'There are plenty of us here. Besides, I'm keeping an eye on you.'

'I'm not about to steal anything.' She half laughed.

'But you already have.' He jerked his chin towards her hand.

'Oh.' She glanced down. She'd forgotten all about the stem of the Monstera plant she'd swiped. Now she realised she was gripping it so tightly it was a wonder she hadn't minced it to pulp. 'That.'

Amusement flickered again, ripping an irreparable tear

in his serious facade, and he suddenly smiled—lopsided—as if it was an unfamiliar sensation stretching on his face. 'Yes. That.'

He reached out and took the frond from her and she just let him because now he was smiling. Which meant that now he was spellbinding. Her heart raced in response to his move closer. She was so aware of him that she had to consciously *not* take a step back. It wasn't that he was a danger but that he was a threat of another kind. A threat that was also a temptation. Especially when he smiled.

'Any particular reason for this?' he asked. 'You didn't want a flower?'

'If I picked a flower it would die sooner.'

'So you *care* about the plants?' he mused. 'This wasn't wilful destruction?'

'Of course not.'

His smile deepened as he stepped closer again and revealed a dimple beneath that perfectly sculpted cheekbone. Rosanna stood immobile as he threaded the stem into her hair. He didn't touch her directly but she couldn't breathe. She remained still even after he'd finished. Because he didn't move. He just stood there looking into her eyes. And she looked back—unable to do anything else. The tension stretched. His expression was devastatingly hot. Was he really flirting with her? Did it happen like this—so quickly? So easily?

Guys never flirted with Rosanna. They never noticed her. And if by some chance they did, it was only to request to borrow her notes or to get something from the lab supply cupboard. And she definitely didn't attempt to flirt—too shy, too wary of awkward rejection. Relationships weren't something she had much experience with. Only right now there wasn't just a flutter of anticipation inside her, there was a fizzing sensation and a temptation to lean closer and say something…*stupid*, probably. Yet she couldn't seem to stop herself.

'You're not going to make me pay for it?' she asked. 'No punishment for petty theft?'

The terrible thing was she was curious as to what sort of 'penance' he might require—might it involve skin?

What was wrong with her?

His eyes widened slightly. That fizzing built the pressure inside her—threatening to explode in a way she wasn't sure would be wise.

'Why would I want to punish passion?' he asked softly.

Passion? An unfamiliar flare of heat swept over her. She felt passion for plants, yes, absolutely. But this was different. He was unbearably handsome, and his all-serious intensity called to something within her. Mortified at her thinking, she glanced away from him. Small talk wasn't her thing either. She'd always been shy, but she had to get herself out of this, quickly.

'It's an amazing view,' she muttered awkwardly.

He didn't reply.

'And it's the most beautiful terrace,' she added, her nerves growing. 'It's weird because you know you're in the heart of a massive city, but it's quiet and secret up here.'

She didn't usually fill silences. She wasn't usually around people long enough for awkward silences to develop.

'You've seen the other apartments?' he asked.

'The ones that are open, yes.' She glanced up at him and couldn't help a burr of defensiveness. 'I've not been sneaking through others. I'm not a thief.'

'No?' Something flickered in his expression. 'How do I know there aren't other things you've taken?'

That glint in his eye ignited a fire beneath her skin. A sense of playfulness—of challenge—filled her.

'You can't take my word for it?' she murmured. 'Or are you going to pat me down?'

She experienced a sudden craving for touch that was so strong and so unlike her that she shivered.

'I can imagine a strip-search.' His gaze grazed down her body as if he had X-ray eyes able to see through the black satin to the plain black underwear she wore beneath.

He was like a shadow in which you found danger—enter depths you might get lost in and thus never emerge into the sunlight again. Rosanna was most definitely lost already.

'The only thing I've taken is the frond,' she said.

'Why that one in particular?' he asked softly. 'I saw the way you looked at the plant—as if it was something precious. What makes it so special?'

How long had he been watching her?

Embarrassment curled. 'The coloration on the leaves. I wanted to see if I could grow it from a cutting,' she mumbled.

'So it wasn't just a whim?'

'I don't tend to do things on a whim.'

His eyes crinkled. 'Nor do I.'

She suddenly smiled because that she could well believe—he seemed too intense to indulge in spontaneity. 'I shouldn't have taken it without asking.'

His eyebrows lifted. 'We're all tempted to take things we shouldn't sometimes.'

His huskiness fuelled the fire of temptation already melting her.

'I won't tell if you won't,' he added softly.

That whisper with its promise of secrecy forged something between them. Something illicit. Something tempting. She had the feeling this guy could get away with almost anything. He had an aura, not just of power or command, but of unshakable capability.

'Do you do that often?' she asked.

'Not tell?'

'Give in to temptation and take what you shouldn't.' That heat scaled over every inch of her skin.

He hesitated for a moment before his smile emerged and went ever so slightly lopsided again. 'Not often, no.'

She believed him—the discipline, the decency, the duty, rolled off his demeanour.

'Although that doesn't mean I can't be persuaded by the right person,' he suddenly added. 'A temptation strong enough.'

That frisson of danger reared again.

'You look strong enough to withstand any temptation,' she said. 'You look like you have a lot of discipline.'

He half laughed. 'Appearances can be deceptive.'

'But not everything in an appearance can be faked.' Breathing, real, right in front of her, there was no dispute that those muscles of his weren't honed. Muscles like that took work. 'Or are you saying you're not as strong as you look?'

'You think I look strong?'

'Yes. That's part of your job, right?'

He cocked his head, that smile flickering around his mouth. 'You look like a cat burglar. You act like one too. Yet you cry innocence.'

Rosanna blushed. She was more innocent than he'd probably imagined. A virgin at twenty-six—basically a mythical creature, right?

She breathed, wishing the heat would ease. Her skin was so pale that a barely heightened heartbeat showed up on her face as if she'd seen the most embarrassing thing imaginable. The merest hint of adrenalin in her system turned her into a tomato, which then clashed with the orange of her hair. Her awareness of it only made it worse. Her mother always recommended she smother her skin in make-up for contouring and complexion control. That way she could obliterate the millions of freckles at the same time and make her appearance smooth and inoffensive. She'd not bothered tonight. She should have.

She shrugged. 'There's nothing else I want to take from here.'

'No?' He almost pouted. 'Now that is disappointing.'

'What did you want me to take?'

'Anything really, then I'd have to apprehend you.' His eyes lit up. 'Or you could just take me.'

That tension twisted.

'I'm not strong enough to take you on.' Nor experienced enough.

'I think you're underplaying your attributes.'

What attributes were they?

But he was watching her, his head slightly cocked to the side, his indigo eyes glinting as they caught that tiny light.

She was swamped by a rush of something so primal, so fierce, it stole more than her breath. The crazy urge to kiss him was so overwhelming it scared her. 'I'd better get back—'

He took her hand, his touch instantly silencing her. That heat thickened. She didn't—*couldn't*—move, though his clasp was loose and she could've broken away easily. She stared up at him, lost in the unwavering blue of his eyes, stilled by the gentle rub of his thumb across the back of her hand.

He regarded her intently, his voice little more than a husky whisper. 'Stay a little longer.'

CHAPTER TWO

IT HAD BEEN a simple invitation, yet there was an underlying suggestion—an offer of something so much stronger that was unspoken. And Rosanna couldn't break from the stillness. It was as if she were locked in a resin sphere—in a perfect tableau of temptation.

'Just a little longer,' he added gently, as if coaxing a timid creature.

A thread of something new pulled tight deep within her. A thread of strength, of defiance. For once she *didn't* want to be timid or silent. She sucked in a breath. 'Why?'

His striking gaze drilled into her, seeming to seek knowledge while impressing his own will upon her. 'You know why.'

Did she? He still stroked the back of her hand with his thumb. It was the softest of touches yet it sent sparks up her veins and she felt a dragging sensation deep in her belly. An inexorable pull towards him. An inevitability that she couldn't deny. The desire—the need—for more of his touch. Only his.

Lust at first sight? Apparently it really was a thing and it was unbelievably strong. Yearning caused her to tremble—like an abandoned animal craving connection. Once again that thread buried deep within tightened. She didn't want to be meek. So yes, she did know why. Because she felt it too. And for the first time in her life she felt like acting on it. Because there was a perfection in the mystery of him—of her. A safety in which she could finally take a risk. To be swept off her feet.

'Please,' he muttered.

Not a whisper, but a low masculine request that both sought permission and promised pleasure.

Rosanna lifted her chin to look him more squarely in the eyes—reading the heat and intensity in his. Keeping hold of her hand, he reached out with his other to cup the side of her face. She so easily could've stepped back to avoid that more intimate touch. She didn't.

She released a harsh breath at the gentle rub of his fingers against her jaw, her lips parting as she exhaled. He stepped closer, an effortless glide into her space. Still she said nothing, nor did he, lost in each other's gaze, in the heat weaving around them, drawing them closer still.

So very slowly, so very carefully, he brushed his mouth against hers. It was the lightest, briefest of kisses. It should have been shocking. She should have stepped back. To kiss a complete stranger within only minutes of meeting him? It wasn't the sort of thing Rosanna did. But the second that mouth of his slid against hers? Rosanna was gone and all that remained in her place was a woman who craved more of the man standing before her. And at her soft gasp he returned. This time his lips lingered and her mouth parted. She heard the sound low in his throat. A growl of satisfaction that stoked something equally primordial within her. An echo of the most basic instinct of all. The drive for physical connection. Lips, tongues, hands. Suddenly they were entwined as the next kiss—kisses—engendered more heat and stoked more want. He released her hand only to immediately place his hand on her waist. His palm was big and sure and she couldn't resist leaning closer. She wanted to feel more of him. She wanted to let him take her weight. She trusted that he could. And he did. He pulled her close and kissed her deep—until she was wax in his hands, warm and willing and pliant. Then he lifted his head and she read the message in his eyes.

Want. Need. Now.

Yes.

It was as if time had entered a small loop creating this

space all of their own. Their understanding was unspoken but she knew this was an escape for him too. She briefly wondered from what it was. He didn't seem as if he ought to have any great concerns, yet she was sure he did. A second later the thought evaporated. It didn't matter. There was only this. Only now. And it was perfect.

Every kiss fanned the flames building within her. The hunger mounted. She rose on tiptoe, pressing against his hard body, rejoicing when he cupped her bottom with both hands and pulled her closer still so his arousal pressed against her, turning her on even more. Awash with sensual excitement, she understood for the first time just what he wanted. She wanted it too. Sexuality. Pleasure. A physical fulfilment. For the first time, she truly ached for it. And her body moved purely on instinct to get it. In the arms of a stranger—it was madness. But she reached higher still on tiptoe, her body tumbling into his. He caught her, as she'd known he would. But then he spun them both and pushed her down. She sank back against the soft cushions of the lounger, exhilarated as he followed, keeping the contact of hands and kisses.

He touched her, saw her. Yet to her own surprise she wasn't self-conscious about her skin—because he seemed to like it, given the teasing way he was tracing the patterns of her freckles. And she knew her uneven waist wasn't noticeable in this dimming light, while her scoliosis surgery scar remained unseen as she lay on her back. She wouldn't have to mention it, let alone explain. Besides, he seemed to be focused on something else—something *within* her. Something far more important. Something raw. Something that sucked all his attention.

That need. That matched his own.

Desire surged through her as if a dam had been released. A froth of foam masked the dangerous swirl of desire deep within—this unstoppable drag towards him. Towards the heat bursting between them. This was new. This was undeniable and it was most definitely insane—a moment of pure risk. But she didn't care. Hidden in this shadowy, verdant corner, there was no stopping this magic beneath the stars. With skilful fingers he swiftly unbuttoned her blouse. Even though the air was warm she shivered and suddenly realised the threat of exposure.

'No one can see us?' she asked breathlessly. Privacy mattered. She wanted this to be theirs alone.

'No and there's no cameras up here,' he assured her. 'Motion detectors, yes. But not cameras.'

'You know your stuff.'

'It's my job to.'

He knew other stuff too. How to kiss her so she trembled. How to touch her so she moaned. He undid her bra, pushing the cups away so he could tease her tight-budded nipples. That hunger and need burned. But she squirmed as he slid those skilful fingers up her thighs.

'At least let me do this for you,' he muttered softly.

She understood he wanted to give her pleasure—and the novelty of someone wanting to do something for her? She couldn't resist—could only bathe in the attention, the wonder. She watched him as he hooked his fingers into the waistband of her panties and pulled, sliding them down and off, exposing her most private part to the air, to his eyes, to his touch. At the light skim of his fingertips across that so private part of her she melted. And when he levered up and slid down the lounger to press his lips to the place where his fingers had just touched…that was when she was lost completely. When he tongued her so intimately she was shocked into stillness and silence. But as his mouth sucked and his hands teased, he stirred the most agonisingly desperate feeling within her and she could only fall into his hold—trusting him implicitly to take care of her. And he did—with lush sweeping relentless caresses.

She knew it was madness for him too—his breathlessness, the slight shaking of his hands, the film of sweat on his skin, the passionate determination to please her. Just at the moment when she thought she could take it no more he slid a single finger inside and his tongue flicked across her most sensitive little bud. She closed her eyes and screamed as waves of ecstasy rolled over her.

Long moments later she was still flushed and shaking, awed by the intensity of what he'd done to her—what he'd made her do—to abandon all caution or reserve. But it had been so worth it. So deliciously, sinfully good—so good it should have been enough. Yet there was a pulsing sensation at the apex of her thighs, a slick hunger not quite assuaged despite the bliss still coursing along her veins. She opened her eyes and saw him looking down at her, his smile that little bit uneven, as if he wasn't used to smiling. But when he did—wide enough—there was that dimple. She couldn't help but smile back. For such a strong, serious-looking guy, he had a sweetness about him when he pulled it out. And if he could do this for her? She wanted the rest. With him. This once. Barely knowing what she was doing, she pulled him back up towards her. He braced his hands on the lounger either side of her, holding back enough to look directly into her eyes. His smile faded as the question flickered in his burning indigo-blue eyes.

'Please,' she muttered.

Not a whisper, but a low feminine plea that both sought permission and promised pleasure.

She felt his muscles flex in response. She lifted her head enough to kiss him, stroking her tongue into his mouth the way he'd done to her over and over. And to her pleasure and relief he met her, matched her, finally lowering to crush her body with his again. She groaned the second he did. *Yes.* This was what she wanted. All of him, encompassing all of her.

She relished in his strength. In the power of his body over hers and in the power she was discovering within herself. That she could make this big, strong man tremble? Make him gasp? Make him moan? All with only kisses and caresses? She felt free to explore his magnificent form—she unbuttoned his shirt, loving the soft silkiness of his skin and the steely muscle beneath. She rubbed against him like that eager kitten who craved touch. She couldn't get enough of it now, couldn't get close enough to him. His hold on her tightened, his sweeping hands soothing her restlessness and the small sounds of desperation she'd barely recognised as her own.

'Easy, sweetheart,' he muttered. 'I got you. I'm not going anywhere until we're done.'

That promise—awesome as it was—still wasn't enough. She trembled with renewed passion. He huffed out a breath, suddenly pulling back to reach into the pocket of his trousers to retrieve a slim wallet. Fascinated she watched him extract a small foil square. Her breathing quickened. She hadn't even thought about contraception. Thank heavens he had. For a heartbeat she contemplated telling him but changed her mind the same second. She didn't want anything stopping this. Her sexual status didn't matter. It was nobody's business but her own, right? He probably wouldn't even notice. And she wasn't worried that he might inadvertently hurt her. He was gentle, generous, his touch like fire. She knew how much he'd wanted to please her just then. And maybe it was crazy, but she trusted him completely with her body.

And maybe, most of all, it was selfish, but she wanted this. She wanted him. Now.

He gazed at her, bracing above her again. Neither of them said anything. The kiss said it all. Here. Now. *Everything.*

She wanted to know what it was like to be had by him. She wanted to be held secure like this in the cage of his arms, beneath the glorious weight of his tight muscled body. A prison, a paradise, a weapon of pleasure that he suddenly, sharply wielded as, with a sure thrust, he took her final secret for his.

She gasped, shocked, and for a split second froze. So did he.

'This okay?' he gritted through clenched teeth, his powerful body rigid around hers. 'You're very snug, sweetheart.'

Releasing a tight breath, she gazed up into his eyes—drowning in that almost purple blue. She didn't want to tell him. Didn't want him to stop. She grasped him on pure instinct, pulling his head to hers. Needing his kiss as she needed oxygen. For life.

And he gave it to her—his lips coaxing hers. He slowed right down, giving her time to accept him, time to be overwhelmed again. She forgot the sharpness of his possession as somehow her own strength surged. That new thread within her scaled up into a cord of steel. And now she'd adjusted to the heady sensation of him pinning her to the lounger, she realised she had him caught too. Instinctively she'd curled her legs around his. He was locked within her body now, within her arms, and it felt so good to move against his magnificent form.

His lopsided smile returned and his eyes gleamed as she arched beneath him, learning to meet him stroke for stroke. He paused, rolling his hips against hers before he thrust deep again, setting off a maddening, delighting sensation that she wanted more of. She moaned as he did it again, her desire for retaliation igniting when she saw his smile of satisfaction widen and that dimple emerge. Her hands clasped him harder, her hips lifted quicker, both caught their breath. He arched, tossing his head with a growl as she flexed on him and felt her femininity surge.

They exhaled deeply in unison as pleasure bit hard. Sensations scurried through her with every rock and thrust of his body. She was melting, disintegrating, her form turning not to dust but glitter—she was a sparkling mass of euphoria. The urgency rose. A burst of energy rapid-fired from him and through her. Suddenly it was passionate and frenetic and utterly unstoppable. They ground against each other in ecstatic agony, seeking the release that was so, so close it was torture. He was so strong he overwhelmed her. His breath was rough and hot in her ear, his groans rapid and unfettered, his possession fierce and relentless until she was the one who came apart. She was the one who screamed, shuddering as the orgasm stormed through her like a tornado, shattering her completely. Only then did he unleash with a final fierce thrust, his guttural groan ringing in her ears.

CHAPTER THREE

ROSANNA'S SKIRT WAS rucked up, her silk blouse open at her sides, her bra undone, the straps hanging like ribbons at her elbows. Her hair was half fallen from its bun. And who knew where her panties were? Honestly, she didn't care. She was utterly undone—a breathless mess of wonderment—and she refused to allow any embarrassment to slither in, and no regrets either. How could she possibly regret something that had felt so good?

He was slumped over her, his heart pounding as arrhythmically as her own. She ran her hands beneath his shirt and across his back, feeling once more the powerful breadth of him. The sweat-slicked heat of his skin, the web of hard muscles beneath. Neither of them was fully naked, but the parts that were, where skin pressed against skin, were where pleasure pooled. He was still locked deep inside her, still feeling every aftershock of emotion shudder through her.

He lifted his head and looked at her and offered that lopsided smile. There was the tiniest hint of rue in his expression.

'That went a little further and a lot faster than I anticipated,' he admitted huskily. 'But it was amazing. Thank you.'

She nodded, unable to answer because she had a lump in her throat the size of Australia. She couldn't hold his gaze either. Not without her truth leaking out. Her emotions. Her gratitude. Her wonder. And already she felt the return of that low aching hunger. *She wanted to do it again.* She turned her head to hide that particular truth from him. And that was when she noticed the light flashing intermittently on the deck beside them.

He turned his head to follow her gaze, his eyes widening when the light flashed again. Abruptly he withdrew from her. Rosanna felt chilled the second he sat up. He stood and swiftly fixed his trousers before reaching down. His phone had fallen from his pocket to the floor. Face up, the screen flashed as notification after notification landed.

As he retrieved it and stood reading the messages, his face was illuminated by the blueish light. He was appallingly handsome—beyond movie star and straight into other planetary perfection. Because men this good-looking didn't exist in the real world…moreover men this generous with their attention weren't real. And sure enough, he was distracted now and, going by the frown deepening on his face, not in a good way.

She took advantage of his distraction to pull herself together—swiftly re-clasping her tangled bra, buttoning her blouse and smoothing down her crumpled skirt. She was still wearing her shoes so was spared the mortification of trying to find them, but she instantly abandoned any idea of finding her panties.

'I'd better get going,' she muttered awkwardly, walking towards the locked elevator before he had the chance to reply.

'Let me…' He huffed out a breath and rubbed his forehead.

She knew he was diverted now and she didn't want to be a bother to him. She didn't want to analyse this. Rosanna didn't talk much to anyone, certainly not about intimate things; she was too wary. 'I really need to get back,' she said quickly.

There was a moment when he looked into her eyes when she saw a hint of regret. But he didn't argue with her. He didn't stop her. Which made her quest to leave asap the right one.

Doing this was a one-off. She needed to execute her vanishing act now before the lights came on and reality was exposed. Because if she lingered the magical facade would crumble and reveal the slightly sad, drab reality. He'd find out she'd lied to him—by omission yes, but it was still a lie and she didn't like to lie. She was a guest, not a worker here. She was lacking in real social skills. He'd not seen her naked, not seen her surgery scar or her pale skin under bright lights. She wasn't beautiful in the way he was—she couldn't match his perfection. And as much as she might want it, there would be no replay—not one as gorgeously secret and somehow *safe* as that had been. So it was best to leave now before any of that morphed to the rejection she was sure was inevitable.

He swiped patterns on his phone and she heard the elevator whirr. Did he have access to the security system on his phone?

'I'm sorry. I have to get back to work,' he muttered. He was still serious and focused, just not on her any more.

'Of course.' She didn't want his apology or any regrets.

It seemed to take an interminable amount of time for the elevator to arrive. She stepped in the second the doors opened. She turned to face him, making herself lift her chin and look at him one last time. Because this was a moment she'd always treasure. But the moment had now passed.

Leo Castle gripped his phone so tightly it was a wonder the screen didn't shatter from the sheer force of pressure. Work was the one constant. It was what he did best. What he needed to do. Always. And he needed to get back to it now.

But he felt a terrible sense of frustration. That fragrant, stolen moment with this woman had given him the most intense pleasure he'd ever had and she tempted him to take more. They'd not even had a whole hour. But more time would mean more talk and from that the truth would slip out.

He'd misled her. He, who was used to other people keeping secrets, who had long ago vowed not to have any of his own. Yet tonight he'd been tired, and so, unusually for him, he'd kept his own truth back. Happy *not* to be Leo Castle for a few minutes. Not the boring, responsible, always working CEO. In a moment of weakness he'd wanted to be someone else. *Anyone* but himself so he could just enjoy a moment with a pretty little thief. Only that moment had become several more moments. Shockingly fast and intimate. Unstoppable. Undeniable. He'd had *everything.*

His half-brother, Ash, was the player, not him. Leo Castle did not seduce strange women in secluded corners. He did not have sex on a whim without even knowing his partner's name.

Tonight he had. Damn it. Tonight he hadn't wanted to be Leo Castle. Hadn't wanted to be responsible and focused only on work. For those glorious moments he'd wanted to forget everything and it had been so easy with her standing before him with her kissable lips and big eyes, her firebrand hair and her breathless, blushing intensity. She'd fuelled the heat in his blood, the sudden onslaught of need that had overruled his reason from a single touch. And her trembling response had rendered restraint impossible. The only regret curling through him now was that he had to let her leave. And that he could never admit to her the truth. Not now. She would be angry with him—rightfully so—and Leo Castle didn't deserve forgiveness.

He never had. Never would.

Leo Castle could never escape who he was—a man who'd *failed.*

He suddenly moved, shoving out a hand to force the elevator doors to open again. 'Don't forget this,' he said huskily.

He leaned in enough to pass her the stem she'd snapped

from the plant. He'd snatched it up from where it had been crushed beneath them on the lounger just before following her.

'Thank you.' Mortified, Rosanna took the cutting, unable to hide how badly her hand shook.

She must have lost it in her dishevelment and had forgotten about it completely as the ramifications of her actions sank in. She'd just given her virginity to a complete stranger in a heated, thirty-minute exchange. Now a wall of heat enveloped her. *She didn't even know his name.* But she didn't want to. She didn't want to trade numbers with fumbling awkwardness. Didn't want to hope that he might get in touch with her…some time. She didn't want that inevitable disappointment. This magical moment was perfect just as it was, right? And it was over.

But he still didn't release the elevator doors. Her heart thudded painfully as he stared at her, the blue of his eyes all but obliterated by the stormy darkness of his pupils, the full curve of his lips almost sulky. He was so intense she forgot how to breathe again. But she made herself mutter.

'Bye.' She knew she was blushing and she willed him to release the doors and let her leave.

Instead he lifted his hand and brushed the backs of his fingers down her jaw. It was the lightest of touches yet that sizzle beneath her skin flared. Her resolve started to crumble and all she yearned to do was lean back into him.

That couldn't happen. She made herself step away, breaking the contact. He straightened and dropped both arms to his sides. As the elevator doors closed the last image she had of him was his gazing at her—fully focused, intense, devastating.

And desolate.

Her heart lurched but at that moment the elevator descended. She didn't stop at the party floor. She repeatedly pushed the button to take her all the way down to the ground, desperate to get out of the place entirely. But she didn't really run, she all but floated, her feet barely touching the ground as she fled with her perfect stolen treasure.

CHAPTER FOUR

Two months later

'I'M A FRIEND of his mother's. Of course he'll see me.'

'I really don't think this is a good idea.' Rosanna hurried alongside her mother, trying once more to change her mind. 'Ash isn't in charge of Castle Holdings, it's Leo Castle you need to speak to.'

'Him?' Her mother blanched. 'After all our years of loyalty, he won't even take our call.'

Rosanna's headache worsened and a horrible taste burned the back of her throat—a sense of impending doom making her physically ill.

She'd decided on the spur of the moment to come to Sydney to check on her parents. She'd been down a couple of times since their accident the weekend of the Kingston Towers party because neither had seemed themselves. Now she had unpalatable news she figured it was best to give it to them face to face. This morning she'd been informed that she'd not got the junior lecturer job she'd applied for last month. She'd really only applied because she knew she 'ought' to progress in her career at the university and at least then the stories her parents spun would almost be true. But she'd not got it—apparently she was 'valuable' where she was. Honestly, she was ignoring the part of her that actually felt relieved she'd not been successful and the fact that she didn't really want to teach those large classes. She'd planned to tell her parents first thing and get it over with, but she'd arrived to find her mother in a rage because Gold Style hadn't won the tender for Castle Holdings' new apartment building in Melbourne and, worse, their current contracts had been cancelled. So now her mother had a battle light in her eyes that put Rosanna on edge.

'Why do you need me with you?' she asked her.

But she knew why. Ordinarily, her parents were a formidable, forceful *pair*. Striking-looking, confident, consummate professionals at the art of mingling and making connections to sell their service. But they'd left her father in a slump at home—it was so unlike him not to want to fight for this. Rosanna hoped it was just him taking time to recover from the accident, but he had a pallor that worried her. He'd not been himself in weeks.

'You saw Ash recently,' her mother snapped as she stalked along the pavement.

'Oh.' Rosanna gulped.

During their interrogation after the Kingston Towers party, Rosanna had made the mistake of admitting to her parents that she'd caught up with Ash Castle. She'd been clutching at straws—desperately thinking of anything to avoid admitting that instead of 'schmoozing' possible clients and being seen by Leo Castle, she'd been upstairs having hot sex with a stranger, a security guard.

She still couldn't believe that had happened. Couldn't forget it either.

But truthfully her conversation with Ash had lasted all of twenty seconds before she'd pulled her 'just got to speak to someone' card to escape the awkwardness. Initially her embarrassment had resurged when he'd brought up what had happened between them all those years ago at school but, now she mentally revisited that brief conversation, it only confirmed her feeling at the time that Ash hadn't been his usual carelessly charming self. He'd been subdued and concerned enough to speak up, something he'd not done at the time. Perhaps he'd changed? She frowned, because she wasn't sure people *could* fundamentally change like that.

'You finally have an "in" with him again,' her mother said. 'He'll listen to you.'

No one had an 'in' with Ash Castle. The guy was reckless in both his business and personal life. He invested heavily in start-ups then pulled the pin the moment he maximised his profits. Plus, he slept with anything with a pulse before rapidly moving on to the next woman. Except for Rosanna, of course. He hadn't slept with her. He'd only asked her out because his dying mother had told him to 'be kind to her'. That truth still made her wince.

Ash Castle had been the glittering mirage of possibility. The 'ideal catch'. Back then Rosanna had wanted to emulate her parents' success—to show she could be the daughter they wanted her to be. That was through acquiring useful contacts, right? Ash Castle had been the ultimate useful contact. So even though she'd not been particularly keen on him personally, she'd cultivated a relationship in the way her parents encouraged and said yes to his invitation to the dance. Worst idea ever.

Because the video of him 'cheating' on her at the school senior dance had caused Rosanna's public humiliation. But it had been the berating, ongoing disapproval from her mortified parents that had wrecked what self-confidence she'd had left by then. It had been her 'fault' for not being a 'good enough' girlfriend to keep him. Nothing about her had reached their standards—she'd been too shy and awkward, too crooked—even post-surgery—and now she'd been a public 'failure' socially speaking. For her parents, where image was literally everything, it was the worst—especially in that 'crowd'.

And maybe she hadn't been a great girlfriend. She'd been flattered that he'd paid her attention and she'd tried, in Gold Style, to make it 'work' for her. But she hadn't *fallen* for him. Yes, her pride had been crushed, of course. But she'd realised that, not only could she never be as socially acquisitive as her parents, she could *never* be who or what *they* wanted. And that was what had really hurt. And while there was little she could do about that, she *had* decided that never again would she attempt any kind of arranged relationship, or put business considerations at the forefront of personal choices. Call her a fool, but she wanted someone to sweep her off her feet…rather as that security guard had.

It was weeks since she'd given that complete stranger her virginity and she still thought about it too often. Late at night when she ought to be asleep, parts of her body burned so badly she'd had to take cold showers. Which was probably how she'd got this niggly flu. And she'd actually caught herself daydreaming when she should have been concentrating in the lab—wishing a tall, muscular man would stalk into work and whisk her away with silence and a lopsided smile. As if that were ever going to happen. It was an embarrassing fantasy she could never admit to.

But that was irrelevant. What mattered was appeasing her mother and Rosanna was certain there was no point in talking to Ash about Castle Holdings business. It was Leo—the man in charge—who was determinedly shaking things up, who'd refused to award them the contract and cancelled all their other outstanding ones. From all she'd heard the half-brothers were fiercely independent and loyal only to each other. Which meant Ash would refuse to interfere.

'It's just one contract, Mum,' Rosanna tried to reassure her. 'You'll get another. You'll get way more.'

Her mother halted so suddenly that Rosanna had to backtrack three paces.

'I didn't want to tell you, but your reluctance leaves me no choice,' she snapped. 'In an attempt to leverage what we'd saved, your father invested everything into a different apartment complex. Not one of Castle's. The deal's fallen over already.'

'What?' Rosanna blinked. 'What do you mean *everything*?'

'Every last cent. While he was laid up with that broken ankle he had too much time to think. He borrowed against the business and our personal home.'

'He *what*?' Rosanna gaped. Her father had put everything they had on the line?

'We've been on the edge for a while. That latest redevelopment we did at home went over budget.'

Her parents were always redesigning their own home. They were renowned for never living more than a season or two with the same style, or even the same home. It was part of their 'brand'. Everything was staged to look perfect and up to the minute. As a child Rosanna had hated the constant change. She'd never been allowed to keep any of the things she actually liked—not even a favourite cushion. Then they'd sell the house and move on to another to start the process over again. They rarely stayed within budget, always picking the best, most eclectic, most luxurious of fittings and furnishings, making the ultimate show home for their design flair. They'd moved from one place to the next in the most coveted suburbs, chasing glittering prizes and awards—masters of reinvention. They refreshed, revitalised, made their homes and themselves perfect all over again. Home—like everything and everyone within—had to be the best of the best.

Rosanna was meant to be the best of the best too. They'd pushed for success at all costs—even down to using their only child. They'd only wanted one because more children would have interfered too much with their creative careers. They'd pushed her ahead of her years at school because they'd wanted her to be bright. They'd straightened, not just her teeth, but her whole spine in an attempt to perfect her scoliosis and been disappointed when it hadn't worked as well as they'd wanted. It was better, but not perfect. Not enough for them. She needed to be an accomplishment. *Their* accomplishment. And when she wasn't good enough as she was, they embellished the truth. They'd always had to do that with her…

The reality was she was awkward and didn't want to get involved with some suitable society guy in a mutually advantageous arrangement or basically a business deal. The one time she'd attempted it, it had blown up in her face. But it was what her parents had done. They had a business merger more than a love match. They'd pitted their acumen together and forged identity with activity. But Rosanna had decided, after the Ash Castle debacle, that if ever she were to marry, it would *only* be for love. Maybe it was naive or romantic, but she wanted to be wanted—for all that she was, and for all that she *wasn't*. Because she wasn't *ever* being a disappointment to her partner as well.

But now…had her parents' tendency to blow the budget finally caught up with them? Rosanna finally realised that not even the heavy make-up could conceal the stress in her mother's eyes. Their livelihood was in peril. It explained her father's dejection.

'So now you know why this is vital and I need you by my side,' her mother added. 'You're friends with Ash. All that money we spent on that school for you has to mean something. We're counting on you.'

Her mother's plan was preposterous. Apparently they would say they were 'just walking past' Ash's office…as if that were ever going to be believable. They had no chance of succeeding. Ash had wanted nothing to do with his father's business. But her mother was so fired up, her father a shadow of his usual self, and Rosanna still loved them and wanted them to be proud of her. She wasn't the son her father had wanted, not the beauty her mother had; she was never going to be some society princess or talented interior designer who could take over the family business. She *had* hoped her job would work out and even that had failed. So, this one last chance? She couldn't say no.

'Okay.' Rosanna nodded. 'Let's go.'

She tried to hold her head high as they walked into the tall building but she was wearing an appallingly pink vintage Chanel suit that was her mother's—as the jeans she'd travelled in weren't smart enough. So she who 'should never wear pink because of her red hair', she who also 'shouldn't wear anything too fitting' because it would highlight the irregular curves of her waist thanks to the wonkiness of her spine, was now wearing both. The imperfect things she was supposed to hide were glaringly on show today. But to Rosanna it didn't matter whether she hid her physical imperfections or not. *She* was imperfect. Yet she'd worked hard to be happy within herself—honestly? She'd been happy when she'd first seen the results of her surgery. It had been enough for *her*. But not them. Never them.

She sucked in a breath, trying to revitalise her low spirits. But she'd not got the job. She wasn't going to see the security guard again. Her parents were on the verge of losing everything. And now she had to face the source of her teenage humiliation for the second time in as many months.

Could her day get any worse?

Ash Castle's offices were in an ultra-modern building in the heart of Sydney. Taking a breath, Rosanna followed her mother and another couple of people into the elevator and pressed the button to take them to the top. It was going to be mortifying but Rosanna had been through worse; she'd survive.

'Hold that, please!'

A peremptory tone made her spine tingle. She obeyed without even thinking, pushing the 'doors open' button down while the man strode in. Not a man—a muscle mountain. Rosanna stared, horrified. It was *him*. Indigo eyes, smouldering sensuality, her *secret*. Her blood began to sizzle but at the same time, she was melting with embarrassment. He was looking down at his phone, frowning again, the way he had that night just after they'd been together. She could only hope he'd keep staring at it for the duration of the elevator ride.

Of course, he didn't. He glanced up and around as the doors slid shut, his blue gaze landing on her after the briefest of seconds. His eyes widened, the pupils surging so quickly they all but swallowed those striking irises. But he said nothing. Rosanna turned to stare straight ahead but her wretched skin burned and she felt herself beginning to sweat. She held her breath but the elevator seemed to be moving stupidly slowly. One person stepped out on the third floor. The other on the fifth. That left just him and her mother. Was he heading to the top floor too?

From her peripheral vision she knew he now leaned against the wall at the side. She felt his gaze on her—burning through her like some horrible powerful ray-gun. Doubtless he was puzzling over why she was here. The real question was why was *he*? This wasn't Kingston Towers. This was Ash Castle's company headquarters.

Her headache was blasted away by a jolt of adrenalin and astonishment. She was acutely aware of her mother beside her. Nervously she shot her a glance only to be hit by another wave of astonishment. Why was her mother suddenly so pale?

The elevator chimed and the doors slid open but none of them moved. It was as if they were all frozen.

'After you, ladies,' he eventually said.

It should've been the epitome of polite, yet there was a drawling sarcasm about the way he said 'ladies'. It was unfathomable. Her mother hesitated then walked out onto the landing. But then she turned to face the man who'd followed them both out.

'You've not met my daughter, Rose.'

Rosanna's jaw dropped. Did her mother *know* him? But her mother didn't do the helpful thing and introduce *him* to her. He was the security specialist, wasn't he?

He glanced at Rosanna. His eyes narrowed and there was a stiffness in his stance that made her even more wary. He looked like a predator about to attack. There was no reason to attack. No reason to embarrass her—surely?

'Actually, Danielle, I *have* met your daughter. We met at the Kingston Towers opening. Didn't we, *Rose*?'

Time stopped completely. All Rosanna could hear was the rush of her own blood pulsing too fast.

'You did? Rose?' Her mother sounded startled and expectant for more information.

But Rosanna couldn't take her gaze off the man before her. How did he know her mother's name? Why did he look so grim? There was no sign of that dimple now, only cold anger. Suddenly she was afraid of what he might reveal.

'Briefly,' she said faintly.

Don't say it. Please don't say it.

That burning nauseous feeling returned. But he was still watching her and something raw flickered in his face before the rigid lethality in his gaze intensified.

'Is there anything I can help you with today?' he asked coolly. His glance flickered from her to her mother and back again.

Rosanna had lost all power of speech. *Why* would *he* be able to help them?

'No.' Her mother pushed the elevator button. It hadn't had time to go anywhere so the doors immediately reopened. 'I've just realised we need to be elsewhere. I've got my meetings muddled. My apologies.'

Why was her mother apologising? Why was she so flustered and in such a hurry to leave?

'Actually, I wouldn't mind a few minutes to catch up

with Rose again. Just *briefly.*' He stressed the word lightly but that lethal look in his eyes didn't lessen as he stepped nearer to her. 'That's if you can spare her, Danielle?'

'Oh?' Her mother sounded shocked and then shot Rosanna a sharp look. 'Then I'll see you at home later, Rose.'

Rosanna was too stunned to move but the moment the elevator doors shut—blocking her mother from view—the security guard grabbed her arm and marched her away from the weirdly absorbed attention of the two women staffing reception.

'What's going on?' she hissed as he opened a door.

He didn't answer. He guided her into a room and closed the door behind them both. Rosanna's uneasiness grew. Worse, so did the awareness within her body.

Who on earth was he and what on earth did he *want*?

CHAPTER FIVE

ROSANNA GLANCED ABOUT the room, desperate to give her eyes respite and her brain a second to catch up. Ash's office was stunning, she had no idea how he got any work done with that view to distract him. Except it wasn't the view commanding her attention now.

'What's going on?' she asked again.

'Isn't that my question?' the tall security man countered as he leaned back against the door, blocking her exit. 'I have the impression you've not told your mother what really went down at the party.'

His choice of words was inappropriate. And deliberate. She fought off the immediate blush and inevitably failed.

'We came to see Mr Castle,' she said, ignoring the reference.

He stared at her fixedly for a moment. 'Mr Castle?'

'Yes. Ash Castle, the man whose office we're currently standing in.'

Why hadn't the receptionists stopped them? Where *was* Ash?

He blinked and lifted away from the door to take a step nearer her. 'Are you applying for a job?'

She bristled at his unfriendly tone. 'No, Mr Castle is a friend of mine.'

'You're friends with Ash?' His frown deepened. 'And your mother is Danielle Gold. So I presume your father is Red Gold, of Gold Style.'

She nodded. She had no idea why her mother had suddenly changed her mind about trying to see Ash. Or why she'd shot her that killer look when she'd left so quickly.

'And you're *Rose*.'

Why was he glaring at her like that?

'I prefer Rosanna,' she said stiffly, still feeling the heat of the flush in her face. Not that it was any of his business. She really didn't want to look into his eyes, but she couldn't break away from the intensity of his gaze.

He was staring at her as if she were a human Rubik's cube with one infuriating square that couldn't be turned into the right place. The silence stretched until she couldn't stand it any longer.

'Look, I'm here to see Ash—'

'He's not here,' he interrupted.

'Why are *you* here?' she demanded, patience lost. 'I thought you worked at Kingston Towers.'

He stared at her for another moment. 'You really don't know?'

'Know what?'

'That I'm also Mr Castle. I'm Leo Castle.'

She stared at him. *'What?'*

The reddening over his sharp cheekbones stunned her even more. People couldn't prevent blushing, she knew well. She blushed when she felt things strongly and when she had to admit awkward things. So what he'd said was true. He was Leo Castle—Ash's illegitimate half-brother. The man whose father had denied his existence for his whole life. Who'd fought for recognition and finally won it—the 'workaholic control freak' who'd taken over the company and terminated her parents' contracts. The man she was supposed to have *impressed* that night. The room tilted.

'No. That's impossible.' But the seriousness in his expression made her pause. 'You're not on the security team?'

'I'm on every team working in Castle Holdings,' he said. 'I'm the captain.'

'But you *told* me you were the security guy.' Her voice was a pathetic whisper, while a wave of anger arced and crashed through her.

'You *assumed* I was the security guy. I didn't correct

you. Just as you didn't correct me when you told me you were working service that night. I soon found out that wasn't the case.'

Service.

She'd given him one sort of service, hadn't she? Oh, hell, it had been the most amazing moment of her life and the most intimate. And now he'd wrecked it—he'd *lied* to her.

'You know I wasn't?' she asked. 'You knew who I was?'

'None of the other waitresses knew anyone who matched your description.'

'You tried to find me?'

His mouth compressed.

It wasn't just nausea she felt now, but dizziness too. She swayed slightly and had to furiously blink.

Bad things came in threes, right? So here it was. She'd not got the job she'd been striving for. Her parents had lost their business. And now she'd come face to face with her one and only one-night stand—only to discover that, not only was he responsible for her parents' devastation, but he'd *lied* to her.

'Did you know who I was?' he asked.

She couldn't comprehend the question. Couldn't believe any of this was real. She'd been coming to see Ash Castle to support her mother. Even when she knew he wouldn't give a damn and would do nothing, at least she'd have tried. But this was Leo Castle himself. The man in charge. And if she asked him? After what had occurred between them? It was horribly sticky. Now she knew why her mother had left so quickly. She'd known they were facing defeat.

'Why did you want to see Ash?' he asked when she didn't answer.

She didn't want to go into it. There was no point.

'Tell me and I'll see if I can help,' he pressed. More than serious now, he was thunderous and definitely didn't sound inclined to *help*. 'Or shall I guess?'

She looked up at him.

'It's about the tender for the Melbourne building. And the cessation of Gold Style's other contracts with Castle Holdings,' he clipped. 'Are you aware of the reasons why they've been dropped?'

The floor seemed to be crumbling beneath her feet. She was suddenly on a precipice without knowledge or power to protect herself. Instinctively she knew he was going to tell her something she wasn't going to like. The way her mother had abandoned her quest with such haste and discomfort?

'They betrayed Castle Holdings,' he said. 'Your father took confidential information to a competitor.'

Rosanna shook her head.

'They didn't tell you that bit, huh?' He watched her relentlessly. 'Moreover that competitor has already had several failed contracts and has been charged for breaking commercial law,' he said. 'I can't have Castle Holdings having anything to do with that mess. I won't have the name dragged into it.'

It surprised her that he cared so much about a name that his own father had refused to give him.

But she had to protect her *own* father. 'It sounds like he made a mistake. Maybe he was desperate and made a rash decision.' She shot him a pointed look. 'Haven't you ever acted on impulse?'

He met her gaze coolly. 'Not only did your father access confidential information that he gave to a direct competitor, he misrepresented his relationship with me to gain financial advantage for himself. There's no place for him or your mother in our structure any more.'

His coldness shocked her. He'd made up his mind and he wasn't going to change it. The awful thing was Rosanna could well believe her father might have talked up his connection to the Castle family. He'd talk *anything* up if he thought it would get him a sale. While he had a brilliant flair for design, he was not so brilliant in business—hence spending all that money on their own redesigns. And it was why the Castle contracts were so important. No wonder her mother hadn't wanted to face Leo. She'd not told Rosanna the whole truth. Yet while she understood how bad it looked, how Leo must feel a sense of betrayal, Rosanna felt awful for her father too. He must've felt desperate.

'You hold my parents' livelihoods in your hands,' she said. 'Their reputation. Their life's work.'

Leo shook his head. 'Your father's own choices have led him to the position in which he now finds himself.'

'He's been unwell.'

'Then why not be honest?'

Rosanna could only answer honestly. 'Because he has a stupid amount of pride.' She sighed. 'They both do.'

'Can *you* be honest?' He watched her. 'Because you've just shown up to talk to my brother, who has *nothing* to do with my business. Who wants no input or influence. And you wanted to ask him to intercede.' His expression was stony. 'Did you know who I was that night?'

In the fairy tale, after her first experience of true lust, her life was supposed to have *improved*. There was supposed to have been some magical change—as if something had been unlocked within her—all positive radiance, right? That hadn't happened. In fact, her world had worsened. Admittedly, *not* because she'd slept with him. Rather because he'd just destroyed her parents' business. She knew it was wrong to hold him wholly responsible for that, yet at his questioning of her character now? She felt *furious*.

'I had no idea,' she said. 'None.'

He didn't believe her. The scepticism was clear on his face and the arrogant judgement of the man grated on her nerves.

'Was I supposed to have instantly recognised you?' she demanded.

'A lot of people do.'

'I'm not like a lot of people,' she said. 'I don't use social media. I don't read newspapers or watch much TV. Forgive me for not knowing your face.' She knew he still didn't believe her. 'Are you asking if I slept with you because of what you might be able to do for me in the future? If I used sex to get what I want?'

'Did you?'

She'd known he was going to ask but it shocked her anyway. 'That might be how you operate, but it's not my style. I had no idea who you were. If I had I never would've allowed what happened.'

'Never?' He suddenly smiled and it wasn't pleasant. 'What is it you think you know about me now that would change anything that happened that night?' He stepped closer. 'Because a name makes all the difference?'

'I think you know better than anyone the difference a name can make,' she replied.

He froze and his expression turned grim again. 'So you wanted to ask Ash to use *his* name and intervene?'

She couldn't answer that—he already knew.

'And why did she bring you along?' he continued sharply. 'Looking so very society princess in your pretty pink suit. Are you the temptation on a platter? The sweetener for the deal? Because you "know" Ash as well?'

That sick feeling swirled in her stomach.

Rosanna worried that in a way that was *exactly* what she'd been here to do. Not to support her mother, but to use a relationship to gain advantage. Only there wasn't quite the relationship anyone thought there was between her and Ash. Never had been. It was Leo who was the one she'd been intimate with. The only one.

Rosanna was feeling hotter and hotter and not in a good way. The perfectly air-conditioned office was stuffy. She wriggled her toes in her shoes but it didn't make any difference. The blood wasn't moving oxygen around her body. That dizziness swept over her again and trying to blink it away barely worked.

'Do you seduce many of your contractors?' she asked.

A spark ignited in his eyes.

'I think we could debate who seduced whom for hours and never declare the winner.' The muscle in his jaw twitched. 'The fact is we both won that night. You loved it. So did I.'

There was a roar of awareness at his assessment of their night. She remembered her pleasure as he'd come apart inside her. But that man was so far removed from the angry man standing in front of her now.

'Is it a weekly thing?' She persisted, refusing to succumb to those memories. 'Monthly?'

Grim. Furious. Still. He glared at her. 'Never before. Never since. You already know that.'

She fought the fierce pleasure his words brought, denying understanding anything of him.

'I don't know anything about you,' she said.

Except he was ruthless and unrepentant about it. And he had an unforgiving streak. He was not the wholly controlled, responsible man that people said he was.

'We'll put it behind us now,' she added determinedly. 'Forget it ever happened.'

'Do you believe that's possible?'

'Of course,' she lied. 'Now please let me leave.'

They didn't need to see each other again. *Ever.*

CHAPTER SIX

LEO DIDN'T WANT to believe her. Maybe he was arrogant, but people knew who he was. Given certain people had spent most of his life brazenly lying to his face, trust didn't come easily to him. Yet…no way was she that good an actress—the shock on her face when he'd walked into the elevator had been genuine.

His blood bubbled, heated by anger and by that other thing he was trying to ignore. But it was impossible to stop the memories spinning. He'd not been able to stop them all these weeks. They teased when he was too tired to resist. For a while he'd wondered if she'd walk into Kingston Towers again. He'd spent too many minutes indulging in that frivolous fantasy. He'd even briefed the security desk that if a blushing redhead ever appeared and asked for a security guy, they were to summon him immediately. She hadn't, of course. And now here she was attempting to go behind his back, to his half-brother, Ash. And what was their relationship, exactly? He didn't like the thought of Ash knowing this woman when he knew how the guy operated.

'How do you know Ash?' He couldn't help asking.

The wash of colour in her cheeks made him grit his teeth.

'We were at school together,' she said.

School acquaintances? Her blush suggested there was more to it than that. Jealousy flared instantly. He froze, furious with himself. Leo had worked hard not to be jealous of the half-brother who'd had everything Leo hadn't—legitimacy, two parents, the best education money could buy. But since getting to know Ash, Leo had learned those things weren't always all that awesome. He and his half-brother had more in common that they'd imagined, so he couldn't let this matter get in the way. His relationship with his brother was more important than this was.

'Ash isn't here,' he said harshly. 'He's in New Zealand with his girlfriend.'

Which was why Leo was in Ash's offices today. Ash had phoned for Leo's help with a work issue and of course Leo had agreed. He was happy the guy had worked it out with the woman he wanted. Even happier now, to be truthful.

Rosanna's eyes widened. Yeah, the words 'Ash' and 'girlfriend' hadn't ever been put together in a sentence before. But even that couldn't wash away the anger at the thought of her with Ash, no matter that it had been years ago. Ash wasn't having her again. *Leo* was. He'd make her forget any other man she'd known. He had to turn on his heel to mentally slap some sense into himself. Since when was he such a possessive brute? Normally he never gave a damn about a woman, never took the time to allow a relationship to develop. He was too consumed with work.

Only when he turned back to face her again there was that awareness in her eyes, an audible edge to her breathing. Electricity crackled—*emotion*. He didn't want *that*. Ever.

And he had no reason to feel guilty about cutting ties with her parents' company, right? That was a legitimate business decision. Her parents had shared sensitive commercial information, they couldn't be trusted, so he'd had no choice. And then they tried this—to go behind his back to canvas his brother and bring their daughter as, what, collateral?

It was unacceptable and unforgivable.

Rosanna hadn't known about her father's betrayal—that had been obvious as well. She'd been mortified. He understood the particular shame of having a parent who behaved badly. And a part of him also understood she wanted to protect and help her parents—that she was desperate enough to dress up in the hope of persuading someone. Leo could almost respect that, because he'd tried for years—doing all kinds of menial jobs to help his mother earn enough to keep them both. When it had got worse, when he'd screwed up, he'd been more desperate than to dress up, he'd literally begged for help. Only he'd failed. The difference here was Rosanna's failure wasn't going to kill her parents. No doubt they'd have another contract shortly, her father was too much of a salesman not to. It just wouldn't be with Castle Holdings.

What to do with Rosanna now? Those memories assailed him yet again, muddying his mind. He remembered the consideration she'd given to the garden, the secret sensual side of her he'd glimpsed.

'Did you grow a plant from that cutting?' he asked before thinking better of it.

Her eyes widened. 'Yes, as it happens. I did.'

It made him oddly angry. 'So, you got what you wanted from me and then you went after the other Castle brother for something else?'

Her pupils dilated even more and her face suddenly paled, making her freckles stand out shockingly against the paleness of her skin. His adrenalin surged as she swayed before him. He moved instinctively, drawing a chair close, concern overriding any anger.

'Sit down.' He cursed and firmly pushed her head down.

Rosanna felt atrocious. She battled to remain conscious and not sink into the velvety darkness. She was not *fainting* in front of this man. She choked back a rising bitter tide in the back of her throat. A glass of water materialised on the desk beside her.

'Drink,' he snapped.

She sipped it carefully.

'Most women swoon at my feet,' he said after a moment. 'They don't tend to turn green and gag.'

She chuckled weakly. 'I've insulted you.'

'Indeed, you have,' he said dryly.

She glanced up but there was no lopsided smile, certainly no dimple. And the mental image of all those women swooning at his feet worsened her head. But she had no right to be jealous.

He hunched down in front of her. 'Better?'

Indigo eyes. Intensity. So near. So gorgeous. And she was so tempted to slide forward and hope that he'd catch her and pull her close.

She sat back instead. 'I'd keep your distance. You don't want this bug, it's nasty. I can't seem to shake it.'

'Oh?' He gazed into her eyes intently, that rich colour deepening. 'How long have you been unwell?'

She shrugged.

'Maybe you ought to see a doctor,' he suggested.

'Maybe I just need to go back to bed.' She winced the second after she'd spoken.

That intensity, bigger than them both, flared. She desperately tried to ignore that summons deep inside—it was like a clanging of a bell in medieval magical times, calling supplicants close. But something else flickered in his eyes and he suddenly reached forward and pinched the skin on the back of her hand.

'Ow! What are you doing?' She tried to pull her hand away but he gripped it tightly, staring at it. 'What is wrong with you?'

'What's wrong with *you* is the more important question,' he muttered. 'You're dehydrated. You've lost weight. You suddenly look like hell—' He abruptly stood. 'Come on.'

She stared up at him, half shocked and a little hurt. And, *no*. She wasn't going anywhere with him. 'What—?'

'Get up. We're going to see a doctor.'

'I am *not*—'

'Either you get moving and come with me to a private clinic, or I call an ambulance and we create an almighty scene in front of everyone. Your choice.'

He was too tall, too implacable and far too calm, all things considered.

Control freak. Her mother had been right. He was serious and determined and he wasn't going to waste time arguing with her.

'Who do you think you are?' she growled, but she stood anyway.

'A concerned citizen.'

The fact was, she felt terrible. Worse now that she'd seen him. 'This is ridiculous.'

She wanted to slink home alone all the way back to her tiny safe flat with her pretty plants and pet fish, far away from this overly bossy man who made dangerous feelings come alive in her traitorous body.

He wrapped his arm around her waist and guided her—as if she couldn't walk by herself. Dreadfully, she realised she did need his support; she was as wobbly as a barely set panna cotta. She was vaguely aware of the wide-eyed stares of those receptionists as they waited for the lift. Once inside he swiped a security pass and the elevator smoothly dropped them to the basement.

His sleek silver sedan wasn't like any car she'd been in. It was seriously low to the ground and the engine utterly silent.

'This is electric?'

'Yes.'

'You like it?' she asked. Distraction was good. She needed to stimulate the candy-floss-like capacity of her brain—it seemed to be dissolving as the seconds slipped by in his presence.

To her relief he actually took the hint and talked her through the specs, filling in the time with irrelevant facts.

It felt like only moments later he swooped into a fifteen-minute car park. They were never going to be fifteen minutes or less at a walk-in medical clinic.

'You'll get a parking fine,' she muttered.

'I don't care.'

To her mortification Leo took over. It wasn't a drop-in clinic, it was *private* and they were happy to attend to her immediately. She was taken to a screening room with a nurse who documented her symptoms and took a few tests. It was ridiculous and unnecessary and she was mortified because now that Leo Castle—she was still getting used to *that* idea—wasn't in the room, she was breathing easier and feeling better. Now, she was embarrassed that he'd dragged her in here and caused such a scene, demanding that she be examined immediately. Not long after the nurse had left, the doctor appeared, closing the door behind him. The expression in his eyes made Rosanna's heart seize. The wariness about him scared her.

'Is something wrong?' She leaned forward.

'I have some results already.'

That was quick. The nurse had left the room only a few minutes ago.

'HCG was detected in your urine sample,' he added without further preamble. 'The blood test will indicate the exact levels and give us concrete confirmation, but it looks like you're pregnant. And that does explain your symptoms.'

Rosanna just stared at the man.

'Rosanna?' He spoke again. 'Did you hear what I said? You're pregnant.'

His voice faded as comprehension sank in. *Pregnant?* That wasn't possible.

'There's been a mistake,' she muttered.

The doctor sat in front of her and smiled. 'Have you missed a period recently?'

She didn't know—it was unlike her not to notice, but she'd been preoccupied with trying not to be distracted by memories of the man out in the waiting room!

'If you like we can do an ultrasound now,' the doctor added. 'That would confirm the pregnancy and give us a clearer idea of your gestation. Would that be helpful?'

She was coming across as an idiot. Shock did that to a person. And the thing was, if she *was* pregnant she knew exactly how far along she must be—she'd only had sex the once in her life!

'Would you like me to invite your partner in for the procedure?' the doctor asked.

Her *partner*? That dizzy feeling swarmed again.

Next second there was a cool damp towel on her forehead and the nurse was watching her. 'You're a little overwhelmed?'

Rosanna drew a deep breath. 'Can I have a moment alone with Leo, please?'

The door opened again only a second after she left. He must've been lingering near.

'What did the doctor say?' Leo asked calmly as he closed the door. 'Or do you want me to guess?'

She stared at him, picking up on something in his tone. He couldn't possibly have known *already*?

But he was staring at her fixedly. 'I'm right, aren't I?'

She was reeling from that test result while he looked like…an automaton. He couldn't know *everything*. No one did. He scared her. Not just how wealthy and powerful he was. But how *different* from the man she'd thought him to be that night on the terrace.

'What makes you so sure this baby is even yours?' she blustered, desperately needing some kind of defence from him.

He hunched down in front of her once more. 'Tell me it's not mine, then.'

She stilled because this time there was burning cold rage in the backs of his eyes.

'Will you lie to my face, Rosanna?' That relentless gaze was laser-like—stripping through her layers to seek the truth. 'Not just a white lie, not just an omission,' he added softly. 'Will you tell a life-changing, damaging lie?'

It wasn't just the shocking question or his masculine beauty. It was the seriousness and will emanating from him. He compelled her honesty by sheer force of personality. He wasn't someone to mess with and his honour called to her own sense of responsibility. He who she knew had been denied for so long in his life.

She couldn't lie. Not to him. Not to their child. Not to herself. Not ever.

'You can't *possibly* be so certain,' she said huskily.

'Why would you want to lie?' His expression was taut.

'Because you frighten me.'

He visibly paled. 'Why? You think I'm going to make you do something you don't want to?'

'I don't know.' She didn't know anything about him.

And yet she also realised that it wasn't him who frightened her. It was how she *felt* around him. Her response, her whole-body reactions were purely instinctive. Around him she behaved in a way that was so unlike herself. *That* was what was scary.

'We'll work this out, Rosanna,' he said. 'You invited me in here just now. You had a reason for that. A good one.'

'They want to do a scan.' She swallowed. 'They asked if you would like to be present.'

She stared at him, but he was so hard to read. How did he feel about it? His chiselled expression was stonier than ever. No lopsided smile. No dimple. But now no fury either.

'Of course,' he said briefly. 'If you're happy for me to remain, then I would like to.'

He was so polite, yet she was sure emotion simmered

within him. But he was so controlled he wasn't going to let it out.

Somehow she survived the embarrassment of having the scan with him beside her. She stared at the enormous screen unable to see much in the swirling grey.

'Okay.' The doctor sent them a bracing smile, pointing at the screen. 'You see that?'

'Is that…?' Finally it appeared even highly competent Leo Castle was lost for words.

'There are two, yes.' The doctor drew a breath. 'Congratulations, you're having twins.'

'That's…amazing.' Leo turned from the screen to her. 'Isn't it, darling?'

Darling?

'You're about eight weeks pregnant,' the doctor added.

'Yes.' Leo cupped the side of her face and gazed right into her eyes. 'How wonderful.'

When he looked at her like that, the oxygen level in the room dropped and every brain cell slithered into hibernation, leaving her with nothing but the desire to lean into his touch. She was that clueless creature seeking heat from the sun.

'It's just incredible,' he breathed.

'Incredible' was correct. How could this have happened? And why was he looking at her as if—?

It's for show. This is for show. He doesn't mean it.

She belatedly realised he didn't want the medical staff thinking this was the shock that it truly was. He didn't want them to think this was a *mistake.*

Rosanna's blush burned because this was nothing but a pretence and for a second *she'd* made the mistake of believing in that look, in that intent. But this wasn't real interest. This was duty and responsibility and honour. Everything he'd fought for before.

Leo covered her hand with his and squeezed as if willing

his strength to transmit through the contact. But it didn't stop the panic seeping into her. This was happening too fast. She hadn't even known his name a couple of hours ago, and now they were acting as if they were starry-eyed lovers celebrating the most longed-for pregnancy ever. The falsity of it was appalling. And the reality?

Terrifying.

CHAPTER SEVEN

ROSANNA COULDN'T THINK. Her not getting that job, finding out her parents' business was falling apart and learning her one-night lover was a total liar—wasn't that enough? But to find out she was pregnant—with *twins*—in front of him? That life as she'd known it had just disintegrated for ever?

She didn't listen as the doctor made suggestions for follow-up appointments. Leo agreed to something and then something else while she was too shocked even to pretend she was listening. Leo held her hand as he smiled and thanked the staff.

Somehow they were back outside. Somehow he hadn't got a parking fine even though they'd been more than an hour. Somehow she was in the car, her safety belt on, and he'd pulled out into the traffic, driving with a certainty she couldn't comprehend.

But in seconds she realised his fancy car was too small. She felt trapped in a myriad ways—on a journey, moving too fast with no idea of the destination or even when she might get a chance to take a breath. There was no way to slow this down.

'Where are we going?' she muttered.

'Somewhere we can talk.'

He'd dropped the facade of the deliriously happy partner the second they'd got into the car and she wasn't ready to talk about this yet.

'I want to go home.' She winced at her breathiness.

'Where's home?' he asked.

'Newcastle.'

'Fine.' He kept driving.

Rosanna stared at him. That was *hours* on the road.

Hours in this too-confined space. 'I'm not driving all the way there with you.'

His jaw clenched. 'Can you just trust me to work this out?'

Rosanna wasn't sure she could or *should*. She should be assertive and take control of her own life but she was so shocked by the news they'd just received that she was almost catatonic. Whereas Leo was all 'action man'—decisive and fast, making it all too easy just to let him. Twenty minutes later they pulled up outside a charter helicopter business.

'It's a forty-five-minute flight.' He glanced at her. 'Give me a moment to arrange it.'

Less than a quarter of an hour later she was strapped in beside Leo while the pilot worked out the flight plan. She should have been excited, given this was her first helicopter ride, but she was too preoccupied to even feel nervous. Headphones muted the engine noise but she still couldn't think. She was so inwardly focused she saw nothing of the view. When they landed in Newcastle there was a car waiting. Leo ushered Rosanna in and took his place behind the driving wheel.

'What's your address?' he asked.

She gave it to him.

He plugged it into the navigation system, then frowned. 'That's the university?'

'I live in a campus flat there.'

'Alone?'

Her heart pounded. 'Yes.'

His hands tightened on the wheel as he pulled out into the traffic. 'What do you do?'

This was how little they knew each other. He didn't even know what she did for a job. 'I did my science degree here and never left. I work as a teaching lab technician at the school of Biological Sciences.'

'What does that entail?'

'As a lab tech I prep experiments for the students, do demonstrations for them. Make sure the equipment and supplies are maintained. I help the senior researchers run their experiments and record data. I also take tutor groups—mostly first year students, drilling into them lab rules and etiquette.'

'Biological sciences is what, plants?'

'More like petri dishes. I mostly work with the microbiologists.'

He asked a few more questions—more details of her duties. And then the kicker. 'Do you enjoy it?'

She hesitated but they pulled up outside her university flat before she had to answer. Rosanna was stunned by his efficiency, but felt no relief at arriving home—in fact she was struggling with having him in her small space. As she watched him assess her lounge with a single swift glance she knew she wasn't going to be able to stay here. It wasn't a place to raise one, let alone two babies. And she wasn't going to be able to hold down her lab tech job either. She was in real trouble.

'How long will it take you to pack enough for a week or so?' Leo asked bluntly. 'Because you can't stay here.'

'I can't leave,' she immediately argued. 'I have work, for one thing.'

'You can't work, you keep half fainting. Besides, you can't work around those chemicals any more, can you?'

She felt control slipping from her—she'd not even thought about that. There were protocols but she sensed Leo was a zero-risk kind of control freak. 'Then where do you expect me to go?'

'Seriously?' He stared at her. 'You know we need to sort this out.'

So the answer was obvious.

'You've not been taking care of yourself,' he added.

'You've had symptoms for days and haven't been to the doctor.'

Doctors cost money and she'd needed to work. She'd not wanted to put a foot wrong before that position was announced.

'Stay with me at least for a couple of days while we talk through how we're going to work this out.'

He made it sound so simple. But it wasn't.

'I'm not staying with you. That's not happening.'

'Then I'll stay here with you,' he said.

That was even worse. Her apartment was one bedroom and tiny and there was no way the man could stretch out on her sofa. Heat built in her cheeks. She refused to feel attracted to Leo. *Refused.* Except her damn body wouldn't listen to what her brain was screaming and responded to him regardless. Her eyes wouldn't stop looking. Her skin wouldn't stop tingling. Those secret parts heated...

'Or do you want to stay with your parents?' he asked coolly.

She froze. She'd forgotten all about her mother, who must be wondering what in the world was going on. The thought of telling them her news made her stomach roil. Not because they'd be disappointed, quite the opposite. She had the awful feeling they'd want to take advantage of her pregnancy with Leo Castle's children in a way that would be ludicrous, because everything to them was about bettering the business, enhancing their reputation and their aura of success and society. They would use this against Leo in their fight to win back those contracts. Suddenly she realised Leo knew that too. He must be *hating* this.

She pulled out her phone and saw she'd missed five messages from her mother. She'd put her phone on silent ahead of that terrible meeting that hadn't happened and, with everything that had gone so catastrophically awry since, she'd forgotten all about it. She quickly tapped out a reply.

I'm fine—will call later!

Then she switched it off. She didn't need to deal with a volley of messages back yet.

Leo watched her the entire time. 'You know we need to talk, Rosanna.'

She leaned back against her counter and moistened her lips with a quick touch of her tongue.

'You can't have nothing to say.'

For the first time she saw frustration gleam in his eyes, but his voice remained measured.

'What was that pantomime at the clinic?' She suddenly burst with anger. 'You were acting as if we were…'

'I don't want people talking.' He shrugged negligently. 'And I won't have what's mine kept from me.'

'What's *yours*?' Something stirred within her—an odd mix of rebellion and primal satisfaction of her mate signalling his protective intent. 'This is *my* body.'

'You're right, it is.' He advanced upon her. 'And I've seen first-hand how an unwanted pregnancy can ruin the life of a mother and damage the child irreparably. I won't allow that to happen to you. I promise you'll have whatever support you require.'

He was saying all the 'right' things yet somehow it made her feel worse. 'So you're saying I've won the unplanned pregnancy lottery?'

'I'm saying you'll never have to worry about whether you have a safe place to sleep, or enough money to feed your children, how to scrape together their sports fees, or pay for the constant clothes because they outgrow everything every three months.'

She suddenly realised that this was a *personal* list—that he'd really meant 'first-hand'. Because *he'd* been that child and those were real crises that his mother had faced. She knew some of his 'myth'—the battle to gain recognition as Hugh Castle's son—but she hadn't fully appreciated the real difficulties.

'I'm sorry,' she breathed.

'So am I.' He stood right in front of her like some fortress of strength. 'But accidents happen. It wasn't either of our fault, we just have to problem-solve the best way through it.'

He was moving too fast. His mind leaping ahead with a speed she couldn't keep up with—talking about clothing and food and shoes while she was still in shock.

'What do you want to do, Rosanna?'

Her heart thudded but her brain slowed again. It was as if his nearness lulled her into a false sense of security. That thread of desire tightened. As if everything would be okay if he kissed it better. It was shocking that, faced with the biggest crisis of her life, all she wanted was his touch. She desperately needed to get away from him so she could sort herself out.

'I need time to think. Space to think.'

He paused, then stepped back towards her sofa. 'Then I'll wait until you're ready to talk.'

'You don't trust that I'll come and talk to you when I'm ready?' she asked.

He briefly hesitated again. 'Don't take it personally. I don't trust anyone. Certainly not with my personal business.'

He was more of a stranger to her now than that night on the terrace. That night he'd been courteous, kind, generous… focused on pleasing her. Now he was revealed as a ruthless businessman with an uncompromisingly hard core. This was a man who'd fought relentlessly for years—forcing his father to accept his existence and claiming all that was rightfully his. He'd done it before so he'd do it again. Goosebumps rippled across her arms. It wasn't that he didn't want these babies. He wanted to be involved. *How* involved?

'Then I'm going into my room for a while,' she said.

'I'll support you,' he muttered as she moved. 'No matter what.'

It made her oddly angry that he was putting this decision all on her. He'd offered everything, yet in some ways nothing. This was life-changing and huge and completely terrifying. As she turned the handle and pushed the door, stepping across the threshold, he called to her.

'Fair warning though, Rosanna. I want these babies. They're mine. And I'll do all I can to convince you to have them.'

Leo watched her disappear into her bedroom, barely holding back the urge to chase her and haul her into his arms promising to do anything and everything to make her say yes to what he wanted. And what exactly was it he wanted? The primary instinct was to *protect*—both her and the babies. But the last thing he wanted was to ruin her life and he couldn't be sure he wouldn't. His existence *had* ruined his mother's life—at least for periods of it. And he'd *failed* to protect her and care for her when he was big enough, when she'd needed him most… He'd gone to his father and begged for his help only to be denied and rejected again and then suddenly, shockingly, it was too late.

So having a family—children—wasn't something he'd ever considered. He didn't think he had the attributes. His bloodline sure didn't seem to make good fathers; he'd figured he was better off not bothering. Besides, he was too busy with the businesses. He liked it like that. And babies? They were for a lifetime.

He released an uncomfortable breath. Everything had changed. That control over his destiny that he'd been so smug about? *Obliterated.*

Too bad. This wasn't about him any more, but those

babies. He was *not* letting them down. Not the way he had his mother.

All his childhood he'd been acutely aware of his mother's financial and emotional struggles even when she'd tried to hide them from him. He couldn't help Rosanna with emotional issues, but he could certainly help with financial. So at least in that way this outcome could be different. It could and would be so much better. It had to be. He wasn't having anyone else suffer because of his mistakes and, while this pregnancy *was* a mistake, he wasn't having his children believe their very existence was a problem or that they were ever a burden—not that his mother had ever said it. But he'd seen her struggle. And his extended family—her family? They'd made them both feel shame and guilt—and *unwanted.*

No, that wasn't happening to these babies. There would only be acceptance and enrichment—literally. At least he could deliver that.

Another wave of panic rose at the prospect of actually parenting. He had *zero* clue how to be a father. His mother had been amazing but his father certainly hadn't. He'd refused to admit he was even his father, let alone engage at all. And Leo hadn't been the amazing son his mother deserved. He'd let her down the moment she'd needed him most. What made him think he could do any better for Rosanna?

He didn't. But the very least he could give them was the security and safety that he and his mother had never had. *Financial* security and the safety of the Castle name would be like a forcefield around them. That had to mean marriage—the old-fashioned contractual kind where alliances were forged and kingdoms shored up. The political kind that ensured the safety of citizens. In this case, two tiny ones.

He just had to convince Rosanna. He glanced around her

small lounge, gleaning what information he could, doing the diligence. Her flat was small but filled with life—literally. By the window was a tiered stand filled with pot plants while on a table in the corner was a tank with a lone, very odd-looking fish. He grimaced at the vitality. If it weren't for paid employees, anything alive left in his care would've long ago died of neglect. He was too busy with work to remember to water things and he travelled for long stretches all the time… Not great attributes for impending fatherhood.

He rolled his shoulders and looked the other way, but there was more greenery. On the dining table was another plant alongside a pile of notebooks. He couldn't resist peeking at the open one. Drawings covered the page—diagrams, to be precise—of the plant on the table. She'd written notes about it in very fine, neat writing. If she was a scientist, that meant she'd see reason, right?

Shut in her bedroom, Rosanna was a mass of contradictions. She grabbed a weekend bag and tossed it onto the bed, furiously dismissing the wicked thoughts that flashed in her mind when she saw her pulled-back sheets. How could she be thinking about getting hot and heavy with him again instead of getting to grips with how life-changing the revelations of the last hour had been?

She was *pregnant*. It was unplanned. She had no true partner. Sure, Leo would be there, but she sensed he meant that only in a business, 'problem-solving' sense. They didn't know each other. Intimately and emotionally she was on her own and, even though he said he'd do the right thing, she was sure that he didn't mean marriage. That 'right thing to do' wasn't required in this day and age.

But she *wanted* these babies. It hit her in a huge wave of emotion and instinct. They were a miracle. Awe burgeoned inside and maybe it was insane to be so rapt at this prospect, given her personal circumstances, but she wanted these children so much she had to suck in a steadying breath. She was just going to have to be clever about *how*. People all the world over were successful single parents. As long as she loved them and they were together, they would be okay.

But she couldn't manage on her own financially. Not now. She didn't have any savings. She'd been a student too long and her technician's salary was meagre. Her debt meant she'd have to continue to work and with childcare costs the way they were…? She couldn't ask her parents for support; they had their own crisis to face. Besides, she didn't want their unfulfilled expectations of her being transferred to her children…

The obvious answer was the one she most wanted to reject. Leo Castle had more money than he knew what to do with, but she didn't want to be *dependent* on him. He had the right to be involved and have his say, but she had to maintain her independence. And as long as she kept her own physical distance from him that would be possible. When he was near, when he was touching her, she couldn't think straight. She could barely think at all. There was no way she could keep her distance while they were here in her tiny flat. But she'd do whatever she had to, to ensure her babies' well-being.

He glanced up as she walked out of the bedroom.

'I think we should go back to Sydney to work through all our options,' she said briskly, as if it were her own idea. 'I'll stay in a nearby hotel.'

Not with her parents. Not with him. *Neutral* territory. She'd begin as she meant to go on.

'I have a spare bedroom. What's the difference?'

She gritted her teeth. 'Space.'

'My apartment is larger than most hotel suites. You'll have plenty of space.'

He wasn't going to give up, he'd argue every point. It was

the 'sensible' thing to do and they did need to talk and no doubt his apartment was massive. Plus, it would save her money. She could control her base impulses, surely? 'Fine.'

'You'll pack your things?'

'I already have. I just need to sort the plants and Axel.'

'Axel?'

'The axolotl.'

'That weird fish?'

'He's not weird.' She put some food into his tank and made a mental note to text her neighbour asking her to check on him while she was away. It would only be a couple of days. Then she scattered some nutrients onto her plants.

'You don't have as many plants as I thought you would.' Leo came closer to watch what she was doing.

She sent him a sideways glance, not sure if he was being ironic. 'It takes effort so I'm judicious about my selections.'

'Really?'

For the first time Rosanna saw his dimple flash and something melted inside her. 'I like the unusual ones.'

'I can tell.'

'There's nothing wrong with something being a bit different,' she said softly. 'Or imperfect.'

'I'm not good with plants,' he muttered.

'They just need a little of the right attention.'

He studied her plant stand, his gaze following the plastic piping she'd fashioned. 'This is quite the set-up.'

'It means I don't have to worry about their heating and watering. It's all on a timing system.'

'You built it yourself?'

'I work in a science lab,' she said coolly.

'So you can make all kinds of clever things from all sorts of nothing?' He turned to look right into her eyes.

'It's just tinkering.' She glanced away from his intensity. 'And I don't have the funds or the space to just go buy a glasshouse. But I don't want them to die while I'm gone.'

She grabbed her current notebook and a tin of pencils, putting them safely into the top of her bag, conscious that he was still watching her closely. It was causing her innards to overheat again.

They didn't speak on the helicopter flight back to Sydney but her heart pounded regardless. She knew Leo wasn't just *thinking*, he was plotting and preparing plans for their future. What he wanted, why he wanted it and why she ought to agree with everything he suggested instantly…

Possibilities circled through her mind and she tried to think of counter-arguments to what he might suggest, only she kept coming up short. With a sinking feeling she suspected she had little leverage. She could only try to hold her own.

CHAPTER EIGHT

THERE WAS SUCH inevitability about their destination, yet even so Rosanna couldn't stop herself asking as the elevator opened to let them out, 'So, this is your apartment?'

Kingston Towers penthouse. Inner-city paradise. Scene of her undoing.

'Yes.'

The worst flush she'd ever experienced swamped her. Her pulse skittered as intimate memories scurried through her mind. That was why he'd been here that night. Why he knew how to operate the slick security system. Why he knew whether there were cameras in here or not. The stunning secret garden with its hidden pool and soft lounger were all *his*. Compelled by memories and magnetism, she couldn't stop looking at him. She was drawn to him in a way she couldn't deny, not even now they shared a massive problem. He was watching her back. No smile, no dimple, but a fierceness in his eyes that made her catch her breath.

'I was going to sell it, but I couldn't help holding onto it,' he said quietly. 'I have a nice memory from the opening night party.'

Now that fiery colour wasn't just staining her cheeks but her entire body. 'Have you made more "nice memories" since then?'

It ought *not* to matter, but it did. Badly.

He slowly shook his head. 'I've had to make do with that one.'

She was swamped by a rush of hot relief and primitive satisfaction. He regarded her with that inscrutable stare and she had the scalding sensation that he too was remembering particular points of that evening and for a split second she thought he was about to—

Suddenly he turned and strode into the apartment. He carried her bag straight down a long corridor and into a large bedroom, devoid of any signs of occupation; she knew the room wasn't his. Still, she also knew his was too near. She should have insisted on staying in a hotel, because the tension simmering beneath her skin was too much.

'It's been a long afternoon.' Huskiness roughened his voice. 'You must be hungry.'

Yet to her the time had passed quickly.

'Rosanna?'

She'd just noticed the bedroom window overlooked the terrace garden and now her throat had clogged. Memories scalded—the scent, the taste… She *ached.*

'I'll go organise something,' he growled and stalked out of the room.

She attempted to think calming thoughts. Rational thoughts. In the luxurious en-suite bathroom she splashed her face with cold water. It didn't work. Her cheeks remained flushed, her mind frantic. There was no escaping the memories both he and the garden stirred.

Finally she walked out to the massive living area. It was dominated by double desks upon which there were several computer screens. All were switched on. His work was clearly his priority. When she finally made it to the kitchen he was putting a large tray on the counter. It was covered with gourmet sandwiches, tiny tarts, crackers, cheese and fruit.

To her surprise her mouth watered. 'How did you…?'

'The chef downstairs delivered it a couple of minutes ago,' he explained briefly. 'Shall we take it outside?'

She couldn't face that garden yet. 'Here is fine.'

With him on one side of the vast counter and her on the other.

Leo poured them both cool sodas and took a seat. Patient yet intense.

'Tell me what you're thinking,' he said when they'd both replenished a little.

She drew a steadying breath. At least now she wasn't blushing like mad. 'I'm not giving them up,' she said. 'I'm keeping them. They're mine.'

It was more than an echo of his own words. It was a challenge and they both knew it. He nodded but didn't smile. He didn't need to—satisfaction then determination flared in his gaze. 'That's a good start,' he said. 'Now we negotiate.'

She didn't think there was going to be much negotiation. There was going to be a decree from him and denial from her.

'You know there's one very obvious, very easy solution,' he began.

She watched him, waiting.

'You can't guess?' he prompted.

'I don't think I want to,' she muttered.

A small smile of appreciation flickered. 'We get married. Immediately.'

She shook her head. 'No.'

It didn't matter if bald, flat rejection was rude, it was a ridiculous suggestion. It surprised her that a man so future-focused and innovative and capable enough to be in charge of two successful companies would have such old-fashioned intention.

'Why not?'

'It's unnecessary,' she all but shouted. 'We can take care of them without being tied to each other in such a complicated way.'

'Isn't it more likely to get more complicated if we're *not* married?' he countered silkily. 'This is the most straightforward solution.'

Straightforward? He had to be kidding.

'Marriage will give these children legitimacy,' he began.

'That shouldn't matter.'

'It shouldn't. But it does. It did for me.'

She'd worried his personal circumstances might weigh on him, but there was a major point of difference that he was overlooking.

'But you're not like your father,' she said carefully. 'You won't turn your back on them whether we're married or not. Their experience will be totally different from what yours was. Our marriage is not essential.'

'I disagree.' Such finality. 'And you don't know—'

'Times have changed—'

'Have they?' he interjected coolly. 'Why would I want to take that risk? Why would I want my children to suffer from even a sliver of the judgement I was subjected to?' He pinned her with a gaze far fierier than his tone suggested. 'Why would you want that for them?'

'*Marriage* isn't about them. They don't need us to be married to have the security you want for them. They could still have your name—'

'It's not *enough*,' he shut her down.

That glimpse of emotion, of anger, made her pulse skip. She saw him draw in a steadying breath, trying to control his reaction. This wasn't easy for either of them.

He was serious and focused, but now the forceful side emerged. 'Do you not believe they deserve the best beginning in life?'

'Actually I'm determined they'll get *exactly* that,' she said. 'But the "best" is *not* shackling their parents together in a sham that will only end in tears and acrimony.' She didn't want an 'arrangement' that she would resent for evermore. Wasn't she allowed to want love?

'Tears?' His gaze narrowed on her.

She sensed him pivoting, prepping for another attack.

'I'm not saying we have to sleep together.' He softened his tone. 'We can live separate lives.'

What did that mean—to be married and yet, not married? Didn't he want to 'have' to sleep with her? Even for that, she wasn't enough. Her anger flared. 'Are you saying you'll cheat on me?'

His mouth thinned. 'Of course not.'

He was too perfect, wasn't he? Too determined not to make the mistakes of his father.

'Then are you saying you can live without sex for as long as we both shall live?' She batted her lashes at him. 'Because if we have to marry at all, then it must be for life, right? Otherwise why are we bothering?'

A muscle jerked in his jaw. 'If you're saying you expect this marriage to last, then that's wonderful. That's exactly what I want. We are in perfect agreement.'

'We are not!' She glared at him. 'You'd settle for a celibate life?'

A smirk slowly spread on his face. 'As I'll be married to you, I won't need to.' Dimples in both cheeks appeared while a glint lit his eyes. 'Our past record makes me think that I won't have to wait all that long for you to ask me to consummate our marriage.'

What? She stared at him, her jaw dropped at his arrogance. And the mortification that he *knew*...so she *had* to deny it. 'You'll be waiting an awfully long time.'

'Will I?' His smile vanished and he shrugged carelessly. 'That's fine too. I don't fool around all that much. I never have.'

'So no partying? No endless stream of beautiful women?' She'd suspected he wasn't a playboy but he really wasn't bothered by the prospect of a sexless future?

'I haven't the time to be frivolous,' he dismissed the question.

'You just work. A lot.' Which concerned her just as much.

'I like work. I'm not going to apologise for that.'

So very disciplined. So very controlled. Her fingertips

itched. She didn't want him to be so damned *perfect* about everything. 'All work and no play…'

'Work *is* play for me.'

'Really?'

'Don't you love what you do in the lab?'

She didn't want to answer that honestly. He sat back, his smile building almost back to dimple point. 'Perhaps you'll use this as an opportunity to figure out something you love doing more?' He mused as if it were all an amazing chance she should be grateful to have. 'You won't need to work, so you can consider anything.'

Was he bribing her now?

'We're not in love,' she muttered.

'What has that to do with anything?' he blithely shot back. 'It may as well be you. Especially given the current circumstances.'

'It "may as well"?' She gaped at him. 'Don't you want to fall in love and get married for real one day?'

'Marriage has never been on my to-do list,' he said. 'But I can adapt when necessary.'

His denial surprised her. Had he never wanted to settle down with a life partner? Yet he was the ultimate catch himself—intelligent, successful, brain-fryingly attractive, not to mention stupendously wealthy. Women must target him all the time.

'You've never wanted a wife and children?' she clarified.

His expression shut down. 'It's not something I'd have gone out of my way to achieve.'

To *achieve*? As if it really was an item on his to-do list. As if, should he decide to, he'd just make it happen—all so easily. Which was exactly what he was trying to do now. He was a person of action and achievement—in every area. She wanted to rebel against that. Because she so totally wasn't.

'But that's what you want?' He cocked his head, something flickering in his bright eyes. 'To fall in love? Are you a romantic, Rosanna?'

It didn't matter. Right now she had to be a *realist*. Because unfortunately the only guy to have swept her away on a tide of desire was standing right in front of her, offering her something utterly unpalatable. She wasn't going to have much opportunity to meet anyone else, given she was going to be busy on double-baby duty. Which was fine. Because she was going to have her children.

Leo looked tense. 'You want a happy marriage like your parents had?'

She nearly choked. Her parents were married to their *work*—and only by extension to each other. Nothing mattered more to either of them than their business, so they were a *partnership* that was far more professional than personal.

He, too, seemed married to his work. So, no, she didn't want that.

'I don't want to be trapped in some political marriage where we don't actually want to be with each other but we're together for societal reasons. That wouldn't be good for the children. They're not stupid.'

'It would only be unpleasant if we were actually warring, which I don't think we'll do.'

So he thought this would be some bloodless, cool-headed, passionless union? That might be true for him, but for herself? The feelings he aroused within her were definitely passionate. Definitely not cool-headed. And while he thought they could still sleep together—maybe—he didn't seem that *desperate* for it. Perhaps that night wasn't as memorable for him as it was her…

He watched her thoughtfully. 'Perhaps there are some other issues that could be solved if you agreed.'

'Oh?' She narrowed her gaze on him. 'Such as?'

'Our children will have security and safety.'

'They can have that without us being married.'

'They're my heirs. I'm a wealthy person. They might be targeted.'

She rolled her eyes. 'We're in Australia, not a lawless state full of bribery, corruption and kidnapping cartels.'

'It's still a risk I'm not prepared to take.'

'Then we live in one of your buildings.'

'I don't wish to be separated from them.'

'You want to be a hands-on father?'

He stiffened. 'I wish to be involved in their lives. For them to know who I am. And that I will do all that I can for them.'

What did that mean, exactly—*all that he could*?

He seemed to turn to stone before her eyes. More remote. More serious. More determined. 'It could be very advantageous for your parents should we marry.'

Her skin iced but deep beneath her blood began to bubble. The irony was that this was exactly the kind of socially advantageous marriage her parents had hoped she'd make. The reason why they'd sent her to that insanely expensive school was to meet the children of insanely wealthy people and foster connections that could enhance their careers. They wouldn't be outraged on her behalf at this proposal, they'd be pushing for her to say yes. The second they found out about the pregnancy they'd probably march over and demand Leo 'do the right thing' and marry her. They would use their newfound, blood-bound relationship to the Castles for professional gain. Use their grandchildren as they'd used her. They'd interfered in her social life once before and it had been mortifying. She would effectively be a bought bride. But under his sufferance too—he'd endure it because he 'had' to 'do the right thing'… and that would be hideous.

'In what way?' she asked coldly.

'They wouldn't need to worry about their work any more,' he said.

'Are you saying you'll renew their contract if I marry you?' she asked, unsure how she was keeping her voice steady. 'Am I hearing you correctly? A bartered bride, that's what you're going for?'

She didn't want to be anyone's burden—not less than one hundred per cent desired. So, no, she was never going to marry him. Never going to have a marriage of convenience.

He paused. 'There's no need to be so emotive. We're floating ideas. It's part of problem-solving.'

'By taking one thing utterly unrelated to this issue and using it as leverage?'

'I'm saying they wouldn't need to worry about losing their house.' He frowned. 'They need never work again. Early retirement, isn't that everyone's dream?'

So he'd not renew the contract. He'd simply pay her parents to go away. The outrageously wealthy man's answer to all problems.

'Is early retirement *your* dream?' she asked.

That frown deepened. Yeah, she didn't think so. Her parents lived for their work, just as Leo seemed to. Paying them to head off into the sunset wasn't any way to coax her into agreeing. And that he'd hold her parents' future fortunes over her made her think less of him.

'None of your reasons are enough to induce me to say yes to a crazy proposal,' she said bitterly. 'I would've thought a successful businessman like you would've been able to think a little more creatively.'

Right now Leo wasn't thinking at all. He was staving off the very basic, very wrong urge to *kiss* her into submission. He'd not known he suffered from caveman tendencies, but they were rising to the fore now and it was horrendous. He shoved them back down, gritting his teeth,. What frustrated him most was that this wasn't even an argument—she'd given a flat rejection from the start and stubbornly refused to entertain any good reason why she should reconsider. He'd come up against brick walls before. In the end he'd battered them down—destroying them in the process before rebuilding something better suited to his needs. He'd have to do the same here—because he'd do *whatever* was required to secure what he wanted.

Except what he wanted right now was off the rails. His body was trying to overrule his reason and push him into action. With the shock of everything today he just wanted a moment to feel good again. Getting close to Rosanna would feel more than good. Instead he stood rigidly, rejecting the urge. Look where succumbing to that lust had got them already.

Besides, he had to back-pedal over his mention of her parents. The fury that had ignited in her eyes? Mentioning them had obviously been a mistake, but he'd felt compelled to use whatever tools he had to secure his win. Except all he was doing was making her angrier and less agreeable. Unfortunately the spark in her eyes was making it hard for his brain to work. The flush in her face was fuel to his own flame, messing with his already reduced ability to rationalise his way out. He just wanted to touch her skin, trace the patterns of her freckles and flushes.

He was an animal, he really was. To be thinking about sex right now?

He had to focus on the imperative *need* of his new responsibility. He would give her and their children the security he'd not had. He would never turn his back on them. But tangible support was all he could offer. Financial security, physical safety and name. Nothing more. Certainly not happy ever after.

Because he was not a romantic. And she? She'd not answered that.

It was too bad for both of them, because marriage was the one and only structure in which all those things could be achieved.

The years he'd spent fighting to prove his own damn provenance? His desperation in trying to help his mother? She'd worked so hard to support him with no help from her family and none from his father. She'd been cast off when pregnant and his father hadn't just refused to admit or accept responsibility, he'd made her situation so much worse by denigrating her character. And Leo *had* been a burden for her—but she'd carried him, cared for him and he'd loved her for it. As soon as he was old enough it had been the two of them side by side together. But he'd been stupidly arrogant and eventually let her down with foolish, youthful laziness.

When she'd died he'd vowed he would get justice for her. To him that had meant proving her truth against the lies of Hugh Castle. It was the least he could do when he'd failed her so completely—failing to get her the help she'd needed soon enough.

And he couldn't help himself from working his ass off to make something of himself in the futile hope of getting just the attention, let alone the approval, of a father who was never going to be interested no matter what he did…

Not being given a chance at all? *That* angered him more than anything. And it felt just the same now, as if Rosanna wasn't giving him any kind of chance with her instant refusal of everything.

'You don't think it's an abuse of power to make such an offer?' She slayed him with the cool fury in her pale blue eyes. 'Maybe you're more like your father than you like to think.'

Cold anger washed through him, equalling the rage he read in her expression. How *dared* she? He r*efused* to be like his father. *That* was his whole point. His offer was the exact opposite of what Hugh had done. She wasn't thinking straight. Nor, to be honest, was he. It had been a long, shocking day. Rosanna needed a break. He, too, needed time to recalibrate and figure out the way to convince her. Firing off now would only worsen things. He refused to lose control of his emotions. Instead he made himself count to ten.

It barely worked. But he steadied enough to inwardly acknowledge that mentioning her parents was a kind of coercion. Even so, he didn't quite care. He'd use whatever it took to secure the future of his children.

He had to draw another breath. He could barely envisage them, or barely cope with the idea of not one but two small babies. Hell, he wouldn't know the first thing to do with them. *Caring* for them? That was impossible. He'd failed at caring for his mother. With devastating consequences. So he *needed* Rosanna to be onboard. He needed *her* there. This, the woman who nurtured broken plant cuttings to new life, all health and vitality. She'd know what to do with the babies. She'd fill the emotional gaps that he couldn't, and he would get her financial help. He'd hire her an army of nannies if she needed it. In this way they could be a good team. She just needed to understand that somehow.

Rosanna stared as Leo's eyes darkened with emotion. Had she scored a hit? Yet she felt bad; she didn't truly think he was anything like the two-faced cheat Hugh Castle had turned out to be. But his offer put her on edge, making her wary of what else he might try.

'It's not an abuse of anything,' Leo finally answered unevenly. 'It's a very generous offer. One you ought to consider seriously before it's taken off the table. You mightn't like what the replacement offer might be.'

Her skin chilled. 'Replacement?'

He shrugged. 'If I start going more "creative" with my thinking.'

A frisson of danger sparked in the stormy atmosphere.

But then he almost smiled. 'I don't want to argue with you.'

'No?' She couldn't take her gaze off him. 'You just want everything your own way.' She stood up from the stool. 'I'm not marrying you. Ever.'

'Why not give us a chance?' He too stood and walked around the counter.

'There is no us,' she muttered. 'There's just a…situation.'

'But there could be.' He advanced closer and the glint in his eyes froze her. '*You're* the one not thinking creatively now.'

She couldn't think at all any more. Not when he was this near, this intense, this determined.

'Why can't we make it what *we* want?' he asked softly.

Want?

Rosanna couldn't breathe. There was lightning now—fully charged attraction that was impossible to deny yet too much to bear. All because he'd come to stand right before her. Of all the people in the world, why did her body want him? A man who was bossy and authoritative and serious? Why this unemotional, ruthless, unforgiving man? Yet she'd just sparked to life.

'Don't look at me like that,' he growled.

'Like what?' she snapped back at him.

'I'm angry too,' he muttered. 'I'm frustrated as *hell*.'

Some long-secret part of her had taken control of her limbs. She didn't step back when he stepped closer. She didn't flinch. Didn't resist. Because the balm of having her body against his? She practically melded against him. It was like that night—when one touch had been all it had taken. His arms clamped more tightly at her wordless response. She couldn't stop staring. His mouth was in a grim pose yet perfect in its fullness. There was the slightest hint of stubble on his sculpted jaw. The angles and planes of him were honed and hard, yet there was a silken quality to his skin. That sizzling ache within soared.

He released a low groan and smashed his mouth over hers. It was the most appalling relief. She was flung into that furnace of molten want. The horrors of the afternoon were blasted away.

This was how to feel better. *This* was the only way to forget everything. She trembled against him, satisfied only when he pressed her hips against the heat of his. Finally feeling that rigid arousal again, she moaned. It was *madness*.

'Say yes,' he breathed.

It was such a hot whisper. But she realised it was seduction. Calculated. The *one* way he could get her to capitulate. Not just to say yes, but to *beg* him to do as he wished. Which meant it wasn't as uncontrolled as it was for her. And it would only be a matter of time before he lost interest. And that would hurt her.

'No,' she muttered back.

It was barely audible even to herself but he heard. He lifted his head and gazed down at her.

'Why not?' There was a gleaming darkness in his eyes now. A possessive wilfulness. He wanted her to surrender to this.

'It would be a mistake.'

'It's what we both want. I can taste your hunger, Rosanna. And I know you can feel mine.'

His bluntness was shockingly arousing and she was unable to deny the liquefying heat he aroused within her. She was so close to surrendering to what she wanted.

'No.'

He immediately loosened his hold before pausing briefly to support her while she recovered her balance. She was mortified that he felt her trembling—that her body gave her away even when her words did not. But he respected her words. He didn't challenge the rejection as a lie. But there was an edge in his expression that made her wonder if she weren't in more trouble now than if she'd given way moments before. Because there was no denying the truth any more. There was only stopping herself from acting on it.

CHAPTER NINE

ROSANNA DREAMT SHE was trying to stop a waterfall with nothing more than a sieve…and there was an inevitability about her own drowning. *Twins.*

Her eyes flashed open. It felt impossible to do alone and she had no other support she could count on, which meant negotiating some kind of arrangement with Leo. A lifestyle that *she* could live with. That was not marriage, nor was it an affair.

She'd gone to her room immediately after that kiss last night. He hadn't stopped her—as if he too had needed respite from the tension. But she was sure his frustration was mostly concern for the future, whereas hers was complicated by the lust overtaking her every time she so much as looked at him. She *couldn't* marry him. Instinctively she knew the magnetism drawing her to him would hurt her eventually. She needed space to settle them into a platonic arrangement. Something peaceful, calm, *unemotional.* That would be best for everyone.

She dressed in loose jeans and T-shirt then opened the door that led directly from her bedroom out onto the terrace to appreciate the gorgeous morning sky. With the door open she could now hear splashing and couldn't resist investigating. Leo was swimming in that small pool. It should've been impossible given the size, but there was some kind of machine humming. He must have seen her because he suddenly flipped to swim onto his back.

'I can set the resistance,' he explained. 'I can make it harder or easier, depending on what I need.'

Clever.

'So you're swimming to nowhere?' She tried not to stare at the bronze skin and flexing muscles on show and opted to tease him instead. 'Expending all that energy only to stay in the one place?'

It sounded hellish frustrating but no wonder he had that broad-shouldered physique.

'It's a good challenge,' he said.

'Yet so unrewarding. Never getting anywhere.'

'It's not about the destination though, is it?' He waded to the edge. 'It's about the process. The benefits of the journey.'

It just sounded exhausting to her. She'd constantly striven to prove herself to her parents, to her teachers, to her bosses…and ultimately her process, her attempted journey to acceptance, had failed. But Leo Castle wasn't a failure. He was the ultimate achiever.

He pulled out of the water and she couldn't stop staring. She'd not seen him fully naked that night. It had been dark and they'd both remained partially clothed. Now, in the brilliance of the early morning sunshine, he was all smooth skin and rippling muscles that gleamed with the promise of heat and silken pleasure.

'Do you feel better for a good night's sleep?' he asked.

What sleep?

Glancing up, she read heated amusement in his eyes. And heard the tone of arrogance.

'I feel marvellous,' she lied. 'What about you?'

'Oh, yes. Fully refreshed and ready for round two of the marriage debate.'

Did he have a knock-out move planned? Rosanna had to dig in for the long haul.

'But breakfast first, hmm?'

That chef from downstairs must've stopped in again because the outdoor table was laden with delicious options—creamy yoghurt, cereal, fresh fruit and still-warm pastries. Rosanna sank onto a seat, unable to resist.

But Leo's phone chimed three seconds after he joined her there. 'Excuse me, I need to answer this.'

She listened as he walked inside. His voice was low and reasoned—problem-solving, answering questions. Apparently the marriage argument wasn't his priority. That was good. Rosanna could appreciate the warmth of the sun and that stunning view across the harbour and the frankly amazing apple pastries.

Ten minutes later he returned. Her resting pulse rate picked up again even though he'd put on a T-shirt. She had to get a grip. But he'd barely sat back down before his phone rang again. As he walked around the terrace she could hear him instructing some poor soul to write up a report and have it to him within the hour. It was early Saturday morning and he was working—almost every minute of it so far.

Fifteen minutes later she carried her used dish to the kitchen, passing through that lounge where the computers were running, their screens filled with data and graphs and scrolling tickers along the bottom. He was now seated at one of the large desks. He controlled not one, but two large companies, which meant he had a lot on his mind. Work was his passion and that was fair enough. But the impact on children? She knew too well how it felt to be low down on the priority list.

Deep in thought, she went back to her room and freshened up. When she re-emerged over an hour later, he still hadn't moved.

'Still working?' she asked as he typed something out onto one of the three computers.

He glanced up for a second. 'Why does that sound like a loaded question?'

'My parents are workaholics. So I know it's not fun for kids.'

'There's nothing wrong with wanting to do a good job.'

'No. But balance is important.'

He sat back, a small hint of amusement in his eyes. 'Will this be your next reason to refuse me? I'm too committed to my business?'

As a child she'd been basically abandoned for business so her concern wasn't as petty as he made it sound. She knew how it felt not to have someone who took the time to *listen*. Who was always preoccupied and too busy at 'more important' appointments to bother turning up to her school events.

'I don't care about your business. If that's your priority in life, that's fine,' she said. '*My* priority is now my children. And I'm not going to let them suffer by having an absent, workaholic father, where everything they do is dictated and determined by how best it is for the business, around your schedule.'

He inhaled sharply. 'But the business is what pays for the food, the roof over their heads.'

'Oh, please,' she sighed. 'You could retire this instant and have enough money to live on for a hundred lifetimes.'

He blinked. 'A lot of people depend on me for *their* work.'

'Because only you can be the boss?' She shook her head. 'Maybe you should hire more people and free up your own time.'

'I'm good at what I do, Rosanna,' he said softly.

Oh, she knew that.

'But isn't it awfully arrogant to assume that no one else could possibly do your job as well as you can?' she asked innocently.

'Not arrogant,' he denied. 'Nobody *cares* about it to the same extent that I do.'

'Again,' she challenged, 'isn't it arrogant to assume no one else could feel things as strongly as you do?'

'They've not invested the blood, sweat and tears that

I have. Or the years.' He leaned back in his seat and surveyed her. 'It's about ensuring the right decisions get made.'

'And only *you* can make them? You need to approve *everything*. I bet you're an absolute micromanager. I feel sorry for your staff.'

'Oh, there's no need,' he said with cool smugness. 'They're very happy.'

'Are they?'

'Given what I pay them, I'm certain of it.'

All the money for all the hours? For being able to drop everything first thing on a Saturday morning and write up some report for a demanding boss?

'What style of management do you think they'd prefer?' He rose out of the chair and strolled towards her.

She was on shaky ground here. 'Perhaps they might prefer a more collaborative approach. Or be allowed more freedom to work on problem areas themselves before coming to you. Perhaps they'd like more trust put in them.'

'And you're a successful manager? Employee? You have a proven track record in such things?'

She stiffened, not wanting to let him know that she'd failed in securing her promotion, yet she felt as if he'd guessed already. 'I just think that any kind of obsession is unhealthy.' She dodged his question.

'Ah.' He nodded and stopped just inside a safe distance from her. 'Perhaps. But obsession is how things get achieved.'

Because it was all about achievement?

'There's nothing wrong with single-mindedly pursuing your passion,' he said intensely. 'Not letting anything or anyone stand in the way of what you want most.'

What did he want most? Was it money and status? Conspicuous success?

Except right now, it felt as if he wanted *her*. And he was embarked on a single-minded pursuit like a hunter who wouldn't rest until he'd captured his prey. But it was only because he wanted her to say yes to the rest of the deal. The fine print of for ever. Inking an agreement that wouldn't do either of them—or their children—any good in the long run. And therefore one that she couldn't agree to.

'What happens when you finally attain it?' she asked. 'For how long does it keep you happy? How long until you start to think…this isn't that great. This isn't enough… what then?'

'There's always another challenge. That's life.'

Right. There would be another woman one day, who would be a challenge for him. And Rosanna wasn't sure she could stand by and watch that.

'So you launch from one challenge to the next. Relentless in your pursuit of achievement. Do you know how to relax? Do you ever take holidays?' She studied him. 'When was the last holiday you took? Never?'

'You make it sound awful when really it's not. I *like* work. I'm lucky.'

'Because you're alone and your single-mindedness isn't impacting on anyone close to you.'

He stiffened as she continued.

'*I* want balance,' she said. 'I want my children to have parents whose *lives* are balanced. Who can be there for them.'

His jaw hardened. 'And I *want* to be there, Rosanna. That's what I'm asking for.'

'A piece of paper isn't being there. Can you be there in the right way?' she persisted. 'Look at you, you're glued to your phone. You work every hour there is. It's Saturday morning and you're present but not really *here*.'

He was still for a moment and then he suddenly smiled. 'You want me to pay more attention to you.' He put his phone on the table and stepped closer. 'That's fine, Rosanna. I can do that.'

She ground her teeth together. Not *that* kind of attention. This man wasn't like anyone she'd ever met. He was structured, disciplined, ruthless and relentless and so damn serious. And while part of her respected him for it, he scared her. She needed to know there was more to him than concern for spreadsheets. 'That's *not* what I meant.'

Leo watched her stalk back to her bedroom. Huffy and beautiful with her fiery hair tousled and emotion staining her cheeks. Of *course* it was what she'd meant. She wanted him. He wanted her. That part of it at least ought to be straightforward. He'd been frantically trying to focus on anything other than her all morning and he'd failed and he was frankly stunned that he was still struggling to secure her acquiescence to anything. The frustration of trying to talk to her while having his own mind hijacked by the demands of his body was killing him.

He'd been buying time to get his head around the situation by avoiding her this morning—giving her space too. Apparently that had been a mistake. But there was no damn rulebook for how to play this situation. The way his imagination slipped was highly unusual for him. Taking those work calls had actually been respite—a breather to recalibrate. His self-control had never been in doubt before and he hated it. And now she was calling him out on his method of *management*?

That frustration rose higher. This was everything he'd never wanted—trying to understand someone, to make a relationship work? He'd never wanted to feel responsible for either the fortunes or happiness of anyone else again. Not after he'd failed his mother and lost everything.

But, damn it, he still wanted to pick Rosanna up, as if he were that caveman, and toss her onto the nearest bed and keep her there until she'd agree to his demands. There weren't many—to let him in, to let him have her…

It was some primitive instinct rearing, right? A ridiculous one at that.

This was not the time. Even though she'd responded to him last night he knew she was scared. He'd seen the strain in her eyes just before and couldn't forget her pallor when they'd been in that clinic yesterday. It had been primal instinct pushing him to touch her—to reassure her that it was wonderful. He'd said it was to stop people talking, but really he'd just not been able to help himself. A twin pregnancy was harder, higher risk, wasn't it? He swiftly searched the Internet for the information he had no idea about. Apparently in early pregnancy she needed rest, good nutrition and little stress. Arguing with him wasn't going to help anything. So he needed to back off and figure out a better way.

While their physical attraction was about the one thing they seemed to have in common, and he didn't think either of them were going to be able to resist it for long, last night she'd said no. Even when he'd felt her fiery response to his kiss. Even though she'd been as breathless and as into it as he. He'd swear on his life he wasn't wrong about that. But that night at the Towers she'd quickly left and never returned. She'd had no interest in learning his name. She'd only wanted to share a brief moment with him… *Why*? She'd obviously not been playing the ingenue. She'd have said yes to his proposal already if she'd had any sort of cunning plan. Which meant she was as unsophisticated as she appeared in those baggy jeans and tee this morning.

He remembered her blushing shyness, her nervous attempt at small talk, then the suck of her breath as he'd entered her snug body. A high-speed one-night stand didn't make sense for her. Maybe she was wary because more than the pregnancy was new to her…? Maybe she'd been more than overwhelmed just by their passion. Maybe she'd had less experience in the intimacy of lovers?

A sharp sensation of protectiveness—of possessiveness—speared through him. That *couldn't* be right.

But his instincts honed in. He *needed* to discover the secrets lurking just beneath her beautiful, blushing surface. Was he right? Because it might explain some things…

Suddenly escaping everything seemed like a fantastic idea. Perhaps he ought to take her criticism as constructive feedback. Perhaps he ought to take a break from work to focus solely on this situation. He could barely work anyway because he was too busy ruminating on her rejection. He couldn't concentrate until he got what he wanted. And now what he wanted was to know her. They could go somewhere warm with water and a beautiful view of things she liked—plants? Weird fish? And no interruptions whatsoever. He'd put all his energy into securing *this* deal. It was like any other acquisition, right? It needed time for negotiations; he needed to make the most enticing offer he could and the other party needed time to adjust to the change.

But there was no professional protocol to be maintained when the deal was this personal. He would protect his children. He would protect their mother. Somehow he would find a way to ensure she couldn't refuse what was right and best.

He phoned Petra—his assistant manager on the insurance arm.

'Sorry, P, I know it's Saturday but this is a biggie.' He gritted his teeth, thinking of what Rosanna had said.

Petra's surprise was audible as he asked her to step in and take over for a few days. But he also sensed her determination whistling down the phone. She wanted to do a good job. He knew he could count on his people, he just… hadn't done it to this extent before.

'I'm going to be out of contact almost completely,' he warned her, bracing against his own discomfort at the thought.

'For how long?' Petra sounded staggered.

'It shouldn't be more than a week, but I'll keep you posted.'

Then he phoned Jake on the Castle Holdings arm and repeated the request. It was only going to be a few days. Surely nothing too drastic could happen in that time. He'd sort out the marriage situation with Rosanna and prove her wrong about his micromanagement tendencies at the same time. Win-win.

He found her perched on the edge of her bed, frowning at a book.

'Did you unpack your bag already?' he asked.

Her eyes widened. 'Um…'

'Pack it again. We're going away.'

Her eyebrows shot up, like a porcupine on instant defence. 'Yesterday's travel wasn't enough for you?'

'I think you were right,' he said briskly. 'We both need time and space to sort this out *together*.'

'What about your work?'

'I can't remember when I last had a holiday.' Fact was, he'd never had one. 'Now is as good a time as any.'

A mutinous gleam shone in her eyes. 'So what's your plan?'

Was that resentment at his authoritative style? He breathed out, trying to slow down long enough for her to get on board. 'Where would you like to go?'

He'd already made arrangements but they could be changed—he could nail *adaptation* for her.

'I'm not leaving the country.'

Her suspicion was sobering. He had a lot of work to do to gain her trust. 'I'm not asking you to,' he said quietly. 'But we could get some fresh air and sunshine.'

'Have you noticed my skin?' She gestured to her face and body with her hand. 'The last thing I need is sunshine.'

Now he smiled, because he *had* noticed her skin. He

couldn't seem to resist fantasising about tracing her freckles. 'Warmth and rest, then. You're exhausted.' He held his breath.

She regarded him steadily for a long moment. And then? 'Okay.'

A win. *Finally.*

CHAPTER TEN

ANY OTHER WOMAN would consider a three-hour flight cosied up in a first-class pod with Leo Castle a dream come true. For Rosanna? It was a nightmare. He was too close; she could smell the freshness of his soap and feel the warmth of his body. Both of which made her want to lean even closer. She didn't, of course. She fretted.

She'd messaged her parents just before boarding, guiltily telling them she'd gone away on an assignment for work. It wasn't altogether untrue. This was a kind of business. And she wanted any future arrangement agreed with Leo before telling her parents. She didn't want them attempting to interfere.

'Why the Great Barrier Reef?' she asked Leo, desperate for distraction from his nearness.

'Why not?' he replied. 'You ever been?'

She shook her head.

'Me either.' He smiled enough for the one dimple to make a brief appearance. 'We can discover it together.'

He was working hard at being agreeable but the truth was there was a slender bond of intimacy growing between them. Not quite the sort she secretly ached for. Right now she couldn't maintain eye contact or she was going to do something stupid. She pounced on the small packet of snacks the air steward passed her. It was exactly what she needed to occupy herself. But the packet was impossible to open. She tried with hands, then teeth, then with pure unadulterated frustration.

'Do you want—?' Leo broke off as the foil finally burst and launched salty rice snacks into the air like confetti. 'A hand with that?' He finished the offer belatedly.

Rosanna stared. *Leo* was the one who needed a hand.

He'd borne the brunt of the explosion. A billion rice snacks now littered his lap. She half expected *him* to explode next. Instead he shot her a sideways look and not one, but two dimples appeared. Next minute, the man was laughing.

Rosanna remained frozen a split second longer, then she too slid into a chuckle—half in relief, then pure ridiculousness. His laugh was warm and infectious and the unexpected merriment multiplied. She giggled helplessly as she felt his shoulders shake in an easy, intimate moment. She helped him collect the morsels, trying not to make anything of the chance to touch him, but she felt her flush building and knew he was watching her expression too closely.

'Sorry,' she muttered.

'I'm not,' he answered in that low, intimate way. 'It's nice to see you laugh. You haven't much.'

She glanced up and was ensnared in his gaze. 'Nor have you.'

Now he was smiling, small and lopsided, but true and unbearably intense. The whisper of want swirled, spinning her closer to him. It would be so easy to tip forward and touch her mouth to his—that kiss last night had sent her soaring. And his smile now reminded her of the gentle humour that night on his terrace at the towers. It had been irresistibly *easy* then. But they'd both been pretending to be people they weren't. That wasn't reality now.

'Next time, let me help?' His gravity washed through her like shock waves, radiating through her body to bone.

Could she trust him to? Did she have any real choice?

In *how* he helped? Yes, she did. She sobered completely and made herself sit back. She had to think more clearly than this.

After the flight they faced a hop by helicopter. They skimmed over sapphire waters, looking down on emerald and gold islands that Rosanna could scarcely believe were real, so gorgeous were the colours. Finally at their secluded destination, she stood on the deck just absorbing the hombre blues stretching before her. The privacy and luxury and untouched wildness were profound.

'Lost for words?' he asked quietly.

She nodded. She'd thought that by escaping the city—his domain, her family difficulties—she'd be able to focus on combatting his will. Only now she was here in this incredible, unique beauty, peace descended. In a place this perfect, there could be only tranquillity.

'We have the hut to ourselves,' he said.

Rosanna smiled. She wouldn't exactly call it a hut. The stunning villa was mostly open-plan with clean lines and soft furnishings that subtly screamed comfort. She'd noted with relief that there were two bedrooms, both with stunning views. They had their own pool as well as that amazing ocean just behind her. But none of these exquisite things were enough to distract her from the man now walking towards her.

'Give me your phone.' He held his in one hand and stretched his other towards her.

'Why?'

She followed him into the villa and watched him open the small safe secreted in the lounge. 'Locking away my phone and my watch. Yours too.' He glanced at her wrist but she didn't have a fancy smart watch like his.

She met the challenge in his gaze and handed her phone over.

'No phones. No moans,' he mocked.

'What?' She coloured at his amused phrase.

'That's the deal, right?' he said softly, standing too close to her. 'No work. No pleasure either. At least, not sexual.'

Her heart beat heavily.

'Because, just so we're clear, that's how *I'd* like to relax,' he said.

He actually looked more relaxed already. More handsome. More tempting.

'You said you didn't really fool about all that much,' she muttered huskily.

'Now I'm here with you I can't think of anything better.'

She tried to breathe. '*Not* going to happen.'

'I know.' He grinned. 'I'm resigned to the fact.'

But *she* wasn't; instead she was already battling the heated thoughts his words conjured. 'You'll never last without your phone.'

'Maybe *you'll* never last,' he countered. 'You'll be the first one to give in.'

'Is that your goal? To make me the one to surrender?'

'Surrender?' His lips curved seductively. 'Why does it have to be a fight when it's something we both actually want?'

'We all want things that aren't good for us sometimes.'

'Sometimes we just need to live a little because who knows what's going to happen tomorrow?'

As they had that night at Kingston Towers?

'How long are we staying?' She desperately turned the topic.

'A week or so? Thought we could play it by ear.'

Her pulse lifted. She was going to be alone with him for *days*. 'Wow. That's a long time for you to be away from work. How are you going to cope?'

'I'm sure I can find some way of passing the time.' Such loaded implication in a quiet drawl. His smile suddenly flashed. 'You enjoyed it, Rosanna. Why not let yourself enjoy it again?' He leaned closer to whisper. 'It can hardly make the situation worse, can it? You're already pregnant. We're already in a mire of complicated. Why do we have to feel frustrated as well?'

So this was merely a source of frustration for him? 'You don't think it will make things worse?'

'I think it will make some things a whole lot better,' he said calmly. 'At least it will be out of the way.'

She stared at him. 'So you think it will go away?'

'When you've had enough of anything, you don't want it any more.'

So *she* would become something he could take or leave without any concentration or effort or will. He'd indulge but couldn't foresee indulging in *her* for too long. It wasn't as if anyone else had ever wanted to. But for Rosanna the amount of will required to resist *him* right now was almost unsustainable. And if they indulged, what if they then became out of sync in the satiation of this hunger? What if he'd had enough before she did and he didn't want her any more? He would find someone else who he *did* want. And… what if she never had enough? What then?

His smile softened. 'I'm going to go cool off,' he said. 'You want to join me?'

She drew a steadying breath. She shook her head. 'I'm going to…eat something.'

She watched him disappear into one of the bedrooms and then went to the sleek kitchen counter. She'd not considered how intimate this trip was going to be. How it *had* to be. She couldn't play a part, she had to be herself. It was inevitable he'd discover everything about her here—it was the point, after all. Which meant she had to show herself as she was—flawed, stilted. Usually she was okay with herself, but she felt a flutter of nerves at him seeing her in a swimsuit. Her loose jeans and cotton tee were enough to mask scars—but she had more than scars to show.

She put together a small plate of delectable snacks from the vast selection on offer in the fridge, then went outside and sat on the comfortable lounger on the deck by the pool. She determinedly lifted her gaze beyond the pool to the amazing water beyond. Remote and isolated, this was an escape from the rest of the world and coming here was truly bucket-list material for her. She couldn't wait to explore the living reef; the aquatic life would be incredible. Except at this moment she was most fascinated by the man tirelessly swimming length after length as if a great white shark were after him. He was in there a long time and, incredibly, her lashes lowered as the sound of the water and the warmth of the setting sun and the oddly comforting closeness of Leo Castle lulled her and suddenly she was fast asleep.

Rosanna stretched out slowly, loath to relinquish the dreamiest sleep she'd enjoyed in weeks. But as she blinked she heard an amused voice from a distance.

'I was wondering if you were ever going to wake up.' Leo stepped into her line of sight. 'You're like Sleeping Beauty.'

She stared at him—his black swim trunks and red tee revealed strength and heat… 'Holiday' Leo looked *fine.*

Quickly she sat up. 'But I'm awake now. No kiss necessary.'

She was still dressed in yesterday's jeans and tee but she had no recollection of getting from the lounger outside to the bedroom. He must've carried her and she didn't even remember it, which was…*embarrassing.*

'You were very sleepy,' he said.

She glanced down beside her, noting the smooth clear space where he'd not slept.

'I took the other room obviously,' he added, revealing yet again he'd read her mind.

She felt that wretched heat fill her face.

'Although you're far more biddable when you're half-conscious.' Amusement kindled in his eyes. 'Like a little limpet. It took some manoeuvring to extricate myself from your sleepy clutches.'

Surely he was joking? But she could well believe her body would burrow close to his given the chance.

'Don't worry, I was a gentleman.' His customary serious expression returned. 'I'm sorry if all the travel was too much.'

'It wasn't,' she said huskily. 'I was just tired.'

He left her and Rosanna resolutely put on a bikini she'd barely worn and covered it with a wrap dress. She couldn't pretend to be anything she wasn't and the sooner she was honest with him, the better. On her way through she snaffled a pastry from the platter on the kitchen counter and went out to the deck. It was a stunning day. Leo had sunglasses on and was pulling together swimming gear from a room by the pool.

'You want to explore the reef after breakfast?' he asked.

'I'd love to.' She studied one of the masks. 'But I'll need to practise in the pool first, I've never snorkelled.'

'No?' He glanced up at her in surprise. 'You grew up in Sydney, right? City of swimming pools and beaches.'

'Yeah, but I stay out of the sun because I burn easily.' She'd covered up even more when her spine problems had emerged. 'And we didn't go on holidays. My parents always had a project on.'

His expression tightened. 'But you're their only child, right? Didn't they spoil you?'

She'd never been spoiled like this.

Awkwardly she undid the cord of her wrap dress. That first night it had been almost dark and since then her clothing had been loose enough to hide the unevenness of her body. It wasn't as bad as it had once been; still, for the first time in ages, she felt self-conscious. She'd never shown anyone her scar like this. Why would she when she'd seen the unveiled disappointment on her parents' faces? She glanced at him.

He was staring at her but behind those sunglasses it was impossible to tell what he was thinking. Where exactly he was looking. So she broached it directly.

'My waist looks uneven because of my spine,' she said briefly.

'I hadn't noticed.' A husky apologetic tone. 'I wasn't looking at your waist...'

He removed the sunglasses and the expression in his eyes was blatantly carnal. A surge of heat scampered across her skin because she recognised that primal expression of *want*. But now she'd pointed out her imperfection to him he blinked and his gaze slowly lowered.

Her scoliosis hadn't bothered her as much as it had bothered her parents. It was their reaction that had hurt her—their shame over something she'd not been able to control and their determination to correct it without anyone knowing. As if her deformity had to be a dreadful secret. They'd hurried her to specialists and demanded correction.

'It became obvious when I was about eleven and started growing. Initially the specialists weren't sure whether I'd need surgery but my parents pushed for it—the argument being that it would prevent it from progressing. Really, they wanted me to be perfect. I never was, of course, no matter what happened with my spine,' she said.

Her truth told, she turned so he could see the scar. It wasn't something that *she'd* wanted to hide—it had been her mother who had wanted her to wear the loose dresses, as if her remaining asymmetry was still an embarrassment. But Rosanna had survived those months of recovery, mostly alone, and so she knew she could endure other hardships too. If anything, she was a bit proud of it—but revealing it to someone else?

That was scarier.

He was behind her now and it mattered just that little bit too much that he was quiet. But then she felt the lightest of touches on her skin as he traced her scar.

'That's a long incision,' he muttered. 'It must've been painful.'

'At the time, very.' She bent her head. Initially after the operation it had been excruciating. She didn't like to think of those first few weeks often. But not only had it stopped her curve from worsening, it had improved it a lot. Just not enough for her parents. 'My parents wanted them to do it again because they weren't happy with the outcome. But I was okay with it.'

'Does it get sore?'

'Only sometimes. Mostly it's fine.'

'It must've taken a while to recover.'

'No sports for a year. I wasn't devastated,' she admitted dryly.

He chuckled. 'No? You weren't all jolly hockey sticks?'

'I was a nerd. Enforced rest gave me time to draw.'

'Will the pregnancy cause you pain?' His voice was very husky now. 'You'll be able to take the strain of carrying two babies?'

She paused. 'When I recovered from the operation they said childbearing should be fine in the future. I guess I should see my specialist when we get back to Sydney.'

His finger pressed a little heavier on her skin. 'We should have done that already.'

'I don't think I'm going to expand all that quickly.' She half laughed. 'And if it does get sore, it won't be anything dreadful.'

'I don't want you to be in any pain.' He lifted his hand away.

She felt the loss of that tiny contact. 'Lots of women have backache when pregnant. At least I'm used to it. And it may not even happen.' She turned to face him again. 'I'm still not perfect but it's better than it was.'

He looked down at her. She felt almost naked in front of him now but there was something in his eyes that her sad brain wanted to read as admiration.

'No one's ever perfect, Rosanna, but you're *strong*,' he said softly. 'You have a steel spine. For real.'

She smiled gently.

'If you can handle surgery like that, you can handle anything.' His hands lightly shaped each side of her waist—one side indented, the other more straight.

It didn't matter though, just the look in his eyes made her feel wanted—and his words? They filled her with a blaze of heat that was new. A *power*. He'd seen and he'd not thought any less of her, in fact he thought along the lines she'd secretly felt. That she had some grit. And now she was struggling to remember what she'd been telling him. *Why* she'd been telling him.

She drew in a steadying breath and remembered. It had been about her *parents*. Because? She felt an instinctive, self-protective need to hold him at a distance. She'd tell him everything. Anything to distract herself from the temptation he posed. Nothing would push him away more than discussion of her parents. The sooner she said it all, the sooner they could move on and he would understand why she didn't want to marry him. Why she *couldn't*. She stepped back from his touch and his hands dropped.

'You have to understand my parents excel in hyperbole and the pursuit of perfection—I got braces, and a steel rod in my spine, to make me…better, so I could be the future face of the business—it's all about appearances, right? They wanted me to be my best, not always what was best for me. Whatever I did was embellished because I wasn't ever quite good enough.' She laughed awkwardly, quickly getting through the worst. 'And I didn't want to let them down. Their work is the whole reason they married. They share a passion for design and they wanted to be the best so they teamed up. It's everything. They always held parties to show off their home—networking events really. I was shy and hid in the background and by the time I was old enough to help out they wanted me to stay out of sight until my spine had been straightened. And teeth. The freckles could be faded with make-up.'

'Didn't they see that all these things are part of what make you unique?' He frowned. 'You're stunning, Rosanna.'

She battled another blush and tried to ignore him. She'd not been fishing for compliments, she'd just been trying to explain where she came from so he'd understand why she didn't want a businesslike marriage.

'They said boarding school was to help me get past the shyness and isolation of surgery but it was more for the connections they could make with the parents there. They wanted me to make connections. Ash Castle attended, as did all the other heirs to the social empire, you know? Future leaders and all those bright young things.'

'They sent you to a school because of who attended?'

'They subscribe to the "who you know" rather than "what you know" school of success. That's what's always worked for them up until now.'

His expression stiffened. 'And that's changed since I took over. I understand their disappointment but they shouldn't have shipped corporate secrets. It was more than disloyal.'

'It was,' she agreed simply. 'The only thing I can think is that he was desperate. Success is everything to them.'

'Is it everything to you?'

'No. Not their definition of it anyway,' she said. 'I was supposed to follow them into the family business. That's why they called me Rose—because my father is known as Red. It was supposed to be a cute marketing plan for Gold Style that I couldn't live up to. I don't have the design flair, I don't have the social skills needed to sell the concepts…' She huffed out a breath. 'When I did well at school that was the one thing they could celebrate. But then they pushed too hard in that and suddenly I'm supposed to be a genius. I was put up a year because they were so pushy and told the teachers I was gifted. I had to work so hard to maintain the grades they told everyone came so easily. They were resigned to my not being in the business only if I then excelled academically. It was a relief to go to university but, honestly, even there I've not done what I "should" have. I was supposed to have been a prodigy, instead I just did my degree and then took a job as a technician because I didn't want to leave…' It had been safe there. 'But that hasn't stopped my parents telling everyone I'm a *professor*. I avoid coming back to Sydney too often so I don't have to disappoint them all over again.'

'Your value shouldn't be based on a list of achievements.'

'Says the ultimate over-achiever.'

'It was survival for me,' he said briefly. 'Do you enjoy your job?' He'd asked her that before, but now, in a way, she could answer him.

'I applied for a lectureship last month so my parents could finally be telling the truth.'

'So you're still trying to please them. Still pushing yourself along a path that's not really of your choosing.'

'I've failed though.' She shrugged. 'Didn't get the job.'

'Did you really want it?' he asked her astutely.

She sighed. 'Maybe not. Maybe I didn't really push for the projects that would've promoted me. Honestly? I was tired after striving so hard all through school to keep those grades. But it's the expectation, isn't it? To fulfil the dreams and expectations of your parents.'

She didn't live up to her potential or the expectations others had of her.

'What about your *own* dreams and expectations? If you never had to worry about money or status or what anyone thought…what would you do?'

'I don't know.' She'd never taken a breath to figure out for herself what she wanted.

'You like to grow things.'

She laughed. 'That's just a hobby.'

'That's a passion,' he corrected. 'And passion is a good thing.'

'You can't make money from plants.'

'Sure you can.' He cocked his head. 'Anyway, you don't need to make money.'

'I don't want to be dependent on you.' Her laughter faded. 'I don't want anything like my parents' marriage, where it's basically a business arrangement and the projection of their image, the look of it, is their priority.'

'We won't have that,' he said quietly. 'This isn't about the look of it. We're working together *only* in the sense of doing what's best for those babies. You're free to find fulfilment in your work, Rosanna. I'll support you in anything you want to do.'

That wasn't quite what she'd meant. Yet he made it seem as if it *would* be different—and that was tempting. He'd already shown her he could cast work aside to focus on the 'family' he wanted to build. But there was still something missing. The *heart* of it.

'Do you have any scars?' she asked, suddenly needing to push back on him in some way. 'Now I've shown you mine.'

'None on the outside,' he said.

'Nothing?' she pressed. 'Not even from some silly scrape?'

No. He was total physical perfection.

He shook his head. 'Millions underneath though.'

She regarded him warily, unsure about prying further but curiosity couldn't be contained. And he was the one who mentioned it… 'Such as?'

Leo studied her, his heart pounding. It was fair enough of her to ask. She'd opened up to him. And it was a way of distracting himself from the desire to kiss her.

'It was hard,' he finally said quietly. 'And I felt very alone.'

'Your mother must have suffered when Hugh wouldn't admit he was your father.'

'Very much so.' He hated remembering it. 'She tried for a long time to manage without asking anyone for help.'

'Where was her family?'

'They'd washed their hands of her.'

'That seems cruel.'

'Very. Unforgiving.' He nodded. He had the same fault—he'd never forgive them. 'I was about eight when she took me with her to face Hugh Castle. She'd got that desperate. He literally closed the door on us.'

'I'm sorry.'

He didn't tell Rosanna it wasn't the first time his mother had tried. Nor was it the worst thing Hugh had done to her. 'It's important to me that our children don't face any uncertainty,' he said. 'That you don't suffer anything in the way of what she suffered. I can't let that happen to you.'

'Where is she now?'

He couldn't answer for a moment. 'She passed away when I was a teenager.'

'Before…'

Everything. 'Before I had any success. Before I proved Hugh was my father. Before I could give her any real security.'

Talking about this wasn't working. It made him want to touch her just to avoid these memories and the misery they roused. He shouldn't use Rosanna like that.

She was trembling but trying to hide it. She stepped just beyond reach each time he brushed too close—hyper aware of his proximity. As he was of hers. That kind of awareness made him wonder about her experience again. Maybe she'd been working too hard for too long and there'd not been the time. Maybe that shyness, that self-consciousness she mentioned had stopped her letting anyone get too close. But now she had no choice.

Yet she wasn't *afraid* of him, he didn't think. She'd trusted him enough to come away with him. To talk to him. But to touch him? She stepped back the very second it looked as if she was about to lean forward and kiss him. As if she were desperately stopping herself.

Maybe that was just desperately wishful thinking on his part.

'I hear what you're saying and I'm sorry for what you went through...but it isn't going to make me change my mind,' she said. 'It can't.'

He felt it as pure challenge. He shouldn't. This *wasn't* a game, there was too much precious at stake. And yet there was that electricity between them that made him want to push closer, to challenge, to make her laugh.

'Stop worrying,' he said, to himself as much as anything. 'I know it's a little complicated, but it could be worse. At least you're not my secret stepmother's illegitimate half-sister's niece or something really scandalous.'

She laughed and his spirits lightened. He liked it when she laughed. And if he didn't step away from her right now he was going to break his promises to both of them.

'Let's go explore,' he growled.

Swimming lazily, snorkelling, taking in the stunning sight of the corals beneath the water. It was a hidden garden, a whole world of beauty and wonder. It should have been the perfect distraction—absorbing them both completely. Then they walked along the shore. Even without getting in the water there was so much to observe. She often crouched, gazing at the foliage of some of the plants, watching the insects. Everywhere she looked there was something even more amazing. She couldn't help pointing things out to him as the joy of discovery overrode her usual quietness. It was lush and vital and unlike anywhere he'd ever been. He felt as if he were living in a wildlife documentary. But the most striking, fascinating creature was the angular, fiery yet pale woman alongside him. She was insightful. Yet also innocent. A pleaser who wanted more for her own children.

He wanted her to stay relaxed and satisfied. Which meant he didn't want her to worry about anything. The anger he'd felt towards her parents' betrayal faded slightly in the light of that and in what she'd told him. He was going to have to work something out when they returned to Sydney. He was going to have to fix it.

Two hours later Rosanna sat in the shade and distractedly doodled in her notebook. She couldn't help thinking about what he'd told her about his mother and his father. It would have been awful, never to have been accepted. That kind of rejection went far further than skin deep. No wonder he had that drive to win. She felt guilty for not cutting the guy some slack. He wanted to do what was right.

He was back in the pool, resting his head on his arms at the edge, the rest of him floating. She sipped sparkling water yet felt that dizzying tingle as if it were champagne. Was she drunk on the mere sight of him? His nearness? Or was it his attention—he'd stayed near her on that walk, looking at the pools she looked into, talking with her at each point. She swept her hair up into a loose ponytail to cool her neck. And now he was looking at her the way he'd looked at the fish she'd pointed out to him earlier.

'I can feel you staring at me,' she grumbled. He was making her hands shake.

'I like watching you.' He sounded amused.

'You need a hobby.'

'Why can't you be my hobby?'

She braved a look at him. 'I've no plans to be anyone's plaything.'

'That wasn't what I meant.' His mouth curved dangerously. 'But it doesn't seem like that terrible an idea.'

'Leo...'

He laughed and her world stopped. He was too gorgeous when he smiled and utterly irresistible when he laughed.

'Sorry if I've made you uncomfortable, but you fascinate me.'

She shook her head in disbelief. 'There's nothing fascinating about me. No mystery.'

'I think you're wrong about that. And I like seeing what you notice,' he added. 'You're more observant than anyone I've met. You discover the smallest things.'

'It's because I take the time to bother. Lots of people are too busy trying to talk or flirt or something.'

A smile flickered but his gaze sharpened. 'You don't like to talk? Or flirt?'

She shook her head.

'There was me thinking redheads were feisty and vivacious and full of spirited temper,' he teased.

'Not shy and awkward and basically mute?' she muttered. 'Stereotypes don't help anyone.'

'You weren't shy around me. Or awkward. Or basically mute.' He leaned closer to study her. 'That night you were the absolute opposite of that.'

She'd been different then. Because she'd lost her reason and let him do anything. Everything.

'You were different that night too,' she said. 'Because, generally, you're more serious than anyone I've ever met,' she said. 'Very focused and rigid.'

He stared at her for a second and then laughed again. 'Rigid?' He drew a breath. 'And yet around you I laugh. Often. Isn't it interesting, the devastating effect we have on each other?'

She swallowed. She didn't want to talk about the effect he had on her and she couldn't stay still with him this close.

She stalked inside and chose a novel from the shelves in the lounge. She desperately needed distraction.

When she went back to the deck she saw Leo in the distance. He'd taken himself for a run. It was almost an hour before he returned, slick with sweat and effort. He briefly stood beneath the outdoor shower and it took every ounce of her willpower not to drool at the display. Then the infuriating, stunning man dived back into the pool. Rosanna tried to read the novel.

'Do you even *know* how to relax?' Rosanna glared at him when he finally paused for breath.

'By relax you mean lie about and do nothing?' He shook his head, spraying droplets of water as he laughed. 'That's not how I relax.'

'I'm lying about doing nothing because I'm *not* doing nothing. I'm reading. Plus I'm growing babies. Tell me how *you* supposedly relax, then. At the office?'

'I enjoy it. It's exhilarating. There's always some new challenge.'

And she'd deprived him of that challenge by daring him to take a holiday. She had the horrible feeling *she'd* become his new challenge.

Surely him busy working would be better than him being fully focused on her? He'd become even more of a temptation with his attention. When he laughed it was as if the biggest fireworks display lit up the dark sky. Brilliance cascaded from him and enveloped her in its spillover, lighting her up. She needed him back on his conference calls or whatever. Not on her.

She couldn't concentrate on the damn book.

CHAPTER ELEVEN

LEO FLOATED, SHOCKED by his uncontrolled thoughts. He was actually jealous of the attention she was giving a *book*. But he wanted her to look at him instead. He wanted her to talk to him some more. To lead him on another stroll along the beach and point out small insects no one else would even spot. He'd had to take himself for a run to burn some of the insane sexual energy he was struggling to contain.

He ought to be worrying about work. About the deluge of emails probably overflowing in his inbox. Instead he was focused entirely on Rosanna. Right now, all he wanted to see was that heat in her eyes that he'd seen that night all those weeks ago. But the uncertainty and shyness she'd shown since being here? That had made him think. What she'd told him of her upbringing—she'd spent long tracts of time alone when recovering, she was a dreamer, not a party creature. She'd liked to draw and read books. Now the creeping suspicion built into a whisper of certainty. She wasn't just shy, she was *inexperienced*. Not just sexually but with emotional intimacy too. In that last the pair of them were alike.

She finally turned the page of her book. Now he thought about it, she was making surprisingly slow progress with it given how much time she'd had her nose in it. He cocked his head as another suspicion entered his mind. Was she even reading it?

'What's it about?' he called to her from the pool.

'Hmm?'

'The book. What's it about?'

'Oh…um…' She flicked to the back.

'No, don't read me the blurb,' he teased. 'You tell me.'

She sighed. 'I don't know. I can't get into it.'

Yet she'd been staring at it so studiously for ages. Which meant she couldn't concentrate on anything either.

It more than tickled him. It gave him hope.

The way their fingers brushed when he handed her a glass of sparkling water. The way his arm pressed against hers when they were seated together in the small boat when out exploring. The way he focused on the small things she pointed out to him. The way his gaze lingered on her when she walked past him. Every instance was so tiny yet so hot and so intense. And every one felt as though it was leading her to something that was inevitable. The chemistry was drawing her closer and closer to him. She shivered with need for more of his touch. It was as if she'd succumbed to an illness and there was only one cure. The only thing that saved her from total humiliation was that he seemed to feel it too.

'Dance with me,' he invited after they'd eaten a sumptuous dinner of fresh baked fish and verdant salad.

She eyed him warily.

'Please,' he added.

It was an echo of that first night together. When they'd danced another way entirely.

'I don't dance.'

'Nor do I,' he said simply. 'But I'm tempted to now.'

A warm spurt of amusement trickled through her. She liked his honesty with her. 'Are we going to stand on each other's feet, then?'

His expression warmed. 'We have better rhythm with each other than that, as well you know, Ms Gold. I think we can do okay.'

He picked up the remote for the entertainment unit. A second later music floated through the hidden speakers. He had that unpractised, uneven smile that she found irresistible. He knew the effect he had on her, didn't he? She studied him, saw the intent in his eyes as he approached her.

'Do you think it's wise?' she muttered.

'Are you afraid I might overstep the boundaries?'

She shook her head. She wasn't afraid of *him* but of herself. 'No. You can tell me over and over that work is wonderful, but it is still *work* and there must have been times when you've wanted to do something else but you haven't let yourself,' she said. 'Which makes you a master of self-control. So I think *not* overstepping will be very easy for you.'

Impossibly his gaze intensified. 'I guess the difference is I don't want to deny myself the pleasure to be had with *you*. I don't want to waste all that effort and energy when it could be used on something so much better.'

From just his words another blush burned through her. It wasn't fair. He knew she couldn't resist his touch. She racked her brains with increasing desperation for some way to put a barrier between them—make him turn away from her.

'You know I kissed your half-brother,' she muttered huskily.

'My half-brother has kissed most of the women your age in the whole damned country, as far as I can tell,' he replied lazily.

He didn't seem jealous at all. Now she felt miffed because the thought of Leo kissing another woman made *her* want to stab something.

'Don't forget to dance, Rosanna,' he chided softly, that smile audible now.

She closed her eyes and felt him draw her closer.

'Rumour has it Ash is a renowned lover,' Leo muttered idly. 'What did you think?'

She stilled and glared up at him.

He stopped moving too. 'You just said you kissed him.'

His tone was all innocence yet there was sharpness in his eyes. Maybe she'd been wrong about that lack of jealousy?

'That was *all*,' she said.

'Oh?' Leo asked, still with that dispassionate tone, yet the angularity of his features tightened. 'Why not everything else? I mean, his reputation is—'

'I didn't want to,' she mumbled, completely regretting ever mentioning it. The truth was Ash hadn't wanted to sleep with her either.

'And yet with *me*,' Leo said quietly, 'a complete stranger, you wanted everything.' He pressed her waist closer against his. 'You, who—as far as I can tell—hasn't really dated anyone, let me have you in almost an instant.'

She suddenly felt his tension—he held his big body in check but he was *wired*.

Fraught, she was vulnerable and exposed. 'That's not something worth discussing.'

'I think it is. I'd like to know why.' He gazed into her eyes. 'Or are you not up to trusting me yet?'

'I do trust you,' she said. Truthfully she always had.

'Then tell me why you let me touch you that night.'

The flush of heat over her body was appalling. She didn't really know why Leo was the only one to press her buttons—only that once he'd pressed them there'd been no off switch. 'I think I was tired,' she mumbled.

'Tired?' He chuckled. 'No.'

'Leo…' A wall of heat enveloped her.

'It's okay.' He cupped her cheek, feeling for himself the way her skin scalded. 'At the risk of coming off like a complete jerk, I'm pleased I'm your only lover, Rosanna,' he said huskily. 'That I'm the only one to have entered your body. The only one who knows how hot you truly run. How silken and snug your gorgeous body is. The only one who's heard those little moans you can't hold back because you're about to come.'

She was appalled that he'd guessed her secret and appalled at the heat washing through her now—it was so intense, so sudden, that she was almost about to come again now. His touch tossed her back into the heated swirl of bliss that only he'd summoned within her.

'Stop it,' she mumbled.

But she didn't mean it. She wanted more—she ached for that easy obliteration of every damn thought, care, worry… all burned in the heat of ecstasy that he could give. She could feel the tension within him. The arousal. It mirrored her own. She was so close to kissing him.

It was overwhelming. And frightening. Because everything was different now. This wasn't one magic moment, one night that could be kept a secret for always. They had complications to deal with. But she couldn't back away from him the way she knew she ought to. She couldn't cope with the intensity of his magnetism. Why was this so immense? Maybe it was the pregnancy hormones making her so sensitive—was that a thing? Or was it a biological urge to cling to the nearest big, strong male because she was pregnant…a primitive need to seek security? Leo was big and strong and powerful. He was also the most handsome man she'd ever laid eyes on. He was also holding her in a way that made her feel *everything*.

'I'm right, aren't I?' he added almost hoarsely.

She turned her head slightly. 'It shouldn't matter.'

'But it does. To you. To me. What's going on, Rosanna?' He shook her gently. 'You didn't think that was something I should've known?'

'How could I tell you?' She looked up at him, her heart burning. 'I didn't think it would matter. You were very courteous. Very…careful to ensure I was having a good time.'

His hold on her tightened. 'I could've made it better,' he growled.

Rosanna stared. As if that were even possible?

His dimple suddenly appeared and the indigo in his eyes lit. 'You don't think it could've been better?'

She shouldn't admit anything more. This was so mortifying. Yet it didn't seem to matter that he knew—and so, yet more of the truth slipped out. 'It was like a dream to me.'

One that had devastatingly real consequences. But now he smiled at her. A full, devastating, gorgeous smile that rendered her spellbound. She was utterly entranced and she couldn't regret that night. Not then, not now, not ever. Not even though they now faced a complicated future because of it. She had to get hold of herself to be able to *think*. Summoning her last speck of resistance, she pushed him. He immediately stepped back.

'What are you doing?' he asked as she raced indoors.

'Getting your phone for you,' she muttered.

'Why?' He stood in the doorway. 'I don't want it.'

He began to laugh as he watched her furiously stabbing the numbers on the hotel safe.

'Sure you do,' she argued. 'You want it. You've been missing it. Aching for it. I bet your fingers are itching.'

'My fingers *are* itching,' he conceded. 'But not to touch my phone.'

'Stop it.' She all but begged him.

His smile was slow and so infuriating and a glint that reeked of smug satisfaction lit his beautiful eyes. 'You can't handle this. You're looking to take me out,' he said. 'I'm winning.'

He was *not* winning. She finally got the safe open. Ignoring her own phone, she snatched up his and turned to face him, holding it in front of her like the temptation she knew it was.

'Rosanna.' His voice was low and gravelly but it wasn't a warning.

There was delight in his eyes and it fired a playfulness

within her. She would catch him out, wouldn't she? Distract him with the thing most important to him.

'Don't you want to come nearer?' she teased him.

'I think it's best if I don't answer that.'

He remained in the doorway. Didn't venture so much as a step closer. Which meant she had to move closer to him again.

She pressed the button to light up the screen and held it up before her like a weapon. 'Look at all those notifications. All those emails. Missed calls and everything.'

'Rosanna…' The gleam in his eye turned feral with the promise of retribution.

A low burn deep in her belly, a strength coiling within her. A hunger. 'Take it, Leo,' she tempted him with a soft sultry tone. 'You know you want to.'

She stopped walking, holding the phone so he could just reach it—but not the rest of her.

'Oh, I know exactly what I want.' He grabbed the phone but didn't so much as glance at the screen before turning to throw it away. It whipped through the air and splashed into the pool behind him.

'What?' Rosanna shrieked and ran past him to the edge of the water. 'What did you just do?'

She stared at the spot where the phone had splashed into the pool and immediately sunk. Then she slowly turned and stared at him.

'You did not do that. You did *not* just do that.' She was stunned. That was him, wasn't it? A man of action. Not passive. She needed to be more like him in that respect and now anticipation scalded her insides. 'Aren't you going to go in and get it? It'll be ruined.'

He had the widest, wildest smile. And she couldn't cope—nor could she tear her gaze from him and that ferociously playful expression in his eyes. His *phone* was at the bottom of the pool and he was…smiling?

'It's waterproof, right?' she checked. 'It's new and fancy and waterproof.'

'Don't know. Don't care.' He stepped towards her. 'But what's very interesting is that you're so keen for me to be distracted by something other than *you*.' He stopped the merest inch away from her and whispered, 'Can't you cope with my attention, Rosanna?'

Her heart pounded as sensual energy scurried around her body. She was so close to surrender and he knew it.

'Don't be mean,' she breathed.

'I'm not being mean, I'm being *honest*. Why don't you give it a go? You might find it a relief.'

She gazed, lost in his eyes.

His *attention* terrified her. She wasn't entirely sure what she was afraid of...getting hurt? In this situation, hurt was inevitable. They were tied to each other for the rest of their lives. They were having children together. That didn't mean they were going to be together. But they'd be connected. Their lives intertwined—through custody arrangement, meeting for handovers, both attending school concerts. It saddened her—which she knew was stupid. Because all of that could be okay. People handled that just fine all the world over. And from far worse situations. At least she actually liked him. But *that* was the problem, wasn't it? And from where her fear actually sprang was that she would want more. Always more. And he didn't want to give it to her. He'd already said, hadn't he? That once he had enough of something, he didn't want it any more.

But at least she'd have had this.

Finally, she appreciated that this might be her one chance. She was doing herself a disservice by denying herself, wasn't she?

'Are *your* fingers itching, sweetheart?' He laughed softly. 'Shall I tell you again?' he tempted softly. 'How badly mine are? How much I ache to touch you properly again?'

She closed her eyes as he stepped closer still, that one last pace until he was pressed against her. His arm went around her waist, holding her close. She refused to listen. Refused to feel.

'You have another phone, right?' she muttered, her eyes still closed, desperately fixating on the phone horror in a final last attempt. 'A secret one hidden in your bag somewhere. You've probably been working while I've been asleep.'

'Oh, Rosanna.' His breath gently stirred the hair at her temple. 'What a highly active imagination you've got. I'm absolutely innocent of all those charges. I *have* been awake though, with my imagination working overtime.'

And he'd needed to dip in that cool water in the middle of the night. She'd seen him.

'Are you going to open your eyes and look at me?' he asked.

The tiredness that had pervaded her mind and limbs over these last two weeks evaporated. It was as if a mist lifted from her and revealed a deep well of energy that wanted to be burned in one way only. Her weak mind presented her with all kinds of temptations. Suddenly she didn't know why she'd felt such a strong need to resist him. Was she mad? Why wouldn't she want to experience this again? It would all be fine. As she opened her eyes he smiled. It wasn't full of satisfaction. It was full of genuine reassurance.

'You look so serious.' He touched her cheek again.

Her lips were horribly dry, her throat tight. 'That's usually you.'

'What's holding you back?' he asked.

The last scrap of truth escaped. 'Because I'm not good at this.' Being intimate in any way with anyone.

'You're good at it with me.'

Heat flushed through her. It scared her how much he affected her.

He cupped her face in both his hands. 'It's just sex, sweetheart.'

She badly wanted to believe that but, considering how overwhelming she found him…

'It won't complicate things any more than they already are,' he promised. 'And it might help us both think more clearly.'

'You can't think clearly either?' she asked. Because thoughts and doubts and dreams endlessly swirled in total confusion in her mind.

'You've been the only thing on my mind for months.'

His admission melted her. In the end there was only the certainty of feeling and the simplicity of truth. She wanted him. She wanted this.

'Kiss me.' Her lips were dry, her skin stretched tight, she was sure he ought to be able to hear the hum in her blood.

'Rosanna?' A broken check for reassurance.

'Please.'

The second he touched his lips to hers she was incinerated by the intensity of their connection. The determination on his face ought to have terrified her. Instead she felt a welcome relief, a burgeoning satisfaction of her own because she understood he intended to please her *entirely.*

He set out to shatter her into total oblivion. She relished being that challenge for him. As he was hers. He advanced on her with nothing but success in his mind. The mantle of respectability was gone, revealing raw lust. The desire to give and take pleasure—the thing one and the same. As inexperienced as she was, she knew there was something about her that pushed his buttons. And as temporary as it might be, there was no denying it now.

'You're so bloody beautiful.'

'You say that as if it's a bad thing.'

'You bewitch me. You did that night. A sprite in amongst the greenery. Like a garden nymph, stealing what she wanted.'

'You still think I'm a thief?'

'I know you are.' He touched her. 'Dangerous and beautiful and utterly irresistible.'

'I'm not dangerous.'

'Oh, but you are *so* dangerous to my peace of mind.' His expression tightened.

None of her concerns mattered any more. The fight to resist him faded. The decisions of their future were forgotten. Because he was here and he was touching her and there was only now. Lost in his kiss, she reached for him, sliding his tee up his flat abs, exposing his body to her hungry eyes, her ravenous touch.

'Not so fast. Last time was fast. This time…' he breathed out '…slow.'

But she needed him now. She needed this awful ache to be eased. She needed that hit of pleasure unlike anything she'd known. Now she'd decided—*surrendered*—there could be no slowing down, no stopping.

He laughed beneath his breath and stopped her by simply picking her up and carrying her to the bed where he slowly but deftly peeled back her bikini.

'Your skin is so freaking amazing,' he growled.

She smiled, marvelling in the pleasure of him finding her so attractive. It might only be chemistry, but it was fierce and strong and so very real. And he took delight in tormenting her—so slowly, until she was literally screaming with her need for completion. She cried out as he thrust home. Finally she felt the fullness she'd craved for weeks. His hands tightened, beneath her, holding her closer as he pushed harder and deeper. And that sweet relief was underpinned by the ache of need. Every layer peeled away to reveal the only thing that really mattered. He didn't need to gloat. He was more serious than that. She saw the determination anew in his eyes.

'I've missed you.' He gazed into her eyes, triumph blazing in his own.

It mirrored the satisfaction flowing through her.

Slowly he moved and kissed her again as he did. A soul-destroying kiss that broke down any defence she'd thought she might be able to rebuild, leaving her raw and vulnerable to him—an open book of emotion for him to devour.

So it was far too late when she realised that he was going to take it *all*.

CHAPTER TWELVE

LEO SAT ON the deck, appreciating the view in a way that was wholly new to him. Rosanna was paddling in the shallows, investigating little fish, noticing the smallest of things as she took those few extra seconds to truly observe. She silently saw so much—feeling deeply, appreciating. He found himself more aware as a result, keen to spot something ahead of her so he could draw her attention to it. In that way, she'd opened up his world. So now he noticed the little lizard sunning itself near his foot. Bright eyes, alert, watching him. He couldn't resist smiling at it and broke off a bit of his bacon sandwich to toss to it.

He ought to be satisfied yet it felt as if a blade were still pressed upon his throat. A sense of threat remained, pushing him to secure more. Physical—sexual—intimacy was easy to achieve. He liked discovering what made her sigh or cry for relief, what make her shake, what made her laugh. But he felt driven to discover *more.* What she'd told him about her life—he wanted to know more of what she wanted. How she felt. It was weird to be so curious about someone. He tossed another piece of the meat to the lizard.

'You've found a friend?' She waded towards him.

'Maybe.'

'Do you have many others?' she asked lightly.

It soothed him that she was curious about him too.

He nodded. 'Ash.'

His half-brother was the closest he had to any kind of best friend. But now, even though he knew his half-brother had chased off to another country after some woman… the thought of him having history with Rosanna burned. It shouldn't matter at all. For a while it *hadn't.* Yet now he couldn't stop himself asking. 'What really happened between you two?'

Colour washed over her skin. He didn't read anything into her blush. It was almost standard when he asked her something. 'You said you'd kissed him…'

'You really want to know?'

Leo glanced away and then back at her. 'It's just that it's not like him to walk away from a woman without…'

Rosanna sat beside him. 'I was hardly a woman at the time.'

Leo frowned. 'When was it?'

'After my surgery.' She swallowed. 'I didn't just have to return to school, but move to a new one miles away from my home. I'd been in hospital, then had several months alone in recovery and, honestly, I just wanted to stay at home for a while and be in one that wasn't being redecorated yet again. But my parents were ready to move onto their next project and decided it was "better" if I was away at boarding school. They said it would give me the stability I'd been asking them for. Plus now I was all fixed up, it was time for me to acquire the social skills they said I needed.'

'Social skills?'

'To cultivate beneficial relationships. It's how they operate, remember?' She rolled her eyes. 'Because they'd talked me up academically, the school did as they asked and put me in a higher grade so I was by far the youngest student in the class. I didn't know anyone, I felt awkward and a huge amount of pressure to maintain my scores.' She bent her head. 'I didn't know it at the time, but my mother had asked Ash's mother to get him to keep an eye out for me.'

'And did he?'

She nodded. 'He hung out with me more than most, and we went out a couple of times. Then he asked me to be his date to the senior dance. It made me instantly popular and, fool that I was, I thought I could do what my parents wanted. Learn how to use a relationship to get ahead in life.' She smiled sadly. 'Ash had an awful lot of sway over people, so it was ideal, right?'

Leo had a bad feeling hearing the bitterness in her tone. 'What happened?'

'The dance didn't go so well,' she muttered. 'He had a… moment with a couple of other girls and it was videoed.'

'A moment?' Leo groaned; he could well imagine the sort of 'moment' she meant. 'He humiliated you.'

'Of course, I felt hurt when I first saw the clip. And that my classmates took such delight in publicly playing it to me. It went viral and became the school's most notorious event.'

'I bet,' Leo murmured.

That would've been enough to send *any* sensitive young woman into a cave for a while. And Rosanna was sensitive.

'But honestly?' She straightened a little to look at him. 'With the benefit of a few years, I can look back on it now and realise a part of me felt relieved. I knew he wasn't into me in that way. And I wasn't into him. It ended all that pressure. Not that *he* put that on me at all. When I think about it now, he was actually lovely.'

'Ash Castle, *lovely*?' Leo joked dryly but his chest had tightened—what *pressure*? Did she mean from her parents?

'Back then he had so much going on and we didn't know the extent. He was trying to be kind but he just couldn't resist, I guess. He was having an awful time and I suppose he needed an escape. I was embarrassed, but I wasn't *devastated* by him getting off with two other girls when he was supposed to be on a date with me. Later I found out he'd only asked me because his mother had told him to. She was so unwell, he'd have done anything for her. Honestly, it was more mortifying that *my* mother had tried to sort out my social life for me by talking to his mother in the first place.'

'Oh.' Leo nodded, his suspicions confirmed. 'Your parents again, huh?'

'They were furious with me.'

'You? He was the one who got filmed.'

'And he was disciplined and never returned to school. Then his mother died. It must have been horrendous.' She drew in a deep breath. 'Meanwhile my parents said I obviously hadn't been a good girlfriend if I hadn't kept his interest. I hadn't done my job or whatever…'

'They blamed you?' Outrage built in his chest. 'What did they want you to *do*, exactly?'

'Better,' she said simply. 'But I don't think it's in me. Not to "work" relationships like that.'

His curiosity bit—she'd been so *abandoned* with him that night, yet he knew she'd been inexperienced. Maybe not just sexually. 'And you haven't dated anyone since?'

Her lashes lifted, revealing shy amusement in her pale blue eyes. 'You think I'm some sort of exotic species?'

'Like some of those creatures on the reef?' He shrugged. 'Perhaps.'

Honestly, he didn't know what to make of her. She was shy yet warm once he'd got past her quiet barrier. She could be clinically detached, yet compassionate and loyal. Maybe she was too shy to ask someone, but he couldn't believe no other guys had ever asked *her* out.

'After the incident with Ash I suppose I was put off for a bit,' she admitted. 'I certainly wasn't about to date anyone at school again. Nor in my class at uni. And I'm *never* going to date anyone I work with.'

Leo half smiled. So now she had a bunch of rules as to who she could or couldn't date? 'Sounds like you know what you don't want.'

'Not some society stud like Ash, that's for sure.'

Right—which also might rule him out. 'No colleagues, no one your parents would approve of?' He worked it through. 'Which makes it hard to find anyone you could say *yes* to.'

She glanced away and then back at him. His skin tightened. It had taken only seconds for her to say yes to him.

'You thought I was a security guard,' he mused. Not a colleague. Not a threat. 'Would your parents disapprove?' Had it been rebellion?

'No, it wasn't that…' She trailed off and that colour swept into her cheeks again.

'Then what?'

'I just… You were…'

'I was just what?' Something hot and fierce swirled in his blood. A ridiculous preening inside pushed him to ask why. 'What was different about me?'

'Chemistry, I guess?'

For a second he was ridiculously pleased. Then it was as if the tide of satisfaction receded and left emptiness. Because she hadn't wanted more at the time. She'd not asked for his name or number. She'd not wanted to seek him out again. He gazed at her and for the first time in his life wished that he could read minds. Never had it mattered what anyone thought of him before. But he wanted to understand why she'd walked away so easily. Because it niggled. Was it because she'd been afraid of his reaction if they'd seen each other fully naked? If he'd seen her scar and reacted in a way that made her think she wasn't good enough for him or anyone? He hated that her parents had put that on her. She was *amazing*—strong and brave. She'd been so that night with him.

That colour built in her cheeks as the silence grew.

Yet he knew she wanted him now. That he'd pleased her. He was about to do it again—was suddenly determined to do it even *more*.

'I didn't know who you were or anything about you,' she said softly, her colour high. 'You just…swept me away.'

'Maybe that meant that with me you could relax enough to let go,' he said gruffly. 'There was no expectation. No perfect performance required for once. In your mind it didn't matter at all. And so…you could relax.'

'You think?' An expression he couldn't quite read flashed on her face. 'Damn, I should have hooked up with a total stranger sooner.'

No. No other strangers. No other guys. He almost roared it as a fierce bolt of possessiveness tore through him before he recognised the teasing note in her voice.

He scooped her up and carried her back to the big bed they'd left only an hour ago and set about sweeping her away again and again. He kissed every inch, taking care to caress her spine. Not just to tease, but to worship every sweet inch of her until neither of them could move. Even then he watched her, still wishing he could read her mind.

She studied the edge of the cotton sheet that lightly covered her, obviously trying not to blush. Failing as usual. 'Why don't *you* sleep with the billions of women who fling themselves at you on a daily basis?'

He laughed at her exaggeration. 'There aren't billions.'

Her kiss-crushed lips pouted. 'Oh, come on, there's at least five a day. I saw three at the airport on our way here. You can't have failed to see how they looked at you.'

He hadn't noticed any. 'I was too busy watching you.'

She bit her lip but the little laugh escaped regardless. 'Smooth. But not necessary. I'm already back in your bed and you've had your way with me twice this morning already.'

It hadn't been a line. It had been simple truth.

She gazed right into his eyes. 'I'm serious. Why aren't you a player? You could be if you wanted to.'

'Most of the time I'm so consumed by work I don't realise where the day has gone,' he answered as honestly as he could. 'I'm absorbed in it.'

'That's the thing that matters to you most?'

'It always has been.' At least since his mother had passed.

'You're that disciplined?'

He saw it not as discipline, but necessity. Since his mother had died it had been the only thing that mattered—work was the one way to make himself a success, to force Hugh Castle to face him, and the impetus behind his need to make something more of that man's empire than Hugh himself had ever made of it That had been everything until recently, when he'd been consumed by thoughts of Rosanna—which in itself was shockingly unnerving. The sooner they agreed their future, the sooner he would return to his usual focused state. Surely now she'd see how much sense it made for them to marry. They had chemistry, they were building a friendship. This didn't need to be that complicated.

But now she studied him in the way she did those unusual plants she was interested in—with that focused curiosity. 'You don't wake in the small hours of the morning and overthink all your most personal things?' She wrinkled her nose. 'Not ever?'

At that he smiled. 'I wake in the small hours and overthink *work*.' But that wasn't entirely true. There were things that came to him then that he hated. 'I never wanted to be like him. Like Hugh.'

'In what way?'

'In his greed. In his cheating.' He sighed. 'I know Ash used to play the field, but he was upfront about it,' Leo said. 'Women knew where they stood with him. But I didn't want any of that complication in my life. I never wanted to make promises I couldn't keep.' He gazed at her sombrely.

'So why did you play that night with me?'

He still didn't rightly know. 'That night had been the culmination of a hard year's work. Stepping in to take over

Castle Holdings. There were times I didn't think I was going to make it and I wanted to nail it.'

'To prove to the world you could be as successful as Hugh?'

There was a shadow in her expression that he didn't understand. 'You think that's stupid?'

'No.' She sat up and wrapped herself in the sheet. 'I don't blame you for wanting to better him. I would too. So you were in a celebratory mood.'

Oddly he hadn't been. He'd been tired and a bit deflated. 'It wasn't normal for me to do that either.'

She glanced at him again. 'You wanted an escape.'

'I was stunned, to be honest. I couldn't believe what had possessed me. I suddenly realised I had a roomful of people downstairs waiting on me.' He laughed a little. 'Maybe it's as you said, just chemistry. We're a perfect compound, compatible in the most fundamental of ways.'

'Is that enough for you?' She looked back at the edge of the sheet. 'You truly don't believe in love?'

He didn't know how to answer without offending her.

She lifted her head and gazed at him, her eyes soft with an emotion he didn't want to analyse. 'You don't think that one day you might meet someone and there'll be something so much more? I wouldn't want to be in the way of that happening for you.'

More?

'That's not going to happen, Rosanna.'

Maybe he should have appreciated her thoughtfulness. Instead her solicitude engendered a flash of anger. He didn't want her concern for his well-being. He was just fine. *This* was all he wanted—a straightforward fix to the situation they were in. This, just as it was, would be a good deal for them both. Companionship, good sex, security.

Or maybe she didn't think it was? Maybe she didn't realise that sex didn't get any better than it was between them… Or maybe, he realised with a hit of discomfort, she wouldn't want *him* being in the way of that happening for *her* either. She wasn't a cool-headed scientist. She had a *romantic* streak.

He couldn't deliver on that. But for what it was worth, he wanted her more than he'd ever wanted a woman and that hunger wasn't easing any. His anger built. So did his determination to get her to agree. It seemed more imperative than ever that he secure this damn deal. He could give her things no other man in her life could.

'No?' Rosanna was lost in the gleaming passion in his eyes. In the growing fervour she'd not seen in him before.

She knew he didn't have random one-night stands, but he didn't understand that for her it hadn't been about the occasion, but the person. It had been about *him*. And she'd felt a little hit to her heart that it hadn't been she who had overwhelmed his control, it had been circumstance causing him to act the way he had that night with her. Of course, that was right. She supposed any woman who'd appeared on the terrace at that time could've ended up in his embrace, the recipient of his attentions.

'Then how lucky for me to have been the one to stumble across your path that night, huh?' she couldn't resist pointing out a little bitterly.

Something snapped in his expression. 'That night you turned up and *you* were the one I couldn't resist. I wanted to forget everything. Who I was. Where I was. What I should or shouldn't have been doing. I just watched you and I wanted you. Just as I want you again now.'

He wasn't slow that time. But the time after? That was when her last little flicker of doubt and disappointment melted. His touch was an achingly sweet relief.

Now she could luxuriate in the week they had left here. In the stillness of their surroundings there was nothing to steal any of their attention away—only the two of them alone in paradise. And when he kissed her she lost all capacity to think or to worry. She liked losing herself in his arms and becoming this creature who only felt good things. Now she satisfied the curiosity and hunger that had held her in thrall for all these weeks. She could expunge those regrets of what she'd not done sooner by doing it all now. Take her time. Take all he had to offer. In this warmth, the gentle breeze, shaded from the burning brilliance of the sun, she fully understood the delight of desire.

'This is something to build on,' he said huskily, hours later. 'I can support you, Rosanna. You can trust me.'

And when he gazed down at her, the epitome of beauty in the world around him shone and she couldn't think beyond him any more.

'Just marry me,' he tempted. 'You know we can make this work.'

That was the thing, it didn't feel like work at all. He offered her a perfect, problem-free paradise. That rough stubble on his face, the tan on his skin, the smile in his eyes, the damn dimple… He made everything seem so easy, tempting her with the promise of happiness and laughter. The off-beat pulse of panic in her blood was drowned by the heat he stirred within her and Rosanna ignored the warning strike against her ribcage.

'Yes.'

CHAPTER THIRTEEN

A FEW DAYS slid by in a mixture of laziness and activity. They snorkelled on the reef entranced by turtles, corals and fish, walked along the sand, boated to cays and other islands. Laughed about little things. He shared in her delight in finding beauty on the reef. It had been the perfect place to bring her. And each afternoon he took her back to bed after lunch, so through the hottest point of the day he was shrouded with her beneath billowing cool cotton sheets. Until there wasn't a part of her he hadn't touched and tasted ten times over.

It still wasn't enough. He was still hungry for her. He'd made a point of indulging her in every act of intimacy, teaching her just how sensitive some parts of her body could be, showing her how the peak of pleasure, a white-hot orgasm, could be achieved in a myriad ways. Then sustained. Then achieved again. Yet still there was more. There was a depth to this connection between them—a profound intimacy in the way she straddled his lap and held him locked tight into her body. He teased her, talking to her, delighting in making her unable to answer coherently. Breathless and hot and restless and so playful—teasing her, pleasuring her, making her ignite. He adored the way she flushed and responded and flipped it all against him. And still he felt a near constant ache for her.

He *should* be fast asleep. He'd already got the win, he should be enjoying the winner's spoils. She was going to marry him. There was nothing to worry about. But here he was, lying awake since the middle of the night until dawn. Overthinking. And for once it wasn't about work. It should be. He'd been out of touch for days. But instead he was worried about Rosanna's agreement. Oddly he now felt her arguments against marriage as a warning he'd not heeded. The responsibility of her happiness haunted him. He wasn't sure he could shoulder it. Here—on holiday—it was easy enough. But ordinarily he wasn't on holiday. He worked. He *needed* to work. His employees depended on him and it was the only thing he'd done for so long. The only thing he really knew how to do. What made him ever think he could be a husband and father? He killed houseplants. He'd never had pets. His children deserved a better parent than he'd ever be. Rosanna deserved a better partner.

He got up, pacing through to the lounge to grab a cool drink and clear his head.

He didn't discuss his father with anyone. Not even Ash. But he'd found himself wanting to explain to Rosanna that he'd never wanted to be the lying cheat Hugh Castle had been. To never take advantage of women—or anyone—in that way or any other. His father had been a controlling, unrelenting bastard. Leo wanted to be better than that and wanted her to know that she could trust him.

Which meant he needed to fix things with *her* parents. They'd wanted her to make a match with Ash Castle all those years ago and now they had to deal with him, the man who'd cancelled their company's contracts. But for Rosanna's peace of mind he was compelled to take action. He could send a message from his watch. She'd never know and if she did she wouldn't mind. He didn't want her experiencing any of the bitterness he'd felt with his father's rejection and no further pressure of difficulties with her parents. That didn't mean he'd forgiven them. There'd be rules and he'd make it clear they weren't to upset or pressure Rosanna in *any* way. It only took a moment to message his assistant but as he returned his watch to the safe he knocked Rosanna's phone. The screen lit up and he saw there were a number of missed notifications. The most recent message was displayed in full.

Ro, crisis at the flat. There's been a flood. Where are you? Call urgently.

The implications took a second to sink in. Then anxiety spiked. All her belongings—her plants, notebooks, weird fish…

He glanced in the doorway to their bedroom. She was fast asleep but he knew she'd worry. He could find out more about the situation first before telling her.

Quietly he walked to the office of the private resort, glad the sun was rising and it wasn't too shockingly early to phone people; glad he had something concrete to focus his worry on. Because there was an unusual amount of anxiety building within—rendering him unable to rest, unable to be easy and just enjoy this. It was stupid—hadn't he achieved exactly what he'd wanted?

She'd said *yes*. To *marriage*.

Only he wasn't sure it was right. Now he questioned whether pushing the proposal had been wise. Having her so close beside him for so long—for ever? Suddenly he felt keenly aware that she was precious—fragile really. And he didn't want to crush her. He didn't want to screw this up.

He stabbed the buttons on the office phone—avoiding the damned inner anxiety by focusing on her real issue. It turned out a water pipe had burst in the flat above her and leaked through and everything was sodden. He thought again of the things she'd put so much effort into. She didn't need the heartache of sorting this out. He could get the clean-up under way and she could have another day without knowing until the worst had been fixed up. He'd get professionals in and it could be sorted by the time they returned. He'd save her all that stress.

* * *

'You're very serious this morning.' Rosanna smiled as they returned to the villa after a couple hours out on a double kayak.

He'd been wondering how the clean-up was going. Was itching to put in a call to check. And he realised he didn't want to lie to her. 'There was a flood at your flat,' he muttered.

Her eyes widened. 'What?'

'The unit upstairs had a burst pipe. The occupant was away for the weekend as well, so no one noticed until it started coming out of your front door.'

'What?' A frown crashed on her brows. 'How do you know?' She folded her arms and glared at him. 'So you've been using your phone.'

'No, that's wrecked from the water. I saw the message on yours when I went to get my watch from the safe.'

'When was that?'

'Early this morning.' He saw she wasn't happy and tried to explain more. 'You were fast asleep. It was easy to arrange a clean-up.'

'That's why you've been distracted.' Her frown didn't lessen. 'When were you going to tell me?'

He didn't know. 'You don't need stress at the moment. You've got enough on.'

'So you thought you'd fix it?'

'That seemed...like an idea.' He watched her warily because now she stomped inside the villa.

She whirled on the top step to face him. 'Is this what it's going to be like?'

His defensiveness rose. Like *what*? 'I just thought—'

'That you knew what was best for me.' She glared down at him. 'That you could make decisions on my behalf. For what was best for *you*.'

'Not for me. I did it for you.'

'Really? I don't need you to do that. I'm not incompetent. Or incapable. Or that useless.'

'I thought I was doing something *helpful.*' He'd been concerned for her welfare. For the health of the babies. Was that so awful of him?

'What did you think might happen if you told me before you fixed it?'

'I don't know,' he growled. 'You've been tired. I just…'

'Do you really think I'm that fragile?' She paused, something flickering in her eyes. 'You said I was strong.'

And she was. He'd just wanted to shelter her from unnecessary stress. He'd wanted to fix it for her.

'I'm not just another thing you're *responsible* for, Leo,' she said when he didn't respond. 'I need you to include me, not decide things unilaterally.'

'That wasn't what I intended.' He growled. 'I wanted to protect you.'

She paused. 'Why?' She came down from the top step so she stood eye to eye with him. 'From what?'

'I don't know,' he snapped. 'But you're vulnerable.'

'I'm *pregnant,* not incapacitated.'

And he'd never felt as frustrated. 'Look, I'm sorry but I can't risk—' He rubbed his forehead and smothered a growl. 'Life is precious, Rosanna. I've failed before. I can't do it again.'

'Failed in what way?'

He froze.

'Failed *who*, Leo?'

He stared at her. The anger was gone from her face—the flash flood of colour had receded and left her paler than usual.

'Leo?'

She was strong and fierce and honest and he realised she needed to know what she was getting into. She needed to know that the man she was marrying was never going to be the kind of husband she *should* have. It was only fair that she understood his limitations so he wouldn't let her down like this again because she'd know what to expect.

'I failed my mother. More than once. Really badly.'

Rosanna's eyes widened in her pale face and in the sunlight her gold hair glinted and suddenly he was tired of feeling frustrated. Somehow he felt compelled to confess everything to her—as if she really were the beautiful angel she resembled.

'You know Hugh never wanted me,' he muttered, needing her to understand just how desperate things had been. 'He tried to bully her into getting rid of me, but she wouldn't and once I was born he refused to acknowledge I was his son. She tried to manage on her own but she needed help. When she asked him for just a little support he threatened to call social services on her for neglect of me. He didn't want me, but if she didn't toe the line, he'd make sure *she* didn't get to keep me either.'

'What?' Rosanna looked shocked.

'Yeah,' he muttered. 'That much of a monster. He wanted us out of his life for good. He was the ultimate in selfish.'

'Your poor mother.'

She didn't know the half of it. 'He actually paid off other guys to say they'd been with her.' Leo watched the distress in Rosanna's eyes build but he couldn't stop himself telling her the truth of how awful it had been. 'He spread the rumour that she was easy and that I could be anyone's bastard. And of course he refused to do a DNA test his whole life.' Leo growled. 'My mother gave up. She didn't have the funds or the energy to fight him in court. Nor did I until much later. But the things he'd said caused a rift with her family. They believed him over her.'

'Leo, that's awful.'

They'd *both* been unwanted then and his outrage still burned. 'He made everyone believe she was a liar. But she worked so hard. It was the two of us against the world. She didn't resent me. I mean, she had every right to but she…' He trailed off, remembering how they'd had nothing but each other. 'She would've done anything for me and she did. I cost her everything she had. In the end, even her life.'

'How?' Rosanna asked softly with a shake of her head.

She didn't believe him. So pretty. So trusting in the best of him. He didn't want that burden any more. He didn't want to crush her when he fell from that pedestal.

'I worked part-time jobs from the age of nine after Hugh had rejected us again.' That was when he'd understood the reality of his mother's struggle. 'Anything to help her out. She always had two or three jobs on the go but even then we were broke all the time.' He sighed. 'In my teens when I was stronger I worked in a cool store. One night I decided to miss a shift at work. Just to have a night out with a couple of mates.'

He'd been working for years and had been tempted to a blowout. It hadn't seemed like a big deal at the time, just one night off after a hard week.

'But my boss phoned my mum, trying to track me down. There'd been an unusually large delivery that night and it needed sorting. Mum had only just finished her previous shift but my boss was angry and told her he'd fire me if I didn't come in.' He bowed his head. 'But I didn't answer my phone to either Mum or my boss. I was a stupid jerk. So Mum went in. She worked the shift for me. But she'd had a cough and working in that cool store for eight hours, being so run-down already, made it worse.' He couldn't look at Rosanna now. 'It only took a couple of days. The cough went to her lungs. She said she'd be fine. But she wasn't. Pneumonia.'

And he'd never missed a day of work since. Not until he'd taken Rosanna to Great Barrier Reef this week. And that had been work too, right? Of a different kind.

'It wasn't your fault.' Rosanna put a gentle hand on his shoulder.

'Of course it was,' he argued, stiffening beneath her touch. 'If I hadn't been selfish and lazy… She worked so hard for me and I let her down.' He hated himself for it. The feeling of helplessness had been absolute. Now the final humiliation spilled from him like poison. 'When it was evident how unwell she was, I went to Hugh Castle one last time.'

He'd wanted to transfer her to another hospital. Fight for second opinions. Anything that might've helped her. Even though he'd known it was too late by then. But he'd been desperate to try anything. 'I actually cried. I begged him for help.'

'And he wouldn't.'

Leo had failed. He'd been determined it would never happen again—he'd never allow himself to return to that utterly vulnerable, helpless position of losing someone he loved, of being unable to help them. It was easy enough when he kept people at a distance. Only now a wave of panic burned in his gut—because he had Rosanna and two children to be responsible for. His breathing quickened and he grasped at what had happened next—distracting himself by telling her the last.

'A year or so later Ash found me. He'd heard rumours and he was rebellious and bitter. He offered up some DNA to do a test. We'd see if we were related and that would be the proof I needed to prove Hugh's paternity.'

'He was angry with your father too?'

'Yeah. Maybe I'm lucky Hugh Castle didn't have the influence on my life the way he did with Ash.'

'But you took his name.'

'*Away* from him. Because it was the last thing he wanted to give me. So yes, I took it.'

He'd taken everything that old man had never wanted

him to have. His name. His company. His whole life's work. 'And now I have his company. He knows—I told him my plans before he died. Ash invited me to see him and backed me fully. Fool that I am, I went. Thinking that perhaps on his damned deathbed he might finally be honest about who he was and what he'd done. That he might feel an inkling of remorse.'

'But he didn't.'

He'd taken pleasure in the man's impotent rage. He'd taken pleasure in making himself more successful than his cheating, denying father had ever been. The old man hadn't been able to do a thing to stop him.

'I've asked myself my whole life what was wrong with him. I've never figured out an answer that made any sense other than that he was just mean. That he liked to be in control and hold power over people. I won't be anything like him. Ever.'

Which meant he couldn't let Rosanna down or their babies down. But *family* wasn't something he'd ever wanted. It cost too much and he didn't know how to keep it safe or successful. He far preferred work, the challenge of making that a success—getting tangible results was something he could do well.

'My original surname was meaningless,' he muttered distractedly. 'Her family didn't support her, didn't believe her. So she left. She called me Leonardo after Da Vinci because she liked his sculptures. It's as good a reason as any. And I took Castle because it's a permanent reminder to everyone who wouldn't believe her that she was right. It's the only way I can honour her now.' He hated that she'd died before the truth had been proven. 'Because it's my fault she passed away when she did.'

'*No.*' Rosanna gazed into his eyes with such compassion he couldn't stand it.

'Her illness wasn't your fault,' she said. 'It was only one night—'

'When she was tired already,' he interrupted harshly. 'When she'd not been eating well because she'd been giving me most of what we had because I wouldn't stop growing. When she hadn't had enough sleep in years. When her asthma was aggravated by the damp house we lived in because we couldn't afford decent heating. That was all because of me. Because she had to make do with less to give *me* more.'

It was *entirely* because of him that it happened.

'And I bet you were the light of her life,' Rosanna said simply. 'She loved you. She wanted you. She fought to have you and keep you. And, yes, she did anything she could for you. That's what love is. It's awful what happened to her—but that lack of support was on her family, on your father. The other *adults* in her life. *Not* you.'

Rosanna watched the emotions flicker across Leo's face until he turned away from her. No wonder marriage and children weren't on his to-do list. The man had been so hurt—by a father who'd repeatedly refused to acknowledge him and then by the loss of his beloved mother, who'd sacrificed everything to have him. And he blamed himself fully for her death. There'd been no in-betweens. It had been so extreme for him.

'You should have been able to have some fun,' she said sadly. 'You were just a teenager.'

'Don't feel sorry for me, Rosanna.'

'Well, I do,' she said softly. 'I think all that just sucks. You were so alone and too young to deal with all of that. It wasn't fair.'

She regretted burning him for being a workaholic. Of course he was—he'd had to be just to survive. And then, because of the guilt he'd felt. It didn't matter what she or anyone said to him, she knew there'd always be a part within him that felt guilty about his mother's passing. Emotions weren't rational. No wonder he'd wanted to stay in control. No wonder he'd wanted to shield her from stress.

'I have a really good life,' he said quietly.

He had a really lonely life.

'She'd be pleased for me,' he added.

'She would. And proud.'

She turned him to face her and wound her arms around his waist. Relief flowed when he rested his head on hers and he accepted her simple embrace. But Rosanna knew pride in achievement wasn't everything. Pleasing someone, making them proud…that didn't really matter. What mattered was knowing that the person you loved was *happy*. That was what she wanted her parents to want for her, as she was sure Leo's mother would want for him. What she wanted for her babies. And, she realised, it was what she wanted for Leo. Honourable, hardworking, loyal, heartbroken Leo. She wanted *him* to be happy. She wanted to do everything she could to make his life better still.

And why was that?

Her heart soared and sank at the same time, tearing her in two with a wave of anxiety that she couldn't stem…

She loved him.

CHAPTER FOURTEEN

THEY DIDN'T LAUGH on the flight back to Sydney. Rosanna didn't spill any salty snacks, didn't eat any—she wasn't hungry. He sat near to her but there was the slightest withdrawal. More than mere silence. Maybe he was thinking about work already and all the things he had to catch up on since being away. But she was anxious it wasn't that. She was anxious about *everything*.

Dinner last night had been an art of distraction. In bed after there'd been his touch again—a silent, desperate touch. She'd clung, unable to hold back her need to embrace him. She couldn't tell him she loved him, self-preservation warned her. He'd been quiet since. So had she. Maybe she was being over-sensitive—feeling vulnerable about her own emotions—but she couldn't help feeling he regretted all that he'd said.

Back at the Sydney penthouse she discovered Leo hadn't wasted any time. She found her belongings had been dried out and sent over. Her cuttings had been brought to the terrace garden, even Axel the axolotl had made the move.

'Is everything going to survive?' he asked.

'I think so.' She smiled at him. 'Thank you. This was a massive effort.'

'Not my effort really. I just got staff onto it.' He watched her ruefully. 'I'm sorry I didn't tell you about it right away.'

'It's okay, I understand why you waited.'

He feared her vulnerability. He glanced away. She felt wariness at this new intimacy. On holiday it had been easy, now there were other issues to navigate.

'We should dine with your parents tonight,' he said suddenly. 'Have you got something to wear?'

The prospect terrified her but she knew she had to face

them. 'I can find something. And yes, I know I can buy something if I want to.'

She waved the bank card that had also been waiting for her at the penthouse. He'd insisted on organising money for her. She'd accepted, now understanding why he needed to do that too. His need to ensure her well-being was part of the deal. But he'd learn that *she* needed independence too. And respect. They could work on that. She knew he was trying—he'd just apologised, after all.

After Leo left to go to his office, Rosanna phoned her boss to let him know to expect her resignation. She offered online support to her students until her replacement was hired. Given her flat was currently uninhabitable, he understood. She emailed her students to let them know and got some immediate replies that made her smile. She'd figure out a job in the future, but for now she needed to work things out properly with Leo. They needed more time to build on the foundations they'd begun to form on their trip away. She went shopping, unable to resist the desire to impress not her mother, but Leo.

He returned from work surprisingly early. She smoothed down the sides of her dress. It was floral silk, sensual to the touch. Slim fitting, but she didn't mind if her slightly wonky waist and lean to the left were obvious.

'Is this okay?'

He hardly glanced at her. 'Gorgeous. Let's go.'

Her nerves built even more. He was definitely distant and her heart shrank.

'I spoke to my mother earlier,' she said as Leo drove them out of the basement garage.

'How was she?'

'She sounded excited on the phone but didn't press for more information, which is unusual.'

Leo narrowed his eyes on the red traffic light ahead. 'I

offered them a deal at a new property we've picked up in Queensland.'

'Pardon?' Rosanna swivelled to stare at him.

'A contract on a resort we're redoing there. It's a new acquisition. Something different. It's not a large project, but we'll see how they go.'

She was stunned. 'So the proposal bargain you made the other day—'

'Was a mistake,' he interrupted her smoothly. 'As you rightly recognised at the time. This isn't a reward for saying yes.'

But that was exactly what it was. And it felt wrong. 'How can it be anything else? You can't give them the contract. Cronyism and nepotism aren't your thing.'

She'd respected him for that.

'They can't be homeless, Rosanna. I can't allow that to happen.'

So he was paying them off?

Her parents were now getting everything they'd wanted—business contracts and a society wedding. Their only child marrying a powerful, wealthy man—creating a permanent relationship they'd always benefit from. But she didn't want them winning all that—they'd have learned nothing from their own mistakes. And she certainly didn't want him feeling obligated to look after *all* her family. It made her not just a responsibility to him, but a burden.

And suddenly she was furious. 'Have you negotiated with them already?'

'I haven't told them about the babies. I thought we could do that together.'

Her jaw dropped. 'You thought?' Her fury flared. 'You've done *all* the thinking on this.'

Just what she *didn't* want.

'I didn't want the contract mess and their problems getting in the way of our wedding,' he said.

He'd gone behind her back. *Again.*

'I thought we'd talked about making these decisions together.'

'This was a business decision. Not a personal one.'

'Rubbish, it's to do with my *parents*,' she snapped. 'You thought you could decide the "best" way to solve this without even discussing it with me?'

She was a pawn, not a person. She had no real voice. She was not a priority. Again.

'That's not how it was.' His frustration sounded. 'I've had a business relationship with your parents for longer than I've known you.'

'But this *is* personal. This is because of me and what's happened between *us*. Otherwise you'd have just cancelled their contract and never looked back. It's everything *you* didn't want, Leo.'

'Things have changed.'

What mattered to him most was the impact on his business. That was what mattered to her parents most too. *She* was not the priority here. And she never would be. Nor would her children. He might think he'd done it for her. But he hadn't.

'I didn't want to upset you,' he said.

'Why would it matter if I got upset? People get upset all the time. Then they get over it. We could have worked it out.'

His jaw tightened. 'I was hoping to save you stress.'

'You've just caused me more.' She was so hurt. 'You're used to doing anything and everything you want, calling all the shots, but that's not how this can work with us. I thought you understood that. Why couldn't you trust me to talk to me?'

They'd got nowhere. She'd been fooling herself for thinking they'd connected not just on a physical level but an emotional one. That he'd opened up to her. That he understood her needs as well as her understanding his. But he'd gone all high-handed boss again. Solving everyone's problems for them as if he were responsible for everyone and everything. He did it without consultation. Without trust. And without that, there could be no future—not the kind she wanted.

In the light of her *own* emotions, her own vulnerability to him, she knew she couldn't do this. She couldn't accept this for her future.

'I thought you didn't want them to end up homeless,' he growled.

Of course she didn't. That wasn't the point right now. 'Why wouldn't you talk to me about it when you knew I'd want you to?'

He glared at her. 'Because I knew you'd say no.'

'So you just did what you wanted anyway? Despite already knowing it's not what I would want.' She was so hurt. 'Because you feel responsibility for me.'

'Naturally I do.' He looked furious. 'I got you *pregnant*.'

It came back to that. Of course it did. And it would *always* come back to that. If fate hadn't intervened, they never would have come to this—to her living with him, agreeing to marry him.

It wasn't because he'd fallen in love with her.

He'd paid a high price for that night. He'd even tried to do the right thing then. He'd used contraception. He'd been courteous. He'd done everything right. When really all he'd wanted was a few moments of escape for himself. She related to that. She really, really did. But now he was stuck with her. And he was a man who took his responsibilities so very seriously.

He should be free and laughing as he had when they were out on the reef. Carefree and having fun. He should be out dating, playing the field. Finding his perfect match. Getting over the heartbreak of his mother's passing. Learning it was okay not to work all the time. Learning that loving again would be worth it.

Not *settling* for her because he felt he had to. Because he couldn't *not* do the right thing. She didn't want to be that person to him. The one he 'had' to be with, who he 'had' to look after. Fate was cruel. The burden of her and their twins was the last thing he deserved or needed.

The worst thing was, she wanted so much more from him. And that was unfair of her, wasn't it? She'd fallen for him knowing she was never going to be the right wife for him. She wasn't who he'd fall in love with. How could he? So now he was working so hard to make the best of it. To make her believe they could make it work. But she wasn't who he really wanted. This was only because of circumstance. He only wanted to marry her because he had to. And it hurt. It really, really hurt. Because now that whole trip felt like a lie.

'This isn't relevant, Rosanna.' He tried to dismiss it.

'It's totally relevant. It's everything.'

'We don't have time to talk about this—'

'We don't have the time not to. This matters.'

'It doesn't. It's fixed.'

'*Nothing* is fixed.' She shook her head at him—at the way he wanted to shut this down. 'You're afraid of emotional conflict.'

He flinched. 'No, I'm not.'

'You don't want anyone to get too close.'

'How can you say that? I told you things I've never told anyone.'

'And you regret it.'

'Right now? Yes. Because you're using what you know of my past to misinterpret my actions now.'

'No, I'm seeing your actions for what they are. You're a straight-up guy just trying to do the right thing. And you'll always try to do the right thing by anyone.'

He stared at her. 'And the problem is…?'

'You don't want people equating you with your father.'

His jaw clenched. 'Of course I don't.'

'That's the real reason you want us to marry, right? Because you don't want to be seen as being like him. Not being there for your children. Not recognising them.'

He didn't deny it.

It was the *only* reason that really mattered to him. He was desperately proving that he wasn't like the man who'd seeded him. He'd do that over and over. This *was* about his past. Not about her at all. Or even what was truly best for their children.

It was still about reputation. Her life would be bound for ever by 'what's best for the business' dictates. Just as her whole childhood had been. She'd never been the priority—not number one in her parents' lives. Not in Leo's either—her future partner's. And that was not what she wanted for her children. To come second to the business. To reputation. To what others thought. The measure of success. To make all decisions upon that.

She'd allowed it to happen. She'd tried to be what her parents wanted. But now she had her own children to think about and she didn't want them trying to live up to—or break away from—parental reputation or expectation. She wanted them to be free. And in order for that to happen, *she* needed to be free. And to do that—she had to be *honest*. And brave.

'There are a lot of factors contributing to the decision for us to marry, Rosanna.'

'But not the usual one.' The most important one for her. The emotional one that he clearly didn't feel.

'You mean…' He trailed off.

'You can't even say it?' She laughed a little brokenly. 'Love. Leo, yes. I'm talking about love.'

'We've both known from the beginning this has nothing to do with love.'

It had *everything* to do with it.

'You think you don't deserve it,' she said. 'Not just because of your mother. Not just because you don't want to mess up a marriage the way your father did. You don't want to mess *anything* up so you don't engage at all.'

'Look who's talking.' He snorted. 'You're the one who hides in a lab all day, still trying to be something for someone else. Who could only have some fun when she pretended to be someone else.'

'It wasn't that I pretended to be someone else,' she argued. 'You were right. That night with you I was able to be myself—with no preconceived ideas, no expectations.' He'd encouraged her to be herself. Accepted her as she was. He'd told her she was strong and she'd believed him. 'I could just be me. And you wanted me then.'

But he didn't love her.

'And I want you now. We want *each other*,' he said grimly. 'So why are we arguing? Why isn't that enough?'

Because it wouldn't last for him. And she didn't want to wake up every morning and wonder if that was the day when he decided he didn't want her any more. 'Because one day one of us might want someone else.'

He stared at her. 'Might that not happen anyway?' he asked cruelly. 'Whether we state we're in love or not?'

His cynicism broke her heart. 'You don't believe in it.'

'No, I don't. There's a decent arrangement, Rosanna. And that is absolutely what we can have. There's loyalty and honouring the contract we'll make. *That's* what marriage is. A contract.'

Purely business.

'So there's no consideration in your life for loving someone? There's responsibility. There's protectiveness. There's passion. What's the missing piece of the puzzle?' She stared at him. 'Why can't you call it what it is?'

'Because it isn't what you want it to be,' he growled. 'It never will be.'

He didn't feel for her that way.

'What if it is for me?' she said. 'What if I said I'd fallen in love with you? And I want you to love me. *That's* what I want.'

'Rosanna…'

'Couldn't we have it all?' She gazed at him sadly. 'Why can't I?'

His face froze. 'I'm sorry. I can give you everything else. Everything—'

'*But* the one thing I really want. The one thing that's *free*.'

'It isn't though.' He scowled. 'I don't have the resources for that in my account. I don't have the means or the capacity to give you what you want.'

'That's not true,' she whispered.

'Not for *anyone*,' he continued harshly. 'I don't have it, Rosanna. Never did. Never will.'

She glared at him. The way he'd retreated behind his wall of seriousness. 'You think you're strong? Focused? It's not discipline, it's *denial*. And it's based in fear.'

'I know what it feels like to have nothing and to lose everything.'

'I know. And I'm sorry, but that doesn't mean you never strive again.'

'I spend my *life* striving.'

'For *one* element,' she yelled. 'The *least* important. Work doesn't matter. It doesn't keep you warm at night.' She was furious with him. 'You didn't want to be like him.'

'It's about responsibility—'

'That's just control in disguise. You want to control what

you give and to whom you give it. Every bit as much as he did.'

'I'm *nothing* like him,' he roared, stopping the car at a red light.

'Are you sure?' she asked bitterly. 'Because it seems to me that he was incapable of giving love. And also of receiving it. And isn't that you?'

His withdrawal was absolute. The rigidity of his expression. The cold anger in his eyes.

'You don't want that from me,' she said. 'You don't want my love.'

'You only offer it because you're confusing lust for love. Because you're tired and emotional.'

'Are you serious? Are you going to say this is hormones talking?'

'Isn't it?'

'Don't tell me I'm tired. I'm fine. I'm strong and capable and I'll survive. More than survive. But I *am* tired of not having my voice heard. Of not being someone's number one. Of not being more important than anything else to someone.'

He froze again. 'Then if what I'm offering isn't enough, don't feel you have to stay.'

Her heart tore as she swung on the door handle and stumbled out of the car, clutching her little handbag close. She frantically waved at a taxi going past.

'Rosanna!'

She ignored him. He'd just told her to go. It was the most honest thing he'd said all afternoon.

CHAPTER FIFTEEN

LEO CASTLE REFUSED to be angry. Rosanna walking out was the best thing. Definitely best for her. And it had been good to remind himself of his painful past because now he remembered what he wanted to be, how he wanted to live—with honour and utter independence. Security and safety for Rosanna and the babies was paramount and his way to help them achieve that was with his work. Always with work.

Finally his cool-headed business brain switched on.

She'd been right in the beginning. There was no need for them to marry. He'd get them an apartment, set the children up with trust funds, ensure Rosanna had more financial support than she could ever need. It was straightforward really. Why had he got so tied up in knots about securing so-called legitimacy and security for them? For thinking that they needed to be *married*? For thinking that *he* was integral to making that happen? Quite the reverse was true. They'd be better off *without* him being overly influential in their lives.

But here he was once again wide awake in the small hours of the night, overthinking his most personal problems. The things he regretted. The moments he wanted to redo but couldn't.

She deserved more. She ought to have felt that spark with someone more worthy than him. Of course he'd failed her. He didn't know what he was doing and didn't think he could ever learn. Because there it was, the fear that, with a father like Hugh Castle, he was missing some elemental aspect of humanity. He could work hard. He could think well. But loving someone the way they needed to be loved? Listening to them? Meeting their needs? No. He'd failed at that. Again.

In his office, hours later, Leo looked down at the list of text messages. Rosanna had sent the same message every day for a week already.

I'm fine. Will be in touch again soon.

She was letting him know she was fine. Not where she was. Not what she was doing. Not who she was with. Just very courteous and polite so he wouldn't worry.

He wanted to throw his new phone into the goddamn ocean. These messages were rubbish. Not enough. Not ever enough.

But he refused to phone her. Refused to track where she might be. Refused to write more than his monosyllabic reply. She'd wanted space. He had to give it to her. And he reminded himself, yet again, that he'd done the right thing. The *only* thing to have done. For *her*. He couldn't give her all that she wanted so he'd let her go. That was right, wasn't it?

Only he hadn't *let* her go, he'd *told* her to leave. And he hated remembering the look in her eyes at that moment.

She would be better off with someone else eventually.

Leo felt capable of violence at the thought of some other man in her life, but he clamped down on every muscle. He didn't want her to be unhappy and she would be eventually, if she were forced to stay with him, living a life in which he couldn't give her everything she needed. He couldn't do the emotional stuff. He didn't know how to.

He should have been feeling better by now. It was over a week already. But he wasn't. And, damn it, he *was* angry. He was freaking furious.

Why had she pushed? *Why* had she asked for more? *Why* didn't she understand he'd offered all he had to give? *Why* couldn't that be enough for her?

But why should she settle for less?

Rosanna Gold deserved the best of everything and everyone.

Only there was that selfish bit in him that still wanted to keep her for himself. That greedy part of him that tormented him every damn minute with memories—teasing him with sensations and sounds. He remembered her lilting quiet comments, that chime of laughter that became so infectious when she let it go, the softness of her pale skin, her slender waist and that one spot on her back where he could feel where steel met spine.

She was strong, the thief in his garden. And she was sweet.

He couldn't believe that she really was in love with him. He'd told her it was lust clouding everything—as it had clouded his world for weeks. Thanks to him, she'd fallen pregnant. With *twins*. She'd fallen out even worse with her parents. She'd had to quit her job. He'd completely messed up her life.

No way could she love him given all that.

Rosanna showered and dressed, glad it was time to get moving. She'd been awake for an hour already and had dwelled long enough for today. She liked to walk to the plant nursery the long way—via the beachfront. She'd found room in a flat share—agreed to a month by month lease, which gave her flexibility for now. And while she'd started at the nursery just on customer service, her boss had quickly realised her knowledge base and had upped her responsibility with the actual plants. So life was going okay, right? Only on the inside, she wasn't quite okay. Not *yet*.

She missed him.

They'd laughed together. They'd discovered they had stuff in common. She'd enjoyed their conversations—she'd found him fascinating and funny. He'd electrified her life. She'd thought they'd entered their own little world on the reef—one that they'd bring back with them. She'd thought that he trusted her…

She'd been an idiot. Leo Castle didn't truly trust anyone and he never would. He'd temporarily allowed her his body, offered her financial and physical stability, even a kind of companionship. As *friends*. But that was where it ended for him. Whereas for her it had been impossible not to make a far deeper emotional investment. She'd not meant for it to happen. But it had. She'd fallen in love with him. So easily. So quickly. So stupidly.

As she neared the nursery she turned her phone on and tapped the screen.

I'm fine. Will be in touch again soon.

She sent the text to him at the same time each day. Then she sent the same to her parents. Then she turned off her phone again—mostly to stop herself hoping she'd get a decent response. Her parents hadn't questioned her as to why she'd suddenly decided to move or why she'd not explained her relationship with Leo. Maybe they were too busy with their new contract for him in Queensland already. And Leo had barely replied at all. The first time he'd answered.

Let me know where you are so we can make arrangements for the future.

She hadn't done that yet. She'd just sent the same message. Since then he'd just replied OK.

She knew hiding was cowardly but right now it was all she could manage. Working was good. Working was a distraction from the brutal fact that she'd asked him to love her and he'd told her to leave. That she'd ruined what they might have had. She'd not been enough—a disappointment yet again. She'd let their children down.

Leo didn't want her with him because she couldn't accept what he could offer. But no more would she accept *less* than she needed. No more would she try to be what someone *else* wanted. Not for the rest of her life.

She'd never been someone's number one. Maybe she never would be. But she'd put herself first and by extension her children too. Because *she* needed to be a better example to them than she'd been until now. She needed to demonstrate self-worth to them so they would grow up strong and happy and capable of loving and being loved.

So at least now she was holding her own in life. New town. New flat. New job. New friends even—her workmates were friendly, her flatmates too. She'd made more friends here already than she'd made at the university in all those years.

But that night as she walked home via the beach path, she turned her phone back on and saw she had a message. Her heart stilled. It was her parents. There was some waffle, nervousness even, but also a note of concern she'd not heard before. And then…

We miss you. Is there anything we can do for you? Anything you need?

Her mum's questions ever so slightly soothed a deep wound. For the first time they'd finally asked what—if anything—they could do for her. They'd asked to know her thoughts and how she felt. And she'd tell them. Soon.

She'd not meant to scare them, which was why she'd messaged each day. But she needed to do this now for *herself.* So she'd build the courage to eventually figure out some kind of working relationship with Leo.

It stung that he'd made no effort to contact her more directly, or to find her. Which meant he was truly okay with her leaving. Regardless of the reputation he cared about so damned much, he hadn't wanted her to stay. And that hurt.

A stupid part of her had hoped he'd turn up, but over the course of the last fortnight that hope was starting to fade. She'd come to realise that right from the start their entanglement had meant something different to her than it had to him. And if he wasn't ready to open up to someone, to her? That had to be okay. She couldn't force him to. It was okay for him not to have fallen in love with her.

Yet while she knew that rationally, emotionally she was *devastated*. She'd opened up to him. She'd given herself to him—she'd wanted to give him everything. But he didn't want it. He didn't want her.

He'd be in her life for ever. He was the father of her children. So she knew she had to work out a way where she could cope with seeing him…and, eventually, seeing him with someone else.

She needed time to build the strength to face that. Time and energy and courage. And she wasn't going to apologise for taking it now.

Leo didn't want to work any more, but he had to. It was the only thing he knew—the only way to hold back the emotions festering inside him. He couldn't face going back to his penthouse—it was filled with her plants—but he'd had to do that too. He was terrified of killing her freaking fish.

For some unfathomable reason he couldn't outsource the responsibility of Axel. He now knew more about the care and feeding of axolotls than he'd ever imagined possible. He'd been working round the clock, even when he was at home keeping Axel company—avoiding any downtime in which he might start thinking about her.

Who was he kidding? He thought about her *all the time*.

Losing someone was the worst feeling in the world. He'd

never wanted to go through that devastation again. He'd never let anyone close enough. But he was devastated right now.

So he went to the office. It was the only thing he could think to do, even though he'd never been more sick of it in his life. Hours later he glanced up at the knock on his door and watched his manager, Petra, come in with a wary look on her face. When he'd first got back to the office he'd learned she'd gone to Melbourne to sign up a new client. Now she'd returned and looked as if she were entering a scorpion's nest as she presented the proposal she'd gone away to deliver.

'You don't mind that I went ahead and did this without consulting you?' she asked as he skimmed the fine print.

Rosanna's words came back to him. She'd said she felt sorry for his staff because he was such a micromanager. He'd scoffed. But maybe she'd been right?

'Of course not,' he muttered. 'I was away. I trust your judgement.' Then he paused and looked up at Petra. 'You enjoyed it?'

'Yeah, once I got past the performance anxiety.'

He felt that twist of guilt tighten. 'You did a good job,' he said.

'So it's okay with you?'

Petra's double-checking for reassurance made him feel even worse. Maybe he was more iron fist and less 'velvet glove' than he'd realised.

'It's more than okay.' A rush of thinking derailed him. Allowing his team greater responsibility would free up some of his own time. 'Actually I'd like you to take a look at the project list and rank a few you'd like to take greater control of. I need to delegate more and I'd like you to be first in line.'

Petra's jaw dropped. 'Seriously?'

'You'll need a couple of assistants too,' he added, thinking it through and feeling the certainty of the direction in his bones. 'Otherwise you'll end up like me.'

Frozen on the inside. Incapable of giving someone the time and emotional support they needed. Wedded to work. Unable to trust anyone. He'd always needed to see it all, know it all, decide it all, himself—to have that total control.

Suddenly he didn't care about work any more. It had lost its stranglehold on him. And he didn't want to be controlling everything for everyone all the time. He wanted a damned break.

He'd been using work as an excuse to avoid intimacy. Using it as a vehicle to prove himself over and over again—but to whom and for what? *What* was he fighting so bloody hard for any more?

Far too late he realised he'd been fighting in the wrong field of his life.

He'd let his mother down, and the impossibility of making it up to her, the impossibility of fighting for his rights—and hers—from his father...bogged him down. He'd failed in all of that.

I bet you were the light of her life.

Rosanna's words haunted him, seduced him, made him feel better. Rationally he'd always known she was right—that he'd been young, that his mother might've got sick anyway, that the far greater responsibility fell on the shoulders of his father.

But *believing* it was harder. Rosanna had said he was like his father too. That he was too controlling. Too afraid of relinquishing control.

Control. Discipline. Denial.

All facets of the same stone that his heart had become. The stone weighed too heavy now and the resulting hurt was unbearable. Because Rosanna Gold was lovely. Kind. Funny. Dutiful, even when she didn't want to be. Loyal to a fault. Even to people who'd let her down. She still tried. Indefatigably trying to do her best for others. For her students. For her damned plants and funny fish. For anyone and anything she allowed in her life. Which actually *wasn't* that many people or things. Because *she'd* been hurt before too.

But she'd wanted to love him. She'd tried to love him.

And he hadn't let her.

He'd turned away from the light that she'd brought him. The light that she was. And now he was in darkness. Now he realised that he wanted that light—that *love*—more than anything. Even though he was terrified of losing it—of her taking it away, or not wanting him any more.

So he'd not believed her. And he'd not listened to her. He'd ignored his own damn actions—and said no to her. The overprotectiveness he'd felt hadn't been about the babies. It was about *her*.

He'd done to her what his father had done to him. The thing he'd said he'd never do. He'd denied her truth—the existence of her feelings. And he'd denied his *own*. He'd not allowed himself to have faith in the thing he wanted most. And he'd hurt her as well as himself. It was the worst thing he could have done to her—when he knew that she ached inside to be seen and heard, to be valued by that one special person who paid attention and noticed the little things. To care for her the way she'd care in return. Openly, unconditionally. For always.

He'd been so *arrogant* to think that his way was the only way. But there was only one thing he was certain of now. He didn't just want Rosanna back in his life. He *needed* her. And he loved her. He just had to convince her of all of that… Because what if he'd hurt her too much to be forgiven?

CHAPTER SIXTEEN

'ARE YOU SURE there's nothing else I can do?' Rosanna called to her boss as she finished watering the seedlings.

'No, you head home. Thank you!'

On her way back through the shop she couldn't resist pausing to tweak the terrarium display. She loved that the shop sold not just plants but terrariums and aquariums as well. They were all so pretty and working amongst them inspired her.

She glanced up as someone stalked towards her—she smiled, expecting it to be a customer. But it wasn't a customer. It was a man she knew.

No. Her heart stopped.

She spoke before he had the chance to. 'I'm at work. I can't talk now.'

'Your shift finished ten minutes ago.'

How did he know that? *Control freak.*

'How did you find me?' she asked, her emotional control slipping already. 'An investigator?'

'You didn't give me much choice.' The faintest smile curved his mouth.

She hardened her heart against it. But she couldn't stop herself drinking in the sight of him. Leo Castle wasn't in a suit. He wore loose trousers and a grey tee and looked as if he hadn't eaten or slept in a month. Deep shadows beneath his eyes highlighted the burning over-brightness of his indigo irises. His voice was as creaky as his appearance—as if it hadn't been properly cared for in days.

He stared down at her, seeming to try to see right through her. 'Rosanna.'

Her heart pounded at the emotive whisper. She willed

herself to look away from him and not be bewitched all over again, struggling to find the strength. He was *here.*

She didn't want to see him. She'd been doing *well.* She wasn't ready and this wasn't *fair.*

'I told you I needed more time—'

'I'll leave if that's what you want.' His voice was so husky. 'But I hoped you might hear me out. Just briefly.'

The problem was she couldn't cope with her own emotions—the initial elation at seeing him again followed by the instant torpedoing of that excitement because she'd remembered, *he didn't want her.*

Why, then, was he here?

'It's Thursday afternoon,' she said. 'You should be at work.'

'I've switched to a four-day week. Thursday is my new day off.'

She stared at him nonplussed—because he looked so damn serious about that.

'It's true. I'm trying to change a few things. I need to.'

'What's that?' She nodded at the strip of green leaf he was holding.

He glanced down and a rueful grin broke the seriousness. 'I noticed it when I was walking along the beach earlier waiting for you to be finished here.' He held it up so she could see it properly. 'I thought you could try growing another cutting.' He regarded the limp thing sadly. 'I would have ripped out the whole plant but remembered you like growing something from not very much. I think that's a challenge you enjoy.' He gazed directly into her eyes. 'And I think you don't want to destroy something in order to create something new.'

'Sometimes you can't get something to grow no matter how much you want to.'

'That doesn't mean you stop trying,' he replied.

* * *

Leo couldn't stop staring at her. She looked gorgeous. In loose trousers and a white tee that was knotted at her waist that still didn't show any sign of the twin secrets growing inside. Her glorious hair was swept up in a messy bun and secured with a white scarf. He'd watched her smiling at customers, insanely jealous of the two minutes of her time that they got. She'd looked happy and healthy and stupidly that had made him angrier. Made him more afraid. That smile had fallen from her face the second she saw him. So now he was terrified.

'Can we go somewhere to talk?' he asked gruffly.

There was a moment where he thought she might refuse. But then she turned.

'You can walk me back to my flat,' she said.

The one he'd learned she shared with three other people. He was jealous of them too.

He'd been awake all night plotting what to say, how to say it, where to say it, but now he was here, he'd forgotten all his great plans and didn't know where to begin. Now he was with her, all he wanted to do was pull her close and kiss her. Exactly what he wasn't supposed to do. Instead he put one foot in front of the other and walked out with her.

'Did you need to see for yourself that I'm okay?' She sounded bitter—as if she thought he'd not believed her messages. 'Because I am.'

'I know and I'm glad,' he said huskily. His heart was beating too fast. He paused on the beach; he couldn't go a step further. He drew in a breath. 'I've asked my managers to take on some of my workload. I'm serious about Thursdays—or whatever day might be best. I'm trying to let go of my micromanagement issue.'

She blinked. 'Good for you.'

'So that's given me more time to think.' He paused because his brain just wouldn't work properly now—every thought had scattered upon seeing her again. 'I've been feeding Axel. I thought if I could keep him alive there might be hope for me…' None of this was coming out right. 'I wish we could go back to the reef.'

Wariness, sadness, bloomed in her eyes. 'You only took me there to convince me to do what you wanted. You just wanted me to say yes to marrying you.'

'I would have done anything to get you to say yes to me.' He admitted it freely. 'But I never stopped to ask myself *why* I really wanted that so much.' He couldn't resist reaching out to take her hand. 'I also swallowed my pride and offered your parents something I said I never would. Why did I do that?'

'Because you thought you had to, to make everything okay. To win. To stave off any future conflict.'

'Again. That's partly true. But *why* did it matter so much?' He needed her to understand. 'I've been in conflict my whole life, Rosanna—'

'I know,' she interrupted softly. 'Fighting the whole time. You must be so sick of it.'

'I thrive on contractual challenges. On problem-solving. But with you there's always been a different edge.'

She fell silent.

'I watched you that night. You were so beautiful, so curious. You appreciated something so small with such intensity. And made me curious and then you suddenly opened up like some gorgeous flower.'

She pulled her hand free of his, her shoulders hunching inwards. 'It should only have been that one night.'

'No. You're wrong. I was wrong for letting you leave then. And for letting you leave the other day.'

Rosanna's blood beat like drums, deafening her when she needed to hear most acutely. 'Why are you here? I offered you everything I had and you didn't want it.' He'd hurt her. 'But I'm fine now. I don't want your excuses. We can just move on.' She blinked back tears.

'I can't move on.'

'Why?'

He took hold of her shoulders and bent his knees so he could see into her eyes. 'Because you matter to me. Because you're everything to me.'

She dragged in a scalding breath. 'No…'

'That night I really liked you, Rosanna,' he said quietly, urgently, his words tumbling. 'Yeah, I took one look and wanted, but when you started talking I wanted to listen. I wanted to be around you. And the more time I had with you, the more I wanted and that freaked me out.' He released a harsh breath. 'I'm not good at building relationships… I don't have much practice and it scares the hell out of me. And for the first time I wanted to do things *other* than work and that was scary too. Because that's not controllable in the same way. I'm sorry it has taken me so long to realise what should have been so obvious. I did all that on the reef, with your flat, with your parents… Not because I felt I should, but because I've fallen in love with you. Only I resisted admitting that the day you left because it terrified me. You could hurt me like no one else. You *did*. I never wanted someone to ever get that close.'

She curled her hands into fists. 'I never wanted to hurt you. *You* did that when you pushed me away.'

'I know,' he said simply. 'And I am so sorry I hurt you.'

Suddenly she was shaking and he swept his arms around her.

'I'm sorry, I'm sorry, I'm sorry.' He whispered it against her hair. 'Because that's what happened.' His breath caught. 'I hurt you before you could hurt me.'

'You sent me away.' It still hurt.

'I was an idiot. I was afraid and that made me angry. I thought you were about to leave anyway…sending you away was me getting in first. Because I couldn't stand the thought of your rejection. I couldn't cope. And I'm so sorry.'

He held her closer, cradling her as the tears finally fell.

'You're number one to *me*, Rosanna. You're *everything* to me. And without you…' His voice broke. 'I don't want that world any more. You were right. I tried to control everything because I was afraid. Losing someone hurts, Rosanna.' He struggled for composure. 'And I'm lost without you.'

She gripped his T-shirt, unable to answer. Her throat was too tight. Her tears too heavy.

'I don't want anything but *you*. You with your fiery hair and freckles and skin that's so soft and so revealing. You with your quiet way of seeing the world. Your eye for detail. You're *my* idea of perfect. Just as you are. I want to steal you away to remote beaches so we can enjoy the sunsets. I want to dance with you—and I've never wanted to dance with anyone before. I want to stop and savour the small moments with you. See the things you see.'

'Leo.'

'I didn't mean to ignore your wishes or belittle your input or make you feel like you weren't my priority. I just wanted to protect you. But I screwed up.'

'And I overreacted,' she whispered, tears tracking down her face. 'I felt insecure and I flipped. I worried you were only doing all this because you felt you had to.'

'I do have to.' He smiled at her. 'Because I love you. But I'm terrified I am going to let you down. I'm terrified I'm going to let the babies down. I don't know how to be a dad.'

'Leo…'

'I couldn't look after my mother. I couldn't help her when she needed it most.'

'You're the most caring, most responsible man I know. You cared for me when I fell asleep on you that first night on the island. I saw you sneaking snacks to that little lizard. You tried to fix my flooded flat and ensured my plants didn't die… I don't know how to look after these babies either and learning might take us some time, but the *desire* to care…that's innate. And you have it no less than anyone else. In fact you have it *more* than most. The only problem is that sometimes you do it without consultation.' She smiled at him with regret. 'I shouldn't have said you were like your father. You're nothing like him.'

'You were right about my need for control.' He closed his eyes. 'There was a lot in my life I couldn't control for a really long time. So then I focused on what I *could* to the exclusion of almost everything else. And now I'm rusty at releasing my grip.'

She sighed. 'I don't want you to ever let me go,' she whispered.

'It might be hard for me not to be overprotective. It's going to take some practice at talking these things through with you and not just going ahead and trying to fix them on my own. But I really want to try.'

She loved that he wanted to try for her.

'I don't want you thinking I'm here because of duty or responsibility. This isn't actually about the babies. I'm here for *you*.'

A moan of raw emotion escaped and he swept her close and kissed her. He was here, offering everything she wanted, and she so badly wanted to believe in him. But she needed more of everything from him.

'Every time I take a breath it hurts because I know you're not beside me,' he said. 'You're not wandering off the path to look at some random tiny thing. You're not showing me so very much in all those little things. You're not there when I get home. So home is hollow in a way it never has been before. Please come back with me.'

'Do you mean it?' Elation slowly filled her cold, cavernous heart—until his love filled it to overflowing.

But she shivered at the thought of what might have been. 'We might never have found each other again if I hadn't come to Ash's office that day.'

'So let's be grateful that we did and not lose each other again. Ever.' He released her hair from its clasp, running his hand through the waves. 'Maybe our paths would've crossed eventually. You were coming back to Sydney. I would've seen you.'

She chuckled. 'You think fate would've intervened?'

'I have no idea. I am just eternally grateful to your parents for bringing you back into my life that day—the best thing they've done aside from having you in the first place.'

She glanced up at him, nibbling on her lip. 'What are we going to do about them?'

He smiled down at her. 'We'll manage them *together*, okay?'

'Okay.' She drew a steadying breath. 'Will you come to my little flat with me now?' she asked. 'Please?'

His face lit up—double dimples, wide smile, love in his eyes. 'Thought you'd never ask.'

She walked faster than she'd walked in years, super-glad her flatmates would all still be at work. She *needed* him.

As soon as they were inside her door she turned to him and he didn't hold back. He picked her up, bracing her against the wall as he kissed her so hard she now understood how desperately he'd suffered through the long hours of loneliness and misery too. They'd endured an awful separation. They never would again.

'Please,' he growled, shaking with the effort to go both slow and fast, gentle and passionate. 'I missed you,' he muttered, pressing kisses against her hair with every other word. 'It scares me how much I missed you.'

She heard the break in his voice and lifted her gaze to see him. The vulnerability in his eyes devastated her.

'I know,' she breathed, her tears spilling again. 'It's been awful.'

He hoisted her up. 'Not any more.'

'No. Because you're here.'

He filled her with his strength and vitality and all that gorgeous, glorious intensity. It was better than anything—more sublime, more intense. The power of him was fully focused on her and nothing, nothing at all, was held back. Out of control completely, she shook in his arms—from pleasure this time, not heartbreak. And he matched her. His arms were like steel bands and it was the sweetest, sharpest sensation in the world.

'Love me,' she breathed almost deliriously. 'Love me the way I love you.'

'I do. That and more, darling. You have *everything* of me.'

He held her so close, making her believe with every kiss, every touch, every vow. Again and again he promised and assured until her belief in his word was imprinted on every cell in her body.

'I'm here,' he growled. 'With you. For you. And I'll love you as hard and as best I can until I'm no more.'

'Yes.'

He was her for ever.

EPILOGUE

A little over two years later

'ARE YOU READY?' Leo Castle strode out to the terrace and saw his wife ensconced at the table, bent over a large piece of paper with a container of sharp coloured pencils beside her.

His heart soared at the sight; he loved it when she was deep in concentration like this.

'I just need five more minutes,' she murmured, not looking up from her drawing. 'This bit is almost there.'

He sighed theatrically and shook his head mournfully. 'And you once told me I was a workaholic...'

At that she glanced up and sent him a laughing look. 'And you're not still?'

'Absolutely not,' he declared with a wink. He tried hard but admittedly there were times when their Thursday afternoon date got pushed back by a couple of hours. Not today, however—today he had *very* special plans. He'd even taken tomorrow off work as well.

'I have a particular surprise. Only *you're* keeping us waiting...' He waggled his brows at her lasciviously.

'Okay.' She chuckled and put her pencil down. 'You've convinced me.' She glanced up at him again with a gleam in her eye. 'You've always been good at that.'

He stepped closer to see the picture she'd been working on. It was miniature perfection. His wife? *Total* perfection. Her cheeks were flushed and there was a smudge of charcoal by her chin and her hair was in the messiest ponytail he'd ever seen. She wore loose linen shorts and a plain, not-quite-white-any-more tee and she was gorgeous.

'I just need two minutes to get changed.' She stood and stretched.

'I'll go see the twins.'

He walked back inside and followed the sound of toddler laughter.

'Daddy!' The stereo call would never get old.

Gracie and Millie ran and clutched a leg each. His soaring heart now swelled to bursting point. They were such delights. He dropped to the ground and they squealed with laughter as he pulled them into a hug and quizzed them on their day.

'How many times did you go down the slide?'

Rosanna skipped to the bathroom and took the quickest ever shower. Time had slipped from her completely. Her parents had taken the girls to the park for an adventure an hour ago and she'd got lost in the garden on the terrace, inspired to do a drawing for her new collection. She'd finally figured out the job of her dreams. Her boss at the nursery up in Brisbane had seen her notebook and loved her botanical sketches. Together they'd designed a limited stationery range to be sold onsite. To Rosanna's amazement it had taken off and since then she'd expanded her sales online. She was still growing her own plants and now she put together terrariums on request for the store to sell as well. Now her little business was literally thriving.

What was more, her relationship with her parents had improved hugely over the last couple of years. While they had gone to Queensland, once there they'd soon decided to retire. It had completely shocked Rosanna, but they were working on their golf handicaps, of all things. They'd actually relaxed and seemed *happy* with each other. They stayed with Leo and Rosanna quite often—helping out with babysitting when they needed it, loving simple trips to the park and time with their granddaughters. Doing the things they'd not taken the time from work to do with Rosanna when she was young.

Rosanna pulled on a silk slip dress in sky blue and slid her feet into summery sandals. Thursday afternoons were their special dates, but Leo had told her that tonight was an extra-special one and she was to pack an overnight bag. She smiled to herself as she fixed her hair. With Leo, they could be going anywhere.

She went to the twins' bedroom and found him on the floor. He was lying on his stomach reading a story to the girls, who were leaning against him like two little puppies. Her heart melted at the sight.

'Ready?' she asked with a teasing lilt.

'Two minutes.'

She chuckled delightedly. That he took time for them was the greatest sign of his love.

She went to the kitchen where her parents were pottering about making an early pasta dinner. 'Thank you so much.'

'No problem.' Her mother had actually spilled pasta sauce on her shirt.

She shook her head as she passed Axel in his tank and went back to kiss the children.

Leo had finished and rose to meet her. He held her hand as they went down in the elevator and got into the car. It was only a few minutes' drive till they parked up outside his usual helicopter service.

'Well?' She glanced at him. 'When are you going to tell me where we're going?'

'When we get there.'

It was a forty-minute flight, heading north. Not in the direction of her old university, but the wine region. They circled over an estate—from above she admired the large mansion and perfect-looking pool. A few minutes later they'd landed.

'I thought we needed a weekend house.' He glanced at her as they walked across the lawn. 'In the country.'

'A what?'

'A country house.'

Her heart pounded. 'Really? As in to keep?'

'As in, yes.' He took her hand and walked around the outside of the house.

'Are we not going in?'

'There's something at the back I want you to see first.' He smiled at her. 'Back when we met, you couldn't afford a glasshouse so I thought you might like one now.'

Rosanna stopped and stared at what had just come into view. At the rear of the house was another lawn and the focal point? A stunning Victorian-style glasshouse that wouldn't look out of place in a city's botanical gardens. White-painted frames, glass, wrought-iron decorations… Her jaw dropped.

'Leo, it's *magical*.'

'Do you mind that I went ahead and bought it without talking to you first?' He smiled at her. 'Because if you don't like it, we can sell it.'

'Don't you dare.' She nudged him playfully.

'I knew you didn't need to see the actual house.' He laughed. 'I knew this would be enough to convince you.' He pulled out a large iron key from his pocket as they walked towards the greenhouse. 'You have to admit it's romantic.'

He unlocked the door and ushered her in.

Romantic wasn't the word. 'Leo…' Again she stared in awe.

'It got shifted here and I had it restored.' He stepped behind her and wrapped his arms around her waist.

She craned her neck to look at him. 'How long have you been planning this?'

His lopsided smile widened.

The glasshouse wasn't filled with plants yet—she knew he'd left the joy of that for her. But there was a set-up in the corner. Silk screens, behind which? A huge bed with soft-looking linen, a velvety sofa, a small table upon which there was a hamper. She already knew it would be filled with her favourite things. They weren't staying in the house tonight, they were staying here—in paradise.

'This is so perfect.' It was gorgeously lush and indulgent.

'Happy anniversary,' he said, cradling her close.

'But I don't have my gift for you with me.' She leaned back against him.

'I know, I'm early. Couldn't wait any longer.'

It wasn't their anniversary for another three days.

'How can I compete?' She shook her head. 'What can I possibly give you that will match this?'

'You've already given me everything.' He spun her in his arms and gazed into her eyes. 'There's nothing more I could ever want in life other than more time with you.'

Her heart melted because he had warmed up so wonderfully. He was incredible—so determined, so loyal, and all she could do was tell him and show him how much he mattered to her. That, she knew, was everything—because it was what he did for her.

So she smiled and rose on tiptoe to kiss him. 'Time to do this?'

'Please. Lots. Always.'

Direct, honest…with that edge of desperation. She knew there was a last little hunger—a need in him that might always need to be soothed. With laughter. With love. With gentle humour and fierce touch. With the certainty that they *both* needed. Because she was the same. But she was here for him as he was for her. And they'd get there—they already had.

'Mmm…' She teased a thoughtful pose before pressing against him with all her passion and playfulness and underlying truth. 'Then, okay, we have a deal.'

He laughed and she melted at the love shining in his eyes. 'I like doing deals with you best of all.'

* * * * *

MILLS & BOON

Coming next month

THE SECRET BEHIND THE GREEK'S RETURN
Michelle Smart

Marisa opened her eyes, going from heavy sleep to full alertness in an instant.

Nikos.

He was alive.

Or had she dreamt it?

A look at her watch told her it was four in the morning.

She threw the soft blanket off and her stockinged feet sank into thick carpet.

Rubbing her eyes, she stared at the sofa. At some point while she'd slept, Nikos had put a pillow under her head, laid her flat on her side and covered her.

She hadn't dreamt him.

Heart in her throat, she found herself in the adjoining room before she even knew she'd opened the door and walked into it.

The light in there was incredibly faint, the little illumination coming from the lamp Nikos had left on for her in the living area. It was enough for her to see the shape of his body nestled under the covers, breathing deeply.

She definitely hadn't dreamt him.

Nikos was alive.

The relief was almost as overwhelming as it had been the first time, and, eyes glued to his sleeping shadowed face, she stretched out a trembling hand and lightly pressed her fingers against his cheek.

The relief was short-lived. A hand twice the size of her own flew like a rocket from under the sheet and wrapped around hers.

'What are you doing?'

Her heart jumped into her throat, the beats vibrating through her suddenly frozen body.

Nikos raised his head and blinked the sleep from his eyes, trying to clear the thickness from his just awoken brain, and stared at the motionless form standing beside him.

'Marisa?' His voice sounded thick to his own ears too.

As his eyes adjusted he saw the shock in her wide eyes before his gaze drifted down to notice the buttons of her dress around her bust had popped open in her sleep to show the swell of her breast in the black lace bra she wore.

Arousal coiled its seductive way through his bloodstream to remember the taste of her skin on his tongue and the heady scent of her musk. He tugged her closer to him, suddenly filled with the need to taste it again, taste *her* again, to hear the throaty moans of her pleasure and feel the burn of their flesh pressed together. It was a burn he'd never felt with anyone but her.

Her lips parted. Her breath hitched. Her face lowered to his…

His mouth filled with moisture, lips tingling with anticipation. He put his other hand to her neck and his arousal accelerated.

It had been so long…

Then, with her mouth hovering just inches from his, she jerked back and snatched her hand away. It fluttered to her rising chest.

'I'm sorry for waking you,' she whispered, backing away some more. 'I was just checking I hadn't dreamt you.'

Continue reading
THE SECRET BEHIND THE GREEK'S RETURN
Michelle Smart

Available next month
www.millsandboon.co.uk

Copyright ©2021 by Michelle Smart

COMING SOON!

We really hope you enjoyed reading this book. If you're looking for more romance, be sure to head to the shops when new books are available on

Thursday 8th July

To see which titles are coming soon, please visit

millsandboon.co.uk/nextmonth

MILLS & BOON

For exclusive extracts, competitions and special offers, find us online:

facebook.com/millsandboon

@MillsandBoon

@MillsandBoonUK

Get in touch on 01413 063232

For all the latest titles coming soon, visit

millsandboon.co.uk/nextmonth

WANT EVEN MORE

ROMANCE?

SUBSCRIBE AND SAVE TODAY!

'Mills & Boon books, the perfect way to escape for an hour or so.'

MISS W. DYER

'Excellent service, promptly delivered and very good subscription choices.'

MISS A. PEARSON

'You get fantastic special offers and the chance to get books before they hit the shops.'

MRS V. HALL

Visit millsandboon.co.uk/Subscribe and save on brand new books.

MILLS & BOON
A ROMANCE FOR EVERY READER

- **FREE** delivery direct to your door
- **EXCLUSIVE** offers every month
- **SAVE** up to 25% on pre-paid subscriptions

SUBSCRIBE AND SAVE

millsandboon.co.uk/Subscribe

MILLS & BOON

THE HEART OF ROMANCE

A ROMANCE FOR EVERY READER

MODERN Prepare to be swept off your feet by sophisticated, sexy and seductive heroes, in some of the world's most glamourous and romantic locations, where power and passion collide.

HISTORICAL Escape with historical heroes from time gone by. Whether your passion is for wicked Regency Rakes, muscled Vikings or rugged Highlanders, awake the romance of the past.

MEDICAL Set your pulse racing with dedicated, delectable doctors in the high-pressure world of medicine, where emotions run high and passion, comfort and love are the best medicine.

Celebrate true love with tender stories of heartfelt romance, from the rush of falling in love to the joy a new baby can bring, and a focus on the emotional heart of a relationship.

Desire

Indulge in secrets and scandal, intense drama and plenty of sizzling hot action with powerful and passionate heroes who have it all: wealth, status, good looks…everything but the right woman.

Experience all the excitement of a gripping thriller, with an intense romance at its heart. Resourceful, true-to-life women and strong, fearless men face danger and desire - a killer combination!

To see which titles are coming soon, please visit

millsandboon.co.uk/nextmonth

JOIN US ON SOCIAL MEDIA!

Stay up to date with our latest releases, author news and gossip, special offers and discounts, and all the behind-the-scenes action from Mills & Boon...

millsandboon

millsandboonuk

millsandboon

It might just be true love...

Unlimited access to all your favourite Mills & Boon romances!

Start your free trial now

Available at

weloveromance.com

Get the latest romance news, exclusive author interviews, story extracts and much more!

blog.millsandboon.co.uk

OUT NOW!

Payback in passion

Available at millsandboon.co.uk

MILLS & BOON

OUT NOW!

Tantalising temptation

Available at
millsandboon.co.uk

MILLS & BOON

OUT NOW!

Playing games

Available at millsandboon.co.uk

MILLS & BOON